PENGUIN BOOKS

FALL OF FROST

Brian Hall is the author of three previous novels, most recently *I Should Be Extremely Happy in Your Company*, and three works of nonfiction. His journalism has appeared in publications such as *Time*, *The New Yorker*, and *The New York Times Magazine*. He lives in Ithaca, New York.

Praise for *Fall of Frost* by Brain Hall

"Flawless, intensely moving, and supremely intelligent . . . *Fall of Frost* is far more than a fictionalized biography, it is a novel as wily, elusive, and deceptively plain as the life it so deftly evokes."
—*The Boston Globe*

"Elegant prose in fiction always grips me, but only occasionally does a novel come along whose language holds me spellbound, makes me forget the tyranny of plot. . . . Hall's biographical novel of Robert Frost is absorbing art worthy of its subject. . . . *Fall of Frost* criticizes a poet's delusions while celebrating what poetry really does, how it really comprehends and enriches life."
—*The Kenyon Review*

"*Fall of Frost* seized my attention, showing me things about Frost I'd never known, never intuited. Brian Hall has done his homework, and then some, getting into the great poet's head and heart. This is a book I've read with pleasure, savoring the atmosphere of Frost, the sense of a visionary poet's life in review. It's affecting work, another milestone in Hall's impressive, unfolding body of work."
—Jay Parini, author of *Robert Frost: A Life*

"Brian Hall's book on Frost offers a fresh approach to Frost's life, not as a work of fiction that pretends to be history but as a work of history that uses fictive means to get at the truth about a complex historical figure. By moving away from temporal narrative to a musical weaving of times and places, he gives a convincing reading of some the central tensions of Frost's character."
—Carl Dennis, Pulitzer Prize–winning poet of *Practical Gods*

"It seems to me that Brian Hall has genuinely caught Frost's tone or tones of voice, especially in the darker range."
—Richard Wilbur

"Is it too early to crown the best novel of 2008? It's hard to imagine that in the nine months remaining in this year I will glean more pleasure from a book than I did from *Fall of Frost*. This is a novel that works on every possible level. . . . I was completely immersed in its world, in the emotional landscape of Robert Frost. Yet I also read it with enough critical distance to marvel, open-mouthed, at the skill with which Hall constructed the book. *Fall of Frost* is a character study in the deepest sense . . . and it is simultaneously an extremely sophisticated meditation on literary form: a novel about poetry which is itself built like a series of exploded and distended poems; an exploration of the writing process that arises from sensitive readings of Frost's work. . . . Hall's novel gets at Frost's character not with the certainty of the biographer but with the elliptical suggestiveness of the poet."
—Bookbrowse.com

"The reviewer's oft-used term tour de force has never been more applicable. . . . What Hall has managed to achieve is a serious, but highly readable, piece of detective work into the mind, spirit, and work of one of America's most recognized poets. . . . One of Hall's great achievements is that the novel never seems like a performance, though in reality it is a brilliant one."   —*BookPage*

"A careful, haunting, bittersweet portrait of America's most beloved poet . . . Hall draws rich connections between Frost's language and the seminal events in his life. . . . For readers desiring a richly poetic treatment of Frost in all his splendid contrariety—kindly/surly, selfish/magnanimous, caring/distant, childish/infinitely wise—this is a book to savor."   —*The Christian Science Monitor*

"Rich and deep . . .What Hall loves most is thinking about the poems. The novel should be read with a fat volume of Frost handy. . . . Frost couldn't have asked for a more generous champion. . . . Out of this stony material Hall has fashioned a warm and lovable book."   —*Bookforum*

"Hall stitches [his] scenes together in the same way Michael Ondaatje assembled his kaleidoscopic portrait of the jazz cornetist Buddy Bolden in *Coming Through Slaughter*. Hall's writing evokes Ondaatje, too: imagistic, elliptical, strenuously lyrical."   —*The New York Times Book Review*

"A deeply researched and intensely rendered portrait of what Hall calls 'Frost's extraordinarily lush and difficult mental landscape.'"
—Christopher Benfey, *The New York Review of Books*

"Hall's stream of Frost's consciousness is deep with detail and treacherous with waterfalls of sudden chronological leaps, but slowly the poet's long and eventful life emerges as a continuous whole."   —*The Seattle Times*

"Brilliant . . . Hall cleverly crafts internal dialogue and conversation attached to real-life occurrences, and consistently conveys sympathy for a talented man whose life was crowded with tragedy. . . . If one purpose of fiction is to enlarge readers' empathy for others, Hall has decidedly succeeded."
—*Star Tribune* (Minneapolis)

"Moving and quite wonderful . . . An almost dizzying, sympathetic evaluation of the great poet, in which the chapters float like Frost's own memories experienced by the reader directly. Few writers could achieve this as deftly and elegantly as Hall."   —*The Oregonian* (Portland)

"Hall does almost everything right in *Fall of Frost*. . . . Sophisticated, daring, and literary . . . Hall treats Frost respectfully and fairly, offering insights into his personality, inspirations, and heartbreak."   —*The Hartford Courant*

"Deeply moving and exquisitely wrought . . . Hall's novel brings Frost vividly to life."   —*The Baltimore Sun*

FALL OF FROST

BRIAN HALL

PENGUIN BOOKS

PENGUIN BOOKS

Published by the Penguin Group

Penguin Group (USA) Inc., 375 Hudson Street, New York, New York 10014, U.S.A.
Penguin Group (Canada), 90 Eglinton Avenue East, Suite 700, Toronto,
Ontario, Canada M4P 2Y3 (a division of Pearson Penguin Canada Inc.)
Penguin Books Ltd, 80 Strand, London WC2R 0RL, England
Penguin Ireland, 25 St Stephen's Green, Dublin 2, Ireland (a division of Penguin Books Ltd)
Penguin Group (Australia), 250 Camberwell Road, Camberwell,
Victoria 3124, Australia (a division of Pearson Australia Group Pty Ltd)
Penguin Books India Pvt Ltd, 11 Community Centre, Panchsheel Park, New Delhi – 110 017, India
Penguin Group (NZ), 67 Apollo Drive, Rosedale, North Shore 0632,
New Zealand (a division of Pearson New Zealand Ltd)
Penguin Books (South Africa) (Pty) Ltd, 24 Sturdee Avenue,
Rosebank, Johannesburg 2196, South Africa

Penguin Books Ltd, Registered Offices:
80 Strand, London WC2R 0RL, England

First published in the United States of America by Viking Penguin,
a member of Penguin Group (USA) Inc. 2008
Published in Penguin Books 2009

1 3 5 7 9 10 8 6 4 2

Grateful acknowledgment is made for permission to reprint the following copyrighted works: Excerpt from "Robert Frost in Amherst" from *Frost: A Time to Talk* by Robert Francis. Copyright © 1972 by Robert Francis. Published by the University of Massachusetts Press. By permission of the publisher. • Excerpt from "For Robert Frost" from *Flower Herding on Mount Monadock: Poems* by Galway Kinnell. Copyright © 1964, renewed 1992 by Galway Kinnell. Reprinted by permission of Houghton Mifflin Company. All rights reserved. • "Robert Frost" from *Collected Poems* by Robert Lowell. Copyright © 2003 by Harriet Lowell and Sheridan Lowell. Reprinted by permission of Farrar, Straus and Giroux, LLC. • Excerpt from "March Elegy" from *Poems of Akhmatova* by Anna Akhmatova, translated by Stanley Kunitz and Max Hayward (Houghton Mifflin: Mariner Books, 2002). Permission granted by Darhansoff, Verrill, Feldman for the Estate of Stanley Kunitz. All rights reserved. • Excerpt from "Babbii Yar" by Yevgeny Yevtushenko, translated by George Reavey. Reprinted by permission of the author. • Excerpt from "Shine, Perishing Republic," copyright 1934 by Robinson Jeffers and renewed 1962 by Donnan Jeffers and Garth Jeffers, from *Selected Poetry of Robinson Jeffers* by Robinson Jeffers. Used by permission of Random House, Inc. • Excerpt from "Annus Mirabilis" from *Collected Poems* by Philip Larkin. Copyright © 1988, 2003 by the Estate of Philip Larkin. Reprinted by permission of Farrar, Straus and Giroux, LLC and Faber and Faber Ltd.

THE LIBRARY OF CONGRESS HAS CATALOGED THE HARDCOVER EDITION AS FOLLOWS:
Hall, Brian, 1959–
Fall of Frost : a novel / Brian Hall.
p. cm.
ISBN 978-0-670-01866-6 (hc.)
ISBN 978-0-14-311491-8 (pbk.)
1. Frost, Robert, 1874–1963—Fiction. 2. Poets, American—20th century—Fiction. I. Title.
PS3558.A363F36 2008
813'.54—dc22   2007033334

Printed in the United States of America • Designed by Nancy Resnick

In memory of

LOUIS ALTON HALL

physicist and father, who recited to me the first lines of Frost I ever heard:

> Home is the place where, when you have to go there,
> They have to take you in

and who kept hidden in his desk, where no one found it until after his death, a copy of Frost's "Revelation."

> We make ourselves a place apart
>   Behind light words that tease and flout,
> But oh, the agitated heart
>   Till someone find us really out.

Who kept watch over the world, who guarded those who drove on through the darkness, sleeping? . . . Was he now placed on guard? Never! never would he be fit for it, he who was incapable of any help, unwilling for any service, he the mere word-maker. . . .

—Hermann Broch, *The Death of Virgil*, tr. Jean Starr Untermeyer

I owe absolutely everything I am to poetry—all I know about the pronunciation and spelling of words, all I know of geography history and philosophy and all I know of true thought and feeling.

—Robert Frost to Louis Untermeyer, October 12, 1939

DONALD HALL: Can you say what you are going to do in the remaining *Cantos*?

EZRA POUND: It is difficult to write a paradiso when all the superficial indications are that you ought to write an apocalypse.

—*The Paris Review*, Summer–Fall 1962

THE FROST FAMILY

Robert Frost (1874–1963)
Elinor White (1872–1938)

CHILDREN

Elliott (1896–1900)
Lesley (1899–1983)
Carol (1902–1940)
Irma (1903–1981)
Marjorie (1905–1934)
Elinor Bettina (1907–1907)

1

"The old man won't be placated."

Franklin Reeve is speaking to Fred Adams outside the door. He hasn't bothered to close it, since the old man is deaf as a post. But the old man doesn't hear half bad when he turns his right ear forward.

His deafness is part ruse. He's always been a slow thinker, and at eighty-eight he creeps. He gets confused. The wanted word fails to come, the riposte wobbles on him (or the thought warns: how many times has he said that?). So he retreats, recoups: "What was that? I didn't hear." A result is, he overhears more now than at any time since he was a boy, when he listened to his parents' voices beyond the door about to be flung open, his ears made acute by fright.

Fred stands before him, assessing how to handle the big baby. The big, spoiled baby.

Well goddamn him! Yes, he won't be placated and why should he be? Dobrynin invited him here. The Russian ambassador said that Frost should say directly to Khrushchev what he'd been saying to him—that it was an inconceivable joke that the world might be blown up over a matter as trivial as Berlin. Does that mean nothing? Russia is top-down, Dobrynin speaks on cue. Khrushchev's man invited Frost to come to Russia and speak to Khrushchev on a matter that might save the world. A plane flew him to Moscow, a Russian car drove him to the Russian hotel.

And during the ride in the car, Frost learned that Khrushchev was not in Moscow. He was vacationing at the Black Sea.

That was a week ago. Frost had flown with Stewart Udall, secretary of the interior, who continued on to Siberia to look at hydroelectric projects. Frost was dragged to an elementary school, a poet's apartment, a palace in St. Petersburg—all the time asking, When will I see Khrushchev? Is he back? Are we going to the Black Sea? I have something to tell him right off, this and that. A proposal. An offer. An invitation. If he's the man I think he is, he'll understand.

Did they lie to him? Were they lying all the time?

Oh, the old man. Humor him.

This morning Frost learned that Stewart Udall had been back in Moscow. One day? Two days? No one told him. Frost also learned that Stewart, this morning, flew to the Black Sea to see Khrushchev. Flew without him! Are they toying with him? He's an old man, half deaf, with sore joints, recurrent pneumonia, hay fever, grippe, chronic cystitis, maybe prostatitis, maybe cancer—are they dragging him halfway around the globe just to toy with him?

"Robert—"

"Don't give me guff about literary triumphs," Frost cuts Freddie off. "Frank tried that. I don't care about any of that."

"I only—"

"They can't understand my poems. This is all for their purposes. I'm a 'people's poet.'"

The people, yes. Everyone mistakes him for Sandburg. Who traipsed around Russia last year, strumming his guitar. Sorry, folks, no banjo with this bard.

"—no, Robert, how can you think that? The audiences have been ecstatic. That crowd last night in the street—they cheered—"

Frost thought Stewart was a friend. He's known him for years. Stewart arranged his reading for Kennedy's inauguration.

Which . . . Frost fouled up. Is that it? He fumbled the ball in the big game. Was Stewart embarrassed? Was this his way of getting back? Drag him to Russia, leave him to rot in Moscow? Sorry, you failed the test. We'll go on without you. Go home, boy!

Well goddamn him!

"—or when you read 'Stopping by Woods' in the Café Aelita, that applause was heartfelt, you knew it at the time—"

"Don't lecture to me, Fred Adams!" Frost shouts. *Goddamn it! Goddamn it to hell!* "Don't you dare lecture to me!"

Fred stops. Stares. Turns and leaves the room.

There he goes again. The old man. The spoiled baby.

Are they right? Are they? They are, aren't they?

2

METHUEN, MASSACHUSETTS

JULY 1900

Doctors: they fill the doorframe, impatience in their faces, their black bags swinging at the ends of their arms with a heavy creak.

They step past you. They pronounce judgment. They wash their hands and leave.

So this is the way the world ends: red evening light (should one say "lurid"? should one say "o'ercast with blood"?), white chickens running free in the yard, and a doctor at the door. Powder House Hill. Is Frost holding the revolver? (Later, he will wonder.)

The doctor steps past. He and Frost mount the stairs (are there chickens underfoot?) to the child's room. Here is Elinor, cadaverous with dread, and the boy, not yet four, lying gray and withered. Four days of diarrhea and vomit. Thirst; cramps. His screams.

Four days! Why did you delay? (The chickens chirr.)

Frost first consulted his mother's doctor.

The man is an idiot.

He prescribed homeopathic pills.

Your mother is a religious maniac with incurable cancer. Her doctor calls on God, not medicine. You knew this.

The doctor straightens. Frost sees it all in that movement. Is he holding the revolver? Might he shoot the man before he opens his mouth? Shoot himself before he hears? "This is *cholera infantum*. It's too late now for me to do anything. The child will be dead before morning."

Elliott. Their firstborn, their baby.

As there is nothing for the doctor to do, he leaves. Hurries, in fact. Nothing for him here.

When is it that night—three? four? In the dark—the boy, the baby, held by Elinor, Frost held off by her. Elinor not saying a word, nor the silent boy: gray and shrunken, a changeling. Where is their baby? They are not sure. Then they are.

Elinor will never say his name again.

"He is gone home," says Belle, Frost's mother, with obscene serenity. *Your doctor's fault!* Frost could wring her neck.

They have no photograph of him. (They have no camera.)

In Frost's mind, an image: Elliott is in the backyard with his father, feeding the chickens. Some are inside the run, others out—there is a break in the wire Frost hasn't fixed. Elliott throws corn kernels, tucks his feet away from drilling beaks, tucks up his curled hands, laughs in fear. He looks back to his father for protection. Behind him, beating upward with a stormwind noise: white wings.

3

NORTH STATION, BOSTON, MASSACHUSETTS

OCTOBER 1940

Out of the clamor of the crowd, the shouts of porters, a Younger Poet boards the Berkshire Limited, bound for Albany. He's just found a seat when down the aisle comes Robert Frost. The Younger Poet prays, and the two seats across from him stay open. Frost sits down, a woman with him.

The Younger Poet imposes on himself the discipline he reserves for his Frost encounters. He divests his mind of trivia—the train, the passengers, their conversations—and opens it to take on the load of Frost. All that exists are the two poets, and the woman beyond, who, as a Frost familiar, must also matter. Is that his secretary, Mrs. Kathleen Morrison? The Younger Poet has heard much. (He refuses to believe the cheap gossip.) He drinks her in. A slight, pretty woman dressed all in gray, with a pleasing voice. How fine it would be to know her!

The Younger Poet waits and watches, taking mental notes. There is a wart on Frost's left eyelid. The backs of his hands are hairy. He seems changed from when the Younger Poet last saw him, seven months ago. His eyes are dark-shadowed and strained; he slumps wearily in his seat.

Frost is searching his pockets for a timetable. "May I?" The Younger Poet hands across two.

"Thank you."

Frost would not remember him. In the past half-year he's met and talked with more people than the Younger Poet will see in a lifetime. But Frost gives him a hard look. "I've seen you before."

"At Mr. Holmes's place. Last March."

"Oh yes." Frost speaks the Younger Poet's name.

The Younger Poet stands up, beams, bows. Frost begins to talk about poetry—Paul Engle, Robinson Jeffers, the *Atlantic*—and the Younger Poet remains in the aisle, attending. He sees a chance to offer up a line of Philip Sidney's: "Good poetry always tells the truth."

"That's a good one," Frost says. "But it makes us fall back on the stock phrase, 'What is truth?' Age-old. Take Keats's 'Beauty is truth, truth beauty.' A fine phrase, as far as it goes. But we know well that truth is not always beautiful. Ugliness is truth. We must remember that."

At Springfield, Frost helps Mrs. Morrison off the train. Passengers whisper as he passes. When he returns, he sits next to the Younger Poet. "My son, Carol, died last night. He killed himself."

"My God! I'm sorry—"

The old poet's face quakes, and he turns away impatiently. "Please don't talk to me any more."

"Of course."

The train begins to move. Autumn slides past the window. Frost never looks. Instead, he begins to talk, and doesn't stop until Williamstown. The Younger Poet calls on his mnemonic techniques. Frost speaks of how to build a poem, of his own books, of his disappointment with *Mountain Interval*, of the sad business of reviews that twist an artist out of shape.

The Younger Poet says he has a copy at home of the infamous article in the *Quarterly Review* that so discouraged Keats.

"You have? Is it as bad as they say?"

"The most bitter words I've ever read."

Frost is avid. "Are you able to quote any?"

He gets off at Williamstown. The Younger Poet stays in his seat, scribbling furiously in the shorthand he's learned expressly for Frost's lectures. He gets it all down. He includes the telling detail of a ragged patch of whiskers under Frost's lower lip, showing he lacked the heart to shave with care that morning.

4

SAN FRANCISCO, CALIFORNIA

MARCH 1874

When the doctor showed up at the front door, your father put his Colt revolver in the man's face, and said that if anything happened to me while you were being delivered, why then the doctor wouldn't be leaving the house alive!

One of his mother's favorite stories. She tells it as she rocks, her voice singsong, partly from Scots burr, partly because this is a ballad she wrote long ago. Maybe it's true. Frost guesses it comforts her to think of William Prescott Frost leveling his gun in gallant defense of his Belle, instead of (oh, say) drunkenly hauling it out of his pants and laying it on the kitchen table to intimate that the next family member who crossed him would get it between the eyes.

Fear didn't protect you. No matter how heaping a platter of terror you offered up to the local deity, your sacrifice was rejected.

He was so proud and attentive. He wouldn't allow me to do any house-work in my delicate condition, so he moved us to a hotel for a time. That was the Abbotsford House, at the foot of Nob Hill.

Actually, Belle did little housework under any circumstances. She hated cooking, was too saintly to notice mess. Frost's father would move the family to a hotel when he couldn't stand the dirt any longer, then move it back to a house when he could no longer bear the hotel guests. Money also played some shadowy part.

Frost would like to picture it better: the night scene (Belle said it was night, and of course it was; difficult births in ballads always happen at night)—the revolver and the lantern, the swinging shadows, the disheveled doctor at the door. It's practically a lithograph. The scene is not the hotel, they had moved to a house on Washington Street, probably better than the later ones. "Near Nob Hill," Belle always said, and why not? All their houses were near Nob Hill.

But to return to the lithograph. Beyond the doctor, bowed in respect before the commanding Colt, Frost can make out the dusty street. The houses opposite are hazy, because when Frost went in search of memories sixty years later (his first time back in the city) there was nothing to give him authentic detail. The whole neighborhood had burned down in the San Francisco earthquake.

And his father—drunk? Oh, let's say no. It spoils the scene. But his being doomed adds glamour, so say he already has the tuberculosis that will kill him eleven years later.

But if Frost admits the turberculosis, maybe he can admit the drunkenness as well. The man is drunk because he is doomed. The Colt wavers uncertainly; the doctor's fear rises. His glance shifts from the one black metallic eye to the two glassy blue ones. And these—William Prescott Frost's eyes—his son can picture with perfect clarity.

They are round, pale-blue eyes, the opposite of deep-set. Does one then call them shallow? They sit on the surface of his angelic face as though to advertise they have nothing to hide. They are innocent. They suggest that whatever William might be about to do, whatever on earth takes shape in his pale, handsome brow, is perfectly reasonable. They are the eyes of Frost's sister, Jeanie, who died in an insane asylum in Augusta, Maine, in 1929.

Robert Frost's eyes are the same pale blue, but they are not the same eyes. In a photograph of his younger self (there are so few; no Frost ever had a camera), closer to his father's age when he died, he can see the difference. He has his mother's large pupils, and his lids are heavier and lower. The effect is not of clear marbles but raw eggs. Not of innocence, but guilt.

At the zoo, you burned monkeys' noses with a magnifying glass. You were playing the unforgiving god.

Anyway, William's got the Colt, and the liquor in him, and that's all the doctor in the doorway knows and all he needs to know. William waves the pistol toward the upper floor. The doctor skirts him and heads up the stairs, where he can hear the woman's yowling. William follows; his toe catches against a riser and he stumbles forward. The doctor leaps up three steps without touching floor or banister.

5

For years, you wondered: were you the yoke? were you the secret?

Your God-smitten mother turned down a minister and married a rake. Why?

There was just the two of them in that little school in that lonely town in Pennsylvania in 1873. He the principal, she the teacher. He needed to learn stenography for the career he dreamed of in journalism.

She gave him private lessons. He left suddenly in June, for San Francisco. Five months later, she followed him.

You always pictured her: stepping heavily down from the hissing train under his dismayed, resentful gaze. He was the runaway horse, she the barn door that had somehow followed him. You were the sorrow that is called, in counter-curse, the joy. You were the burden. As in Job it is written: "By the breath of God frost is given." Mary called her burden the breath of God in the Bible's prettiest scandal story: pretty because, through sheer power of poetry, mistress Mary made herself into the wife of a good man and the Mother of God.

Nothing pretty in sinful San Francisco: a hasty marriage, a husband Belle would flee from two years later (but she would return: he was her duty, her punishment), and two backward children.

You always knew: you failed to make them happy.

Did it run in the blood—the heat, the wildness? Your mother's mother, in Scotland, was called by her father's family a hussy. Her father was a sea captain, and Belle was born in a port town. You always assumed: a brothel. A sad, low-slung house, one in a line along a certain street off the harbor, smelling of low tide. The upright sea captain went down in a storm a month after your mother was born (but you always wondered: did he really escape to the sands of Araby, to farthest Ind?) and the shameless whore abandoned her baby. Your mother was raised by the sea captain's parents, who filled her to the brim of her mind with the piety appropriate for little bastards.

Did it run in the blood? You, you bastard, kept after Elinor, on picnics by the Merrimack, when she only wanted poems and flowers. She wanted Wordsworth and you gave her Shelley. You kept after her until she yielded.

Did she ever forgive you? Although she wasn't pregnant when she married you, did she marry you only because she'd yielded to you? Her duty, her punishment.

6

When was it? Where? His earliest memory:

He wakes—
A hand on his leg. "Get up. Hurry!" It's Aunt Blanche.
He slips down from the bed. A long aisle between berths; curtains closed; dim light. A train. "What's wrong?"
"We have to get off."
"Why?"
"Shush!"
At the end of the car his mother is holding baby Jeanie. The conductor swings open the door and stands aside, mute. Are they being thrown off? Robbie hangs back in fear. Aunt Blanche snatches him up and carries him, upside down, down the steps into darkness. He begins to cry. "Shush!"
They stand on the cinders. It's the middle of the night. Their luggage is in a pile next to them. The train creaks and sighs. It's leaving without them! He cries harder.
"Oh, for goodness' sake!" Aunt Blanche snaps.
The baby is crying, too. They are alone by the empty track.
Only his mother is calm. She has two long thick braids of hair. She stands serenely in the dark and cold, as though a shining Station were at her back, and Comfort piled in heaps beside her, instead of their jumble of tossed-out luggage.

7

His mother's Scottish "o," so round and dark Robbie wants to nestle in it, drown in it, its dozen different meanings, each with its own inflection: "Oh, Robbie . . . ," "Ohh, I don't, I don't know," "Oh, that's lovely, that is," "Oh! William!," "Oh, you're the little man," "Oh! I think you *do* know."

> I may sleep in the cold open fields
> Along with the raggle-taggle gypsies, O

8

You hinted:

> Be her first joy her wedding,
> That though a wedding,
> Is yet—well something they know, he and she.

Something there is. "The Lovely Shall Be Choosers" is your only poem in free verse. You wanted to show the up-to-daters you were not *always* averse, when it was apt. Free verse for free love. Those two were playing tennis with the net down.

You wrote the poem in the mid-twenties, and it wasn't a year or two later you learned you weren't a bastard after all. A letter of your father's came to you when Jeanie died; written from San Francisco back east in July 1873.

> My Darling Wife
> Am I selfish, darling, in my intense longing to have you come to me, and does my selfishness blind my better judgment?

So the illicit pregnancy was wrong, the heavy steps from the train, the anger. You had to erase all that. You discovered they had married in March, in Pennsylvania, a full year before you were born.

But that raised another question: why, when Belle had God, Jesus, and the angels to eat, sleep, and talk with, why did she marry William Frost?

Another letter from your father, when he was courting, maybe gave an answer:

> For a long time . . . I obstinately refused to acknowledge to myself that I loved you. As well might I have disputed my very existence. And when once I did acknowledge it, my love pervaded my whole being. It has ennobled me, it has given me higher aspirations; it has almost seemed to me that when we have been talking together on religious questions, my love for you drew me so close to you in spirit that I could believe with you in Christianity, in the love of God, in the divinity of Christ—things which are to you precious truths, to me enigmas.

Crafty devil! Tempted by her flesh, he tempted her back with Spirit. Christ's Body for hers. A soul to save, her Christian duty.

> Your answer to this will mark a turning-point in my life.

The savage on his island awaits the missionary. Fire burn and caul-
dron bubble.

Do you see in me that which you can love? that which you
can rely upon as a support in the rugged ways of life?

How chilling to read those words while remembering scenes from
San Francisco.

9

WASHINGTON, D.C.

THURSDAY, MAY 10, 1962

"I'm as Russian as you are. I was born in old Russian territory. You
might have heard of it. San Francisco?"

"Is that so? I'd assumed you were born in New England."

"We Russians, you know, we're canny about origins. Look at
Rurik. The first Russian, and *he* was a Viking."

Speaking with Anatoly Dobrynin, the Soviet ambassador to the
United States, Frost is doing what he always does with a new
acquaintance—staking out common ground. It's like Indians' sacred
ground, the only place two tribes could meet without killing each
other. For an Indian, every man was either an enemy he'd do anything
to butcher, or a brother he'd happily die for. When Frost was a boy, he
imagined he really was an Indian.

"You probably know," Dobrynin is saying, "that Stalin was Georgian."

"And isn't your Khrushchev half Ukrainian?"

"Oh no, although—"

"Tell me, is that a Ukrainian folk custom? Part of a traditional dance?"

"What?"

"Pounding your shoe on the table."

Frost's old friend Stewart Udall had called him a week ago, while Frost was down in Washington consulting for the Library of Congress. Stewart said he was going to Russia in the fall to take a look at hydroelectric projects, and in advance of that he was hosting the new Soviet ambassador for dinner. Since Frost had so many strong opinions about Russia, perhaps he'd like to join them?

"Me? Strong opinions?"

"Come on, Robert. You never miss an opportunity to knock them. But you might like this new ambassador. He speaks fluent English. And he even has a sense of humor."

Now, as they stand together by the fireplace in Stewart's living room after dinner, Dobrynin seems unsure how to respond to the Khrushchev jab. Frost is contrite. "Don't let me fool you. I'm being wicked. Actually, I have an idea Khrushchev might be a great man."

"Yes, I read the article in the *New York Times* that quoted you saying as much."

"He's my enemy, but I admire him."

"And Soviet citizens admire President Kennedy."

"Quite a pair, aren't they? The prince and the peasant. Don't get me wrong, I'm all for peasants."

"No need to apologize. My father is a simple plumber."

Frost takes an assessing look at Dobrynin: tall, heavy-set, balding, with witch's-cap eyebrows that make him look mischievous, an "Irish" double chin. He looks like that Russian-American novelist who got himself famous a few years back for writing the dirty book. Stewart was right: Frost does like this young man. All the U.S. ambassadors he's met are rich boys, country-clubbers iron-clad in a social ease Frost can neither imitate nor stand. He was disarmed by a story Dobrynin told during dinner, how he and his fellow Soviet diplomats-in-training were taught table etiquette at the Kremlin, so they wouldn't pick up the wrong fork or mop their plates with their bread at official dinners in the West. Their instructor, a disinherited Russian princess, named the dishes as they were brought to the table: vichyssoise, lobster Thermidor, boeuf en daube. But the plates were empty. This was 1946, and food was still scarce. The trainees used the correct forks on the invisible food and daintily sipped the airy soups, growing hungrier and hungrier.

"Look, now," Frost says, feeling his affection rise, "I want to talk to you about Berlin. Surely your Khrushchev isn't going to blow up the world in a squabble over half a city?"

"The Soviet Union merely wants to regularize the situation. A peace treaty with the German Democratic Republic, and the rights of West Berlin guaranteed as a Free City. You must admit that the current arrangement is unnatural."

"So's a grain of sand in an oyster. That wall you've built is turning the grain of sand into the most valuable pearl there is—a symbol. Someone's going to crack open the oyster to get it, and then where will we be?"

Dobrynin smiles, his witchy eyebrows pinching up. "To adopt your lovely metaphor, I'd say that it's rather a stream of sand, flowing out of East Germany. No country can be expected to accept the loss of its own population."

Frost is impatient. "Any country that makes its own people want to leave is not much of a country. Look"—he forestalls Dobrynin's reponse—"we both know these arguments. That's politics. What we need is someone powerful who'll cut through them. Forget the reasons, do something that shakes the whole pile of sticks, just knocks 'em down. Something great."

"I agree. But it is hard for people to act boldly before it's necessary. We have a saying in Russia: 'Until it thunders, the muzhik won't bother to cross himself.'"

"For a nation of atheists, that sounds awfully religious. In America we talk about closing the barn door after the horse has got out."

"And for you optimistic Americans, that sounds fatalistic. I should say it almost sounds Russian."

Who is fooling whom? Frost is liking this man more and more. Really, the Russkies must be all right if they send this kind of fellow over. "Our countries should be rivals in sports, in the arts, in economics. Not in petty squabbles."

Stewart has materialized, hostlike, by their elbows. "You two look like you're having a lively exchange."

"A most enjoyable one," Dobrynin says.

"I've been telling the ambassador how Khrushchev can save the world," Frost says.

"I think Mr. Frost should go to Moscow and tell the premier himself. It would do 'a world of good,' as you say."

"I think that's a fabulous idea. Robert, why don't you come with me this fall on my trip to the Soviet Union? You could come as a special ambassador."

"What was that?" says Frost, splashing suddenly in cold water. "I didn't catch it."

"I said you could come to the Soviet Union with me this fall."

"To Russia?" Alarm bells are ringing. The collectivists? The utopians? The one-shot-in-the-back-of-your-headers? Frost is too old. And he's sick.

Dobrynin is beaming down at him. "An excellent idea! I'll ask my government to invite you."

Who is fooling whom? The eyebrows do a happy devil's dance. *Goodbye, Mr. Frost! Goodbye!*

Frost only manages a stammer. "I . . . I don't know if . . . I'd be up to it."

Pretty Kremlin guide, herding tourists: "Here, ladies and gentlemen, lies John Reed, author of Ten Days That Shook the World. *Next to him is the American poet Robert Frost, author of the classic 'Pausing Next to the Forest During a Snowstorm,' who died of violent deracination while on a goodwill visit in 1962—"*

At the door, as Frost is leaving, Dobrynin says, "Please do consider it. I agree with what you said about the need for creative thinking vis-à-vis Berlin. Before I became a diplomat, I was an aircraft engineer. Engineers will try something new, something maybe strange, because they wonder if it might work. I often think diplomats only try something new in order to prove that it *can't* work."

If Frost goes, he dearly wishes Dobrynin would go with him. He looks up at this big young man, who speaks English so well, and Russian, too, who's lived forty-odd years in Russia and not been shot in the back of the head once. "You probably don't know," Frost says, "that I was born in San Francisco. Near Russian Hill."

"Ah. Is that so?"

"So in a way, I'd be going home."

10

You lied: before you knew you weren't a bastard, you lied to protect your mother and yourself. In 1915, when fame first came to you in the person of a newspaper reporter, you considered: your life is becoming public property. They will ask: where were you born, when, your parents' names? alive? childhood happy? not so? teachers proud? prophetic?

In 1915, you believed this: your parents married in San Francisco in November 1873, and you were born on March 26, 1874. You assumed: all marriage records and birth certificates were destroyed in the San Francisco fire. You said: I was born on March 26, 1875.

You made an honest woman out of your mother.

And now admit: you enjoyed the lie. So many questions! What had they to do with your poems? In England, where you published your first books, no one had pried, but America was founded on Puritan prying, its symbol is eagle-eyed egalitarianism. America is where the famous make themselves endlessly available (*this is my blood, drink*) or are scorned for their arrogance and thrown down from the pedestal. You intended staying on the pedestal, so you played the game. Come, questioners, all! Did anyone say the answers had to be true? *This is my eyewash, drink.* That's a deeper American game, the Yankee game. And part of the game is to hint at the lie. *Are you smart enough to catch me?*

You left clues. You wrote a poem called "The Lockless Door." You told all who asked that it was based on a real incident, when you were frightened one night by a drunk knocking on the door of a mountain hut you were staying in for a few weeks. You waited to see if anyone was reader enough to figure out that it was more a metaphor for your belated fame, and the demands of your public:

It went many years,
But at last came a knock,
And I thought of the door
With no lock to lock.

I blew out the light,
I tip-toed the floor,
And raised both hands
In prayer to the door.

But the knock came again.
My window was wide;
I climbed on the sill
And descended outside.

Back over the sill
I bade a "Come in"
To whatever the knock
At the door may have been.

So at a knock
I emptied my cage
To hide in the world
And alter with age.

You'd originally ended it with the line, "And alter my age," but that was a giveaway. Still, the import seemed fairly obvious. Yet no one figured it out. You were disappointed. You already knew editors couldn't read your poems (those who'd rejected your offerings when you were a nobody clamored after the same poems the moment you were a success). Now you had to wonder if your readers couldn't read your poems, either. *A poem would be no good that hadn't doors*, you wrote somewhere. *I wouldn't leave them open though.* Yet, since they're lockless doors, a lonely author can only hope some reader, somewhere, will think to try a knob.

You kept hinting. In another poem, you put words in the mouth of a swinger of birches:

> So if you see me celebrate two birthdays,
> And give myself out as two different ages

In the years since your birthdays became public rituals, how amusing that the galas mounted for your talismanic fiftieth or sixtieth rested on a lie that made their symbolism hollow. You wrote:

> I am going to let you give me that triumphal dinner on my fiftieth birthday if it is understood beforehand that I don't much deserve it and that I don't necessarily have to look or act exactly the age.

And:

> It is very very kind of the *Student* to be showing sympathy with me for my age. But sixty is only a pretty good age. It is not advanced enough. The great thing is to be advanced.

Admit it: in your egoism, you've enjoyed the fact that no one understood, you've lorded it over their misunderstanding, as Jesus lorded it over those who couldn't fathom his parables. Did you really want anyone to come in?

Your biographer figured it out. Not because he could read your poems or fathom your parables, but because he unearthed documents that showed the discrepancy in prose. Being bad at the game, he refused to play and insisted instead that the rule book be read.

You sighed. Rule No. 1: Find out what your enemy knows. "When was I born?"

"One year earlier than you say you were."

You allowed yourself to smile. (Let him try to read it.) "I thought so."

Your biographer is Lawrance Thompson. Though an atheist, he is more Puritan than you. Though from New Hampshire, he is less Yankee. He has never understood your fooling. You suspect that by the time of this exchange (it was 1949, and you were seventy-five, having just aged a year in a day) he already hated you.

11

THE DERRY FARM, NEW HAMPSHIRE
1900–1909

The "brook interval," the sunburned Yankee selling the farm calls it. Robert and Elinor are in flight out of Methuen. Elinor holds the baby; Robert is the donkey.

Down from the two-acre mowing field the seller points, down to where the alders line the base of the neighbor's hill, and says, "The brook interval would be yours. The stone wall on the far side marks the edge of the property." The family walks among the alders and finds a course of wet rocks, roots licked clean, an inch of yesterday's rain pooling and trickling westward. It is September; a new century. *Ours is the brook interval.* Which must be New England dialect for "intervale." The San Francisco boy is struck.

Ours is the interval. What he and Elinor desperately need: a nook in time, a place to hide. Elliott is dead. They've fled the Methuen farm on Powder House Hill as cursed, and come to Derry to bury themselves, to die to the world. *Derry, down derry.* Elliott is dead, but they have a daughter, Lesley (seventeen months old, with her father's sea-blue eyes). Within a year another child, Carol, will be on the way. Then Irma, then Marjorie. Fill the interval.

Shipwrecked, their desert island is a rocky thirty acres. There's a white clapboard farmhouse with an attached barn, a garden in the north yard, blackberries, raspberries, and grapes on south-facing walls. On the east is an orchard of apple trees, a scattering of pear, quince, peach, and cherry. There will be chicken coops for three hundred White Wyandottes (little he knows about breeding layers and broilers, but it's all he does know, and he's afraid of cows). Across the unbusy dirt road there's a little pasture with a big grove of trees, and a big pasture with a little grove of trees. Just south is a cellar hole, grown over with lilacs. In the northeast corner of the mowing field there's a gate that leads to a road no longer a road. Two stone walls that once edged it now slouch side by side through green maple woods. Rusty oak saplings grow in the roadbed. More cellar holes on either side—other families that came, oh, a hundred years ago, that farmed an interval and left for good.

The Derry farm is the center of the world. The brook is the Brook; the road, the Road. The Road begins here. At the front door, step down from the granite sill (take note of it: this headstone is all that will remain when the house is a cellar hole fringed with lilacs). Turn right, and you're walking north along the Derry Road. Two miles to the village. Turn left and south, and you're on the Windham Road.

The Brook flows out of the east, out of the bog of Nowhere, whiles its way through the alders, ducks under the road, wanders down the big pasture to disappear into the swamp of Nothingness in the west. In spring it has a summer mildness; in summer it dies like an autumn leaf. Did it ever have a name? The sunburned Yankee didn't say. Too small to name, or the namers all dead.

Proof that the farm is the center of the world: sunrise and sunset are equidistant from the porch rocker's view, and at absolute noon the sun is straight overhead, looking down on the one house, on all the apples in the world ripening, the hay making, the grapes warming along the wall, the one Woodpecker fretting another hole in the maple tree by the empty road.

They leave us so to the way we took,
As two in whom they were proved mistaken

Go out and die! his grandfather said (or did he? it seems as if he did), when he bought the farm for his ne'er-do-well grandson. Frost's father had died when he was eleven, and Frost and his mother, Belle, and his odd, marble-eyed sister, Jeanie, had come back east to his father's family, the upright seventh-generation New England Frosts, with a San Francisco fortune worth eight dollars—gold dust that, as soon as the sun set, turned to dirt.

Robert Frost and Elinor White were co-valedictorians at Lawrence High School and they should have achieved a settled existence by now, with Rob (oh, say) a foreman of a Lawrence mill, and Elinor active in the local church. But it turned out Frost didn't believe in work, and Elinor didn't believe in God. It turned out Frost loved nothing but poetry and Elinor. And it turned out Elinor loved her father, who quit his own secure job (he'd been a minister who didn't like to talk, and who didn't believe in God, either) to poetically pursue his hobby of woodworking, and she disliked her mother, who left her father for leaving his job, and rejected his rejection of faith by becoming a Christian Scientist.

Five years after graduation, the high-school stars were destitute.

Go out and die! If he didn't say it, he thought it. Grandfather Frost *was* foreman of a Lawrence mill. Every inch of him. He bought the Derry farm. And when he died a year later, he didn't give his estate outright to his only surviving descendants, Frost and his sister. No, he didn't trust these Golden Staters enough for that. He set up a distrust fund, dispersing so much each year, like wages to mill hands. Thus everything Robert and Elinor have in the world—the mowing field, the orchard, the house, the pastures, the brook—does not belong to them.

Well, Lesley belongs to them. And the children on the way, and each other, and a dozen poems, and three hundred chickens. And the memory of Elliott, which will bind Robert and Elinor forever like a secret never told, a guilt no one else can share.

In April (one April, all the Aprils) Frost warms at length in the rocker in the first soft spring sunlight on the south-facing porch, gazing down to the brook interval and the alders, where the mist rises from the pebbled snowbanks. Last night the spring peepers were shouting in chorus, pulsing like crickets in summer, but with spring music, with a shivery shimmer, as though the head-heavy snowdrops were swinging, ringing, or like distant sleighbells, like the last dissipating ghost of the Christmas season, yielding to spring heat, spring love. Where do the peepers go, he wonders, when they run out of song? Does anyone know? Today there are hundreds in this little brook, but by June they will be gone, every one. Do they rise up in mist like the snow? Or sink beneath the ground along with the brook in the heat?

Hyla crucifer is the scientific name. *Crucifer,* for the indistinct X (squint! imagine!) of darker mottling on the frog's back. And *Hyla,* for "wood" (tree frog?), or for "matter." Perhaps, flowing out of Nowhere and flowing into Nothingness, they were believed by the ancients to be matter primordial, formed from the April mud. Mud that sings for its brief interval, before it bakes dry. The idea appeals to Frost.

He remembers a Greek story: Long ago, there lived a beautiful boy named Hylas, son of Theiodamas, king of the Dryopians. Hercules demanded an ox of Theiodamas, who refused, so Hercules killed him. He abducted the boy to be his companion. The two journeyed together on the *Argo* in quest of the Golden Fleece. (Golden, at any rate, in the light of the setting sun.) When the ship beached at Mysia, Hercules went in search of a tree from which to carve an oar, while Hylas went to fetch water from a spring. The boy approached the fountain with the full moon shining on him. He was silver-fleeced, radiant with beauty. He bent to fill his bronze ewer, and as the water gurgled across the lip and the hollow bronze rang, the nymph Dryope, enamored at the sight of him, rose from the water and put her arm around his neck. She kissed him gently on the lips, tugged him by the elbow into the water. Still kissing him, she drew him down. All that was found afterward was the bronze ewer lying in the grass by the spring, pearled with water drops. In a frenzy, Hercules ransacked the woods, thrice-calling Hylas's name. He threatened the Mysians with destruction if they didn't continue the search after he left. And so, once a year, the Mysians take to the woods, calling "Hyla! Hyla! Hyla!"

This was a favorite story of the ancients. Theocritus writes of it:

> "Hylas," he bellowed three throat-wrenching cries.
> Each time the boy replied; but his voice came faint
> From the pool, as if he were calling from a distance

And Virgil:

> *His adiungit, Hylan nautae quo fonte relictum*
> *clamassent, ut litus 'Hyla, Hyla' omne sonaret*

A favorite story, these beautiful boys (Bormus is another) lost by the edges of streams, submerged by nymph-love. (*Derry, down derry.*) Do they record accidental drownings? Poisonings from tainted wells?

Frost doesn't own his own farm, but he owns this:

> I am like a dead diver in this place

And this:

> I dwell in a lonely house I know
> That vanished many a summer ago

He rocks on the porch, warming, shuddering. (He has all day. The brook dwindles, the tree buds swell. The road is as empty as life.) One thing, at least, he knows: the brook in the interval, under the alders, is good. And it shall be called Hyla Brook. Elliott is dead, and Elinor will never say his name. Instead, the nymphs, those animal wives whose interests are not our interests, call *Hyla!, Hyla!, Hyla!* in the April mist. And the hyla breed sing, with lustiness and lust, of the brevity of mud.

12

Is he holding the revolver? "Goddamn you, get back in the house!"

Jeanie is shrieking in the middle of the road, waving her Delphic instruments, a china cup in one hand, a saucer in the other. She drinks coffee by the quart—she tells the children she drowns herself in it—until it makes her eyes roll and she spins out weird rigmaroles.

Robert is bellowing. "Get back in!" The workers at Derry Depot will be coming home. The road won't be empty, people will see. His tainted blood. "I'll—I'll—!" Is he holding the revolver? Later, he will tell his biographer, Larry, that he is; that he brandishes it paternally; that Jeanie shrivels on the instant, crumples into beaten girlhood; skulks back toward the house.

She had taken Lesley on her lap on the parlor sofa, with Carol and little Irma on either side. A homey scene, a lithograph: the aunt comes for a visit, the children listen to a story. She was looking out the window, across the brook interval, pointing. Robert paused by the door, wary. She was whispering. He leaned closer. ". . . a graveyard up on the hill. See the stone there, between the two trees? That's a gravestone. Soon we'll all be buried up there. We'll all be in a row! Won't that be nice?"

He burst in. "Shut your mouth!" Coffee splashed on the sofa, Lesley fell from the lap. Jeanie ran to the porch. "Come back here!"

Did he fetch the revolver? Is he training it on her now, as she scurries back up the driveway, to pack her bags and get the hell out of their lives? (Her second visit in seven years; her clothes are too fine for a schoolteacher; she models for artists in Boston and lives with a woman; what sins are on her head?) Is he ready to blow her brains out if she misbehaves?

Or is there no revolver? Is the memory of it merely his own word-drunkenness? A Frost family disease. The Colt of Belle's birthing story captures all wild San Francisco and her own runaway horse to boot. And "revolver" exerts its own magnetism: fortune's wheel, the cycle of revenge, time come back around. The son chases the sister down the road holding the father's weapon, aiming for the sweet spot right between the father's blue marble eyes.

Yes, he is holding the revolver.

13

Tainted water: all those children, through millennia of human history, dead by waterholes where the springbok bathed, by the village laundry pool, by the brook splashing snow-white down from the cow pasture hidden on a higher slope. All the young, bright, loved children. Surely nymphs took them, took them gently, kissed them as they went. Surely animal mothers are taking them even now onto their laps and singing to them in some other world.

You confessed to Larry that you called the competent doctor too late. You told him it felt like murdering your own child. You didn't confess the other thing: the gaps in the chicken run, the Wyandottes running free through the yard and in the house.

Was it your laziness? No, that was the summer your hay fever first hit you. Barely able to breathe, you felt like an old man. But yes, it was also your laziness. The chickens ran free, and you thought, What harm? A hen or two lost to dogs, a dozen chicks to the chicken hawk. But consider (do not look away): he died in July. *Cholera infantum* is a summer disease. Why? Because then the wellwater is sluggish and warm, milky. Cholera is gastroenteritis.

Was it your selfishness? In the summer of Elliott's second year, you spilled milk in the well at the rented house in Amesbury, and, fearing contamination, you resolved to empty it. You descended a ladder and stood barefoot in the cold water for an hour, filling pail after pail, and afterward suffered chills and chest pains. Another doctor stood like death in the doorway and asked about a family history of tuberculosis, and you said yes, your father died of it—your father, who took arduous swims out to a buoy off a point north of San Francisco, in the cold Pacific water, while you stood on the shore guarding his bottle of whiskey, terrified he would never reappear (you were alone, with nothing to comfort you but the sound of seals barking on a distant headland). He would climb the ladder up the buoy's side, to wave exultantly to you and prove fruitlessly to himself that his illness and his alcoholism weren't killing him. Perhaps, then, on Powder House Hill, as three hundred chickens ran wild, you feared a recurrence of the chest pains if you cleaned the well and you told yourself, What harm?, when you knew damn well what harm. You would say that God punished you, except that Elinor's answer to that is forever in your ear: "What a dreadful egoist you are! If there *were* a God, and He cared a jot for anything you did, He would have killed *you*."

Perhaps God punished you for your egoism.

Isn't "God" (anyway) your word for a superstitious belief in a third universal force, after gravity and electromagnetism, called retribution, or What Goes Around, Comes Around? (It guides the stars in their courses, and plots the trajectory of the fall of a sparrow.) Isn't it the child's certainty that the smallest half-thought thought of rebellion will be pierced through on the instant by the blazing sword of the father's gaze? (And when the rage falls for no thought at all, in retrospect the child sees that there must have been a quarter-thought, an eighth-thought, and his worst sin was not acknowledging it.)

When your mother said "God," she meant it. She came to live with you that year on Powder House Hill. She was dying of cancer. (God's little gift.) While Elinor was busy with baby Lesley, Belle would take Elliott on her lap and tell him Bible stories: Jonah and Job, John the locust-eater, Jesus at Cana. Elliott drank it in. One dark day when the sun broke through clouds, he pointed and said, "God is smiling at us."

Elinor was indignant. "This is her campaign."

Your mother had been saying you'd lost your faith reading William James at Harvard. "I lost my faith in Harvard, anyway," you answered.

"And Elinor—" she began.

"Don't say a word about Elinor." (You've never allowed anyone to talk about her.)

So that summer you wheezed and hacked and wondered what visitation this was, and the chickens tasted freedom, and Belle told stories. And in July, on the evening of the seventh day, the doctor straightened from the boy's bed and pronounced like a hanging judge, "It's too late now for me to do anything."

Afterward, you tore into your mother: "All those Bible stories! 'God smiling!' Did you tell him the good one about Korah? Did you? I was brought up on that one in San Francisco!"

Four months later, Belle lay on her deathbed in the sanatorium at Penacook, and serenely said she was going home. "Home," you repeated, wondering what the word meant.

"I know, Rob," she said, "that for the moment you prefer to believe there is no life after death. Soon I will know which of us is right."

You retorted angrily, "If you're wrong, you won't very well know it, will you?"

She died with no one at her bedside. Even Jeanie, who never lost an opportunity to call you a selfish bastard for not visiting her more often, wasn't with her. Was Jeanie posing half nude for her artist chums? (But that was later.) You were crating apples at the new farm in Derry. The Powder House Hill farm, with its poisoned well, was now the second in a line of cursed homes. (The first, San Francisco, was literally swallowed by the earth.) You and Elinor carried to Derry the baby Lesley, and your three hundred chickens, and not a thing of Elliott's. If you had a photograph of him, Elinor would protect it with her life. But it would be too holy a relic ever to look upon, its name unpronounceable. It would remain wrapped thrice at the bottom of a locked trunk. Whereas you might destroy it, in a rage at the lie—this immortal child, smiling at the camera's chemical light.

But you have no photograph. You have only your mind's eye, the boy turning to you for protection, and behind him the white wings beating upward.

14

Home Burial

". . . Amy! There's someone coming down the road!"

"*You*—oh, you think the talk is all. I must go—
Somewhere out of this house. How can I make you—"

"If—you—do!" She was opening the door wider.
"Where do you mean to go? First tell me that.
I'll follow and bring you back by force. I *will!*—"

15

SAN FRANCISCO, CALIFORNIA
1879

Papa comes to play with Robbie, who's done with his bath, but still sitting in the tub of scratchy metal. The water is cold and dirty. Papa doesn't notice because he wants to play. He tousles Robbie's head. He cuffs and splashes him. "Dukes up, little man." Mama says to be careful, but Papa doesn't like that. Robbie should be brave, but water gets in his mouth. It tastes bitter and scares him, so he tries to stand up. Papa by accident pushes him too hard and he falls. Something under the water slices his knee. Oh! it hurts! He starts to cry. Papa scowls. The game is spoiled. Blood in the water mixes with the gray suds, and the sight of it, kind of rusty and greasy with his dirt in it, makes Robbie throw up.

16

SAN FRANCISCO, CALIFORNIA

1879–1885

While the children of Israel were in the wilderness, they found a man that gathered sticks upon the sabbath day. And they that found him gathering sticks brought him unto Moses and Aaron, and unto all the congregation. And they put him in ward, because it was not declared what should be done to him. And the Lord said unto Moses, "The man shall be surely put to death: all the congregation shall stone him with stones without the camp." And all the congregation brought him without the camp, and stoned him with stones, and he died.

Now Korah and Dathan and Abiram rose up before Moses and Aaron, with certain of the children of Israel, and said unto them, "Ye take too much upon you, seeing all the congregation are holy, every one of them, and the Lord is among them: wherefore then lift ye up yourselves above the congregation of the Lord?"

And Moses spake unto Korah, saying, "Even tomorrow the Lord will show who are his, and who is holy. This do: take you censers, Korah, and all your company, and put fire therein, and put incense in them before the Lord tomorrow: and it shall be that the man whom the Lord doth choose, he shall be holy."

And Moses sent to call Dathan and Abiram, who said, "We will not come up. Is it a small thing that thou hast brought us up out of a land that floweth with milk and honey, to kill us in the wilderness, except thou make thyself altogether a prince over us?"

And Moses was very wroth, and said unto the Lord, "Respect not thou their offering."

And they took every man his censer, and put fire in them, and laid incense thereon. And the Lord spake unto Moses, saying, "Speak unto the congregation, saying, 'Get you up from about the tabernacle of Korah, Dathan, and Abiram.'"

And Moses spake unto the congregation, saying, "Depart, I pray you, from the tents of these wicked men, and touch nothing of theirs, lest ye be consumed in all their sins."

So they gat up from the tabernacle of Korah, Dathan, and Abiram, on every side: and Dathan and Abiram came out, and stood in the door of their tents, and their wives, and their sons, and their little children. And it came to pass that the ground clave asunder that was under them, and the earth opened her mouth, and swallowed them up. They went down alive into the pit, and the earth closed upon them: and they perished from among the congregation.

As it is written in the book of Numbers, chapters 15 and 16, and told on the knee to the five-year-old, and to the six-year-old, and even to the ten- and eleven-year-old, for this is a backward child, whose head hangs, whose stomach hurts, who does not go to school, who does not read, who learns tales only in his mother's voice, on his mother's lap, in rented rooms on Eddy Place, and Sacramento Street, and at the Abbotsford House, and the Inglewood Hotel, and on Steiner Street, and at Grace Terrace, and in Leavenworth Street, all of these dwelling places being nigh unto Nob Hill. And Russian Hill also.

17

Midnight.

Frost stares out the window, seeing nothing, deep in thought.

Human speech. The immortal commonplace. Why does it move him so?

The line that stirs him most in *Comus:* "Shall I go on? Or have I said enough?"

In *The Land of Heart's Desire*: "The butter's by your elbow, Father Hart."

In *Hamlet*: "So have I heard and do in part believe it."

18

A Younger Poet publishes a poem in the *Springfield Republican and Union*:

Robert Frost in Amherst

Robert Frost is here in town again.
I saw him on the street just yesterday,

The grayest, greatest, man of all our men,
Gray the way a great boulder is gray.

Somehow that brief view of his weathered face
Made our thin air a sturdier atmosphere.
Home is a sounder, more enduring place.
Yet airier too, now Robert Frost is here.

The Younger Poet writes in his diary:

Thus was the first pop-gun fired in my private campaign
to establish a significant relation with this most significant
man in town. Meanwhile my essay, "Robert Frost, Master
of Humor," is about half done.

19

When Margery died horribly, begging for life, you and Elinor diverged on the paths you'd worn grassless before.

"God, what a woman! And it's come to this,
A man can't speak of his own child that's dead."

"You can't because you don't know how."

You wrote that many years ago. Of course it was about Elliott, but you always said it was about a different child. You never read it in public. You'd as soon stand naked on the stage.

"I can repeat the very words you were saying.
'Three foggy mornings and one rainy day

Will rot the best birch fence a man can build.'
Think of it, talk like that at such a time!
What had how long it takes a birch to rot
To do with what was in the darkened parlor."

You softened it for the poem—you made the woman speak. You managed to have out your fight with her, whereas the real Elinor was too far away to halloo to, shout at, comfort, curse, or shoot with the revolver.

Then it came around again. And of your four children it had to be, again, the baby.

Long ago at Amherst you'd read Blackmore's "Dominus Illuminatio Mea" to the student Christian Association:

In the hour of death, after this life's whim,
When the heart beats low, and the eyes grow dim,
And pain has exhausted every limb—
    The lover of the Lord shall trust in Him.

When the will has forgotten the lifelong aim,
And the mind can only disgrace its fame,
And a man is uncertain of his own name—
    The power of the Lord shall fill this frame.

When the last sigh is heaved, and the last tear shed,
And the coffin is waiting beside the bed,
And the widow and child forsake the dead—
    The angel of the Lord shall lift this head.

For even the purest delight may pall,
And power must fail, and the pride must fall,
And the love of the dearest friends grow small—
    But the glory of the Lord is all in all.

You'd been talking to the wide-eyed Christian colts about escapism, and you left it to them to notice (you don't think they did) that with each quatrain Blackmore constructed a pitiless three-part syllogism of earthly despair, after which, in the fourth line, he waved a wand and pulled out the rabbit Redemption. Back then you were amused, but when Margery died you looked at the poem again and saw how it would read if you snatched the providential Popsicle stick out of the poet's hand and left him just his triple-locked boxes. Using a similar four-beat line, and the same rhyme scheme, you wrote:

> The witch that came (the withered hag)
> To wash the steps with pail and rag,
> Was once the beauty Abishag

It became "Provide, Provide," in which you laughed your worst laugh. Here was no God, nor any good, only goods. Only human providence: what a man might grab for himself and, white-knuckled, keep—riches; a throne so deep no one might knock him out of it; friends whose allegiance had been bought and paid for.

Then you told everyone it was about a charwomen's strike at Harvard, that it was all about political grievance and the blandishments of the New Deal, and you cracked jokes when you told it. You never said a word about the grief.

See, you're a performer. The show must go on. A poem slides on its own greasepaint. "I'll go down joking," you say before reading the poem. Or you say, "This one's horrible." Sometimes you say both. Sometimes this seems heroic to you, other times despicable.

Abishag is the birch fence that rots in three lines, and Elinor will never understand how you can do it, or why you'd ever want to.

20

Frost sits in his room with his fears. (He must always be left alone before a lecture.) Fear of what will happen when he launches himself on his audience. He never writes out his talks, never has notes. He walks a highwire. Or, more perilous than that, a chain of associations, a plank that could end with every step. If he falls, will they catch him? Will they forgive him?

For courage he's downed his two raw eggs. Anything else would make him queasy. He glances at his watch, gauges the murmur from the distant hall. A full house? *You old fraud—haven't they been full for decades now?* But after ten thousand talks he still half expects a sea of empty seats, a scattering of slumped forms. The first questioner, jumping to life: *Who the hell are you?*

Bicycling Jesus! Is he really going to Russia? He said he would go if the president asked him. Did he say that because he secretly didn't want to go? Stewart telephoned the other day to say the president liked the idea. Frost will have to say yes. Did he say he'd go if the president asked him because he knew the president would, which would force him to go even though the idea terrified him?

Russia! The frozen north! He feels sure he will die there. When Voltaire was a mere eighty-two years old, he left his hometown to launch himself on the crowds of Paris, and perished on the trip. Never discount superstition. It's metaphor in disguise, and metaphor springs from intuition, which is often a better prophet than reason. Frost is eighty-eight. (Not eighty-seven; even the wide-eyed world knows that now.) He has declared for forty years that he intended to live to ninety, like the English poet Walter Savage Landor. Frost first read about Landor in some Lawrence school primer, and that number—ninety—struck the fatherless boy. It seemed Biblical, heroic. Frost's father, for all his talk of manly vigor, couldn't stand up to a fifth of whiskey and died at thirty-four. The Romantic and Victorian poets of Frost's youth celebrated lovers' brief blaze of passion and the pathos of early death, but Frost, watching his mother struggle alone in Lawrence, teaching schoolchildren she couldn't control and enduring the contempt of her dead husband's family—Frost thought poets might have something to say about the long arm of marriage (in which law and love are one) and the muddied triumph of *not* dying.

Walter Savage Landor. Oh, did the schoolboy Rob love that middle name. And Landor wrote a fine quatrain when he was seventy-five:

> I strove with none, for none was worth my strife.
> Nature I loved and, next to Nature, Art:
> I warm'd both hands before the fire of life;
> It sinks, and I am ready to depart.

Frost enjoyed the irony: Landor, the old savage, fought with everybody—his teachers, his government, his wife, his children, his neighbors, his servants. Once when his gardener offended him, he threw the man out the window. Then repented and rushed to look out, to see if he'd landed in the flower bed. There's something about that kind of ardency that deeply stirs Frost. Love or hate, fire or ice. None of the tepid in-between. Live your damned life as though it matters. And why? Because it *is* a damned life. Because, at core, it *doesn't* matter.

Ninety years. *When Abram was ninety years old and nine, the Lord said unto him, I am the Almighty God; walk before me, and be thou perfect.* Be thou upright. Ninety degrees.

There's a metaphor Frost has toyed with for years. It means something to him, but he's never managed to turn this particular lump in his throat into a lyric: We're born as though at zero latitude, from out of the earth's wide girth, and at first we're simply whirled, ignorant of where we are. Our pole star is invisible. As we age, we climb the ladder of the latitudes, and our star rises with us. As we leave our twenties, we pass out of the torrid zone. We become temperate in the forties. Our pole star keeps rising. We keep climbing heavenward, and our own poll turns snowy as snow mounts to our knees. Skin pales, limbs stiffen. We become the frozen north. Our goal is ninety degrees: Landor's End. At the North Pole motion stops. All times are equal, all views are into the past. The pole star shines straight down. When Frost gets there, he'll look up and hold his arms out and, spinning on his axis, he'll lift off like one of those helicopter wheels launched with a string, he'll rise and disappear.

Who do you think you are? Elijah?

A tap on the door. A head thrusts in. "Mr. Frost? Are you ready?"

Who do you think you are? Frost turns away, flinches almost. He picks up his battered old copy of *Complete Poems*; also the brand-new one, the thin one: *In the Clearing.* Nerves make him brusque. He should acknowledge this young man, high-school teacher or amanuensis or maybe younger poet, who looks frightened. That clever New York City fellow, Trilling, called Frost "terrifying," but he's not! Just a snow-crusted deaf old irredeemably damned Yankee. "Ready or not, here I come."

The young man gestures him by, trails at his elbow. Outside, they descend the porch steps. Where's K.? Doc Cook, the director, is hurrying toward him along the path: "I'm sorry, Robert, I was delayed, I sent Mr.—" From the left, here comes someone else. They're converging on him.

Rise and disappear. Like Henry Hudson. He *did* write a poem about that—his tendency to indulge fantasies about vanishing into thin air. Such as after one of his father's beatings (savage), while his mother shut herself in the next room and prayed. *I'll run away, and then they'll be sorry!* He called it "An Empty Threat." He imagined a speaker who wasn't going anywhere, forever, but who dreamed eternally of escaping to the Canadian fur trade, of climbing into a skiff no bigger than a zinc washtub and paddling off into the blue vastness of the bay that took Hudson's name and swallowed the rest of him.

Maybe he'd get lost trying to find the lost explorer. Seals would bark from an icy shore. Were they Hudson's doomed men, calling?

Hudson Bay is itself an empty threat. A frozen hole like that in the heart of the Promised Land calls God's plan into question. Like all the Northwest Passengers, Hudson erred in assuming the divine intent of those waters was in favor of commerce. Maybe God is all for obstruction. Maybe He loves a wall. In other words, Hudson forgot his Job. Winter caught him, and, come spring, some of his sailors mutinied. They put Henry and his son and seven men in a skiff, committed them to God's silence, and sailed for home. Not a bone found, not a buckle.

Frost and Doc Cook and a couple of outriders are approaching the Little Theatre. The low evening sun is lighting up Bread Loaf Mountain under dark clouds. Where the hell is K.? They step up onto the thumping side-porch, and here she is coming out through the glass doors (hello, lovely!). He growls, "Where've you been, I've been looking for you." She ignores that, makes sure he has his glasses, his books. "I'm not that decrepit!" he snaps. Through the doors, Doc Cook saying something he's not in the mood to catch, and up three steps (slowly, puff, up my knee!) onto the stage. Applause like rain, then thunder. The older and deafer he gets, the louder they clap. And they always stand now, the moment he comes in. They're thinking, Christ, he's on his last legs; this could be his last hurrah. You and I, Henry.

> It's to say, "You and I—"
> To such a ghost,
> "You and I
> Off here
> With the dead race of the Great Auk!"

He almost died this January, of pneumonia. He can't help feeling that he was saved for a reason. Some last job to do.

They won't stop until he sits. So he doesn't sit for a moment. Yes, a full house. Humid with expectant breath. People in the aisles and out the doors. Last chance, everyone! He's at eighty-eight degrees north!

Christ, is he really going to Russia? He clutches his thin new book. (He's not taking Larry. Larry will be furious.) He sits.

Doc takes the podium. "Ladies and gentlemen, welcome to the opening lecture of the 1962 session of the Bread Loaf School of English. By long tradition, for which we are immensely grateful and by which we are profoundly honored, the first talk is given by the most famous and celebrated poet in America today—"

Frost tries not to listen. It usually irritates him, what people say about him. Either they don't praise him enough, in which case he suspects they're making fun of him, or they praise him too much, in which case he suspects they're compensating for some previous occasion when they made fun of him. Yes, paranoid. Frost knows it. But you can know you're color-blind and still not be able to tell green from red. Doc's a friend. Frost doesn't want to be irritated with him. If he was as deaf as he pretended, he'd turn off his hearing aid. But he doesn't wear a hearing aid, so he props his head against his right hand, covering his good ear.

Russia, Russia. Where writers live brief blazing lives, ending in show trials and executions.

> If well it is with Russia, then feel free
> To say so or be stood against the wall
> And shot. It's Pollyanna now or death

But that was in Stalin's time. This Khrushchev fellow seems better. Frost liked the shoe-banging. If he had to sit through all that United Nations talk he'd bang his shoe, too.

When Frost was sixteen, seventeen, when words on the salty page seduced him like animal wives, he read Turgenev's *A Hunter's Sketches*. Those stories are still what Russia means to him: endless forests of fir and birch; the woodcock in the grove, the snipe in the bog; landowners like drunken sultans; wraithlike dogs whose masters never feed them, tail stumps wagging, ribs staring; peasants as destitute as *King Lear*'s Tom. Hunting, for that hunter, was an excuse to escape into the woods, to look for the hidden valley. Gimcrack, crackbrained Marx-Leninism is just a tarnish on that old silver. In 1845, Turgenev invented the twentieth-century short story—closely observed, withholding judgment. Why? Because he had to. He wanted to denounce serfdom, but had to evade the censors of Czar Nicholas I. Like Jesus's parables, the *Hunter's Sketches* separate readers from nonreaders, the savable from the unsavable. Nicholas's censors, nonreaders to a man, read all two dozen stories and never figured out what Turgenev was doing. Ha! Crafty Russian Yankee!

Applause. Frost looks up. Introduction over. Good; no idea what Doc said. He stands, walks to the podium. Cheers. *Admit it, old man, you love it.* He does. He basks. Love me now, before I speak! He grips his new book. New poems by an old man, and old poems he never collected before. Because they weren't good enough? Has he lowered his standards? Was he just too goddamn desperate to squeeze a last book out? Convince the crowd he wasn't dead yet? Thirteen years since his last book. More famous than ever, more listened to, more raptly—*This is* Meet the Press, *and our guest is Robert Frost. Mr. Frost, will you tell us what freedom means?*—he's grateful for the position his country has given him. But is he worthy of it? Does he have anything to say? What service is asked of him? In going to Russia is he answering the call, or sailing toward the mouth of the whale?

Sit down! He gestures. They sit, settle. Class come to order. The hush. All eyes. They want value.

Now what? A moment's blankness. A blink of panic.

"Suppose I just decided not to read any poetry at all but just tell you stories. That would be new, wouldn't it?"

Murmur. They're uncertain. Disappointed?

"I might spend the evening just reading out of my new book, but I don't want to wear that out in a hurry." It being such thin material. "Suppose I told a story or two."

> Listen, my children, and you shall hear
> Of the midnight life of a man of fear

Turgenev's got him thinking about stories. A good eye that man had. There's a moment in "Raspberry Spring"—the hunter's dog on a hot summer day "polishing" his master's heels, trudging just behind with his tongue lolling. The master chides; the dog wags his tail, embarrassed, but will not pick up the pace.

"I heard of a boy back in the 1830s who must have been full of what America was."

Long ago, in England, before Frost discovered he could make a living with his endless talk talk, he started a novel, thinking it might pay better than poetry. But he couldn't sustain it. He can only write when the fit is on him. And prose feels like an opponent who won't put his dukes up; the form doesn't push back at you. Frost needs his own censors—meter, rhyme. He calls them the tennis net, but they're also the net below the highwire act.

". . . a boy from upstate New York, middle state. He had sailed before the mast." Where's this story from, anyway? "And in Saint Petersburg, when the ship got there, he said to his captain: 'I wish I could see the czar.' And the captain said, 'I'm afraid that would be difficult.' 'Well, I want to see him.'" From the same school primer that told the life of Landor? Frost has recounted the story off and on for years, but has never found anyone who knew the source. It couldn't have been his mother. Outside the Bible, she stuck to stories of the Scots: Rob Roy, Robert the Bruce. The north in her stories meant the land of mist and mystics.

"The captain spoke to the consul in Saint Petersburg, and the consul said the same thing: 'That would be very difficult. I don't suppose that would be possible.' And a message came from the czar presently for the boy to come see him. And he came before the czar—the American of these days; I can just feel him, the kind of boy—with his hand out like this." Frost holds out a fist. *Is it a gift I have for you, or a punch in the mouth?*

Why does he so like this story? "And he said: 'I have a present for you. It's an acorn that fell from a tree that grows beside the house of George Washington. He was a great ruler and you're a great ruler. I thought you might like to plant this by your palace.' The czar sent for a shovel, and they went out together and planted it. And then the czar said to him—in a splendid way, too!—'Anything I can do for you? That's a great thing you've done for me.' And the boy said, 'I always wanted to see Moscow.' So the czar gave him a cavalcade of horses and sent him up to Moscow. And his ship sailed without him. I don't know how he got home."

The boy went north and disappeared. Got his wish, vanished. Something about that—

The boy's czar must have been Turgenev's—Nicholas I. The handsomest ruler in Europe, and the most autocratic. Of him it was written, "One could not be more emperor than he." Perfect, then, for the fable—the Platonic ideal of Emperor confronted by the Platonic ideal of Boy. The Boy, holding out the acorn, is himself an acorn, and the Oak to whom he appeals recognizes him. *You and I.*

A common sort of tale: the powerless winning over the all-powerful through pluck and charm. Stealing some of his power by binding him to a promise. "Whatever you want, my boy! Ask and, on my honor, it shall be granted!" Among the tents of the Bedouin, in the jasper halls of Baghdad, in the pleasure gardens of Kubla Khan. And the always unexpected request that must be fulfilled: your daughter's hand in marriage; the head of John the Baptist on a platter; one grain of rice on the first square of the chessboard, two grains on the second, four on the third. . . .

Something about those stories. A Freudian might say— Oh, but Frost detests Freudianism. Freud was a frustrated novelist. His system is a form of Swedenborgianism, taking good metaphors and petrifying them into dogma.

Where is he? His mind is wandering. The audience in the Little Theatre swims before him. "Now, I was thinking about glorifying America. What does that word mean? This comes from Washington. Somebody wants me to do something to glorify the space age and our part in it. That's prophesying, and I charge more for prophecy." They laugh. Frost soldiers on. But his thoughts won't gather. They laugh too quickly. They've come determined to enjoy him whether he's enjoyable or not. "Space" leads to "the spacious age of great Elizabeth" (was that Tennyson's line?), then Drake, then Columbus. Then the planet Mars. He has no idea where he's going. Out of the solar system, apparently.

A poem on the space age! Good God, he's no court poet. What do they expect, something about beating the Russians to Mars? (It seems clear they're going to be first to the moon.) He's already written his hymn to the space age. It's called "Build Soil":

> Keep off each other and keep each other off. . . .
> We congregate embracing from distrust
> As much as love, and too close in to strike
> And be so very striking.

Once he tried playing court poet to the United Nations, when his friend Ahmed Bokhari invited him to write a couplet for the Meditation Room. It was going to be inscribed on a block of iron ore donated by Sweden. The block was Dag Hammarskjöld's darling. God knows what he expected. Well, no, Frost figures he expected some version of swords-into-plowshares. The peacemongers' favorite verse. They like to forget the Bible also tells us to beat our plowshares into swords. Because, wouldn't you know it, millennial peace comes at the price of killing everyone who won't go along. And wouldn't you know it, Swedish iron ore was beaten into German weaponry through all of World War II. So Frost wrote a couplet not about reconciliation, but about strife, about the need to take a side that seems built into the very structure of existence, the commandment inscribed on every splittable atom. Hammarskjöld hated it. Bokhari rejected it. Bastards!

But where, oh, where has he got to now? He's leaning hard on the podium, taking the weight off his feet. He already feels like he needs to pee again; it's a phantom; it's that bladder trouble. Prostatitis. Operation recommended, knives like nibbling small-fry up his penis. Not on your goddamned life. A woman in the front row with a pile of wavy hair is sitting with her legs stretched out, crossed at the ankles. She's a mermaid, looking up at him through the murk. From Mars he's moved to Prometheus, then teaching, then kindergarten. Now he seems to be on Thoreau and one-worldism. ". . . Thoreau talked that stuff all the time. No property. He could enjoy everything that belonged to other people. He could eat their meals, too." A big laugh. Do they have any idea what they're laughing at? Does he? He can't keep rambling like this. They'll eventually admit to themselves he's not giving them what they came for.

Time to fall back on his poems. "Now I'll read you a little. I'm going to begin with some of the little ones that I have in my head; old ones, too. Suppose I just go back to one or two of the old ones first. I'm groping for what I want. I want to get the mood." Before it gets him. There it goes, galloping into the twilight! Catch it!

He fumbles with his *Complete Poems*. God, he hates that title. If it's complete, what's this other book on the lectern? (Don't answer that.) The pages open automatically to the poems he's said a million times. Up my knee! He reads "Mowing"; "The Tuft of Flowers"; "Into My Own." Friends tell him he reads too fast. They're probably right, but the groove is worn so smooth. And some he has to speak fast, with his mind half elsewhere, or he can't get through them with composure. Poems written sixty years ago. He remembers writing "Mowing" in the middle of the night at the kitchen table in Derry, with the revolver on the table next to him. (Was it really there?)

Old pages opening automatically, completed old poet saying the same old poems over and over. Because he's lazy? Maybe. And because he's old. And because all the audiences in all the halls in all the towns want the same old poems. If he doesn't read "Stopping by Woods" and "The Road Not Taken," they clamor for them at the end. And as of last year you can add "The Gift Outright." It both pleases and bothers him. Didn't he always say he wanted to lodge a few poems like burrs where they'd be hard to get rid of? These three are lodged like bullets.

Ironically, he himself has begun to forget some of them. He's found lately that if he says "Mowing" without having the book in front of him, a line might slip away. This must be how a poet turns his face to the wall. If every month counts as five minutes of latitude, he's at eighty-eight degrees, fifteen minutes.

He snaps shut his *Complete Poems*; opens the other one. "Suppose I skip from there to some of the later ones in the little book. This little one's called 'Away!' " He starts to read it. Oh, gee! Is it any good at all? Isn't "An Empty Threat" better? Why did he collect these poems? Sheer vanity? He wanted to beat out Thomas Hardy, that's why.

Frost is swept with a feeling of nausea. He wants to run. But they came to hear him. He soldiers on, through doubt and fear of failure, fear of them, self-disgust. He reads "Accidentally on Purpose" and "Peril of Hope" and "A Cabin in the Clearing," and the audience keeps laughing and clapping, and Christ, the book can't be that bad, it has sold more copies than any of his others, and K. tells him the reviews have been good (but he can't trust her, she knows how much bad reviews upset him). He starts to read "How Hard It Is to Keep from Being King When It's in You and in the Situation," but partway through he's overwhelmed by the fear that the poem maunders like an old man's thoughts. He stops mid-line. "I'm not going to read any more." He rubs his eyes. "I'm not seeing too well. I seem to be having trouble with my glasses." He's not lying. His eyes are watering. The audience sways in the dark, the glass doors glow with cobalt dusk, his reading lamp glitters and dances. He stares at the page, but the letters are scattered legs of squashed bugs. He's back on his mother's lap, eight or nine years old, trying to read something (Bible? primer? his father's newspaper?), but the words won't form, and then the tears form, and the letters melt away and his stomach hurts.

He looks up, closes his eyes. "Let me say something without reading."

What? Prophesy, damn it! Inhale the poisonous fumes, fill yourself with the insane god.

> "I opened the door so my last look
> Should be taken outside a house and book. . . ."

Don't think, don't question. Speak! Only speak! He continues through "One More Brevity," but behind his closed eyes he's back on that platform in the cold sunshine, with the sharp wind making his eyes water, and sixty million people (they said) watching him, and he can't see a thing. The sunlight burns off the white page and the vice-president with a face like a bloodhound holds his hat out to offer shade, but now it's too dark amid the glare. What a fiasco! The president asked him, and he had his great chance, his one chance, to hit the home run in the last inning of the final game, to win the foot race against the champion, and he blew it, and he had to put aside the poem he'd sweated blood over (occasional poems! why do they ask? bastard poetry!) and fall back on "The Gift Outright," chanting it, keeping the demons at bay.

Fumbled. Game's over. Go home, boy. (His father's voice: "What is it *now*?") He soldiers on. He says "Choose Something Like a Star." He talks about Catullus. He hears himself apologizing for his new book (Frost is in the clearing! He's got the ball! He's crossing the eighty-ninth parallel!) and his eyes clear up enough for him to read a couple of other poems. Then he stares into the darkness and says, "I guess you've had enough of me," and the darkness applauds.

But it wants more. It claps and stomps. So he says "Stopping by Woods" to keep it from asking for it (and damn! it's a good poem; can anything he's written in the last twenty years touch it?). Then it asks for "The Gift Outright" and "The Road Not Taken." (Bang! Bang! Bang! His three shots.)

He failed the president. The young Galahad. A fine young man. No liberal saphead like Adlai Stevenson. Frost predicted he'd win the presidency before he'd even declared for the race. He heard later that Kennedy, on the campaign trail, was ending his speeches with "Stopping by Woods"—saying he had promises to keep, and so on. A sort of thanks to the poet. Frost was charmed. And now maybe he has another chance. Go to Russia for Kennedy. Hold out his thin new book to the czar and ask for a favor. "Ask anything, my boy, and on my honor, it shall be granted!"

"Give me the world on a platter."

Frost will admit it: he has been guilty of making light of the Bomb. An old man's vanity, maybe. Elliott is dead, and Margery is dead, and Carol is dead, and Elinor is dead, and Irma is insane. Frost has survived it all by believing that all times are equally perilous, that if you turn "woe is man" into "woe is me" you're tying lead weights on your shoes in the universal stream whose interest is ever to drown us. People say, Look at this terrible century! And Frost says, Look at the Black Death. Look at what happened to the Indians.

But right now he isn't so sure. They say a single hydrogen bomb could wipe out New York City. Eight million people vaporized in a few seconds.

Nations will always be different, and nations will always have reasons to fight. A world without fighting for things you believe in is hell. But what about a world in which a hundred million people burn (and their wives, and their sons, and their little children) because half of a former enemy's ruined city is islanded in the present enemy's camp, and no one knows how to either rescue it or give it up? Where Troy is itself the Trojan Horse, carrying Armageddon in its belly?

> Haven't you heard what we have lived to learn?
> Nothing so new—something we had forgotten:
> *War is for everyone, for children too.*

He cared plenty about bombs when he wrote that fifty years ago. And those were only TNT bombs. But his own children were children when he wrote that. Hell, his own children were *alive*. "There's nothing like a good map," he tells the darkness. All he can see are the backs of his hands in the light of the reading lamp. *I know this country like the—*

Suddenly he feels as though he really is prophesying. Which means he doesn't know what he means. But there's something there. A good map. You over there, me over here. The space age. Maps, boundaries, witness trees. Bearing witness—

> Listen my children, Beware! Beware!
> My flashing eyes, my floating hair!

He speaks with urgency—"And the evidence of that is that *we've* got a good map, from the Atlantic to the Pacific, laid out as neat, however we got it, by hook or by crook, I don't say." All those dead Indians, even their hidden valleys overrun. A greater power unleashed; a world ended. "It's a great map. And Berlin is the worst map the world ever saw. See, bad maps make bad troubles."

Something there is—
Something wicked—

"Maps do it—that's all." It's vitally important that they understand. He holds up his thumbs. He repeats: "Maps do it. Good night."

He bows his head.

Out of the darkness, thunder.

21

1964

A Younger Poet writes:

And as the Presidents
Also on the platform
Began flashing nervously
Their Presidential smiles
For the harmless old guy,
And poets watching on the TV
Started thinking, Well that's
The end of *that* tradition,

And the managers of the event
Said, Boys this is it,
This sonofabitch poet
Is gonna croak,

Putting the paper aside
You drew forth
From your great faithful heart
The poem.

22

1961

The Biographer is convinced: the old man planned it from the start, had the dedication poem typed out in large print—oh, my eyes, you never know, I'm an old man!—and all along never intended to read it. The entire thing a performance, a tightrope walker wobbling to make the audience gasp, make them applaud when he *doesn't* fall. All eyes on him, he steals the show again, this time from the president of the United States. The old bastard tricked them all!

23

SAN FRANCISCO, CALIFORNIA

1884

Isabelle Moodie Frost, daughter of a whore and daughter of God, scorned by Scotland and all her Presbyters, now a San Francisco Swedenborgian blessed with second sight, patient wife, incipient lunatic, embryonic writer, returns from the theater (the magic! the color! the fantasy!), passes blindly the dank kitchen (she never cooks, hardly ever eats), drops her coat and hat on the floor (never notices; husband or son will pick them up), sits at a table strewn with her husband's empty beer bottles (doesn't see, doesn't smell), and works on a tale she calls *The Land of Crystal.*

In fairyland lived two sisters, Merrilie and Sombreena. Their bodies were crystalline, their hearts visible. Merrilie's heart was in the form of a pure white dove, radiating light, whereas Sombreena's was a fiery tiger from which sorrow flowed. ("And what do you think was the cause of it, children? I will tell you: a bad heart. With every beat of a wicked heart, there goes out into the world somewhere a throb of pain.") Merrilie said to Sombreena, "My own dear sister, why did you get so angry today? I saw the terrible tiger that haunts you in those moods, and he looked larger and wilder than ever before. I fear he will carry you off one of these days, if you do not try to woo back the white dove, with a kind and gentle soul." Alas, Merrilie saw too truly. Sombreena cleaved to her self-willed ways until, one day, she was transformed into a tiger, and banished to the dark wilderness, where vipers crawled on the ground, and hyenas crouched in their dens ready to spring upon whoever approached. . . .

Robbie Frost, ten years old, son of a saint and son of a sinner, sent to bed without his dinner, lays him down and dreams a dream:

He is running away. To the end of the block, around the corner, away from Nob Hill, from Russian Hill, away from the boys' gang he bloodied himself to get into but whose every member he fears, past the monkeys with the burned noses, past the point on the beach where his father swims out to the clanging buoy. He is going north, toward the land of magic and heroes, past the Golden Gate, into the highlands. He winds upward, crosses a ridge, asks directions, finds that he is lost. It is growing dark, and Robbie is afraid. He stumbles across a trail he can scarcely see and follows it up and up, away from farms and pastures, into mountains. He comes to a gap between two cliffs. Steeling himself, he works his way into the darkness. The path descends. Now the light strengthens, and he sees ahead a green valley, hemmed in by peaks. Figures approach: wild savages! Indians! They are the only inhabitants. Long ago they escaped from their enemies through the mountain door. They venture through the pass to make raids on their old tormentors. They are always victorious. In their secret green valley, they live happily and at peace. They welcome Robbie as a hero and adopt him into their tribe.

24

SAN FRANCISCO, CALIFORNIA

1883

His father is holding his forearm, lacing up the glove. From the headland he can hear seal cubs crying. They sound human, unearthly. "You can take this kid easy. Keep your hands up, head in. He's bigger, so he'll try for a clinch, throw you down. Keep away, look for your chance. If you hit him in the nose or mouth, he'll bleed, and that will unnerve him."

Bright light on the water, the beach sand loose and deep. Robbie shuffles in it, his heels too low, his balance off. He looks over the gloves at the other kid. Not a friend of his, or an enemy, either. The son of his Dad's friend O'Donnell. Is it Kevin? Well, Kevin, here we are, you and I. In this together. I'm gonna beat the living crap out of you.

The four men stand at the corners of the invisible ring. "Ready! Fight!"

Forgetting everything, Robbie churns straight at him, swinging wildly. Kevin backs up flailing and Robbie's on him. They spin around, stumbling, landing blows, missing. Robbie gets smacked in the mouth. His left ear pops and the pain seems to run down his neck, like a waterfall of nerves. "Get your hands up! Hands up!"

"Come on, Kevin!" The generals whoop and laugh, the soldiers fight. The soldiers are crying along with the seals. Robbie is ashamed. His father never cries. He does forty push-ups on his fingers. He wins races.

Shame: the bright blue sky, the whirling sun. Kill Kevin, kill him. The taste of iron in his mouth, the flow of brains down his neck, the hot tingle in his forearms where his father held him, lacing on the gloves.

25

AMHERST, MASSACHUSETTS
1935

Enter, bow and scrape. An audience with the king. King King, the Shoe King. Stanley King, president of Amherst College. They say he made a million dollars in the International Shoe Company before he was thirty. A King Midas, turning shoe leather to gold. "Robert. So pleased you could make it. Have a seat." Right there, my boy, the perfect height for cutting off your head.

The previous Amherst presidents, Olds and Pease, were literary men, they understood Frost's anomalous arrangement with the college, under which he lectured occasionally and met informally with students, but taught no regular courses. But this King is an efficiency expert. Each cog does his part and the clock ticks merrily, counting the golden seconds.

King Stanley wants the faculty to be one big happy family, like his corps of whistling cobblers back at his Boston factory. He's decreed the monthly faculty dinner, at which he holds court with his wife, Stanley Queen. Frost avoids it, partly on principle, partly because he senses the resentment of the other professors, who actually have to show up in the classroom in order to draw a salary. But there should be no square cogs, no fifth wheels, no fifth columnists. Bad for business! Frost has been expecting the ax for three years now.

Frost sits. King smiles like a cannibal. Frost hasn't even been doing the little he's supposed to, these past two years. There was the horror with Marjorie; Elinor's collapse; Frost's own illness. He knows he's been remiss, he knows! He deserves the ax. But not from this man, who hasn't suffered a day in his life. That rich man's ease!

> "You may throw billiard balls or bricks at it,
> And they will leave no mark," one citizen
> Had said; and several had agreed with him.

Look how Robinson pads that third line. From *King Jasper*, for which Frost is supposed to write an introduction. Poor Robinson, dead of drink and gloom. Frost must be kind. But *Jasper* ain't a good poem.

Robinson once had a president in his corner, Theodore Roosevelt, who landed him a sinecure in the New York Custom House. That was in the years when Frost was drowning at Derry and having all his poems rejected, and yes, he was envious. Ever since, he's wanted a president in *his* corner. His friend Dwight Morrow tried to hook Calvin Coolidge for him, reasoning that he was a fellow Vermonter, and an Amherst trustee to boot. But Cal never read a poem in his life. So Frost has had to settle for sinecures with the lesser presidents, the ones heading colleges. But even the literary ones he can hardly stand. Poets and the powerful—can they ever understand each other? The poet is powerless before his Muse. He can only stand and wait. Frost's grandfather, the factory foreman, thought poetry was a bad word. Laziness! He had a phrase for what he liked: "Business more than usual." Christ, Frost hated that.

The poet's only power is to escape. *You can't fire me! I quit!*

But the smiling King is speaking: "These past three weeks have abundantly demonstrated how much you bring to this institution, Robert. The trustees and I are very pleased."

Ah. Well.

"Your speech at Commencement—a much-needed political state-ment." King said something last fall about Amherst students' not hav-ing enough opportunity to get acquainted with their poet-in-residence. Which meant, "Come out of your burrow, groundhog." King arranged three lectures by Frost, and in the last, the poet sat up on his hind legs and prognosticated: six more years of winter if Roosevelt was re-elected. ". . . not enough people, especially in academia, are sounding the alarm about his socialist agenda. I wonder if we might print your talk in pamphlet form, run off a few thousand copies, distribute them where they might make a difference. . . ." And the factory is off and running. Yes, poets and power can't understand each other. The poet says no to socialist oppression, power hears yes to capitalist compulsion.

Frost interrupts. "I wonder if I might ask a favor."

What he has in mind is freedom. Freedom each year for a student of his selection, some Amherst boy who seems to own the power of deciding his mind for himself. A year's scholarship with no require-ments and no duties. The student must only go somewhere, any-where. He must run away. Find a place where no one knows him, and sit down. The Bo Tree Fellowship.

"Whatever you'd like," King says.

Frost holds out a fist. "Even to the half of thy kingdom?"

"Even to the half of my kingdom."

26

1938

For two days in March he paced the hallway outside the bedroom in which Elinor lay dying, but she never asked for him. The doctor stood in the doorway. "Her heart is very weak; she mustn't be ex-cited." By recriminations at the sight of him? Sitting bolt upright, pointing a harpy's finger at him, *For all I've suffered I damn you to hell!* All that he needed to say to her, all he needed to apologize for, the pregnancies that weakened her heart, the moves in pursuit of jobs, or fleeing hay fever, when always, always, she wanted to stay where she was, sink roots, become a tree.

Sometimes he could hear her voice through the door, but not the words.

He couldn't bear the cursed house in Amherst, so he sold it to the college, and he couldn't bear the college any longer, or King's disapproval, so he resigned. The Gully House in Vermont groaned with Elinor's ghost, Lesley refused to let him live with her, and Irma was out of the question. He stayed with Carol, but that couldn't last. He tried to bury himself in a dead language, dead poetry, by offering himself to Pease, who'd left Amherst to become head of the Harvard Latin department.

"I want to go live under thatch," Elinor had said about the family's move to England in 1912, and it wasn't lost on Frost that she was saying she wanted to be buried. Rob wanted to drink the air of the land of *The Golden Treasury*, while Elinor wanted to lie down with the dead poets. Now she was ashes, and Frost thought he might go live under ivy. He could read bone-dry two-thousand-year-old poems to dewy twenty-year-olds, see if any of them had the power to raise the dead. "Do you get my dream exactly as I dream it?" he wrote Robert Hillyer, a poet on the Harvard faculty. "It would be for boys who had had not less than three years of Latin and who could make their own translations preferably into verse or at worst free verse."

> *His adiungit, Hylan nautae quo fonte relictum*
> *clamassent, ut litus 'Hyla, Hyla' omne sonaret*

No idea what the tones of speech of a dead language were. Can undergraduate English bring blood back to the cheeks, loosen the tongue, make the silent speak?

> And thus he sang of Hylas,
> whom sailors left by the spring,

> then shouted for till hoarse,
> till all the shore re-echoed
> Hylas
> Hylas

That was in July.

Then came August, the first August day that ever was, the blazing day in the sun-fired woods with K., the birds singing above, Frost and she below, buzzing with the bees, a bare few feet from the path. Now he's not sure he wants to die after all. Now he'd rather translate Horace on jealousy than Virgil on loss.

More to the point, he has a letter from Pease, responding to his offer to the Latin department. Pease says he loves the idea and heaps praise, saving the kicker for the end: wouldn't Frost like to have John Finley to teach the course with him? Finley could be responsible for technical details of the language, leaving Frost free to concentrate on the poetry.

John Finley: Eliot Professor of Classics at Harvard. Speaking of Eliot (of course it's the same family), you can be damned sure they wouldn't set a watcher over Tom, to make sure he could tell his elbow from his ablative. Finley would be their spy. *Watchman, tell us of his plight.* They're pretty sure he'd screw up, those Harvard boyos.

Go home, boy.

You can't fire me, I quit!

27

The snow, the sun, the scrubbed white banister before him like a gleaming bar; tears from the glare and the cold.

"Summing—"

Christ! Muffed the first word!

"Summoning artists to participate
In the august occasions of the state—"

—maybe is a bad idea. Jesus. Is the page on fire? Magnesium flare. "Praise"? "Poetry"?

"This tribute to be his that here I bring
Is about—"

What's it about? The bright light of a new page—new age? Thermonuclear blast overhead? Sixty million people listening.

Frost listens to the silence. "No," he says out loud, but more or less to himself, "I'm not having a good light here at all." He tries to go on.

"Is about—the new order of the ages—"

Novus ordo seclorum. That's right, isn't it?

"—that God—"

Shit, he skipped a line—

"—that in their Latin—"

"Their" Latin? "The" Latin? Whose Latin? Is there a Latinist in the house?

"—our founding sages—
God—"

God help— Goddamn— God strike—

"—gave—"

To give; I give, you give, he gives. *Dona nobis.* Give 'em hell, Harry.

"—His approval of—"

—bombs bursting in air. Atomic fireworks. Go, Harvard!

He complains to God: "I can't see in the sun."

Blind prophet. The tall Texan appears, holds out his hat. Ten gallons of shadow pour over the poem. Frost reaches for the hat. "I'll hold it," the Texan says.

Frost grabs it and tugs. "No, let me have it."

Struggle. The Texan is playing Texas hold 'em.

Laughter. *Why are you laughing, children?* Children of the new age. Augustan Age. And he its Virgil, turned back at the gates of heaven. *Go home, boy.*

More or less to himself, he says, "I'll just have to get through as best I can." He faces the sixty million. "I think I'll say—this was to be a preface to the poem I can say to you without seeing it. The poem goes like this."

He launches into "The Gift Outright." Thank God for ten thousand readings. He could recite this one with real bombs falling on his head. His body blown to pieces, his Orphic head would sing on.

He gets through it.

But he's failed Sir Galahad, the Harvard boy. All the Harvard boys are laughing. The old man's not up to it!

Must conclude. Must step down. (*Go home!*) "And this poem— what I was leading up to was the dedication of the poem to the president-elect—Mr. John Finley."

He slinks away.

28

WASHINGTON, D.C.

MONDAY, SEPTEMBER 10, 1962

"Why did he have to say that?" Kennedy demands, exasperated. (His back is killing him.)

Stewart Udall struggles to find an answer.

29

SAN FRANCISCO, CALIFORNIA

1882–1884

His father's paper-white face, blue below the eyes, the red coins in his cheeks not a sign of health. The face tipping back, raw membranous eyelids closed, the tin cup to his dry lips. He's at the slaughterhouse, drinking blood smoking from the slit throat of the steer.

Did this really happen?

Robbie was a witness. His father would stop by the shambles while campaigning for city tax collector. Robbie fought the urge to throw up.

Taking a flyer about the Democratic candidates into a saloon, pressing in a tack, backing it with a silver dollar and throwing the whole package at the ceiling. The weight of the coin would drive the tack into the ceiling board and the dollar would fall to the waiting hand, while "Vote for William Prescott Frost" or "Vote for Grover Cleveland" remained aloft to excite support, not to mention speculation about how it got up there.

Could his father really do this?

Frost remembers his father describing the trick to him, and he *thinks* he remembers seeing him do it. He remembers the narrow doorway into the saloon, the gate swinging open to reveal the hidden pass, and it seemed dark until you stepped through, and then you saw the glittering mirror behind the bar, the sparkling glasses and brass taps. He remembers the free-lunch counters that lured the drinkers in. His father was one of them, and he tipped his pale face back, glass to his parched lips.

Even mistier is his memory of performing the coin trick himself, although he told Larry (and not only Larry) that he could do it. He remembers wishing he could do it. His father was a natural athlete. Powerful swimmer, fast pitcher, long-distance walker. Even if Robbie didn't see him do it, it was certain that he could, and probably every time on the first try, too. Boom! That flyer sticking like a burr to the high ceiling, where no one could dislodge it. What he told Larry, actually, was that he, Robbie, was so good at the coin trick that all the regulars in his father's favorite saloon admired his skill. (You could say they adopted him into their tribe.)

Grover Cleveland won, a great day for Democrats. Celebrations in the streets. Torchlight parade. Glorious 1884. But William Prescott Frost lost. *Go home, boy!* Only he didn't go home. For four days he went missing, drinking in some hidden saloon Robbie couldn't find.

This really happened.

Another memory: the famous long-distance walker Dan O'Leary came to town and challenged any man who was man enough to go against him in a six-day race. Sleep as much or as little as you choose. O'Leary would give his opponent half a day's head start. If his father hadn't taken the challenge, would some other San Franciscan have girded his loins? William Frost didn't give anyone the chance to find out. He snatched the gauntlet before it hit the ground.

This really happened. It was in the papers.

And did Robbie's dad, an amateur with no standing, weakened by tuberculosis—did he beat the professional, the national champion? That's what Frost told Larry (and not only Larry). But was it true? It's indisputable that his father came in first. (Look it up.) O'Leary claimed, though, that William Frost had repeatedly broken the rule about always having part of one foot on the ground. William swore it was a damned lie. Frost told Larry that Dan O'Leary privately admitted to his father that he—O'Leary—had lost fair and square.

Now, that's the part (if you're keeping track) that's probably not true. Frost thinks he remembers his father saying that. But why would O'Leary admit such a thing?

Admit it (but not to Larry): it would be exactly like his father to win a walking race by running.

Another memory: a dreadful sight in the doorway—a boy holding a jack-o'-lantern.

Robbie's not afraid of the boy (his best friend), and he's not afraid of the jack-o'-lantern. What he's afraid of is this boy and this jack-o'-lantern standing in this doorway.

The half-thought thought, the half-muttered muted sidelong complaint of the ungrateful, wicked child: Robbie told his friend earlier that day that he and his sister were never allowed to make jack-o'-lanterns at home because his father couldn't abide the mess. And what did his blundering friend do? (His friend is an amateur, Robbie is the professional.) He brought the treason to Robbie's front door, he rang the bell, he stands there holding in his hands a replica of his own brainless smile. "I made this for you."

Oh, you fool. Can his father see? Where is he? One room away, one door between. (When he isn't home, you never know where he is;

when he is, you know to the inch.) That door is opening. Home life is about to meet outside life.

Robbie slams the front door in his best friend's face.

"What's going on?"

"He had a jack-o'-lantern. You said I can't have one." Not that Rob's complaining! What he means is: He's the rebel, not me. Here's his name, his address.

"So you slam the door? What are you, a wild Indian?"

"He had a jack-o'-lantern!"

"You trying to make me look ridiculous, boy? With your friends, is that it, the tryannical old man?" His father doesn't have a weapon of choice. He grabs whatever is to hand. A magazine, a ladle, a shoe. Robbie's unlucky this time: a metal dog-chain. Pants down, legs bleeding.

That did happen.

"Oh, it couldn't have," Belle said. This was years later, in Lawrence. His father was living under thatch up on the hill.

"It did."

"Your father did punish you, but he would never—"

"He did."

"Where was I?"

"There."

"Then I know you've imagined it."

"You were in the next room."

"I would have seen."

You never saw, never heard. You had your own door, a canal lock. You raised the water in it and floated, dreaming, a mermaid.

"Rob, you always had a vivid imagination."

Did it happen? You told Larry it did. Were you lying?

It happened.

"It didn't," says Belle.

30

Life magazine has sent a photographer to catch Frost in his natural element. All staged, of course. This time it's a bald fellow with a bow tie named Alfred something. He spies half a dozen waiters lounging in their off hour and rounds them up. Young people! Warm blood! He marches Frost and the kids out behind Treman Cottage to a boulder in a field, tells Frost to lean against it, the kids to group around his feet. Frost is supposed to look like he's passing on to the new generation some granitic truth. What guff.

Alfred fusses with his camera, circles around with a light meter. Frost is grumpy with embarrassment. But the young people seem happy to be here. They're in their late teens, early twenties. It's a sunny day. "Hello," he says, and they laugh. They're here on work fellowships. Young poets and writers. Some might end up doing good work. He's out of touch, doesn't know a thing about them. There's only one girl. Frost chivalrously asks her if she's a poet.

"Yes," she says. She's wearing a white dress and smoking a hand-rolled cigarette. A couple of the boys are smoking the same thing. Simplicity's all the rage; roll your own.

"What's your name?"

"Anne Sexton." She laughs as though it's the funniest thing in the world. All the boys laugh with her.

Frost is charmed by their happy youth. But also wary. "Children," he asks, "why are you laughing? You're not laughing at me, are you?" Their cigarettes give off an unfamiliar smell, like burning field brush.

"Oh no!" a young man exults, waving his arms, beaming at the sky and all around. "We're just happy at the day!" They all howl with laughter.

Ah, youth!

31

THE DERRY FARM, NEW HAMPSHIRE

1905

Lesley wakes. Her father is shaking her. "Get up!"

It's dark. The floor is cold. "Follow me."

She sleepwalks down the stairs. Her father turns into the parlor. She trails after. In a straight line, three rooms ahead, as down an aisle, she sees a light. Her father's a shadow in front of her. She follows him into the dining room, into the kitchen. Her mother is sitting at the kitchen table, crying. In the light of the lantern on the corner table, faces are paper cutouts. Eyes are dark holes.

She turns to her father, all in shadow. He steps into the light and raises his arm. Light glints on the revolver. He points it at her mother, then at himself. "Take your choice, Lesley," he drones. "Before morning, one of us will be dead." She cries and cries until she falls asleep.

She wakes. Winter morning sunlight fires the ice on the window. Cold floor!

She's six years old. The house is quiet.

A dream?

32

Fern leaves of frost on the window at thirty thousand feet. Two o'clock in the morning by Frost's watch, five o'clock on the waves below.

Christ, he really seems to be going to Russia. Crazy at his age.

Flying is still new to him. He's too old; he never quite believes it will work. Freefall, fireball.

The cabin is dark. Everyone else is sleeping, but Frost can't, not in a seat, not on a plane, not on his way to see Khrushchev. Ask him this, then that. One-two punch.

We will bury you. He scared a lot of people when he said that. And his boasting about his rockets that can reach any point on the planet. And Sputnik. And banging his shoe on the table. People thought, is he a madman? But Frost has a feeling about him. Crafty Russian Yankee. He's the new kid on the block, he needs to prove himself. Wants to keep you guessing. Frost understands that. More powerful than any king, but at heart he's still a peasant trying to learn the names of the dishes at the dinner table. The son of a miner. Dobrynin's father was a plumber. And this Yuri Gagarin, who circled the earth last year in a tin chariot sixteen times faster than Apollo's, is the son of a carpenter. Frost hates their shiny-penny utopian fantasies, their gulags on the obverse, but he loves this: rural and working-class boys showing up the rich men who play the world like a game of golf, this little nation in that little hole, the Lord Churchills and Lady Roosevelts.

Perhaps you intended to give me a "going over," to impress me with your strength and might so that my knees would bend; if so, I am ready to go home here and now.

Perhaps you think we're poor relations begging for peace.

These are Khrushchev's words, but they could be Frost's voice in his own head. And the contrition, too, that comes polishing the heels of the flare-up: *I beg your indulgence if I've committed any slips of the tongue.* This was after he turned purple at a press conference and called Chancellor Adenauer "sick" and "senile."

Short and fat, in a shapeless white suit and dented Panama hat. Making crude jokes. Laughing hugely as he feels the potbelly of an American citizen on his U.S. tour. Tickled pink that a Russian rocket reached the moon before the Americans got one in orbit. *We are as good as you now. Soon we'll be better. We will bury you in our surplus wheat. Once you could spank us, but now we can swat your ass.* Lenin was a dagger; Stalin was Frankenstein's monster. Maybe Khrushchev is a madman, but at least he's a man. He wants respect. And why shouldn't you respect a man who can destroy the world?

He and Frost will understand each other.

He peers out the window, over the tips of the frost ferns, but he's not sure he sees anything. That spot of lighter fluff, is that a cloud, or rheum floating across his cornea? If a cloud, he's seeing it from the wrong side. He feels the vertigo you get when you hang your head backward off the bed and imagine walking on the ceiling, stepping out the front door and falling into the bottomless blue.

He pulls his eyes away. Thirty thousand feet high, in a hollow bird's bone. He glances around at the young men sleeping in the other seats, ties loosened, legs pushed out, weight on the smalls of their backs. His translator, Franklin Reeve, is across the aisle. Frost had a good long talk with him tonight, got to know him a little. A smart boy. Getting his beauty rest.

Larry will never forgive Frost for not being brought along. This trip will be the capstone of his biography. Either because Frost saves the world, or because he dies in Russia. Frost forced himself to write a letter a couple of weeks ago. "Larry, Larry," it started. The sound of trying to placate a man who won't be placated.

Who's told you that I was afraid that I had hurt you by not
bringing you with me to Russia?

And that's the voice he shares with Khrushchev—invoking his fears in
order to claim he doesn't have them. (He only ever recognizes it afterward.) But bringing Larry was out of the question. The two of
them can't stand each other. Unfortunately, Larry doesn't realize it.
He thinks the hatred he feels for Frost is exasperated affection. He
can't read himself any better than he can read poems.

That's where, years ago, it all went wrong. Larry was a handsome
lad, bright and devoted. He'd mounted an exhibition of Frost first
editions at Wesleyan; they corresponded, met. Frost needed an official biographer to get the gnat-cloud of unofficial ones out of his
eyes. This was—oh Lord—1939. (Poor Larry! He's been waiting
more than twenty years for the old man to die, so he can come into his
inheritance.) When Frost likes people, he likes them immediately. He
trusts his intuition. With Larry, he made an impulsive decision.

Then Larry wrote *Fire and Ice: The Art and Thought of Robert Frost*,
and the honeymoon came falling out of the sky like an artillery shell.
Larry was in uniform, first down in Key West training, then on the
high seas trying to swat the asses of the Huns. Frost was proud to
have a friend in the fight. He wrote to him,

You are my one soldier at the front in this war, and my
clearest reason for wanting to win.

You are my one— In retrospect, scales fallen from his eyes, Frost has
asked himself: did he imagine, convince himself, overindulge in the
metaphor, that Larry Thompson was somehow Edward Thomas
come back from the dead? Thomas was Frost's dearest friend; inspired by Frost, he wrote poetry that was all his own, and England's
proudly to own. He went off to fight the Huns in the previous war,
wrote poetry in the trenches of northern France, wrote letters to
Frost that Frost was lazy about answering (Frost has never been good
at writing letters, he needs to see the expression on his listener's face),

and was killed by a German shell in 1917. Leaving Frost to apologize to his ghost in a thousand unwritten letters.

If Thompson was supposed to replace Thomas, Frost sees now that it was an unfair assignment. And *Fire and Ice* was Larry's unwitting way of breaking the spell. He proved what he shouldn't have had to—that he was no genius English poet reborn, but a thoroughly mediocre American professor of literature. Frost wrote to him,

> I have read enough of the book to see I am going to be proud of it.

Forgive him—he was writing to the soldier, who might die any day.

> I take now and then a dip into a chapter, gingerly. I don't want to find out too much about myself too suddenly.

Could Larry read between those lines? Apparently not.

Critical commentary on any poem is always more or less a desecration. Or maybe a better word is indiscretion. It can only put into words what the poet deliberately chose not to say. Frost knows this. Maybe Larry's no worse than another academic reader. But why did Frost pick an academic reader, when he hates the academy? Was Larry supposed to fight the academic war for him, too, swat the asses of the French critics, the French-influenced Eliot and Pound?

But no. Back up—Larry *is* worse than some academic readers Frost could name. Frost will never forget the shock of looking at the title page of *Fire and Ice* and seeing that Larry had misquoted the first line of "Fire and Ice":

> Some say the world will end *with* fire
> Some say in ice.

What kind of ear could fail to hear the loss of the parallel? Whose hands was he in? Gingerly he glanced at the opening pages. The first poem Larry discussed was "Stopping by Woods on a Snowy Evening," and—he did it again! Instead of "the darkest evening of the year," he had "the *coldest* evening of the year." He even discussed the "tragic implication" of this cold.

Yes, there was a tragic implication: Frost's biographer was an idiot! "Darkest evening" suggests the winter solstice. Christmas is coming. "Promises to keep"! *Read!*

So Larry didn't have the respect for either Frost or himself to take a few moments to check a poem before publishing comments on it. Then handing the book to the author who was entrusting to him the reading of his very life. *So no, doting old man*—Larry is not Edward Thomas reborn. And Thomas was killed by a shell, whereas Larry sailed through his war without a scratch. The luck of fools—

But enough of this. Frost shifts in his seat, mentally shakes himself. *You'll drown in your own bile.* He takes a few deep breaths.

Looks across the aisle again at Frank. The little pillow is slipping out from under his head. Should he—? No, it might wake him. Frost was sorry they had to end their conversation. But Frank could barely keep his eyes open. The pretty stewardess is nowhere to be seen. She must be sleeping, too. A cot somewhere behind a curtain? Presumably the pilot is still awake.

Fall, fireball.

He looks out the window again. Somewhere up here, higher, in the blackness and silence, are the Sputniks. And the spy satellites. Amazing (to an old man): Newton's apple thrown so high it falls like the moon, in a never-ending circle. Actually, an ellipse: a circle with two centers. Which Frost has long thought is the perfect figure for representing motion. The revolution of the mind around two opposite statements, equally true. Or the two poles of a rhymed couplet. He tried this idea out on Niels Bohr, but Bohr didn't seem to see how attractive it was.

Up here, too, the ballistic missiles hurrying on their errands would pass each other. They'd pass in perfect amity, in perfect mutual understanding. Going as fast as Gagarin, falling not in elliptical curves but parabolas, and very much ending. Fall and fireball. Goodbye, New York! Goodbye, Moscow! Goodbye, goodbye!

The shell that killed Edward Thomas weighed—what?—thirty

pounds? Multiply that by seventy, you get a ton. A company of Edwards. Multiply again by a thousand, you get a kiloton; a Coventry of Edwards. Multiply by twelve, you get the Hiroshima bomb, and multiply by another—what?—eighty?—and you get a megaton. Which makes . . . a hell of a lot of Edwards. All England under thatch. It means so much, it stops meaning anything. How can a poet grapple with that? Frost has no idea. He's too old. And maybe all the other poets are too young.

Is that why we name our missiles Titan and Atlas? The Titans are the parent figures of myth. Keats called them the gods and goddesses of the infant world. Giants against whose law no appeal is permitted. The only recourse is overthrow. Our missiles, like parents, are both protectors and chastisers. *Bad children.* And once on their course, once they've picked up the stick, the belt, the chain, nothing can stop them.

These new ones they're developing are called Minutemen.

> Listen, my children, and you shall hear
> Of the midnight ride—

And the ones on the submarines are called Polaris. Presumably because they fly north, over the pole. In that direction, Russia's practically our neighbor. *Heading for ninety degrees! It's . . . world's end!* Rising out of the sea, flashing their tails like mermen. Their interests are not our interests. Meeting and passing each other in perfect peace, high up in the dark.

Kennedy campaigned on the Russians' being ahead. But Joe Alsop published a column last fall saying the missile gap was actually in our favor. So who fears whom? Who's fooling whom?

Celtic giants: Kennedy hurls a boulder across the world at Khrushchev, Khrushchev hurls one back. Old-stone savages armed. K. and K. King and Kaiser. *The parents are fighting. Hide, children!* The Giant's Causeway they're building is the flat swath of rubbled cities. Fallout raining, radiation rising, dogs scavenging, children rotting. His great-grandchildren turn to him as the bombs fall, "Save us, Grandpapa!" The white flash, the stormwind roar!

Frost, alone in a hollow bird's bone at thirty thousand feet, has frightened himself.

(Breathe. Frank sleeping.)

No, instead of a missile, Kennedy has hurled *him*. A whitehead instead of a warhead. *Nervous joking, old man.*

Frost has always avoided action. When the Lawrence mill strike was on in 1912, he hunkered in Plymouth, seventy-five miles from ground zero, while people he knew fought in the streets. In 1915, he fled England, left her to fight her war. That's why he wouldn't speak up, as Louis Untermeyer wanted him to, during World War II, sign manifestos, man the paper barricades. In his deepest heart he feared he was a coward, and the most despicable thing in the world is a coward who stands back in safety and eggs on the fighting men. If he wouldn't put up, the least he could do was shut up.

And now here he is, riding a missile to Russia, trying to save the world.

> A golden age of poetry and power
> Of which this noonday's the beginning hour

Is there something to that, something genuine, or is it just inauguration-day hokum? A vain old man wooing President Galahad. A vain old poet who's failed each year to win the Nobel Prize for Literature, so he's angling for the Peace Prize. Is that it?

The golden age was Saturn's reign. Our stern parental Saturn rockets, meeting and passing their cheeky Sputniks.

Can we talk?

33

From farm to farm, through dell and over hill, they're making their sweeps. It's a great war we're having, and the Germans have taken Mons. It'll be over by Christmas, but we need more men willing not to be there when we open presents under the tree.

They go in cartloads. Mostly farm laborers. Their wives still make their "obedience" to their social betters, bending the knee and bowing low. Frost could hardly believe it, first time he saw it; but to them that likes it, it's a pretty performance. Now their husbands are obeying the lordly call. The wheels rumble and shudder down the lanes. Tonight he was in Ryton and he stood along the cobbled road with other villagers and watched them go. A half-dozen men held the sides of the tumbrel, swaying. He recognized two or three. One was as old as he was, with a boy Carol's age. The horse was going fast. Lives to waste, but not time. The thought they might soon be dead made strangers and enemy neighbors into family, and the departing waved their hats at the home front. *Goodbye, England! Goodbye!* One of them was trying to get a song started. "God save—"

The horse pulled them eastward into the dark.

34

"Let me walk you home, John," Frost says. Eight blocks from the hotel to John Bartlett's house. Past midnight, the city silent. The stars burn. The air cures you.

As they walk, the two men discuss ethics, existence. Then poor Marjorie, who developed a crush on her doctor at the local tuberculosis sanatorium and got her heart bruised. John is one of Frost's boys from way back, a favorite student at Pinkerton Academy, in Derry. Captain of the football team, but with Frost's own affliction: weak lungs, pneumonia, asthma. Frost used to worry about him every time he got wet.

Frost played Cupid for John and another favorite student, Margaret. They reminded him of himself and Elinor when they were students at Lawrence High School. John had been courting Margaret, but Margaret worried she was too young for anything serious, so she avoided John for a week. Frost had to put an arrow through her. "Go talk to John, Margaret. He's miserable." Now they've been married twenty years. Have four children, just like their old teacher.

Pausing by the front door of John's house, they keep talking. Frost wonders aloud if he should stop writing poetry. "Why go on and obscure what's already been done? Too many writers bury themselves in the rubbish of their old age." He feels blessedly free with John. He knew him back before anyone knew or cared who he was. Under John, Pinkerton Academy beat archrival Sanborn Seminary, six to nothing. Frost wrote on the blackboard:

We didn't pretend to outweigh 'em
So we simply had to outplay 'em

He should turn to go, but he keeps hesitating. Back at the hotel there's only Elinor. She'll be either sleeping or pretending to.

Maybe John sees it. "Let me walk you back to your hotel, Robert," he says.

So they go back the eight blocks, talking now of Carol. Frost has been thinking about buying him a sheep farm here in the Rockies. Alone on a hillside, crook under his arm, playing his panpipes where no one within a hundred miles can hear or criticize him. Cure what ails him. This gets Frost thinking again about bad poetry. He tells John an idea he's been toying with, a new writing project. Scraps of dialogue; things he's heard through the years while lecturing. Tones of voice and what they suggest. Threats, carping, curiosity, stubbornness, friendship. "Just pieces end to end. Like those boulders down there." Frost and John veer down the slope and climb up on the rocks, stepping from one to the other until they reach the edge of Nederland Lake. "But on across. See. The Giant's Causeway. The giants threw those boulders with no thought about where they'd land, but then they looked and saw a way across the water. Life's like that. You hurl experience ahead of you, and it somehow makes a road. Crooked, maybe, I'm not saying. No idea where you're going. But there's the road. Like you coming to Colorado, then Marjorie years later in the sanatorium three blocks from your house. Which brings you and me together, here, twenty years after Pinkerton."

They reach the door of the hotel. It's past one in the morning. He really should go in. He should. "I'll let you go, John. You need your rest."

"Robert, it's been—"

"Hell! Let me walk you home." And back they go, talking, under the stars.

35

He left it too late. Christmas is three days away, everyone's short of money. The merchants spent their last cash on gifts for their own children. None to spare for the lazy play-at-farmer come late to market with his eggs.

The unsold flats fill the seats and footwells of the little red sleigh. Eunice steps along smartly, unguided. She knows the way home. Six in the evening and full dark for over an hour already. Snow began to fall as he left the village. The air is still humid with late autumn, with the unfrozen centers of ponds, and the flakes have tangled on the way down into lacy knuckles that pat against him, softly exploding. Comforting child's hands, or the tap-tap of conscience?

Goddamn his laziness! What's wrong with him? And what possessed him to tell Lesley what presents she, Carol, and Irma were getting for Christmas? Maybe it was this red sleigh he bought a few weeks ago. Something about him being Santa Claus, some foolish vanity on his part, made him say to six-year-old Lesley that it was really Papa and Mama who give the presents, they just say it's Santa for fun, and you're going to get this and that, and don't you think all those things will be nice? *Don't you love me?*

He did buy the brass horn, and he made the doll's pine table and chair, and the playhouse (all hidden in the hayloft). But he still has to buy the picture books, and the eggs were supposed to get him the cash.

Christmas morning, kids! Raw eggs! Don't be shy! Throw them at me! Make it a merry Christmas!

How can he face Elinor? He's dropped the reins. The snow is falling thicker, beginning to accumulate in the ruts. If he hadn't bought the sleigh, he'd have plenty of money for presents. He'd rather play Santa than be one. Rather play at farming. Rather play at poetry. He hasn't sent out a poem for years. What's the point? They all come back. His early promise lost. And can't keep his promises to his own children. Six-year-old Lesley, three-year-old Carol, two-year-old Irma, baby Margery. Oh, gee.

You're wallowing.

Well Christ, can't a man wallow?

Eunice can read his mood. She's slowing down as the snow falls thicker. The night has turned moth-gray, moth-silent. Eunice takes a last couple of steps, stops. Drops her head. Frost sits unmoving. Snow falls. It falls on the good and the bad, on the frozen and the liquid. Not forgiven—sent to bed, tucked in.

Eunice stopped because she knows. What he has to do. His shoulders hunch, his teeth bare. He bawls. Can't a man bawl? A man can and does. Sheltered by the snow and the woods where no one can see.

For two, three minutes he cries it out. Then he's done. He feels better.

He looks around at the enclosing curtain of snow. So what if he's a failure? So was his father. So were the farmers who came before him. Their cellar holes like open graves, their restless spirits walking the earth. Eunice stamps a hoof, and the bells jingle. He picks up the reins. Where is he? About a mile from home. West-running Brook runs under the road here. The widow Upton's cottage is there under the elms. The one lantern in the kitchen. She's by the stove. Singing to herself? Dozing? Even such a little cottage is too much for one old woman to keep. Paint gone. Sons out west. Husband dead forty years. He was Derry's first Civil War volunteer, so when he fell somewhere (Fredericksburg? Gettysburg? Frost should know more about the Civil War, his father was so passionate about it), the village paid for a marble headstone. Thus George Upton glows angelic white among the scraggly teeth of slate Uptons across the road from the cottage. And since marble dissolves in rain, his is the only name you can't read.

Graven in her heart, Frost presumes. She never remarried, and won't join her sons. Waiting instead to join her first love across the road. Sentimental? He hopes not, he wrote a poem about it a few months back.

> And if by guide-post sent astray,
> At eventide one passed that way
> And paused for sadness—

He chuckles. (He does feel better.) That's graven in *his* heart, anyway. And like George's name on the stone, he guesses no one else will be able to read it. Ah, the hell with it, who cares. If God doesn't care, he doesn't care. Christmas is coming. He flicks the reins. "Pause for sadness over, Eunice. Let's get home."

36

The Younger Poet writes for a national magazine:

> Why does the man not say what errand he is on? What is the force of leaving the errand generalized? He might just as well have told us that he was going to the general store, or returning from it with a jug of molasses he had promised to bring Aunt Harriet and two suits of long underwear he had promised to bring the hired man. . . .
>
> Can one fail to sense by now that the dark and the snowfall symbolize a death-wish, however momentary, i.e, that hunger for final rest and surrender that a man may feel, but not a beast?

The Biographer writes:

The most obvious correspondence would suggest the analogy between the specific experience of the rural traveler and the general experience of any individual whose life is so frequently described as a journey; a journey including pleasures and hardships, duties and distances. . . . There is even a slightly tragic implication suggested by "the coldest evening of the year." Yet within this bitter cold occurs an elementary revelation of beauty which lays claim on us as existing nowhere else.

The Thousandth Epistolarian writes:

Dear Mr. Frost:
Why did you repeat the final line? What are the promises you're referring to? Please answer as soon as you can, because my wife and I have argued over this.

The Critic writes:

He does not want or expect to be seen. And his reason, aside from being on someone else's property, is that it would apparently be out of character for him to be there, communing alone with a woods fast filling up with snow. He is, after all, a man of business who has promised his time, his future to other people. It would appear that he is not only a scheduled man but a fairly convivial one.

The Encyclopedist writes:

Early interpretations of the poem tend to understand those "promises" as an affirmation of the traditional American—and especially New England—value of duty.

The woods, an image of indulgence and corruption since the days of the Puritans, are seductive but eventually rejected by a speaker mindful of his obligations. . . . More romantic readings have retained the same opposition but reversed its poles: In forgoing the transcendent experience of nature, as represented by the woods, the speaker is perceived as less dutiful than harried; and in the ambivalence of his decision to continue, he can be seen as resigned to remaining alienated from the natural world and, by implication, from himself. . . . Recent critical theory has not yet deconstructed "Stopping by Woods" in ways significantly different from more traditional readings, but some new insights emerge from renewed interest in the poem's self-conscious play with both the freedom and limitations of language. . . . As Frost's only extended use of the technique, the horse and the speaker's projection of his thoughts on it deserve more attention than they have received. . . .

37

BREAD LOAF SCHOOL OF ENGLISH, RIPTON, VERMONT

JULY 1954

The Little Theatre, the lectern lamplight, the lovely deep dark around:

"... And miles to go before I sleep."

The hush, the fullness. Frost feels it right between the eyes. He takes a steadying breath. "That one," he says, and pauses—"that one I've been more bothered with than anybody has ever been with any poem, in just the *pressing* it for more than it should be pressed for. It means enough without its being pressed." Only the windfalls, the bruised, the stubble-spiked, get pressed for cider. This golden apple is right off the tree.

But remember, old man. These are high-school teachers you're talking to.

"That's all right, you know. I don't say that somebody shouldn't press it. But I don't want to be there." He picks up his book (his bat, his ball) and goes home.

38

THE DERRY FARM, NEW HAMPSHIRE

1900–1909

Frost sits by Hyla Brook. An April day, a May day. A new century. What year? Can you tell, O Man, from the apple blossoms, the bumblebees?

> Sing derry down derry!
> It's evident, very—

He's alive. Somehow he didn't throw himself into that black December pond. The revolver on the kitchen table at midnight never found its way to his temple.

Today he woke at eleven, milked the cow at noon. His snickering neighbors are right, he's no farmer. He's a gatherer of flowers. What used to be called an anthologist. He spent all afternoon in the cranberry bog hunting orchises. Now he sits (the sun says it's about 7 p.m., but is it 1902, 1904, 1906?) on a glacial erratic of million-year-old granite, his muddy boots in the water that took ten thousand years to round the rock into a ball, the water taken gently by the elbow, pulled down by gravity as old as the universe, which is—how many years?

By a bank as I lay
Myself alone did muse, Hey ho!
A bird's sweet voice did me rejoice.
She sang before the day.
Methought full well I wot her lay,
She said the winter's past, Hey ho!
Down, derry down,
Down derry, down derry,
Down, derry down, derry down,
Derry down, down!

The bells are ringing. Winter is past. Elliott is dead, Rob is alive, and Elinor's somewhere in between.

For months when they first moved to the farm, no curtains were hung, no rugs unrolled, no furniture was placed. They camped in the house as in a caravan, mid-waste. Elinor never cooked. Her mother visited and opened her well-oiled mouth. "Don't say a thing against her," Rob warned.

Elinor wanted only two things done, which Rob did: he painted the kitchen red and hung rose wallpaper in their bedroom upstairs. The red kitchen made Elinor think of Christmas, of close lantern light and silent burial in six feet of snow. And the roses were her frozen spring, waiting forever where she could gather them from her bed.

They leave us so to the way we took,
As two in whom they were proved mistaken

He married her for the flower that she was. She was even less worldly than he, even dreamier, a lily of the field, neither toiling nor spinning, only reading poetry, letting it gather on her like gold dust, a fructifying pollen carried on the wind. Oh, she was fragile and silent and black-eyed and beautiful, and she had the best ear for poetry of anyone he knew. All his poems—all of them—are for her; not to keep, but to return with comments. They are the flower-children he brings to his white lily: is this one hardy enough, here's a slight bright one, here's an odd one with a hanging lip. Once a poem pleases her, he doesn't want to hear a peep of complaint from anyone else. It's *her* poem now, and don't you say a word against it.

When Elliott died, Elinor went underground. Rob had to follow her. Dante Rossetti wrote a good poem about grief:

> The wind flapped loose, the wind was still,
> Shaken out dead from tree and hill;
> I had walked on at the wind's will—
> I sat now, for the wind was still.
>
> Between my knees my forehead was—
> My lips, drawn in, said not Alas!
> My hair was over in the grass,
> My naked ears heard the day pass.
>
> My eyes, wide open, had the run
> Of some ten weeds to fix upon;
> Among those few, out of the sun,
> The woodspurge flowered, three cups in one.
>
> From perfect grief there need not be
> Wisdom or even memory;
> One thing then learned remains to me—
> The woodspurge has a cup of three.

That's what saves you. Grief takes so much away, but with the left hand it gives you naked ears, wide-open eyes. The woodspurge, the bluet nodding in the breeze of your own breath, the crater of the ant: they brand you. You can't read the mark, but oh it hurts, and the pungent pain, the sweet smell of the burning wake you. You turn from the pond, you put down the revolver, as too uninteresting. Some while ago he wrote a poem about a diver trapped in underwater gloom, entangled in weeds, drowning. He clutched a white lily he'd pulled down with him. Terrible stuff; it ended with the fish coming to eat him.

Frost had felt that way. But instead children came, and they were steps up out of the underworld, nearly one a year. Carol in 1902; Irma in 1903; Marjorie in 1905. (Thus, it seems, it cannot be 1902 or 1904. With the children, Time is reborn.) And each spring, in synecdoche, the children's birthdays come like steps up out of winter, at exact lunar intervals, a moon for each child: Marjorie's birthday on March 29; Lesley's on April 28; Carol's on May 27; Irma's on June 27. As gifts are made and candles lit and each child's birthday lingers longer into evening, as each round burgher moon rises or each infant sickle moon sinks (cradling the translucent ghost of its mother), how can Rob not take each step upward, or look up from the ant crater at the sound of their voices?

But Elinor, after surfacing, gets a haunted look in her eye and returns below, where the flowers painted on the underground vaults will never die. And he, Orpheus, can send songs down to her, but he can't bring her up. Is it because he cares too much? Demands too much? Is it love itself that keeps her down?

Virgil invented the unhappy ending for Orpheus and Eurydice. In all versions before his *Georgics*, Eurydice is rescued. And it's Virgil's notion that love dooms her: Orpheus cannot bear not to turn, and so the jealous earth reclaims her. Does Virgil sing in praise of Epicurean detachment? The bachelor was wary of love. His most quoted line is *Omnia vincit Amor* but it doesn't mean what everyone thinks it means. It doesn't mean that the man who only loves enough will get the girl, or the mother who only loves enough will save her child. It means that man and woman both are powerless before the Love-god, whose province is madness, whose interests are not our interests.

Orpheus embraces Eurydice, Aeneas embraces his father, and both find only vapor in their arms. The poet calls spirits from the vasty deep, and they do come when he calls, but they are visions, not substance, buoyed solely by song. Must come the dying fall.

Late late yestre'en I saw the new moon
Wi' the auld moon in her arm,

And I fear, I fear, my dear master,
That we will come to harm

Or as it's said in the good old New England way, on spalling slate gravestones sinking sideways into thistles along abandoned roads, as pure a line of poetry as anyone ever wrote:

'Tis a fearful thing to love what death can touch.

"Daddy!"

Frost looks up from the brook, turns. Margery, calling down from the yard pump. "Daa-ddy!" She is three years old. (So it must be 1908.)

The sun is setting. He pushes off from the rock, rubs his sore backside, heads up the slope. Venus glimmers in the west. Half a moon grins down from the top of the sky, where even the cow can't jump over it.

39

THE DERRY FARM, NEW HAMPSHIRE
1906

At some uncounted hour in the middle of the night, Frost sits at the kitchen table. Walls and floor are incarnation-red. Stove feebly warm, gurgling and sighing like a cow's stomach. Wife and children asleep. Nearby creaks are house joists cooling, but what about scurries and thumps from the distant barn? Thus the revolver, which he has taken down (hasn't he?) from the high cupboard and placed on the table next to him.

He's pulled the lantern close. To get *something* on the sheet of paper in front of him, some ray to bounce off the white, penetrate his eye, fire a thought. Two nights, three lines:

> All out of doors looked darkly in at him
> Through the thin frost, almost in separate stars,
> That gathers on the pane in empty rooms

A poem about an old man living alone. His children gone, his farm too much for him. Overgrown; the earth swallowing it. His life's sacrifice unaccepted. Something about that. His children grown and gone. Unneeding him. The feeling has come back to Frost off and on ever since that night a while ago—was it last winter?—looking at the widow Upton's cottage in the snowstorm. The lump in the throat, the prick behind the eyes. Something about the cellar holes, before they become holes. Something about holding on; what's kept.

What *is* kept?

Another noise from the barn. Mouse, hoof, wind rattle?

Tramp? He sees the tramps on the road in daytime. Circling to the kitchen door, wary of the dog, Schneider. Knocking with a hard-luck story. It proves there must still be a few New Hampshire farms, because farms are still failing. Or the man's a logger who's run out of woods, or ruined his back. Or a millworker up from Lawrence on a long, lone strike. Give them nothing and they'll burn the barn down. Give them something and they'll sleep in the barn and take a souvenir on the way out at dawn. If wishes were horses. Close the barn door afterward.

Waiting for inspiration. What *is* kept?

> The wind flapped loose, the wind was still,
> Shaken out dead from tree and hill;
> I had walked on at the wind's will—
> I sat now, for the wind was still.

That's good, the way Rossetti doesn't say it—the poet as dead leaf. Sitting in front of a dead leaf. Waiting for the wind to lift him, move him. Waiting for resurrection, for the flush of maple sap along the stem, down veins to fingertips. Fountain of youth.

> A boy's will is the wind's will,
> And the thoughts of youth are long, long thoughts.

He's always been a slow thinker. Can do nothing but wait. Neighbors snicker. Between poems he has no idea what to do with himself, except fight irritability, love guiltily the children he snaps at. When he's out of ideas, with no purpose in life, no place, feeling like an old man alone. Wait. Sleep late. Milk the cow at midnight. She gazes at the moon. How high? Can she make it? Can he?

What is kept?

He tilts the lantern, looking just past it so that the red curtain comes down, the blaze of blood vessels in his own eyes. How even dim light can blind you. He angles the lamp again, looks down, watches the light slide over the words on the page. Thin frost like separate stars on windowpanes. The old man can't see the real stars. He can't see out. He's holding the lamp too close to his eyes. Trying too hard.

> The Frost performs its secret ministry,
> Unhelped by any wind

"Frost at Midnight." Hard not to think of it. Coleridge's beautiful concluding lines:

> Or if the secret ministry of frost
> Shall hang them up in silent icicles,
> Quietly shining to the quiet Moon.

See, the old man in Frost's poem, he hasn't kept his children, or his youth, but he's kept his icicles. He's kept his moon.

What's beheld is held.

Milking the cow at midnight. When his neighbors can't see. His secret ministry. But the question is, the pain is, can the old man keep on keeping? He's aging; forgetting. He can't see out. Perhaps he's heard a thump, come to a spare room, forgotten why he's there. What is kept when the keeper dies?

Thump.

Jesus! From the barn again. That *was* something.

Thump.

Frost is frightened. Has he summoned something? He's always most susceptible when he's writing. Four lockless doors between the kitchen and the barn. Any moment the last will burst open, violence pour in. He can't flee, he has children. *Coward!*

He takes the lamp. (Does he also take the revolver?) He opens the door to the laundry room, shrinking back, thrusting the lamp forward. Only shadows moving. Next door, woodshed; next, grain shed. He must check the privy in the corner. He bangs the door open, his heart banging. Nothing.

The last door is here, into the barn. He listens. Then eases the door open a crack.

Coward!

He opens it full and stands in the doorway. Holds up the lantern. Shadows up in the loft, in the deep corners. There ain't any goddamn way he's going to take a step further.

Eunice fumbles to her feet and looks at him over the wall of her stall. Well if anyone's in the loft, they know he's awake. That'll show 'em! He clomps back to the kitchen, making noise on purpose. Watch out, Night! Coward on duty!

The moment he sits back at the table the next sentence comes to him.

> What kept his eyes from giving back the gaze
> Was the lamp tilted near them in his hand.

He writes two more sentences and starts a third. It's not quite right, but it's close. He notes down, for later, "icicles, moon" and "sleep; soul to keep; moon to keep?" Then writes one other line, at the moment floating free: "A light he was to no one but himself."

When he puts out the lamp, he sees through the window the gray light just beginning to wash the blackness thinner. Silhouettes of his neighbor's pines on the hill.

To bed! At this rate he'll produce enough poems for a slim volume every decade. If he ever finds a publisher. Thin Frost! He'd better live till ninety.

40

An Old Man's Winter Night

All out of doors looked darkly in at him
Through the thin frost, almost in separate stars,
That gathers on the pane in empty rooms.
What kept his eyes from giving back the gaze
Was the lamp tilted near them in his hand.
What kept him from remembering what it was
That brought him to that creaking room was age.
He stood with barrels round him—at a loss.
And having scared the cellar under him
In clomping there, he scared it once again
In clomping off;—and scared the outer night,
Which has its sounds, familiar, like the roar
Of trees and crack of branches, common things,
But nothing so like beating on a box.
A light he was to no one but himself
Where now he sat, concerned with he knew what,
A quiet light, and then not even that.
He consigned to the moon, such as she was,
So late-arising, to the broken moon
As better than the sun in any case
For such a charge, his snow upon the roof,
His icicles along the wall to keep;

And slept. The log that shifted with a jolt
Once in the stove, disturbed him and he shifted,
And eased his heavy breathing, but still slept.
One aged man—one man—can't fill a house,
A farm, a countryside, or if he can,
It's thus he does it of a winter night.

41

THE DERRY FARM, NEW HAMPSHIRE
1905

Bossy is cropping grass in the little pasture, advancing splayfooted, her jaw revolving like the slow wheel of time, grinding exceeding fine. Under a pine tree in the grove, Lesley's got a board across two rocks to serve as a store counter. (Frost really should build her a playhouse—lazy bastard.) She sits on pine needles behind the counter and sells mounds of dirt on cast-off dishes to three-year-old Carol and two-year-old Irma.

"What are you selling?" her father asks. He's thinking, Cake? Chocolate?

"Dirt," she answers tartly. "Carol! Let Irma come up to the counter."

"Do Carol and Irma want dirt?"

"They like it!" Carol and Irma nod eagerly. "I sell all different kinds of dirt. Who's next?" Carol and Irma crowd close.

All they could ever want, right here. See it, touch it. Their older sister's attention, her momentary lack of scorn, every variety of delicious dirt they can imagine. Frost wanders away, near weeping.

42

You always were a slow thinker. In conversation you hear the other fellow, but he'd never know it, a response occurs to you a week later, a year later. When you're pouring out words, you keep on past having anything to say, you make a fool of yourself unless someone speaks and saves you. (You only see later that you were saved.) When you were at Derry you could hide among unspeaking Yankees, but now you're famous. Pilgrims come to burn their problems at your altar, take away Pythian wisdom. Yet the seer's as slow as ever. (They call you granite; another word for blockhead.) So you orate. This is good stuff. Are they taking notes? (Too often, behind your back, they are.) Later, you fear, they roll their eyes.

> In the lamplight
> We talked and laughed; but for the most part listened
> While Robert Frost kept on and on and on.

But you can't help it. You are needier than they. *Don't leave me.* Because without them, it's only you, your appalling age, your cave, and the glass cage you swing in.

43

The Younger Poet writes:

Robert Frost

Robert Frost at midnight, the audience gone
to vapor, the great act laid on the shelf in mothballs,
his voice is musical and raw—he writes in the flyleaf:
For Robert from Robert, his friend in the art.
"Sometimes I feel too full of myself," I say.
And he, misunderstanding, "When I am low,
I stray away. My son wasn't your kind. The night
we told him Merrill Moore would come to treat him,
he said, 'I'll kill him first.' One of my daughters thought things,
thought every male she met was out to make her;
the way she dressed, she couldn't make a whorehouse."
And I, "Sometimes I'm so happy I can't stand myself."
And he, "When I am too full of joy, I think
how little good my health did anyone near me."

44

Frost could kill Walter. Maybe it's his shot nerves from the flying he did in the Air Corps, all the friends killed. Maybe every girl for him has become the girl back home, something he deserves for his suffering, his ruined youth. But Irma's only fifteen. (She's the pretty one.) "I'll watch the children," he said, so Frost and Elinor went down to New York City to visit Lesley.

Irma sketching in her room with the door closed. Him knocking.

I'll watch the children.

Elinor said, "He gets along beautifully with the children."

45

The kitchen's the only heated room in the apartment Frost shares with his mother and sister, so he locks himself in to work on his butterfly poem. Hide; keep it a secret. Why shouldn't people laugh? No reason to have faith in him. Twenty years old, high-school valedictorian, and here he is a substitute teacher in a one-room school in South Salem. He can't afford the train, so most days he walks the five miles home.

His fiancée, Elinor White, has gone off to college in the far north of New York State, probably hoping he'll forget her. He attended Dartmouth for half a semester, then ran away, then trimmed lamps at the Arlington Mill, then ran away again. (He likes to think of himself as a lone striker, but that's a bit pathetic, isn't it?)

All the back alleys he runs down, forever escaping gangs, lead only here: a kitchen table in a shabby ground-floor apartment hard by the Lawrence railroad tracks. Is it official? Is he riffraff? Nothing to his name but a few scraps of unpublished poems, this gouged table and a lock on the door.

But he thinks he may have something:

My Butterfly

> Thine emulous fond flowers are dead, too,
> And the daft sun-assaulter, he
> That frighted thee so oft, is fled or dead:
> Save only me
> (Nor is it sad to thee!)—
> Save only me
> There is none left to mourn thee in the fields.

The lone mourner. He's writing in part to Elinor, of course. She might say he was the assaulter who frightened her. But he's sorry! He's changed!

> Since first I saw thee glance,
> With all the dazzling other ones

Her gaze is what always struck him. The deep hurt look in those black eyes when she wouldn't speak to him.

> Thou didst not know, who tottered, wandering on high,
> That fate had made thee for the pleasure of the wind,
> With those great careless wings

A boy's will is the wind's will. To make a Shakespearean pun. Letting him kiss her in the secluded grass by the river, she gave him long, long thoughts. But no, he's changed! Really!

Anyway, this poem is better than anything he's done before. Maybe it will win her back.

A knock on the door. "Rob?"

His sister, Jeanie. Screw her! "Robert, open the door!" He keeps writing. Doesn't say a word. She rattles the knob. "It's cold out here, let me in!" He is the Silent Poet.

> Then when I was distraught
> And could not speak

"Let me in!" Now she's pounding. What is she, a fishwife? Her fits of crying. How can anyone work with all that going on? It's a mad-house!

She circles to the back door. Sorry, he's locked that one, too. Stay out, wolf! The shepherd's piping. She starts to kick the door. Crazy bitch.

> I found that wing broken to-day!
> For thou art dead, I said,
> And the strange birds say

Fly away, strange bird! Leave this worm alone. She's making strangled sounds. Is she having an attack? Third this week. This poem is good. Robert feels good.

> I found it with the withered leaves
> Under the eaves.

46

Halloween, and Lesley has chafed all day, wanting to turn the clock hands forward. At last it's dark, and Carol and Irma and Marjorie clamor and dance, asking if it will be before supper or after. "After, surely," says Papa.

"Before!"

"Wouldn't you rather wait?"

"No!" Everyone is in the kitchen, and the rest of the house is dark, and Marjorie's invited to go first but she's frightened, so Carol goes first. When he comes back he says he likes the one in the hall best. So of course when Irma and Marjorie come back they say they like the one in the hall best, too. (Children!) Then it's Lesley's turn. The dining room is pitch-dark but there's a glow from the sitting room, and that's where the first jack-o'-lantern is. It has a frowning mouth with square teeth. She goes through to the hall, and the one there has a very big grinning mouth, and the children probably liked that one because it's friendly instead of scary. But the one at the top of the stairs—oh, that one *is* spooky! The eyes, nose, and mouth aren't cut quite through, so it glows like a ghost, and in the dark on the top step it seems to float like a head with no body. You have to pass it to get to the last one, which is in the children's room. That one has large pointed paper ears on it, and looks like an elf.

Lesley likes the elf best. And when Mama goes, she says she likes the elf best, too!

Papa goes last, and he says he likes best the ghost at the top of the stairs. He pretends it's all a surprise, and he says the elves must have carved them and snuck them in the front door when no one was look-ing. The children believe him, but Lesley knows Papa carved them. That's why he was in the barn all afternoon, instead of picking apples that should have been taken in a week ago.

47

"I'm going out in the alders to see Santa Claus," Papa says.

"Can I come, too?" asks Lesley.

"No, I have to go alone."

"Why do you have the ax?"

"I need it."

"Why?"

"Can't tell you. Between me and Santa Claus. Don't follow me, now." And off he goes, down the snowy slope toward the brook.

Lesley knows not to follow him if he says not to. So she gets Carol and Irma, helps them with boots and coats, and they go out to the mowing field. From there they can see Papa far away down below, go-ing in and out among the alders. "Santa Claus is coming!" Lesley shouts, and Irma and Carol take it up. Then they call, "Where's Santa?" a few times, until Papa shouts up from the brook, waving the ax, "Go home! Santa won't come with you out making that noise!" So they go home, and when Papa comes home he won't say what Santa said.

Lesley doesn't figure it out until Christmas morning, when she comes down to the front room and sees the Christmas tree with all the candles lit.

48

In winter in the woods alone
Against the trees I go

Lo, he's low. Frost gazes out the car window, rain streaking the glass, at the mud and rubble of a demolition site, another one poking up behind it, somewhere in Moscow (the driver's lost), wishing he could have a heart-to-heart with Thomas Hardy. Younger poet to older poet. Ask him, Hardy, old man, how did you manage it? How did you act your country's poet-sage for thirty years without making a god-damn fool of yourself? (How's he going to face K. when he gets home? Her voice in his ear: *What did you think you'd accomplish?*) When Frost lived in England, oh, fifty years ago, an unpublished waif, Hardy was the best English poet alive. Moated at Max Gate, pronouncing through his poems on aging, fate, war, he'd planted himself on the wrongs that can't be righted; immedicable woes. The avant-gardists spurned him, but he didn't care. He was the main army. He had his castle and his art and his stonemason's heart that sweated tears from its own coldness.

Frost's guides are looking for a school. But all they seem to find, block after block, are buildings being pulled down or thrown up. *We are the future. We'll bury you in wet cement, oily puddles, rusted rebar.* Son of God, he's tired. Two days of interviews, long dinners of vodka conviviality (he asked for perry, but it was never available; didn't touch the vodka), lively talk—all in Russian. He didn't want to go anywhere this morning—*Let me sleep, let me die!*—but his guides, his keepers, said the children were expecting him. It's a special school for English. They're fluent, he'll be astounded, now he'll see what Russia can do.

Why are you laughing, children?

"We all laugh in the same language," he said at the press conference when his plane landed. The comment had to be translated. They all laughed.

The driver is arguing with one of his keepers. This language is all "zh"s and "vlya"s and "ost"s with dark, chthonic "o"s (more "aw" than his mother's ethereally round "o"), grave and lovely, gentler than he expected, with drawls and caresses in it. Here he is among the cellar executioners, and all their conversation sounds like love talk.

The two executioners stalk along over the knolls

Lovers' quarrels. Unlike so many Americans, they aren't afraid to argue. They revel in it; their anger has zest. Frost likes that.

Look at him. He's back to listening through the closed door. The sound of sense. Take the driver, now, as he gesticulates. They're arguing over where in hell they are. The guide talking is Elena. The other is Frida. The Pendragons, Frost calls them. Pen-ladies from the Soviet Writers Union, and dragon-ladies, too. They'd tuck him in at night and bounce him out of bed each morning if he allowed it. They're probably reporting every word he says to some apparatchik (pen in one hand, revolver in the other) in some cellar.

The two executioners stalk along over the knolls,
Bearing two axes with heavy heads shining and wide

—then a line about the toothed saw that he can't remember, and a forced rhyme with "knolls," what is it?—Christ, his memory these days—then the next line,

And so they approach the proud tree that bears
the death-mark on its side.

"Throwing a Tree" is the last poem Hardy ever wrote. Not one of his best, maybe, but— It appeared after he died, in *Winter Words*. The tree is partly Hardy, of course; the executioners, his biographers. A tree is best measured when it's down. Best kicked, too.

The driver is backing up.

"You all right?" Fred asks him. Fred Adams is an old, old friend. He knows Frost well, and he gets nervous about the tetchy old man. It gets on the old man's nerves.

"'Course I'm all right," he growls. Can't find the way to school? What he always wished for as a boy. A wrong turn, a hidden valley.

> Then the whining schoolboy, with his satchel
> And shining morning face, creeping like snail
> Unwillingly to school

Four centuries of agreement on this simple point, and they're still sending everyone to school.

The driver's speeding now into the next block. Ignoring intersections. Good thing the streets are empty. Maybe no one can afford cars. Or there's a gasoline shortage. Frost sinks back in his seat, shuts his eyes.

Hardy and his would-be biographers. He knew all about the danger of standing on a pedestal. Not that they'll knock you off—no, they're happy to leave you standing there, making a spectacle of yourself. What you don't know is, they're changing the inscription. Hardy's wife was a silent woman, like Elinor, but unlike Elinor she tried to speak from the grave. She left a manuscript, "What I Think of My Husband." Hardy burned it. A year later he married his secretary and had *her* write his biography. But they say he was the real author. Now there's an authorized biography.

And here, by contrast, is Frost, leaving the hammer and chisel in the hands of a man who can't stand him. *What I Think of Robert Frost*, in three volumes. Volume three, final chapter:

HOW ROBERT FROST ABANDONED ME, FLEW TO RUSSIA, AND DESTROYED THE WORLD

OR

HOW ROBERT FROST CAUSED HOLOCAUST

Stanley Burnshaw, at Holt, asked Frost some while back why he didn't take away Larry's authorization. "I gave him my word," Frost answered. A question of loyalty.

But it's more complicated than that, isn't it?

It's your self-hatred. You suspect you deserve it.

Or: *It's your self-love. As you said to Trilling, "No sweeter music can come to my ears than the clash of arms over my dead body when I am down." Larry will abuse you, others will defend you. You will lie fly-encrusted like Patroclus, a glittering prize, still causing the sweet deaths of others.*

Or: *Larry has been like a son to you. More than he guesses, since all you know are failed sons who resent their fathers. You have a father's duty: keep arguing with them until they either kill you or kill themselves.*

He came into this world being beaten by his father, and he'll go out with a thrashing from his son. Such consistency argues that he really does deserve it. The idea makes him chuckle.

"At last," Fred breathes. "They've found it."

Frost opens his eyes. A forbidding stone building, grimy and worn. The school. *Be nice to the children, goddamn you.*

Up the stone steps, passing beneath a cratered stucco keystone, the brown brick showing through. Reporters and photographers from the two other cars crowd behind. "Mr. Frost is here." A woman at a massive wooden desk looks alarmed. Another confers and hurries down the hall in heavy shoes. A pale woman dodges and weaves, then seems to want to head them off. Frost glances at Fred. "We're not expected," he says.

They are too sudden to be credible

"Surely—" Fred falters.

"Maybe the phones are down." Plus, it's too rainy for smoke signals. *Now* he'll see what Russia is capable of.

A woman is clacking with quick strides toward them. Straight-backed; armored in tight tweed; iron hair pulled back into a rock perfect for crushing skulls. The headmistress.

"Yes! Meester Frust!" Pretending she knew all along. Frost quailed under her type as a schoolboy. The less they understand, the more violent they become. *I don't care who*—(whack). *Don't tell me*—(whack). Did Frost actually back into Fred? It seems he did. "Please, this way." Frost hangs back, but the crowd of reporters pushes him onward. She turns for a moment to skewer him with a look. *You are keeping me waiting.*

But proof *(Ha!)* that Queen Ruler doesn't know what the hell she's doing: she leads them to a classroom of maybe seven-year-olds who don't speak a word of English. As Frost enters, the teacher throws a panicked glance in his direction and barks, the children pop up like marionette soldiers, the boys in what look like sailor suits, the girls in widow black. All with red neckerchiefs. What is it, the Soviet flag wrapped around their necks? Forty of them, they stare at him, silent and overawed. Since they have no idea who he is, it must be his centurian age that stuns them.

I am your future, children: oily puddles and rusted rebar. Why aren't you laughing?

The comedy of adult whispers lasts a minute or two before they're all back in the high-ceilinged hallway, following their infallible leader toward an assuredly better future. Flashbulbs pop. *Sudden Frost Descends on Middle School No. 7. Telephones Fail. Students Freeze.*

There are slogans in English on the wall. Something about the Motherland. One about glorious Gagarin. Another about washing your hands after you piss.

Another classroom invasion, another platoon of children jolted to attention as though wired to the door. Older, maybe twelve or thirteen. The same uniforms, the red nooses, the palpable fear. Frost wonders how much longer he can stand this. The times he came home heartsick and stomach-aching from school, squalling to his mother that he'd never go again. The desks in lines, the children in rows. The questions, and he always too slow-thinking to answer, and the rods and switches and rulers.

The teacher has introduced him, and she's called on some poor red-haired boy in the front row to ask a question. Apple-cheeked from embarrassment, he won't look up; he's actually trembling. Frost wants to say to him, *You and I, kid. Let's make a break for it. Hudson Bay in a skiff. Your arms, my heart.* The boy finally squeezes out, "What think you—" He flinches. "What does you . . . think of Cosmonaut Gagarin? His flying?"

"I think it's great," Frost says. The boy's at a loss to go on, so Frost tries to help him. He lobs him an easy one. "Don't you think so, too?"

But this frightens him. "Of course!" Jesus, he thinks Frost is questioning his orthodoxy. Wanting to apologize, to send him courage, Frost winks at him.

Uh-oh, now they're conspirators.

Frost turns to the class. "How many of you would like to go the moon?"

A long pause. They're all wondering, Is this a trick question? What's the right answer? Of course that goes on in American schools, too, but here the principal's office is in the cellar.

> And I keep hearing from the cellar bin
> The rumbling sound
> Of load on load of apples coming in.
> For I have had too much
> Of apple-picking

A couple of hands go up. Since no one falls on those children and drags them out of the room, a few more go up. The reporters are taking notes, but they're smiling, so more hands go up, and all of a sudden everybody's hurrying to get their hands high lest they be dragged away for lagging. The photographers take pictures. *Frost Asks for Volunteers to Follow in Heroic Footsteps of Russian Space Dog Laika.* Frost says, "You want to get away from here any way you can."

Silence. Now he's really terrified them. He meant the school. But they probably couldn't admit to that, either. "I'm kidding you."

More silence. "'Kidding' means joking. You make jokes, don't you? You're allowed?"

Profound silence. Worse, they still have their hands in the air.

"Perhaps Mr. Frost would recite for us a poem," the teacher says.

"Sure thing," Frost says, angry.

> "Hey diddle diddle,
> The cat and the fiddle,
> The cow jumped over the moon,
> The little dog laughed to see such sport,
> And the dish ran away with the spoon."

"Um, I think they'd like to hear one of *your* poems," Frank says.

"Oh, is that what she meant? Lemme see. . . ." The children's clipped bird-wings are finally coming down. Gee, these poor kids. Frost would love to play Orpheus, in his incarnation as the Pied Piper. Lead this whole unhappy flock out of the blighted city, hide them somewhere up in the hills. "Here's a poem called 'The Pasture,'" he says.

> "I'm going out to clean the pasture spring;
> I'll only stop to rake the leaves away
> (And wait to watch the water clear, I may):
> I sha'n't be gone long.—You come too.

> "I'm going out to fetch the little calf
> That's standing by the mother. It's so young,
> It totters when she licks it with her tongue.
> I sha'n't be gone long.—You come too."

He looks at them, full of hopeless hope. Has the magic worked? Are they his?

But they seem uncomprehending. They're waiting. For him to continue, or for some signal. The teacher speaks to them in Russian.

"What's she saying?" Frost asks Frank.

"She's explaining the poem to them."

"Oho! I know what that means." *The clear water of the pasture spring represents Marxist-Leninist teachings, and the leaves that must be raked away are the Trotskyite chained dogs of the Western imperialists. . . .*

That's it—Frost can't take any more. "I think we'd better go," he says to Fred. "I don't feel very well." His old standby; what always got him out of school when he was a boy. *Out of my way, or I'll puke on the lot of you!*

Out of the classroom, down the hall. He parts the Red sea, shaking hands. He's polite. "Thank you. I've learned a lot." *Don't punish the children.* "They were very impressive. As an educator, I was astounded. Let me put it this way, *now* I've seen what Russia can do." He gains the front door. Wan daylight, woolly sky, somewhat fresh though sooty rain! "Thank you, thank you!" Down the steps, toward the car. He pulls his overcoat close around him.

Now he can be angry. He rounds on Freddie. "That was a damned fool errand, wasn't it?"

Freddie holds up protective hands. "Yes, it was!"

Back at the hotel, after lunch in his room, Frost lies down, thoroughly depressed.

No word, they told him while he was eating, had come from the south. Not a word from Khrushchev.

He said to his captain, "I wish I could see the czar." And the captain said, "I'm afraid that would be difficult." And the consul said the same thing: "That would be very difficult. I don't suppose that would be possible."

All his life, exceptions have been made for him. Institutions have bent over backward. He's been given jobs without duties, students without classes. Money has come mysteriously, from a secret fund, an anonymous admirer, a colluding collector. When he has hinted after prizes, committees have gone down on one knee to hand them to him. He, who played sick from school most of his childhood and never finished college, has been awarded so many honorary degrees he had the hoods sewn into a quilt, and at night he sleeps under it like a Celtic Pendragon warmed by the skins of his enemies. Each time he has hinted, connived, covered his tracks, hinted again, he's got what he wanted, and each time he's felt guilty, and vindicated, and mean, and undeserving, and long overdue.

He's read to sixty million. He's befriended the president of the United States.

Now all he wants to do is save the world. Is that too much to ask?

"I don't suppose that would be possible."

"Well, I want to see him."

Nicholas was every inch the emperor, whereas this czar has gaps in his teeth, ears that stick out, a double chin. His pants are up under his armpits and his hairy shins show. And still he beams, *I'm a clown, but Russia is mine and Hungary is mine and the moon is mine and maybe Berlin will be mine.* He wants respect, and he knows the country-clubbers won't just give it to him, not if he looks like a Polack steelworker bowling with his chums on Saturday night, a greasy kielbasa sticking out of his back pocket. Only he sent the bowling ball to the moon. A nine-hundred-pound sphere of metal on top of a four-stage rocket. It hit the moon at seven thousand miles an hour. An astronomer in Sweden saw the strike, he saw the plume of moondust it kicked up. A hammer and sickle were carved in relief on the ball, so the Russians were branding the moon as theirs, stamping the silver coin, and maybe it alarms Frost, but he has to like them for it, too. It shows panache. On a grand scale, it's driving the thumbtack into the ceiling where no one else can reach. *There's* a rivalry worth carrying on. Whose science is better? Whose emblems will survive? Whose metaphors? When you walk at night with the moon on a leash, imagining another world, what do you see?

What a journey the man has made. They say he was a shepherd boy, later an itinerant harvester. So he and Frost have both swung a scythe, they've both trod a haystack. In Turgenev, the sure sign of the poorest peasant is that he wears bast sandals instead of boots, and Khrushchev has said more than once, red-faced with anger, waving his thick fists at the West, *Do you think we still wear bast sandals?* No, Mr. Khrushchev. But Frost knows the premier remembers wearing them. Watching his sheep, walking country lanes to the next field, scythe on his shoulder, going to meet his father emerging black and coughing from the Ukrainian coal mine. His sandals woven from tree bark, like woody bandages, falling apart in the rain. He remembers dreaming of the highest good he could imagine, a pair of boots. And maybe he was thinking of bast sandals when he pounded his shiny leather shoe on the UN table, saying, *Listen to me!*

He crushed Hungary. *Are you listening?* There's no doubt he's a ruffian. *Hungary sticks in some people's throats like a dead rat,* he said. A cruel thing to say. He's a street brawler. He cut Berlin like the Gordian Knot. He fought in both world wars. He plays killer badminton. They say he's got an indoor court attached to his dacha on the Black Sea. He invites diplomats to lunch and a game, and he smashes the shuttlecock straight at their faces. The fat man has surprising agility.

Americans didn't treat him well on his trip to the U.S., back when illiterate Ike was president. They watched his motorcade go by in silence. The press asked him needling questions. They thought it was funny that he wanted to see Disneyland, hilarious his disappointment when he couldn't go. *Bast sandals!* And his peasant wife, with her moon face and crinkle-eyed smile, trying to straighten the lapel of his sloppy linen suit. Next to her, Mamie Eisenhower dolled up in a designer dress.

That was petty blackguarding. America invited him, and aren't we strong enough to be hospitable? This was the man who denounced Stalin. Who has enemies at his back, but it doesn't seem to touch him. Who chose Dobrynin as ambassador.

Hospitable. Frost lies on the massive carved bed, on top of this strange green Russian blanket that's like a big down pillow inside a sheet. It slides off the bed at night and he wakes up freezing. *Goodbye, Mr. Frost!* Was he really invited here? Or was it all a mistake? Did Dobrynin speak out of turn? Does Khrushchev even know he's in Russia? Or who the hell he is? Maybe right now Khrushchev's lying on a beach on the Black Sea, making plans for Berlin, for the moon, and his third assistant secretary is tossing the telegram in the trash, commenting with a shrug to the fourth, *The old fool actually came, what do we do with him now?*

So this time, finally, he's asked for too much. The three sisters—not

Chekhov's, but the Fates—don't love him enough. Fine, forget about love. What about justice? Because hasn't he always felt (it's indefensible, it's arrogant, it's infantile, but he has *felt* it, and time and again he's willed it to be true) that the superficial world owed him some consolation for what the underworld had taken away? And if he's sometimes had to wrest it, well, isn't that less arrogant, less infantile? Not some delusion that the world agrees with his sense of justice, but simply *I want it and I will pry it out of your hand, as you once broke my fingers.*

And where has it got him? Instead of a son, he has a quilt.

Stop wallowing.

He can tell, when Fred and Frank look at each other. *The old man's lost perspective, fame's gone to his head. Does he really think . . . ?*

So here he lies. He's taken the ornate glass whorehouse-shade off the lamp on the bed table so he can read, and so his room won't feel so submarine, so drowned in the past. *We are the future, but what we really love is the nineteenth century. What we really love is Czarist Russia. Our Stalin the Terrible. Our Khrushchev the Liberator.*

A sign in America when his motorcade passed said *Khrusch crushed Hungary, and he will crush us.*

He needs a nap. He turns off the bedside lamp. The brocaded curtains in the deep window wells glow grayly. Here he lies, in his green pasture.

> In winter in the woods alone
> Against the trees I go

"In Winter in the Woods Alone" was the last poem he wrote for *In the Clearing*. He composed it all in a few hours, one balmy January day at his Florida cottage, where his garden wall is made of coral. It was the day the book's manuscript had to be sent to press. A man with an ax goes out on a late Vermont afternoon, as the low sun is just beginning to redden the fresh snow; he chooses a maple tree and fells it; returns to his cabin as darkness comes on.

That's all. The simplest odyssey—a venture out, an act, a return.

Frost placed it last in his last book, so readers might notice how it balanced his first poem in his first book (with "Into My Own," so long ago, he ventured out; all his poems between are the wielding of the ax; with the last poem, he returns):

> One of my wishes is that those dark trees,
> So old and firm they scarcely show the breeze,
> Were not, as 'twere, the merest mask of gloom,
> But stretched away unto the edge of doom.
>
> I should not be withheld but that some day
> Into their vastness I should steal away

The willful boy that he was then intended never to return. There was no need; others, missing him, would surely follow. Whereas the old man he is now knows too well no one would come looking. They'd turn to their affairs. So he attends to his: he cuts the tree; retreats to his lit room, to warm himself by the fire of last year's tree.

Another reason he placed the poem last was so that someone might realize it was a response to Thomas Hardy's final poem, "Throwing a Tree." Instead of Hardy's two stalking executioners armed to the teeth for murder, Frost sends out a lone man. Hardy's poem ends,

> The tree crashes downward: it shakes all its neighbours throughout,
> And two hundred years' steady growth has been ended in less than two hours.

Maybe that's the English view: cowed Nature and conquering man. But Frost's American needs that tree to warm himself against the next storm. Nature has no use for his pity or tenderness. She'll answer his ax's blow with a blow of her own. As they say in New England, *It's coming on for a blow.* In other words, a noble rivalry.

He tried to hint: "winter in the woods" echoes Hardy's title, *Winter Words*. He refers to the tree's "overthrow," which points to "Throwing a Tree." The rhyme scheme's the same. But no one noticed. (Edward

Thomas would have. He and Frost walked the Malvern hills, quoting Hardy.)

Poetry is usually a young man's game, and Hardy was proud to be hardy, to be an old poet who was still a good poet, like old savage Landor. With pardonable (one might almost say human) vanity he wrote in his introduction to *Winter Words:* "So far as I am aware, I happen to be the only English poet who has brought out a new volume of his verse on his eighty-eighth birthday." As a prophet, he should have known never to speak without enigma. He died before the birthday came. Frost (just as proud to be frosted) made sure that *In the Clearing* was published on his own eighty-eighth birthday. And since he maintained his silence, he survived for another blow: eighty-eight candles.

Here lies Robert Frost: an old poet, indisputably. And still a good one? Oh, let's not ask. Let's think of England fifty years ago, when Hardy was alive and Frost was unknown, a poet by night, father of four and husband of one, groping down a Malvern hillside on a misty evening with Edward Thomas, both alive, both poets, Hardy lovers, both lost. He and Edward came upon a lunar rainbow that, strangely, didn't retreat as they advanced. Instead, it rose from the ground and formed a ring around them. Frost had never heard of such a thing; it seemed miraculous. As though they were marked by the moon as hers. He wrote a poem about it called "Iris by Night."

> And we stood in it softly circled round
> From all division time or foe can bring

Is there a more beautiful word than "pasture"? Upland pasture. *He maketh me to lie down.* Come, Edward, step through with me. Into the clearing. (Frost is dozing.)

Ring around the rosie.

Hurry! It's dangerous here. Something is falling.

But Edward isn't there. The rainbow circle has turned into a net. Frost is holding a tennis racket too heavy to lift. The net is too high. On the other side is Khrushchev, his arm stretched behind him for the smash of the shuttlecock into Frost's face. The cock is in the air, floating, falling in a slow parabola toward his opponent, and Frost can't raise the racket to protect his face, and Khrushchev, dressed all in seaside white, shining, is floating upward like the full moon.

49

You always expected too much from a friend. You always were disappointed.

Edward Thomas died early and avoided the fate.

50

THE DERRY FARM, NEW HAMPSHIRE

APRIL 1903

Come spring, the gaps in the stone wall down by Hyla Brook make Frost suspicious. "*Something's* doing it. Or somebody. Why would they?"

"It's de frost," his neighbor Napoleon Guay says, chuckling. "Near de brook, de ground, she's wet. Frost swell her. Round rocks, dey roll right off. Only frost."

Frost is irked. Is Guay making fun of his ignorance? *You ought to know frost, Frost.* But he likes Guay. His comical Canuck accent takes the curse off the fact that he does know more than Frost about almost every aspect of farming. And he's generous with what he knows. He gave Frost a lecture about ax helves, then made him a good strong one just for the pleasure of doing the job right. He calls them "elves." "Machines don't make good elves," he said, and Frost thought at first it was some quaint Canuck saying about industrialization and the natural world.

They walk with the wall between them, each picking up the stones on his side. My stone, your stone, our wall. A way for a couple of men to socialize, mending a wall, as women gather in a sewing bee to mend socks. Wall as bridge.

Hyla Brook and its alders are on Frost's right, and across the wall to his left rises Guay's hill, mostly rocky and bare, but with a scattering of adolescent white pines and some beautiful old chestnut trees. "Your hill used to be all pine," Frost says. Guay bought the property only a year ago. "A pity you don't see mature white pines anymore. In colonial times they belonged to the king, you know. Masts for the British ships. One of the reasons we fought the war was for the right to use our own white pines." Is he saying this to get back at Guay? *Maybe you know farming, Napoleon, but you don't know America.* If so, it's cheap of him. But Guay doesn't seem to notice. Some mischief continues to work in Frost. *Pun on my name, will you?* "The British needed all those American white pines so they could beat Napoleon."

"Hm," Guay says, lifting a stone into place. His hands are thick and rough. A real farmer's hands.

In case he didn't hear, Frost says it again: "They took all your pines to beat Napoleon."

Guay still doesn't laugh. Maybe he's not listening. His hand hovers for a moment over the placed rock as though to say, *Stay there.* "Leas' I still got de chestnuts," he says.

51

Frost wakes before dawn in the bedroom with the rose wallpaper. One of his children is crying. Margery? He gets out of bed. By the time he reaches the door he knows he was mistaken. But he must see them, anyway.

Four children! How could he have made them?

How selfish he's been. For him, they're steps up out of darkness, but for her, with each one the world has seemed more perilous. She could not lose another.

Four children, four directions, four elements. Lesley is south and fire; angry warmth. Carol is north and earth; stolid and remote. Margery east and air: angelic sunrise. Which leaves Irma west and water. Sunset and hidden currents? Does the metaphor hold? Or does it only leave poor Irma what's left? Fluid she isn't.

In this haphazard household of caravaners (meals, if any, at all hours, father to bed at 3:00 a.m., mother up at 6:00), no telling who's sleeping where. At bedtime the children choose. Bicker, cast lots. He opens the first door: Margery tucked against Carol, who's near falling out of the bed. In the other room, Lesley lies fearlessly face-up (though she's the one most plagued by bad dreams), arms at her side like an alabaster queen on her tomb. Irma drawn away from her, scrunched in a ball.

All sleeping. All his. How possible?

He returns to his bed. He knows, of course, what he heard. The crying of seals.

52

THE DERRY FARM, NEW HAMPSHIRE
OCTOBER 1905

Papa wants Lesley to write her story every day. Tonight her hand is bandaged (she fell on a stick and hurt it very badly), but she's a responsible girl, so she writes anyway, about the walk she and the children and Mama and Papa took to the big grove, where the children ate partridge berries and she played puss-in-the-corner with Mama and Papa.

> . . . and on the way ofer we fond the ston wall nokt down in
> to plasys and carol fond a shell that they emty out after the
> little bulits have gone out he fond that and pickt the shell
> and i wisht i had won . . .

53

BEACONSFIELD, BUCKINGHAMSHIRE, ENGLAND
OCTOBER 1913

After midnight in the cottage by the coal fire, the dull English rain outside, Frost in his Morris chair with his lapboard, sick to heart for Derry, for stars, for his kitchen table, his woodpile, his orchard, his stone wall that hasn't been mended for years and must be in a terrible condition.

The work of hunters is another thing:
I have come after them and made repair
Where they have left not one stone on stone,
But they would have the rabbit out of hiding,
To please the yelping dogs

54

THE DERRY FARM, NEW HAMPSHIRE

MAY 1908

The spruce tree has died, and the children are crying all over again. O Schneider! Barker up trees and down holes! Mild warner of tramps! Lover of open road! Confederate of cows!

Frost is digging out the dead spruce over Schneider's grave. He transplanted it here, in the front garden, from the woods a year ago March. Maybe too small a rootball, or not enough spring rain. Or cursed by the three sisters. Not Lesley, Irma, and Marjorie, but the Greek ladies. The lesson for today: *Death is for children, too.*

O Schneider! Defender of hearth and home!

It's hot. A hummingbird is rising and dropping slow like a jeweled bee among the coral blossoms in the quince hedge. Full feet five thy good dog lies. Frost doesn't want to move his bones (*cursed be he*), or even see them, he would find it upsetting, so he's digging shallow and cutting the roots with the spade. He wrestles with the trunk, trying to pull the tree over, but he hasn't dug enough.

Lesley's crying, anyway. The others are too young to remember clearly.

Carol, Irma, and Marjorie all learned to walk by winding their fingers in his hair and lurching after him. Pulling those plows, he was a patient ox, grinning, and when they fell he'd turn and sniff them, lick their ears. Whenever the cow got out, Lesley would peal, "Snider! Get the cow!" and he'd leap like Ajax off the porch—and run his own way, up the Berry Road, barking joyfully.

Bossy! Get Schneider!

The children chasing him around the meadow. He was a collie, uncatchable. He ran like water flowing. He ran the way Frost, in his dreams, dreams *he* can run. Over the river and dryshod into the woods. You'll never catch me, Bossy!

One of the first things Lesley wrote, when she was five, was about crossing the road to the pasture and the pine grove.

    snider will come ufu with me and bark up trees

He was after sqrales, which he never caught. Elinor wrote out for Lesley: "squirrels."

And there were certain holes in Nat Head's woods he always ran to.

    he likes to run up in nat heads woods he has sevrel squirrel
    holes up ther he likes to bark down them. but he cant catch
    them becas they can run faster then he can

She was six when she wrote that; Frost was pleased she'd noticed. And the image appealed to him: barking up trees and down holes. Ceaselessly looking for something you'll never find. A year later, in the kitchen after a midnight walk, when everyone else was asleep, he found a spare notebook and a stub of pencil and started a conversation with his seven-year-old daughter, older poet to younger poet.

    Schneider met a squirrel and the squirrel said, "If you don't
    catch me, I'll show you another squirrel fatter 'n I be. . . ."

In the story, Schneider foolishly agrees, and what the squirrel shows him is a hole in the ground. If Schneider can catch the fat squirrrel in it, well then, he's welcome to eat him. Meanwhile, the first squirrel runs up a tree. Schneider is left looking down the hole with disappointment, and up the tree with a sense of betrayal.

Frost read his story to Lesley and a couple of days later she answered. Not for her the thwarted longings of middle age, but the cheerful violence of youth, and tenderheartedness for her dog:

> one day snider went up the berry road and he saw a wood-
> chuck with a rat in its mouth good morning said snider
> good morning said the woodchuck you've got a good
> breakfast havent you said the woodchuk oh no said snider i
> wouden't eat you for the world you've got a nice rat to eat
> better than an old bony woodchuck and i am going to make
> friends with you come home and i will give you a little table
> to eat on and the woodchuck came and snider put him and
> the rat too in the oven and when he thought they were
> done he took them out, and ate them.

The winter after that, a stranger dog came into the yard, and Schneider didn't run up the Berry Road. He stood his ground and did his duty. The other dog was chased off, but Schneider was badly chewed. The town was in the middle of a rabies scare, so Frost put him in a pen in the barn and tended him there, keeping the children away. After two or three days, his eyes began to glaze over. He looked horribly like the roughly teased and maudlinly coddled dogs of Frost's childhood, when his father fed them whiskey to watch them lurch and fall. Then his breathing got heavy, and one morning he just stood there sightlessly with his mouth open, panting. Then he died. Frost paid for the knacker to come and cut off Schneider's head, so he could send it to a lab. The results were negative, but the children still say he died of rabies. Which maybe is more comforting than thinking his death a mystery, or the result of bungled doctoring.

So they buried his body here, and his head elsewhere, which is how you can tell he's a hero. Robert the Bruce was buried without his heart so Douglas could carry it to the Holy Land. Frost wrote a poem about that.

Thus of old the Douglas did:
He left his land as he was bid
With the royal heart of Robert the Bruce
In a golden case with a golden lid

This was after reading about his namesake to the children one night. Gee, but his mother loved to read to him, when he refused to go to school, out of Porter's Scottish Chiefs. Who stood and fought, who died. Douglas never reached the Holy Land because he stopped in Spain to fight the Moors.

The heart he wore in a golden chain
He swung and flung forth into the plain,
And followed it crying 'Heart or death!'
And fighting over it perished fain.

So may another do of right,
Give a heart to the hopeless fight,
The more of right the more he loves

Not run up the Berry Road, barking joyfully and living long.

He slashes a few more times at the roots, sweating, then grapples with the trunk again, and now it starts to heel over. He hauls on it, resets his grip, hauls again and the last roots rip and it comes out sideways. He stands it up on its rootball. Ugly, spiky gray corpse.

He wipes the sweat out of his eyes. Farmer Rob.

He looks up in the tree. He looks down in the hole.

55

The Younger Poet drives Frost into the courtyard of Dublin Castle. Frost mentioned offhand on the first day of his visit that he was curious about the Frost coat-of-arms. Typical American! This is the Younger Poet's surprise. "Where are we now?" Frost asks.

"In Dublin Castle."

"What does one do in Dublin Castle?" (Frost has no interest in sightseeing.)

"If one is an American, one goes into that office and asks for a genealogy."

Frost grins at him. He's touched. The Younger Poet remembered a comment, made a personal gesture. "I'll do it!" Frost says. He lays odd emphasis on the words. As though the decision takes courage.

It's only a joke. Something Americans like to half believe. Living in modern flats on a numbered avenue, or on one of a thousand Main Streets in a house they bought last year from a stranger—look, on the mantelpiece, there's the icon from the old country that (they tell themselves) tells them something about themselves: a lion passant; a George cross; three shields, gules, on ermine; horseshit on a field of blarney.

"Lincolnshire Frosts or Somersetshire Frosts?" asks the man in the office.

Frost says he doesn't know. Which is interesting, because he does know. He's told the Younger Poet his family came from Devonshire. Maybe he *does* know it's all a game. But why the nervousness? The Younger Poet is quite sure he's nervous.

"What Christian name is usual in the family?" the man asks.

"Robert."

Also not true. He was named after Robert E. Lee. His forebears were mostly William.

"That would be the Lincolnshire Frosts."

"Good, yes," Frost says. "Will you tell me what arms I get?"

The man pulls down a volume, turns the banner pages, rotates the book toward the American to see. A gray squirrel and a pine tree.

They climb back into the car. The Younger Poet drives them through quaint olde Dublin streets, to which Frost pays no attention. If he was fooling, why does he keep talking about the squirrel and the pine tree, his face wreathed in delight?

56

CAMBRIDGE, MASSACHUSETTS

1946

Frost has been sending manuscripts and mementos to a collector, for his hoard of Frostiana, and he feels like a charlatan, an Indian swami—*Here is my urine, drink.* (But not enough not to cash the monthly checks the collector sends him to keep the flow coming.) Is he becoming a fossil? All that count now are his relics? And in the long run, signed books and birthday-dinner programs worth more than his poems? *The long run.* Christ on a crutch, he feels the length of it. Not his seventy-two years, but much more, the passing of generations, the yielding of children to grandchildren, the hundred-year cycle of pasture to steeplebush to timber forest to pasture. His new book will be called *Steeple Bush*, and he's dedicating it to his grandchildren, who seem a happier lot than his children. His poem in there about the hundred-year cycle is really about them. (Not that anyone will notice.) It's called "Something for Hope."

He's got another poem, called "To an Ancient," and maybe it should be subtitled "You and I." It was inspired by an article he read about a stone-age gravesite, a single human bone and a single stone tool found, and all the guessing the archaeologists did about the life of the man.

Sorry to have no name for you but You

And there was a cave he saw out west, years ago, high on a cliff wall, miles from anywhere. The image kept coming back to him—that stain on the stone wall, maybe cut wider with a stone ax, maybe darkened by cookfire. Human grime, human toil, the nameless toiler, who had food to find, and his own thoughts to wonder at, and the dark to fear as he climbed the wall in the setting sunlight to reach his hole.

I see the callus on his sole
The disappearing last of him
And of his race starvation slim,
Oh, years ago—ten thousand years.

You and I, old man. Two callused souls.

57

CAMBRIDGE, MASSACHUSETTS

NOVEMBER 1949

Now Margaret Bartlett is dying!

His old student from Pinkerton Academy days, John Bartlett, for whom Frost played Cupid, died in 1947. Margaret wrote then to ask about publishing Frost's letters to them, and he felt the usual chill. Now she's writing again, asking again, because she herself is dying of cancer. Will he outlive them all? Will his immortality be all that matters to them, a ticket to their own? *Drink and be—* Especially from his oldest friends, his most human friends, this grieves him. He cannot save them.

Dear Margaret:

All the more in an emergency like this I seem disinclined to let you make a publisher's venture of the letters I wrote you and John in the simplicity of the heart back there when none of us was anybody

58

1984

The Editor writes:

The notebook containing the eighteen stories Robert Frost wrote for his own children on the Derry farm is among the most interesting manuscripts of the Robert Frost Collection in the Clifton Waller Barrett Library at the University of Virginia Library. . . . The twelve stories in the first, pencil-written part of the notebook, in which Schneider is a canine antihero, must have been written by February 1907, when Schneider the collie died. . . . The children's stories can be seen as a vital stage of his development towards his first fully mature work in *North of Boston*. . . .

The notebook is made up of thirty leaves of white wove paper measuring 129–34 X 202–13 mm. The leaves have two holes on one of the shorter edges, about 85 mm. apart and once used to thread the leaves into the notebook cover, which is open on the end. Now, the holes are frayed and the leaves loose. Because they are also unpaginated, a problem arises as to their sequence (see the following section). . . .

59

THE DERRY FARM, NEW HAMPSHIRE

1900–1907

Solitary the thrush,
The hermit withdrawn to himself, avoiding the settlements,
Sings by himself a song

Maybe Frost is still half buried. He writes poems only at night, when no one can see. No one reads them but Elinor. He lays the pages away in a chest, a strongbox at the bottom of a bog. He tries writing prose—essays about chicken farming for a poultry journal, for a few dollars each—which always for him will be an admission of a loss of confidence. He milks the cow, feeds the chickens, candles the eggs. He wanders the woods at night. He goes down to the cranberry bog to hunt for orchises.

I fled forth to the hiding receiving night that talks not,
Down to the shores of the water, the path by the swamp
     in the dimness,
To the solemn shadowy cedars and ghostly pines so still

Whitman has never been a favorite. But maybe those lines were part of what inspired him, years ago, to flee to the Dismal Swamp. He was twenty years old, and Elinor had broken off their engagement. He only knew the name; he knew it was somewhere in Virginia. He wanted to die, but was too cowardly to kill himself. Dismal Swamp! Obviously the earthly approximation of the Slough of Despond, and he was despondent. No revolver needed. The swamp would close over him like a healing wound.

He took a train to Norfolk, then asked directions from the locals. They pointed and he walked to the village of Deep Creek, as the sun declined. (Shades of Bunyan lengthening.) From Deep Creek he took a wagon road to the swamp, just as darkness came on. He had no plan. He was waiting for the swamp (or maybe he meant Poetry) to decide.

It turned out that the road to the swamp continued into it.

> True, there are by the direction of the law-giver, certain good and substantial steps, placed even through the very midst of this Slough . . .

Should he turn off, find an evil black tarn, weight his pockets with stones? But that was interfering with fate. (Or perhaps, prosaically, he was too scared.) He continued on the path until he reached a place where high water covered it as far as he could see into the darkness—

> . . . but at such time as this place doth much spew out its filth, as it doth against change of weather, these steps are hardly seen; or if they be, men through the dizziness of their heads step besides; and then they are bemired

—and really, now, did this part happen to Robert Frost (he will tell his biographer that it did), or is this pure Bunyan? He saw a narrow plank walk stretching across the water, and he went along it, and yes, he felt dizzy. And yes, he had a burden that weighed him down, a satchel, which he lightened by tossing out two books (titled *Sin* and *Despair*; or were they Whittier and Bryant?) and some extra clothes. At midnight he came on a canal boat, and the canallers took him in, and in the morning the boat picked up a party of duck-hunters, and the duck-hunters took him in. He ended up going clear through the swamp and out the far side, and ended up at Kitty Hawk, lighter than air, where he met a man in uniform on the beach, an officer of the coastal Life Saving Service, who asked Frost if he'd given his heart to Jesus. That's right—he met Evangelist.

Maybe Elinor didn't love him, but the Dismal Swamp did. Ever since, he's been fond of swamps.

> From deep secluded recesses,
> From the fragrant cedars and the ghostly pines so still,
> Came the carol of the bird.
>
> And the charm of the carol rapt me,
> As I held as if by their hands my comrades in the night,
> And the voice of my spirit tallied the song of the bird.

In winter, Frost takes the children out to the frozen cranberry bog. He feels through the snow with his boots to find where the ice is smooth, sweeps clear a path. Lesley, seven years old, runs and slides a dozen feet. Frost slides thirty. Carol stomps and shouts and laughs. Irma won't try it; she stands apart and watches, and soon is saying she's cold and wants to go home. "All right," Frost says, but before they go he takes a last run down the rise of ground and casts himself onto the path. Leaning back on his heels, his arms straight down to lower his center of gravity, hands straight out in case he falls (he looks like a figure in an Egyptian frieze, frozen on a tomb wall for five thousand years), he slides clear across the bog.

They trudge home. Smoke from the chimney. Elinor has stayed in the house, with baby Margery.

Is it true to say that Elinor is always in the house? Not strictly. Sometimes she visits a neighbor, or goes shopping in Derry Village. She takes an evening walk with Rob when it's not too cold. But yes, let's say it: Elinor is always in the house. In the parlor giving lessons to the children, in the bedroom going to sleep early, in the womb-red kitchen by the heart-murmuring stove, waiting for her family to come home. In spring, the children bring her flowers. Lesley spells it "boka," and Elinor corrects it, "bouquet."

the first we fond were inercins and next were hapaticas and
vielets and singcwafoles and at last eneminys

They gather the flowers in the pasture across the road, or on Guay's
Hill, and bring them, bruised and wilted, to the granite sill that might
say *Here Lives Elinor Frost*. The children don't know it, but they're doing what their father did years ago, when Elinor was first pregnant,
with the child not yet named, now never named. As Elinor grew heavy,
she grew silent and sad. She stopped taking walks with Rob. Maybe she
was in the throes of prophecy. But at the time, he suspected she felt regret at tying with him the knot that in a few weeks would become Gordian. He wrote an apology that was at least as much a reproach:

Flower-Gathering

I left you in the morning,
And in the morning glow,
You walked a way beside me
To make me sad to go.
Do you know me in the gloaming,
Gaunt and dusty gray with roaming?
Are you dumb because you know me not,
Or dumb because you know?

All for me? And not a question
For the faded flowers gay
That could take me from beside you
For the ages of a day?
They are yours, and be the measure
Of their worth for you to treasure,
The measure of the little while
That I've been long away.

Encased in that poem lay the wounded seed that had written on it, *You
come, too.*

Now that they have a home they more or less own, Frost doesn't only pick flowers for her, he digs them up and carries them on a shovel and replants them around the house. Cellar holes are good places to find unusual varieties, because the people who once lived there went out themselves to search for the unusual—a double-petaled rose, a lilac, a clematis. And when those vanished people searched, they knew to go to the cellar holes of their day. Thus flowers, Poetry's emblems of transience, outlive the generations of men, who carry them (bees dusted with pollen) from cellar hole to cellar hole.

When proud old Yankee families gather for a reunion, it's not to some country manse they repair, but to a hole in the ground. Cousins come from towns and cities, from farms in states with better soil, and rent rooms from failing farmers, set up tents in orchards, and on the day, they walk up a road no longer a road, a scratch on the granite knee of a mountain, and they gather round the hole and bark down it. What do they see? A glimmer of broken jam-jar glass? Some truth about themselves?

> "Tell me why we're here
> Drawn into town about this cellar hole
> Like wild geese on a lake before a storm?
> What do we see in such a hole, I wonder"

(Frost will write this later, sick with longing, in a modern bungalow in England.)

> "Oh, if you're going to use your eyes, just hear
> What *I* see. It's a little, little boy,
> As pale and dim as a match flame in the sun."

White wings beating upward. A few laggard chickens scatter when Frost takes Lesley, four years old, out with him in the evening to the henhouses. He lights a candle from the lantern that he hangs by the door under the low ceiling, leads her down the stove-murmuring line of brooders. The space is cramped, warm, straw-gold and feather-white, bedding-sweet and dropping-sour. He inserts the candle in a little device with foil in a bowl to brighten the light, and a cupped holder in front. He slips a hand under a hen, removes an egg, secures it with his forefinger in the cup. Kneeling, he draws Lesley to him and puts the device before her eyes. "Do you see?"

The egg glows the way the whole henhouse glows when she comes before bed to get Papa and he's inside with the lantern lit. Lesley peers, loses patience, then jumps with excitement. A shadow! A flutter! "Yes!"

"Then it's good." Papa slips the egg back under the hen, pulls out another one.

Sometime later, when Lesley is asleep, he sits in the kitchen and works on another story for *Farm-Poultry* (he needs the fifteen dollars they will pay him; Lesley and Carol and baby Irma make three):

> Welch usually had his chickens out early, and the showing season seldom found him unprepared. But one year his first hatches were so exceptionally fine that the gods fell in love with them, and they died young.

60

THE DERRY FARM, NEW HAMPSHIRE
1909

For three years now he's taught English at Pinkerton Academy, in Derry Village. His real job: a teacher, like his mother. The boys and girls sit with wide-open eyes, and he fills them with stuff that would only be of use to them if they thought it up themselves. He was never really a farmer. He escaped into the cloud of white wings; he climbed the ladder out of sight among the apple boughs; he hid in the high meadow grass, his scythe whispering only to him.

And not a poet, either, apparently. *Teacher! teacher!* the ovenbird accuses him every summer, when he tries to forget. He is at Dante's midpoint, thirty-five years old, not lost in the wood but running toward it, fleeing the exposed meadow where the chicken hawk might drop on him. He asks himself, is this really his life? Is he, in fact, this diminished thing? He, who ran from the classroom, now running it?

It's time to move the family to the village. His work is there, and though Elinor would gladly stay on the farm while the briars grew over it, even she can see that the children, growing up only in each other's company, odd Frosts begetting each other, are getting odder. Rob loves them, but he fears for them if not transplanted from the cellar hole to the trodden path. Lesley's prickly, Carol's sullen, Irma's anxious, Marjorie's shy. It could be a nursery rhyme.

In July, they pack their things. Leave some of the furniture for the man who'll rent the farm, but take table and chairs, beds and dressers, books, the children's essays, Frost's poems. The horse and the cow and the last of the chickens have been sold. The meadow needs haying, the orchard pruning. The garden is a mass of weeds.

They were here for a decade, and Frost never repaired a thing. House paint peeled, roof shingles blew down, windowpanes cracked, porch steps sagged and broke. He *could* say that this was all his plan, that by neglecting maintenance he supported his family on very little. (This is what he will say to his biographer.) But the truth is, Frost has never really felt that they lived here. They bided. Even when the furniture was finally in place, they never invited anyone over. This wasn't their home, it was their cave.

Not that Frost is not grateful. He owes his life, his broken life (such as it is, such as it might become), to this cave. He huddled by the fire and painted flowers on the walls, and the rain and wolves were kept out. Standing on the empty road, about to turn his back on the farm and shuffle off to his teacher-teacher's life in a rented apartment, Frost has a pale foreboding of the intense nostalgia he will feel for this place once he is gratefully free of it. He will also feel a deep sorrow, and no little shame, that he did nothing for it in return but darken it with his grime.

61

Does she love him? She won't say. Always been frail; she was two years older than her grade in school because she'd been at home for slow fever. Doesn't like the act. Never did. Maybe that's normal in a woman. Fear of childbirth. Hard on her heart. After the first, the doctor said she shouldn't have another. Hates the intimate probing the doctor does during labor. She says it robs life of its grace and charm. Note the word she uses: rob. Six children he's made her bear. The last one died after three days. As though to say, Enough! Enough with her pain, enough with his selfishness. A man's a beast.

There's a poem there—her frigidity, his rough treatment. She'd never let him publish it. And he wouldn't want to. Why write it, then? To punish her, he supposes. Make her read it. What's the pistil for, the stamen, the bee? The question's absurd. We exist.

> See the mountains kiss high heaven
> And the waves clasp one another;
> No sister-flower would be forgiven
> If it disdain'd its brother

Would some other man awaken passion in her? Well, Christ. He's what she's got. Maybe she should have set her sights higher; but she didn't. When she gave herself to him, it was the first for them both, and the only forever. A covenant as sacred as marriage, as jealous as the God of Israel. *You shall have no one before me.* Which is why he was horrified when she dated another man at college and returned his ring. Didn't she realize this was divorce? Whoredom? Fire should rain down, the earth open to swallow them.

But he got her to see. Love was only part of the question. There was also duty and consequence. She had no choice any longer. She'd made her choice.

See. It hurt her. And he gave her a child who half killed her when he was born and half killed her again when he died. But he also gave her four more children who are her only reason for living. (He doesn't kid himself.) And he gives her, outright, his devotion. She knows there's no question. He can't bear to be apart from her, couldn't live without her.

It's late. He's alone, able to think his own thoughts, not crowded, jostled.

> All discourses but mine own afflict me; they seem harsh, impertinent and irksome.

That's Morose speaking. A line to keep in. He's writing a short version of a Ben Jonson play for his students at Pinkerton to perform. (Turns out he's good at teaching.)

> Her silence is dowry enough.

A private joke. The play is *The Silent Woman*. Like his poems, like everything, this is first for Elinor, and only distantly for anyone else.

Morose wants to find a wife who will never speak, something Jonson considers a comic impossibility. The further joke is, the Silent Woman that Morose marries turns out to be a boy. Part of the fun is figuring out how to take one of the bawdiest plays ever written and adapt it so that American children can act it in front of their parents without getting their teacher thrown in jail.

> If you had lived in King Ethelred's time, sir, or Edward the Confessor's, you might perhaps have found in some cold country hamlet, then, a dull frosty wench would have been contented with one man.

Elinor will notice that. And this, where two lawyers argue the principles of marriage law:

> CUTBEARD: There is *affinitas ex fornicatione.*
> OTTER: Which is no less *vera affinitas* than the other.
> CUTBEARD: *Quae oritur ex legitimo matrimonio.*
> OTTER: *Nascitur ex eo, quod per coniugium duae personae efficiuntur una caro.*

The Latin will protect the parents' ears (it had better!), but Elinor will know what it means.

> CUTBEARD: There is the relationship arising from fornication.
> OTTER: Which is no less a true relationship than the other.
> CUTBEARD: Yes, no less than the one that arises from legal marriage.
> OTTER: It follows from this that through their physical union two people are made one flesh.

Sometimes, writing at night, he feels like it's the only time he's getting through to her.

62

AMHERST, MASSACHUSETTS

1918

Teaching to pay the bills, he's got no time for poetry. He's dragged his family down from Franconia to live in a rented house. He returns from campus at midnight to find them all asleep, scattered in strange rooms. He sits by the window, reading Emily Dickinson's *The Single Hound*. From right here, if it were day, he could look down Main Street and see her Homestead, a brick pile no wolf could ever blow down. Home, home, nothing but home for her, and for him the road and the rented room. Her hound barks at him, he shrinks from the kitchen door. He runs into the woods, she retreats to the bedroom. He fears the dark, she fears the bed. The tramp, her shadow, reads, lonely, with pained delight:

> In Winter, in my room,
> I came upon a worm,
> Pink, lank, and warm

63

THE DERRY FARM, NEW HAMPSHIRE
JUNE 1938

Frost insisted on doing this alone. He drives up the Derry Road. It's still dirt, but better graded. There are hill cuts he doesn't recognize. He thinks he's there, but when he goes around the curve he isn't. He hasn't been back since 1911. Hasn't wanted to. Everything has stayed clear in his mind.

The house is a shock. Has no one painted it in all this time? The quince hedge out front bristles with maple saplings. The hydrangea and dahlias are gone. The barn door's open. Some old jalopy in there. Lawn needs cutting. Christ, the lower pasture's swampy. The ditch must have collapsed.

Frost trips on the broken step of the side porch, knocks on the door. Will Schneider bark, fool this tramp into thinking he'll get chased down the road? Are there any animals here at all?

A woman opens the door. "Excuse me," he says. She looks suspicious. "My name's Robert Frost. I used to live here. Thirty years ago."

He'd been hoping his name would mean something to whoever he found here. An open sesame. *Robert Frost! Let's walk by Hyla Brook and along the wall, I've mended it every spring, where hunters haven't left one stone on stone and two can pass abreast, it's all the same, all, all the same!*

The magic fails. The woman says, "Yeah?"

No horse in the barn, no poems in the house. No kitchen table, no red floor, no Glenwood stove. No children asleep upstairs or playing in the pine grove. The house is silent. How old is this woman? Thirty and barren? Twenty and aged by overwork? The house is silent, but the road is not. Every minute a car rumbles by, kicking up dirt. It never quite settles before the next car comes.

Frost is forced to explain. See, he had a wife and the house kept her, you can still see *Here Lives Elinor Frost* carved on the sill beneath the front steps if you squint hard enough, and surely you saw her haunting the brook in the moonlight, she was the worn-down woman in the house dress with the close-set eyes that got closer and darker as the years went by. Now she really is dead, and she wanted her ashes spread by the brook, not because she believed in an afterlife, but Christ did she believe in memory and regret, and Hyla Brook cries day and night with it. "Hyla?" Never mind. He just means the brook under the alders, maybe you don't have a name for it—? No, he didn't think you did.

"I guess that'd be all right," the woman says. "But I'd have to talk to my husband first, and he ain't home right now."

Oh, that's all right. There ain't no fucking way Frost is going to do it, anyway. Not after this. He's not sure he believes in an afterlife any more than Elinor did, but he believes in poetry, and her ashes aren't going to be trod into the mud of a brook denuded of its name by an ignorant woman and her nameless paramour. But what he says is "Would you mind if I walked down to the brook? I don't have the ashes with me, I'd bring them back later."

"I guess that's all right." She closes the door.

You guess. Don't know nothin'. Brook? Farm? Is this my hand? Is this my soul?

He can't find the path down the slope that the children wore. The orchard hasn't been trimmed in years; the trees won't be bearing anything marketable. The alders are overgrown. The bridge he built over the brook is gone. The wall is tumbled and humbled and mossy.

Guay? Where are you? Did the elves take you? You go the way of the chestnut trees, old boy?

All he finds is part of the rock dam he built, still holding back some water, and a plank nearby that he nailed in a tree fork, for Elinor to sit on. So she could listen to the crying.

Well is she listening now? No, he's not crying. (Splash the brook in his face.) He gave that up a long time ago. Rage is more his style.

It's the only thing that gets him back to the car.

64

ROUTE 28, NEW HAMPSHIRE

MAY 1953

The most famous poet in America travels to Dartmouth College twice a year to speak in the Great Issues Course. (He's the star attraction.) When he's coming up from Boston he's often driven by a friend, which makes the ride a pleasure (someone to talk to)—except for one stretch. North of Windham, there's Kilrea Road, and then there's the Old Lowell Road coming in from the left and the dip toward the brook. Frost closes his eyes. "Tell me when we've passed by." It takes only a few seconds. (The road is paved now.) But it doesn't really help. Because he sees on his eyelids what he saw the one time he looked: the house unpainted, the orchard cut down, even the grass gone, all gone. The mowing field has been turned into an automobile graveyard. The soil poisoned. *'Tis a fearful thing.* But he closes his eyes anyway, and he puts a hand over his closed eyes. Anything else would seem too weak.

65

THE DERRY FARM, NEW HAMPSHIRE

AUGUST 2004

The Novelist makes a pilgrimage. Route 28 parallels Interstate 93, traversing land developed as suburbs for Manchester, Nashua, Lawrence, and Haverhill. The two-lane road is busy and dangerous, traffic going too fast over abrupt hills and around blind curves. The Old Lowell Road, which crosses Route 28 half a mile south of the farm, is now named Frost Road. *For Robert from Robert, his friend in the art: take that!* Going too fast, with a tail-wagging truck polishing his heels, the Novelist almost misses the small sign, *Robert Frost Farm,* and the house (neat and white, recognizable from photographs) that appears suddenly on his right, but he brakes hard and manages to scurry into the far side of the driveway as the truck slams past.

The Novelist is the only visitor except for a Latino couple who come into the barn, glancing sidelong at the photographs on the walls and asking puzzled questions. They want to buy produce. This is a farm, isn't it?

The guide takes the Novelist through the house. Lesley Frost Ballantine was adviser for the restoration of the interior. Glass washboard, soapstone sink, Glenwood stove. Phone box on the wall with a crank. The kitchen floor is red, and so is the wallpaper above the beige wainscoting. The front upstairs bedroom has roses on the walls. The furniture is tastefully arrayed, the clean curtains are hung, the vacuumed rugs spread. The china is stacked in the cupboard and neatly set on the dining-room table. The guide says it's the right pattern, and the Novelist believes her. But the place feels wrong. Not so much that it feels empty, but that it feels like an empty home. It doesn't feel like a cowering caravan retarded mid-waste by a sandstorm between a couple of oases, both of them fata morganas.

The Novelist walks the grounds. It's a beautiful sunny morning. The visitors' parking lot (the Novelist's Toyota) stands where the orchard used to be. Dozens of truckloads of oil-and-gasoline-soaked soil were removed twenty years ago, and topsoil brought in to restore the mowing field. Now the right kind of grass grows out of the wrong farm's dirt. The alders down by the brook are advancing up the hill. It has been a rainy summer, so Hyla Brook still trickles over roots and rocks. There's a place where stones make a dam with a gap in the center, and the water gathers behind it, bubbling, before falling a foot into a small pool. The Novelist would very much like to believe that this is It, a gesture of Form from the very hands. Frost Falls.

Back in the barn, he buys a copy of *Family Letters of Robert and Elinor Frost* and a T-shirt with Frost's face on it. Looking at the photographs on the wall, he lingers over one he's seen before. (There exist only two photographs of the family from the decade they lived on the farm.) The caption is "The Frost Children at the Derry Farm, 1908." The photo belonged to Lesley Frost, who became the family historian. (Carol burned his letters. Irma, one could almost believe, ate hers.) The Novelist has always wondered who took this photograph. Since the only other from the period is also dated 1908, it's possible that both photos were taken on the same day—some acquaintance, name long forgotten, who paid a rare visit. The photographer stood across the Derry Road and shot the house and barn, with all four Frost children in the foreground, running forward, toward a point off to the left—presumably the little pasture, where they often played, and where Lesley had her playhouse under the pine trees.

> Some shattered dishes underneath a pine,
> The playthings in the playhouse of the children.
> Weep for what little things could make them glad.

The children are just starting to cross the dirt road. Their arms and legs are blurry with speed. They don't need to look before they cross. The girls are blonde and dressed in light-colored smocks. They shine against the dark quince hedge at the front of the house. They are wearing leggings. Carol is in overalls. Three-year-old Marjorie, the family angel, is in front, and the Novelist could swear she is holding a wand tipped with a star. Aptly, Lesley is in the middle of an exuberant leap, and equally aptly, Carol seems to be lagging. Marjorie's shadow is half again as long as she is, angling south-southeast, so it's late afternoon at a time of year when the sun sets to the north. If this was taken on the same day as the other photograph (Robert Frost is sitting behind Eunice on a hay rake, looking remarkably like Robert F. Kennedy), it's perhaps July, after the first haying. But it occurs to the Novelist that the children are heavily dressed for July. Perhaps he's wrong. Or perhaps Elinor, who always worried so much about her children's health, overdressed them. Or perhaps she knew, in her old-woman's fairy-tale cottage under thatch, that Frost Children must be swaddled, or the summer sun would melt them.

Before he leaves, the Novelist watches a short film about Robert Frost and the Derry years. There are shots of the stone wall, the brook, the sun rising, water dripping from house eaves, mist on the mowing field, spring blossoms, tree buds, snow. A narrator recites "Stopping by Woods on a Snowy Evening," "An Old Man's Winter Night," "Nothing Gold Can Stay." An actor, whose face is never shown, walks around pretending to be Frost doing farm chores. Predictably, the filmmakers cast an old man in the role. They've given him the famous tussock of white hair, the thick hanging hands, the low-slung egg shape. (Public, meet preconception.) The effect is startlingly painful. This figure that, as in nightmares, never shows its face, could be the ghost of the battered man, returned to the scenes of its young manhood and finding them all a museum, all dead. As it gazes over a stone wall, or hobbles down a line of autumn maples, or looks vaguely into the depths of a milk pail that has seen no use in years, it might be searching for its lost children.

66

Two roads converge in new snow. Dusk is falling fast on the exposed hillside, three miles from the campus. He comes up here often for the valley views, the stripling Merrimac frozen silver, the square white buildings of the Normal School where he teaches. White ground, steel sky, black trees. He likes the feeling that it's all his. Even a day or two after a snowfall, neither this road nor the one it crosses up ahead shows more than a dog's or deer's tracks.

Wordsworth is running through his head.

> She dwelt among the untrodden ways

He walks to work off his anxiety, his doubt. What is he, teacher or poet? He's nearly thirty-eight.

> She lived unknown, and few could know

When Silver became principal here, he brought Frost up, because Frost has become almost famous in the state for his teaching. The students listen to him, look up to him. He gives talks to educators, and though it still scares the daylights out of him, he's getting used to the fear, the nausea. The applause afterward is less of a surprise, the words of praise don't sound quite so condescending. But . . . a teacher?

> —Fair as a star, when only one
> Is shining in the sky

It wasn't so bad when he was a failure. The tribes of Lawrence—relatives, old friends, teachers—left him alone out of embarrassment. Now they sense something. The late bloomer's blooming.

A violet by a mossy stone

They want to press him while he's impressive, screw him down in the frame. Principal of some stone institution, state commissioner for pickling souls. They'll kill him with the best intentions.

Run! The fit's been on him lately, the fire descending and flowering, he's been writing poems but can't find the time. Rising late, late for class. (Students laugh behind their hands.) He's got some money from the sale of the Derry farm. Run! The question is: which way? In the west is John Bartlett, his favorite student from Pinkerton. Injected with promise and his family's best intentions, John went to Middlebury, and like Frost at Dartmouth he smelled the pickling salts and hightailed it out of there. Flew to Vancouver, did handsome John.

Elinor wants to go to England. Find a cottage near Stratford. Leaded windows, thatch, swans floating down the Avon.

She dwelt among the untrodden ways
Beside the springs of Dove

By any reasonable measure, it's the better choice. If he's going to write, try to get published, there's nothing in Vancouver. Except John. How strongly Frost wants to see him again! And how much he worries about him and Margaret. Bless the union, cure the asthma, conjure a child.

Principal Silver is living with the Frosts on campus, and he's complained about Elinor's housekeeping: dishes left all night, nothing for breakfast. A mama's boy. "Here's all a man needs for breakfast," Frost said, swallowing a raw egg. After a dinner party he gave, Silver reported with a schoolboy's pink-cheeked chuckle that so-and-so said Mrs. Frost seemed lacking in personality. Which made him Frost's enemy forever. "You've no right to speak of her!" he shouted. "She's *mine*!"

> A Maid whom there were none to praise
> And very few to love:
>
> A violet by a mossy stone
> Half hidden from the eye!

Then he came up here in the snow to trample out his wrath. Another reason to leave.

Blue dusk deepening to violet.

> But she is in her grave

Coming up on the point where the two ways cross, Frost is startled to see a man walking along the other road. He's never seen anyone out here. The man's about Frost's height, bareheaded like him, wearing a similar coat. At the rate he's walking, he and Frost will meet at the crossing. Frost keeps coming, eyeing the other man as they converge. His coat is *exactly* the same. And he's got the same unkempt hair. Who is he? Maybe it's the dusk, maybe it's the tearing in his eyes from the cold wind, but Frost has the strangest sensation that he's watching his own image reflected in a slanting mirror. A doppelgänger? That old literary device? He can hardly believe it. With no sound of footsteps in the snow, it's as if they were floating together, like two flat images that pop into three dimensions when you uncross your eyes.

Later, Frost will regret what he does, he will berate himself. But really, how typical—he quails. Ten feet short, he stops. The other walks past without a glance in his direction. Which seems the uncanniest thing of all. After a moment, Frost goes on, looking over his shoulder. Now the roads diverge, and the other man disappears into the darkness.

It simply can't be true, but poetry insists. If Frost had not been Frost—that is, if he'd been brave (maybe that was Robert the Brave walking by)—he would have kept on to the collision, which would not have been a collision. One form would slide into the other. There would be a vibration, a weird jiggle, and eyes would look out of eyes. East and west, all directions would be the same.

But—Frost is Frost.

> She lived unknown, and few could know
>   When Lucy ceased to be;
> But she is in her grave, and, oh,
>   The difference to me!

67

Edward Thomas to Robert Frost, December 15, 1914:

I will put it down now that you are the only begetter right enough.

Robert Frost to Edward Garnett, April 29, 1917:

Edward Thomas was the only brother I ever had.

68

Alone with his fears. He's locked himself in his hotel room. His first reading in Russia is tonight at six, in the Pushkin House.

Which adds to his fear. What does he know about Pushkin? A duel, a few poems in translation. Nothing more. It makes the question painfully pressing: what will his audience know or care about *him*?

He had lunch today—dinner, really, a big spread—with Anna Akhmatova. Frank Reeve was thrilled. You could see him glancing back and forth between them. On the drive there (it was out of town along the coast, one of those dachas Frost has always pictured as grand summer homes, but this was a cottage), Frank explained, "She's your counterpart, the leading poet of Russia, of a whole national tradition," and he went on to talk about Henry James and Turgenev a century ago, and the deeper understanding possible between writers. It sounded dewy-eyed to Frost, but he liked Frank for it.

A century ago. When Frost was a boy. And now he's a man, and Akhmatova's a woman, and he was driven out in style in a long black car, a ribboned carriage on his way to a marriage, the old-fashioned kind, the sort that kept order in ordered societies, where the bride and the groom meet for the first time at the altar.

A seaside cottage with a wooden fence and a garden far better tended than Frost can ever stir himself to do. Not hers—the cottage was somebody else's, Frost can't remember whose, a Russian professor, but he remembers her, when she arrived, his blind date. She was dignified, even grand. She wore a dark simple dress and looked at him with hooded eyes under the sort of forehead they used to call noble. There was something distant and incommunicable about those eyes, and it made Frost feel right at home, even affectionate, because he'd lived with a gaze like that for forty years. And he thinks he maybe made her feel a little better. She was a girl next to him, a spring flower of seventy-three. And maybe it's Frost's laziness, his self-indulgence, his open-road American luck, that's taken his face off guard, loosened it, given it bags and jowls. Whereas her skin was taut, stretched smooth over cheekbones and sharp chin and thin lips as though pulled back and fastened with clips at the back of her head. A death mask, though without anything ghoulish about it; a face of privation, of the Russian strategy of retreat, of that stoic Slav suffering—she was exiled for a time (Frank had explained), her work banned, a husband executed, a son sent to a labor camp for fifteen years—which makes Americans seem, when they suffer, like suffering children. (Like *his* suffering children. Like his suffering, as a child.) Exiled. Like Ovid to the Black Sea. Not America, but Russia is the true heir of Rome, with its subject nations, its slave hordes laboring on colossal public projects, its czars and commissars banishing poets to windswept outposts for unstated offenses.

They talked about Rome, he and Anna. (He didn't call her that, but really, now that they're married, he should.) She had less Horace and Virgil by heart than he did, more Catullus. Frost had read a couple of her poems in a Russian anthology he'd brought with him from the U.S. He had no idea whether she was a good poet (poetry is what's lost in translation, he's said a thousand times), but at least it seemed possible, it seemed there might indeed be something living beneath the death mask of the English lines.

> I used to think that after we are gone
> there's nothing, simply nothing at all.
> Then who's that wandering by the porch
> again and calling us by name?
> Whose face is pressed against the frosted pane?
> What hand out there is waving like a branch?
> By way of reply, in that cobwebbed corner
> a sunstruck tatter dances in the mirror.

He likes that "sunstruck tatter." He can only wonder what the Russian is, the sound of it. Does it tap that dance, seem almost to pirouette? Does "sunstruck" call up "dazed," "God-smitten" (prophecy), and does "tatter" suggest clothes (privation) and cloudwrack (dream)? That's where poetry lives. Which is why a poet in a foreign land is a foolish thing. (K.'s voice in his ear.) Why praise of him is empty. Or worse, political. For the Russians' purposes, he is America's poet of the laboring classes. And maybe for American purposes Anna is Russia's poet of the private vision, the unassimilable self.

So Frost's emotions at lunch were confused, on edge. He felt a real connection to her, but it was grounded on their shared inability to understand each other. The guests broke into a full-throated epithalamium, the Russians singing praises of the bride,

> Her golden leg, her coral comb,
> Her fluff of plumage, white as chalk

and Frost saw Frank stir, saw him glance anxiously in Frost's direction (why, *why* does everyone seem to think he's such a touchy old bastard?), and sure enough, Frank rose to sing the antistrophe, the potency of the groom, his flashing eye and virile hand, and it seemed empty and cheap, and Frost snapped at him, "No more of that, none of that, you cut that out."

Frank blushed, blinked. "I was only—"

"Cut it out."

Would he say a poem, the Russians asked.

No, he wouldn't. The mood wasn't right. Anna would have no way to judge it, yet would be forced to say something. He waved the audience in her direction—though he couldn't bear to hear her empty praise, he was willing to praise her emptily if that allowed him an escape. She said a poem. He listened to that lover's language, drowsy and zesty, and he thought he could hear an added melody, and the melody seemed pure because it meant nothing (*down, down derry, down*). So his praise, though without significance (since not to utter it was unthinkable), was not, after all, empty. "It's very musical, you can hear the music in it. It *sounds* very good." Frank had paraphrased the poem in English, but Frost paid no attention. That meant nothing. This was an old-fashioned marriage, they would cohabit comfortably without communicating. She'd produce her children in the kitchen, he'd till the fields for his. For dinner she'd hand him his—what? oats? groats?—and he'd look at her death mask and she'd look at his quivering imp's face and he'd sing to her "The Keeper of the Eddystone Light," and she'd sing to him a Russian lullaby.

All of which strong feelings (as he now remembers them with surprise in his hotel room) suggest how much he misses K. Her and Ted's daughter, Anne, is competing one of these days in a cross-country horse race, and he's been hoping K. would cable to tell him how she did. Not because the event matters, but because K., by seizing on this excuse to cable him, would show she knows how much Frost wants to hear from her, would show she cares enough to do this simple thing to make him happy. But she hasn't done it. Torturing him. Getting back at him for shaking up her life. Waking her up from her Ted-tedium.

Or just not thinking of him. (All alone, with his fears, in Saint Petersburg.)

He looks at the clock. Twenty-five minutes till Freddie comes.

He refuses to call it Leningrad. This is the royal city, where the American sailor-boy came to extract a favor from the czar. Frost was taken to a palace yesterday. They drove him out of the city and walked him up a terraced ramp with fountains and waterfalls. At the top sat a Baroque music box. The guide started in on the number of windows and the pounds of gold on the domes, and Frost got unendurably bored. Did the czar live here? he asked.

Yes, Peter the Great built it.

How about Nicholas?

Nicholas I or II?

Not the one you shot in the cellar, the other one.

Well, he mainly resided at— Some other palace was mentioned. Then the guide said that *this* palace had been destroyed by the Nazis and rebuilt by the U.S.S.R. Frost turned away, disgusted. "I suppose it's all very grand." Now where was the goddamn car? He did not want more evidence that these people, like Adlai-addled liberals back home, didn't have the courage of their convictions. Rebuilding the country clubs! What for? So Khrushchev could wander the halls, inspect his reflection in a gilt-edged mirror, try his backside on a golden throne? Frost wants to believe Khrushchev is not that sort of man.

He checks the clock again. Twenty-two minutes.

Jesus! Saying his poems to a roomful of Russians! This is crazy! What's he doing here? Waves of nausea foam up from his stomach. Get a grip, old man! He gets up to pace, taking deep breaths. He picks up a book and flings it against the wall. Communication. Come on. Isn't it possible? He flings another book, and it sails through the chandelier, rattling the brilliants. Lovely sound of destruction. Come on. Don't be a coward. He finds a third book on the bed table, but doesn't throw it— he was looking for this one. It falls open to a passage he's read many times through the years. Listen, my children, and you shall hear—

It was a glorious July day, one of those days which only come after many days of fine weather. From earliest morning the sky is clear; the sunrise does not glow with fire; it is suffused with a soft roseate flush. The sun, not fiery, not red-hot as in time of stifling drought, not dull purple as before a storm, but with a bright and genial radiance, rises peacefully behind a long and narrow cloud, shines out freshly, and plunges again into its lilac mist. The delicate upper edge of the strip of cloud flashes in little gleaming snakes; their brilliance is like polished silver. But lo! the dancing rays flash forth again, and in solemn joy, as though flying upward, rises the mighty orb. About mid-day there is wont to be, high up in the sky, a multitude of rounded clouds, golden-grey, with soft white edges. Like islands scattered over an overflowing river, that bathes them in its unbroken reaches of deep transparent blue, they scarcely stir. . . . In the evening these clouds disappear; the last of them, blackish and undefined as smoke, lie streaked with pink, facing the setting sun; in the place where it has gone down, as calmly as it rose, a crimson glow lingers long over the darkening earth, and, softly flashing like a candle carried carelessly, the evening star flickers in the sky.

There. See. Just as there's more religion outside of church than in, more love outside marriage than in, there's more poetry outside of verse than in. (Even if you didn't know Emerson wrote poems, you could tell he was a poet by reading his essays; you could tell, in fact, he was a better poet than an essayist.) So who is this poet of the perfect day? Guess who, children. Do you give up? Turgenev.

Frost first read this, the opening of "Bezhin Meadow," at Derry, when happiness seemed something he'd never see again. Thirty-five years later he wrote "Happiness Makes Up in Height for What It Lacks in Length" and among the many things nameable and unnameable that breathed life into his poem, one bright cluster was those golden-gray clouds high up in the sky, blessèd isles of respite in the deep drowning blue. He was trying to get at the life-saving memory of that, both of another writer's words that give you reason to go on, and of the thing itself,

> one day's perfect weather,
> When starting clear at dawn,
> The day swept clearly on
> To finish clear at eve

See. Somehow, communication happened. The Russian Yankee hurled his boulder across the Atlantic and hit the American Yankee on the head. And the American, nursing that obscure hurt, hurled a boulder back. And maybe it sailed over everyone's head, but Frost would like to imagine it thumped the old man's grave, made his bones dance. That's the kind of rivalry Frost can stand. Meeting and passing, up high in the silence. Free-fall, flower. So gird your loins, old coward. Pick up your stones. Remember that sunstruck tatter. Maybe that wasn't Anna's poetry, but she had enough artistry to inspire poetry in her translator.

He looks at the clock. Fourteen minutes.
Whereas . . . Yevtushenko . . .

> I am
>> each old man
>>> here shot dead.
> I am
>> every child
>>> here shot dead.
> Nothing in me
>> shall ever forget!
> The "Internationale," let it
>> thunder
> when the last anti-Semite on earth
> is buried forever.

Frost likes Yevtushenko, but . . . could that possibly be good poetry in Russian? Or rather, Frost is charmed by Yevtushenko, but doesn't know what to make of him. His poems sound like Sandburg, but Sandburg's an idiot, a genuine innocent, from his baby-silk hair down to his oversized shoes—whereas Yevtushenko's playing a complicated game. He's the Young Turk, poking the establishment in the ribs and maybe making it feel benevolent because it doesn't punch him back. He acts his part like a Greenwich Village beatnik, slim and high-priestly; the cigarette between his lips isn't dangling, it's anchored precisely at the regulation dangle-angle.

Frost spent a weary late evening in his apartment, sitting at a corner table and watching the Left Bankers. Yevtushenko kept coming over to him, sometimes almost on bended knee, other times as the Tatar host, holding the liquor bottle out at the end of an irresistible arm—Drink! (Frost resisted.) Frank was there having fun, and the other Russian poets were youngsters, and they sprang up to declaim their poems. Yevtushenko out-acted them all, head thrown back, arms conducting his own music. Ah, youth! Urgency, self-love; sweet, steaming horse manure. Frost wondered afterward how much of his mixed emotions sprang from jealousy. He remembers the night train up from Moscow to Saint Petersburg, when he couldn't sleep because he's an old man who has trouble sleeping in unfamiliar places, but was far too tired to get up because he's an old man who needs his sleep, so he lay dazed and depressed in the dark and listened to the next compartment, where Frank and Freddie and Jack Matlock, from the U.S. Embassy, were drinking whiskey and telling stories and breaking into laughter that grew louder and gayer and echoed ever more unhappily in Frost's head as the night wore on.

Ah, youth.

He looks at the clock: nine minutes. He slings a hated tie around his neck (Freddie will help him tie it), tucks in his shirt, swipes at his hair in the mirror. Speaking of youth, Yevtushenko kept talking about Cuba. They all do. Seems to be an obsession here. It surprised Frost at first. How could a little island of sugarcane and tobacco fields matter to Mother Russia? But he thinks he sees. Just as Khrushchev keeps saying he can swat America's ass because in fact he's afraid of America, he keeps saying America is old and Russia is young because the truth seems to be that the Russians don't feel young. They've come out of World War II and the Stalin era looking like Anna Akhmatova. Maybe Russians *have* lost the courage of their convictions. They rebuild the palaces of the czars they shot, and want you to admire their stucco-work (*now* you'll see what Russia can do) at the same time they want you to emulate their contempt of same. What's their revolution today but fat men on a dais in Red Square and schoolchildren standing in fear? Then here comes this tall bearded young fellow in green pajamas, just out of the mountains, waving a virile cigar. Ah, youth! Just what old Mother Russia needs, a spoonful of Castro oil.

Frost steps away from the mirror. Seven minutes. He's still nervous as hell. Jesus, here we go. He slumps on the edge of the bed, hands slack on either side. He gets through the last awful minutes by thinking of K.

one day's perfect weather

He wrote "Happiness Makes Up in Height" shortly before Elinor died, thinking of a day with her on their delayed honeymoon, when they rented a summer cottage in Allenstown, New Hampshire. His friend Carl Burell, an amateur botanist, had planted flowers all around the cottage, and he took Rob and Elinor out into the fields and bogs to acquaint them with species they'd never noticed before. He showed them how cunningly certain flowers attracted just the right insects, the only insects that could help them carry on their sex affairs. It was a whole new world to Rob, or two new worlds, one mirrored in the other: rampant, multiform floral concupiscence, and the guiltless carnal joys of married life.

Well. Gather ye rosebuds while ye may. One day! Maybe it was a few days. Elinor was in her sixth month, and she seemed blithe, even frisky. Then came heaviness, sadness.

Now (forgive him, Poetry!) what comes to him when he says the poem is an August day in the Vermont woods, four months after Elinor died, when he rounded on K. to show her he wasn't a harmless old impotent grieving widower she could squireen around so shamelessly, and to his surprise, and his blazing, erupting gratitude, she not only kissed him back, but lay back on the moss among the coy parasol mayapples and looked up at him with eyes that were not at all distant, stoic, or suffering.

> The day swept clearly on
> To finish clear at Eve.

69

A photograph of the Bungalow. (Whoever took it?) Elinor calls it their "dear little cottage." It's only four years old, not thatched, and barely on the road to Stratford, really at the outskirts of London. But it's cozy. Or maybe cramped is a better word. They had to make the dining room over into a bedroom, and the kitchen is a closet, so the little parlor is for reading, eating, talking, playing, quarreling, midnight fears, midnight writing. Table, cheap wicker chairs, Elinor's rocker, Rob's writing chair, all so crowded together you could cross the room without touching the floor.

In the photograph the light is dull, the tree bare, the sky a flat gray. The children, standing in front, are dressed warmly. They've taken time to pose themselves. Marjorie, Carol, and Lesley form an overlapping group by the front door. To their left stands Irma, separated from her siblings by five declarative feet of empty space.

70

You've always been touchy about those three years in England. Larry isn't the first to think you planned it all ahead of time: go to England and market yourself as a Yankee poet, then return to America and market yourself all over again as a British-approved product. You shouldn't blame them (Larry and the others), since that's pretty much what happened. But you didn't plan it. (And you do blame them.) Who would believe how you stumbled into it?

Yet that's how reversals of fortune come, how the wheel revolves. You fell down the rabbit hole and found a land of topsy-turvy, where you were famous instead of a failure, lionized instead of despised. The wild Indians lowered their arrows and welcomed you, and before you knew it, they were electing you chief.

No, nothing was planned. You had only run away. Three years, like the three days of a fairy tale, after which you were reborn. It happened so suddenly. American editors who'd shut their doors to you for twenty years now competed to print the very poems they'd rejected. Which maybe is why you've never since been able to believe in the sincerity of anyone's praise, except Elinor's.

Poor Elinor didn't get her thatch, or her swans on the Avon, but the Bungalow was more a two-door burrow than a house, and she did like that. One night you spread your poems out on the narrow patch of floor between the two chairs by the dying coal fire, and they looked like they made a book because there wasn't enough room for them not to. You'd stumbled on the Bungalow by seeking advice from an ex-bobby who wrote a "rural walks" column for *T. P.'s Weekly*, and you stumbled on your publisher through the same ruddy, genial, pipe-smoking fellow. (England's genius loci, the seer on duty.) When he mentioned the firm of David Nutt, you recalled seeing Nutt's name on a volume of Henley's poems. Nutt's office was three blocks away.

A poetic choice. Henley was another Walter Savage Landor, a man who dearly loved his friends and dearly loved a fight. His friend Robert Louis Stevenson (whom later he fought) based Long John Silver on him—he'd lost a leg to the pirate tuberculosis. He was thirty-nine when he published his first book of poems, and you were thirty-nine when you walked the three blocks to Nutt's office. Three years, three blocks. (Maybe it was four blocks. Maybe you were thirty-eight.) Henley wrote lines you'd muttered to yourself ever since you were a teenager with no money, very little home, a dead father, a loony mother, a crazy sister, and a whole lot of chip on your shoulder:

It matters not how strait the gate,
　　How charged with punishments the scroll,
　I am the master of my fate:
　　I am the captain of my soul.

So you marched the three blocks, you mounted the three steps. The portal gaped. You gulped and entered the gloom and discovered that Mr. David Nutt was . . . not. Floating before you was his animal wife, lithe and untamed and unplaceably erotic, dressed all in widow's seaweed black. "I will speak for Mr. Nutt," the mermaid said in a weird accent, never explaining that he was dead (had she only just finished drowning him?), and never giving her own name, no doubt because she didn't have one.

Well you gave her your firstborn, you surrendered to her your will, and she made you a poet. *A Boy's Will* lay brown and pebbled in the palm of your hand, and it certified you as a modern poet because it said right there on the title page in plain English, "Series of Modern Poets." And "Mr. Nutt" was an animal wife to the end. It wasn't that she drove hard bargains; she didn't bargain. She took your book and dived back into the sea. And *North of Boston* went tumbling after. A few bubbles rose to the surface, but no gold of fay or elf. She never paid you a penny in royalties.

And she was jealous! When you mentioned contracting with an American house, she exploded in mermaid fury. "You American money-grubber!" *You*—oh, you . . . *human.*

Well bless her. She made a poet out of you. And years later you heard she'd died poor and alone back in the grotto she came from, which turned out to be France.

Now your fate was in others' hands, and you stumbled into luck again. At Monro's Poetry Bookshop you met Flint, who by chance knew Pound (he of ersatz sterling), and Monro knew Gibson, who knew Abercrombie and Hodgson, and Hodgson knew where the pot of gold lay: he knew Edward Thomas. Lucky, yes—the circle was small and somehow you were in it, and they were all critics as well as poets, they reviewed each other's books, and they loved you really by chance (you can see that now, though you'd hate to hear anyone else say it). They loved you for being an American who didn't seem "American" to them—you neither sounded barbaric yawps nor drumbeat chanted the forest primeval. You reminded them of the Greek and Roman pastoral poets (New England to them was as misty as Arcadia), whom they particularly loved because England was poisoning her own pastures. London lay under a cloud of coal soot that never blew away, and in Beaconsfield, twenty miles off, after dusk you could see the top of that cloud glowing from the city lights, so that London every night seemed a bonfire, a vision of the future—

> about the towns where war has come
> Through opening clouds at night with droning speed

Edward! You'd always wanted a brother. All you had was Jeanie, who was the paranoid part of you, the paralyzed part. You wanted a blue-eyed brother who'd be the other half, the walker, the seer. You and Edward birthed each other, twins in the womb, not fighting for priority, but urging each other on. You showed Edward, in his prose, where he was already poet, and Edward, seeing in your poetry his own blossoming future, reviewed your books (he was the most prominent critic of the lot) in a kind of ecstasy which proved contagious. You were two larks ascending, wing to wing, each shielded by the other from contrary winds.

Rise and fall. Edward the Brave.

It wasn't your war. At long last you'd started on your career, and a third book in England would clinch your success, but instead came the catastrophe. You'd never pretended to be anything but American, and you had four American children whose war it wasn't, either. And hadn't you promised Edward to take his son, Merfyn, with you, to get the boy out of his father's shadow? And didn't it also take bravery to ship home when the Germans were announcing imminent blockade and unrestricted submarine warfare? (*War is for everyone, for children too.*)

I shall set forth for somewhere,
I shall make the reckless choice

You walked down the gangplank. You and Elinor and the children and Merfyn, by captain's orders, lay in your bunks fully clothed with life jackets on as the blacked-out ship slipped from the Liverpool dock. The belly of the whale. Next to you in convoy was the *Lusitania*, which ten weeks later would go down with a thousand lives. And your own ship was the *St. Paul*, which made you wonder if the christener knew his Bible. Surely that name was as bad an omen of shipwreck as *Davey Jones* or *Arthur Gordon Pym*.

Goodbye, England! Goodbye! But you were a lucky bastard. The Teutonic torpedoes stayed in their tubes, the titanic icebergs stayed in their fields, and three times three days later you were vomited up by the whale on the Forty-second Street pier in New York City. February 1915. You stretched and inhaled the American air, you blinked in the American sunshine. Not your war. You stepped off the pier and walked up Forty-second Street toward Grand Central Station, family in tow, and at the very first newsstand you glanced in the very first magazine and saw a review of *North of Boston*. Your new life as American Poet had already begun.

That's how you remember it, anyway, and that's how you tell it— the walk up from the pier in the new city, your future success cried out by the wheeling seagulls. You remember visiting your American publisher (your mermaid had budged a millimeter) that same day, and being handed a check for forty dollars for a poem in *The New Republic* you hadn't even known was submitted.

It's true, isn't it? But isn't it curious—your story sounds like someone else's, a famous walk up from baptismal water; not the Forty-second Street pier, but the Market Street wharf:

> I have been the more particular in this description of my journey, and shall be so of my first entry into that city, that you may in your mind compare such unlikely beginnings with the figure I have since made there. I was in my working

dress, my best clothes being to come round by sea. I was dirty from my journey; my pockets were stuffed out with shirts and stockings; I knew no soul nor where to look for lodging . . . I walked up the street, gazing about, till near the market-house I met a boy with bread. I had made many a meal on bread, and, inquiring where he got it, I went immediately to the baker's he directed me to, in Second Street, and asked for biscuit, intending such as we had in Boston; but they, it seems, were not made in Philadelphia. Then I asked for a three-penny loaf, and was told they had none such. So, not considering or knowing the difference of money, and the greater cheapness nor the names of his bread, I bade him give me three-penny-worth of any sort. He gave me, accordingly three great puffy rolls. I was surprised at the quantity, but took it, and, having no room in my pockets, walked off with a roll under each arm, and eating the other.

Lucky the man who finds the place that, through force of metaphor, has to take him in. Philadelphia embraced Ben Franklin like a loved brother, and all America took you in, tired and poor prodigal son, through her golden door. With your first magazine review under one arm, and eating your royalty check, you waved your family off at Grand Central Station (they were to stay with the Lynches on Garnet Mountain in New Hampshire till you found a farm somewhere) and turned back into the city to continue your conquest. You lucky, lucky bastard.

> I shall set forth for somewhere,
> I shall make the reckless choice

You walked down the gangplank. Reckless of others, maybe. Reckless of duty. Two roads diverged. Edward went east to his falling shell, you went west to your meteoric rise.

> We both have lacked the courage in the heart
> To overcome the fear within the soul

And go ahead to any accomplishment.
Courage is what it takes and takes the more of
Because the deeper fear is so eternal.

You wrote that in your *Masque of Mercy*, and isn't it curious that the masque takes place in a bookstore in New York City, with Saint Paul a customer, and Jonah bursting through the door, fleeing God. You've always felt you needed God's mercy to forgive you the injustice of having received His mercy in 1915. Edward and you were brothers in cowardice—that fear in the soul that tells us our sacrifice may not be found acceptable in heaven's sight. Edward, if anything, was more fearful. But unlike you, he pierced his heart to tap the courage to overcome his terror.

And the fact that he died at thirty-nine, his heart shaken until it broke by the concussion of the shell—does that mean his sacrifice was accepted or rejected? Does the distinction have any meaning? Have you never found a way to talk about this that isn't playing with words?

It's the survivor's burden to wonder, every breath a sigh.

71

LITTLE IDDENS, LEDINGTON, GLOUCESTERSHIRE, ENGLAND

APRIL 1914

Out of the bungalow, into the byre. Still no thatch for poor Elinor, but the cottage called Little Iddens dates from Shakespeare, with blackened timbers in a buckling wall, and a brick floor undulating like the Avon. Half the ground floor is a cowshed.

The Frosts moved here to be near the Georgian poets Gibson and Abercrombie, and from the moment they arrived, the weather has been magical for England: clear and sunny. Frost has never seen such daffodils. Abercrombie says they were planted here in medieval times for a dye industry, and have spread ever since. There are miles of them, foaming over the hill-waves; in the sunlight they throw so much yellow upward the distant air has a greenish cast, and every man that walks loves butter. Frost and Edward Thomas palely loiter through these fields of asphodel, the flowers swaying and murmuring, bowing their heads in sorrow or prayer.

Frost is just getting to know Thomas, who's visiting for a week. He's brought along his new book, *In Pursuit of Spring*, about a bicycle trip he made last year. The poor fellow works on any assignment that comes his way, anything that might interest some dullard editor to the length of a pound or two. When Frost first met him in London last fall, he was trying to write a book on ecstasy, which made his friends chuckle. He soon gave it up and spent the winter working on the opposite subject, his autobiography.

Long ago the dye works were supplanted by cider mills. This is orchard country now, and the apple and pear trees are in blossom. Frost and Thomas walk together, stopping by stiles or sprawling on last year's papery tussocks under the hedgerow elms to talk about poetry. Thomas eats, drinks, and breathes English poetry, and the well of talk never runs dry. He's read far more than Frost. He can quote with tender pleasure the one true line out of five hundred false decanted frothing by a seventeenth-century parson-poetaster of Somerset, or a sentimental balladeering sea captain from Land's End. He shares Frost's admiration for Hardy, but argues convincingly, quoting with abandon, that Hardy has a rustic's superstition that he's modernized only to the extent of assigning motiveless malignity to Fate instead of faeries, and that his stiff-necked perversity on this score can at times be laughable.

Frost forgives Thomas for winning the argument. He thinks he might forgive him anything. Thomas puffs on his clay pipe, his blue-gray eyes searching, alighting on whatever detail can hold them in the scene—the curve of that hill, the color of that copse. Frost notices, in profile, what its handsome straightness obscures head-on: how large his nose is. Eyes deep-set and melancholy, with long pale lashes that catch the light, looking like tongues of flame. Apostle's fire.

They walk back in the dusk, silent. Frost is thinking of Herrick.

> Fair Daffodils, we weep to see
> You haste away so soon:
> As yet the early-rising Sun
> Has not attain'd his noon.
>   Stay, stay,
> Until the hasting day
>   Has run
> But to the even-song;
> And, having pray'd together, we
> Will go with you along.
>
> We have short time to stay, as you,
> We have as short a Spring;
> As quick a growth to meet decay
> As you, or any thing.
>   We die,
> As your hours do, and dry
>   Away
> Like to the Summer's rain;
> Or as the pearls of morning's dew,
> Ne'er to be found again.

There are times (such as now) when Frost wonders if "To Daffodils" isn't the most perfect lyric in English. Say it to yourself a dozen times. Notice how natural the language is, how unobtrusively it fits the complicated scheme. Admire in particular the first sentence of the second stanza, how it leads unerringly to that startling "any thing"—so often a filler, but here so full. And praise him for the awful "Away," where it stands alone, twinned with "We die," both evaporating like morning dew into the margins.

A volume of Herrick's poems was the first Frost ever took notice of. Not because he knew the man's poetry, or could even read yet—he was seven or eight—but because the book was a jeweled something from a treasure chest: bound in leather, with engravings, gilt pages, marbled endpapers. It came addressed to his mother. He remembers her happiness on turning it in her hands, opening it. Here was another Robert to set alongside Burns, two Roberts who gave his mother pleasure. Friends in the art.

Now, looking back, Frost figures his mother must have been reviewing the volume for one of the city papers. She tried to make extra money that way, since all his father's salary was disappearing into saloons and whorehouses. Belle read Herrick, while William lived him.

> Gather ye rose-buds while ye may,
> Old Time is still a-flying

Robert follows Thomas over the last stile, turns up the dark lane toward the cottage. Elinor is in there. Sometimes it seems as though England has revived her. For a week or two she'll almost enjoy company; then she pales again. But she finds Thomas wholly lovable, as most women would—his beauty, his deep, wounded reserve. "We'll scare up some supper," Frost says to him. When Elinor's down, he does the cooking.

Thomas silently hands him a toffee. He seems always to be carrying a bag of sweets in one of his large pockets.

Frost turns at the front door. The elm branches are in silhouette. A chaffinch darts.

Away

72

Boarding the SS *Parisian*, bound for Britain with his family, ten-year-old Carol has never seen a gangplank before. He pauses at the verge and gapes at the descending board with its series of rounded cross-ties. "Look at that!" he exclaims. "Chicken stairs!"

73

Frost, alone by the window in his brown study on Brewster Street, gazes down on the cold green mercury lights and empty sidewalks of his tidy, professorial neighborhood and thinks of dead poets.

Dear Vachel Lindsay was more child than man. Out of the mouths of babes. Throwing his head back to chant his poems, he could never fathom how obscenely his long neck swelled. His eyes rolled up and fluttered like snapped window blinds.

The lame were straightened, withered limbs uncurled
And blind eyes opened on a new, sweet world.

Hallelujah, amen. He tramped the Midwest, trading rhymes for bread and talking with the angels. He wandered (lonely as a crowd) in enthusiasms, picking up by the wayside new-washed plots for saving the world, or failing that, turning his hometown of Springfield, Illinois, into the New Jerusalem, where poets would rule and virtue bloom. He planned an epic on the American turkey, a fowl more beautiful, he insisted (neck lengthening), than the peacock or the griffin.

He entered heaven by drinking a bottle of Lysol.

The woman he loved, with a boyish, virginal love, was Sara Teasdale, who verily believed her skin was one layer short. Dancing through life with only six veils, she had a lifelong fear of colds.

> If you have forgotten water-lilies floating
> On a dark lake among mountains in the afternoon shade,
> If you have forgotten their wet, sleepy fragrance,
> Then you can return and not be afraid.

She fled her angel lover and married a shoe merchant named Ernst (seriously!), then fled him. Briefly, she kept a secretary who was something more than that. Yes, that old trick; Virgil pulled it with a boy. She swallowed a bottle of sleeping pills and slipped beneath the waters of her bath.

Good, gray-souled Edwin Arlington Robinson drank and drank, alone and more alone, like his own Mr. Flood, toasting himself from his stone jug in the autumn moonlight.

> He raised again the jug regretfully
> And shook his head, and was again alone.
> There was not much that was ahead of him,
> And there was nothing in the town below—
> Where strangers would have shut the many doors
> That many friends had opened long ago.

Eben Flood: and the ebb and flood of taste has nearly obliterated Robinson's memory. Tight-lipped, feline, fearing women, he resembled no one more than Tom Catty Eliot, who holds Robinson's poetry in contempt (no doubt because Tom's poetic nightmares owe so much to it) and has taught the minions of the Eliotic Age to agree with him. Robinson drowned himself, you might say, in bathtub gin, and Eliot can purr and purr: *Mistah Flood—he dead.*

Frost wonders. Poets didn't use to kill themselves in such numbers. Is it the prosaic motorcar? The ad campaign? The lecture circuit? No era is much worse or better than any other, yet how flattering to think you live in the worst. And poets have always been as vain as . . . turkeys.

Harlequin Hart Crane jumped, vestigial wings flapping, from the back of a steamship into the Gulf of Mexico. Like the others, he'd already written his epitaph, in "To Brooklyn Bridge":

> Out of some subway scuttle, cell or loft
> A bedlamite speeds to thy parapets,
> Tilting there momently, shrill shirt ballooning,
> A jest falls from the speechless caravan.

The beau geste of a jester? Is this metaphor run wild, to act out your poems? Or is it the modern poet's ad campaign? For example, today, reported in the afternoon newspaper, cannily wicked Dylan Thomas has succeeded in drinking himself to death. Should one raise a toast? His soul and his stock rise, hand in hand.

Frost's own vanity, fiercely held, is this: he will survive. Or to quote another drunkard: he will not merely endure, he will prevail. The steeple is not for directing eyes heavenward, it's for climbing, and Frost will remain at the top—partly by kicking, when he has to, other climbers in the face, but mainly (so simple!) by not leaping off. Maybe he's got a lover's quarrel with the world, but you don't walk out on a quarrel. Frost believes in marriage.

Perhaps Carol, too, had written his epitaph. But he burned all his poems.

74

Thomas is back! He's come for a month to Ledington with his wife, Helen, and his three children, and they've rented rooms in Chandler's farmhouse two fields away. The walks and talks resume. Apples and pears swell on the trees. Dessert plums nestle in net bags. It continues uncannily sunny, day after day. So much warmth and light! Is this England? Is this a dream? "There's a passage in Turgenev," Frost muses to his friend. "A description of a summer day, the opening of 'Bezhin Meadow.' Do you know it?"

"Aren't there boys around a campfire in the dark?"

"Yes, later on. And horses' faces. They appear in the firelight, disembodied, when they raise their heads to champ the high grass."

"The boys are telling stories—"

"Of animal wives. There's a nixie curses a carpenter—"

In russet light under an elm, Thomas is eating a windfallen cider apple that has yellowed prematurely off the stem. Smokes his clay pipe. Turgenev and tobacco rise like incense to the weather gods. The apple core is tossed, the men get to their feet. "May Hill or Malvern?" Frost asks at the path fork and, amused, watches Thomas agonize. Whichever way they go, they're sure to miss something good on the other path. May Hill has the lone poplar and the view of Wales, Malvern has the hamlet of White Leaved Oak and the great old pagan tree like a troll in the dusk, hung with votives.

"Oh . . . Er . . ."

"May Hill?"

"Well . . ."

"Malvern?"

"Lord . . . You decide."

"May I?"

"You may."

"May Hill it is, then."

They head down the south fork. Passing along a blackthorn hedge, Thomas pauses—"Hold on, old man"—to mark a shoot with his knife. His intent is to return later to strip and cut it for a walking stick—although, like a squirrel with its far-flung caches of nuts, he sometimes never comes back. Blackthorn, holly, hazel. He sands and polishes the stems, fits them with ferrules, adds them to his large assortment, from which, for a walk on another day, he will choose one, heft it, tap it against the floor, palm and repalm the handle, recall its exploits, waver, put it aside, choose another.

After an hour of hard walking, they rest at the top of a knoll. Thomas lays down his staff and takes out his pipe again. His pipes are another fetish; an equally large collection, all clay. When one grows sour, he sweetens it in whiskey; when it gets stained, he buries it in the embers of a fire, rakes it out an hour later white as bone. Sitting next to him, Frost gazes on all his fussing—the knocking against the side of the heel, the probing, the pressing of the earthy tobacco, the striking of the match, the sucking and biting, the rattling of the stem across the teeth as he shifts the pipe from one corner of his mouth to the other—and thinks, *Things*. Thomas's pipes are smooth and round and pendulous like the bottom lip of an orchid; he cups them from below as he cups from above the polished handles of his walking sticks. Things to hold on to, to keep himself from floating away.

As quick a growth to meet decay
As you, or any thing

Frost has read, since April, Thomas's book, *In Pursuit of Spring*. He was astonished by it. Which isn't to say that it was good, exactly. Rather, it was encouragingly strange. It was the work of a man of strong artistic gifts who before your eyes was drowning in the wrong art form. Around the time Frost finished the book, he got a letter from Thomas. "I wonder whether you can imagine me taking to verse," he wrote. "If you can I might get over the feeling that it is impossible."

That might be the motto on Thomas's coat-of-arms: *Impotentia!* The impossibility of fighting off his melancholy when it stoops and catches him in its talons. The impossibility of taking two different paths while remaining one traveler, or of fully enjoying one path when you know what you're missing on the other. Thomas is an over-worked hack prose-writer with a poetic heart and a despairing soul. And it moves Frost beyond words that he imagines the key to his salvation lies in Frost's own imagination. That Frost might *dream* him into existence as a poet. (Their coats-of-arms, side by side: Thomas's, *Impotentia!* Frost's, *Fiat Poeta!*)

They had a talk a week ago. Dreaming is always the easy part; Thomas needed something more concrete. Frost opened *In Pursuit of Spring* and pointed to a paragraph. "*That*, Thomas, is a poem. Tone, cadence—it's all there. You only need to write it out *as* a poem. I don't have to imagine you as a poet: you already are one." Since despair scoffs at the idea of change, it needs convincing that no change is needed.

What struck Frost about *In Pursuit of Spring* was how little it contained of a prose-writer's "poetry": no word-painting, hardly any metaphors. Also—what made it so strange a book—there was no discernible theme; only page after page of description, so close it seemed made with crossed eyes. Which is why it could be turned into poetry. Because you can tell that Thomas is trying to save his life with what he sees. (The two men rest now at the top of May Hill.) Facts as the sweetest dream. What keeps Thomas, on any particular day, from raising the revolver to his temple (yes, the revolver is real—Helen said he walked out one day with it in his pocket, returning twelve hours later with it still in his pocket) is that a boy, holding his father's hand in a railway station, tries to get him to run and fails. That in a dark wood near London there's one isolated bent larch of acrid green. That on a March morning east of Alderbury six sand martins flit in narrow circles, looking like butterflies. That in the flint church of Orcheston

Saint George a tablet says that John Shettler of Elston, aged fifty-two, died on December 6, 1861, "from the effects of an accident." That a corn bunting's song on a dead poplar sounds like a chain of pebbles dropped dispiritedly. That on a drizzly morning in western Wiltshire a keeper walks heavily through a field of turkeys while his chained retriever stands and whines after him. That along the quay in Bridgewater, the *Arthur* is waiting for a cargo and the *Emma* is unloading coal. That Norah Muriel Sweet-Escott, aged twenty, died in South Africa of yellow fever, and on the hills above her seaside church in Kilve, in the dusk, the flowering gorse bushes look like a flock of golden fleece.

any thing

This isn't just Thomas, God knows (and Frost knows). There's something British about it. Americans love their country for what it could be; their "America" is a vague idea they hope to realize, and the harder it is to see, the easier to argue over. But the British love Britain for what it is, so they love it with stubborn particularity. The celandine by the track to town, the daffodils in April and cowslips in May, the odd old British names, the song of the rising lark, the chiffchaff in the coppice, the linnet in the coombe, the nightingale in the hedge. (On his visit in April, Thomas cocked an ear every night, and his greatest disappointment was that no nightingale sang distinctly when the two men were together. "You must hear it," he kept saying, "there's nothing like it." Frost never did.) But it's not just a national pecularity. *In Pursuit of Spring* is also distinctly "Thomasinine," as he ruefully describes himself when the dark descends and he's overcome with self-doubt and world-doubt.

> From perfect grief there need not be
> Wisdom or even memory;
> One thing then learned remains to me—
> The woodspurge has a cup of three.

Where does Thomas's grief come from? As well ask: Where does Frost's paranoia come from? Where do poems come from? A divine fire descends, either of inspiration or of vengeance. Not knowing which, you either hold up an iron rod or run for the woods. Either you make it, or you don't.

(The sun is setting; the sunburned men descend May Hill toward home.)

Other, lesser answers are: Thomas's father is a choleric, carping bureaucrat with a small store of fixed opinions, one of which is that his oldest son is a worthless fellow with no spine or character. None of Thomas's five brothers are remotely like him or understand him in the least. Thomas, in turn, doesn't understand his son, Merfyn, who's no poet, or a naturalist, but an automobile-nut, a tinkerer, lazy and distracted without being dreamy. Thomas gets angry with him, and the boy grows sullen; Thomas rages, and then runs from himself, which in practice means running from the boy. Thomas feels more Welsh than English, but speaks no Welsh, and believes Wales can never be a home to him since he wasn't raised there. (*In Pursuit of Spring* ends with Spring dancing on Winter's grave, Thomas on the coast of Somerset; before turning back toward London, he sees in the far distance, under a rainbow, the blue hills of Wales.)

Oh—and there's his wife, Helen.

Helen! What to say? A goodhearted woman, strong in body, launcher of a thousand projects, bustling, cleaning, cooking, tending the children, talking and talking, dressed always in red. She's the thoughtlessly, tirelessly shining sun to Edward's shrinking, changeable moon. To wax, he must get away from her, so he cuts and polishes another walking stick, always searching for the magical one that will transport him . . . somewhere. Or (for speed) he inflates the tires on his new-fangled bicycle. Or (for permanence) he goes to the beach and swims straight out to sea, out of sight, frightening everyone. He crisscrosses England, this England that is not his England, and whatever direction he goes in, his shadow stretches in front of him, cast by Helen Helios but ineluctably shaped like Edward Thomas, and up ahead, past the coppice where the linnet sings, forever receding with their rainbow, are the blue hills of Wales.

75

Thomas and Merfyn arrived by bicycle on August 3, 1914. The war arrived by telegram the next morning, and news of the first shots by village gossip that evening. (You and Thomas were sitting on a stile; the stars were out. You listened for the guns across the Channel; you heard an owl.) Helen and the two girls arrived by belated, redirected train in the early-morning hours of August 5. The village policeman stood in your doorway on August 9, notebook in hand. The villagers had remarked on the midnight arrivals. They'd already noted the foreign Frosts and their suspicious hours. The villagers figured you all were German spies. "The villagers would think a man from Herefordshire was a German spy," you said. And after the policeman left: "If he comes nosing around here again I'll shoot him."

Would that be with your revolver?

You *hate* it when people wonder who the hell you are.

And your neighbor from over the hill, who put his arm around Lesley and gave her a searching squeeze, he had his patriotic doubts, too—maybe the incriminating papers were in her breast pocket. You caught him one night on the path behind the house and wanted to thrash him. Was he spying on the bedroom windows?

That was so long ago. And now Lesley says you poisoned Irma's mind with your suspicions.

That hurts.

Well, she means it to hurt.

You wonder sometimes if she's right. But she's frightened. She's got her own two girls, and since her divorce she knows she's left them too much on their own. Good girls, but strange—frosty wild. Better to believe her father poisoned the well with words than fear that the water, in its essence, is tainted.

76

The morning was wet but the clouds broke up in midafternoon and bands of brightness pass over the trees, making the perry pears and cider apples smoke. It's hot, and will be dry and hot tomorrow, this un-English summer of dusty herb-scents on the agitating wind, of toasted hayfields and tough-skinned sweet fruits. "This year's perry will be excellent," Thomas says. The two men stop at a pub for the beverage, which Frost never drank before this summer, and will rarely drink after. Sweeter than cider, straw-gold—perry will always be, for Frost, the taste of companionship, of pairing. Another pub beckons. A man is parched, the sun bruises, the farm girls are brown, the fruit on the tree is glad, and English sweethearts and brothers are dying in golden fields nearby.

What to think about that? Whence this sudden war, and whither? How long, how great the need? "The hour of obedience has come," a German philosopher said last week, and everything that propels Frost out of his house, pocketing as he goes his invisible revolver, makes his hackles rise at those words.

Back out to the bright path, the steep descent, the plank across the stream. Frost sees a straight shoot in a hedge and cuts it for a spear. As he and Thomas cross the next field he pauses, hefts it, throws it ahead. He's good at it. He was teaching Merfyn the other day. The two men come up to the fallen spear and he throws it again. It always lands near the path. "Did you learn that from the Indians?" Thomas asked him two weeks ago.

"You mean the ones that captivated me as a boy?" Frost said. "Maybe I did."

But this is not Frost's war, and deep down, despite whatever guilty bravado he may have occasionally indulged in, he knows perfectly well he's going to get himself and his family the hell out of here. The question is—can he lure Thomas with him?

Thomas is thirty-six, the father of three. Surely his duty to his family is as great as that to his country. Frost has been thinking furiously. Thomas won't come to America unless there's a chance to do there what he can't do here, which is to make a living. Frost knows (and God knows) that whatever small audience exists for Thomas's fact-besotted books is a thoroughly British audience, so what can vague America (whose dreams are her sweetest facts) offer him?

Here's his idea: teaching. Americans believe in self-improvement. Maybe they have no use for poets, but they love the idea of learning to write poetry. Frost has connections in New Hampshire, he has a reputation as a teacher. He will buy a farm in the north, near Garnet Mountain, and Thomas will buy the neighboring farm (a path from the back door, a descent, a plank across the stream, a rise, and there's his door). They'll both write poems in fall and winter, and every summer they'll make their real money—a summer school. In their thousands, the well-off asthmatics come to the White Mountains to breathe free on the porches of the long hotels, to play tennis and pinochle, to grow bored with the view, to yearn vaguely for self-improvement. Step right up.

When Frost first mentioned his plan, Thomas laughed. The second time, Frost put the case with all his eloquence, and Thomas puffed his clay, unspeaking. The third time (magic in the land of faeries), Thomas admitted it might be possible.

Come away, O human child!
To the waters and the wild
With a faery, hand in hand,
For the world's more full of weeping than you can understand.

Rather, Thomas understands too well—a moth drawn to the flame. The war, for Thomas (Frost sees, Frost fears), could be the revolver at his temple, the swim far out to sea. Frost must sing to him, draw him away. New Hampshire!

They're climbing May Hill for the dozenth time. The sun has just set and the undersides of the banded clouds are red, the trees black. In a great meadow curving down out of view a tall Lombardy poplar stands, alone except for one small tree by its knees, and Thomas always stops here to feed on the sight. Tonight, with the two trees in silhouette and the red mottled sky shifting behind them, he sits and smokes his clay for a long time. "A *C'est l'Empereur* scene," he finally says.

"What?" Frost asks.

"A painting by Hugh de Glazebrook. The trees remind me of it. A soldier sleeping on sentry duty in a meadow is just waking, and he sees Napoleon standing over him. 'It's the emperor!'"

Frost sees where that's heading. *Come away!* "I wonder if the smaller tree is an oak."

"Mm. I can't tell from here. Why?"

"There's an American story. About a boy who brings an acorn to the czar of Russia . . ."

The first stars are coming out as they continue upward. May Hill is a thousand feet high, mostly meadow, but at the top a grove of Scots firs was planted for Queen Victoria's Diamond Jubilee. The trees are now some thirty feet tall, and under them is a full Scots dark. The two men grope through in silence. They come out the far side, back into lilac dusk. The view west stretches for miles across farmland, the Wye, the Forest of Dean, the Monmouthshire hills, the mountains of Wales. The evening is warm, and the grass crisps when they sit on it. The last redness licking the cloud bottoms looks tropical. "This earth, this realm, this un-England," Frost says, as Thomas presses earth in his clay.

Thomas smokes, Frost broods. A cloudmass lifts away from the horizon. Yellow light gathers along its underedge as though lightning loitered there, then a spark gleams, spreads, congeals into the edge of the new moon, which bit by bit slides out in a curve, unsheathing itself from the cloud. It floats free in the air of this world, drying, turning orange as it sinks toward the mountains.

"Look at the betony," Thomas says, pointing with his pipe.

Frost can just make out the purple flowers by the verge of the queen's trees, a few feet away. Two leaves on each side, a straight stiff stem.

"They look like they're standing sentinel, don't you think?"

That again. Guards of the Scots Highlanders. Frost would like to sing, New Hampshire! But it seems wrong to press it, so he remains silent. He finds small stones among the grass roots and throws them down the field. Rooks farther down, invisible, are cawing, a steady rhythmic chorus they've kept up all day. A couple of hours ago, Thomas said, "They sound like sheep bleating."

"Or like crickets," Frost says now, with the dark thickening. He tosses another stone and goes on:

> "Further in Summer than the Birds
>   Pathetic from the Grass
>   A minor Nation celebrates
>   Its unobtrusive Mass."

"That's good," Thomas says.

"You bet. It's Emily Dickinson." From his and her minor poetic nation. The Land of Near-Poesie. And she lived . . . near New Hampshire!

More silence. The low-slung belly of the moon is just touching the mountain.

"The soldiers along the Meuse can't see that moon," Thomas says. "It's already sunk for them."

Frost doesn't say anything.

"One thing I can't do," Thomas says, "is hate the Germans. That's what my father . . ." He takes his pipe out of his mouth, continues in a harder voice. "My father breathes that—the vile air of the newspapers, all that blackguarding of the Germans. I told him a German could love his country as honestly as an Englishman, and he would

174

have thrown me out of the house if I hadn't slammed the door in his bloody face." He sucks on his pipe again, glares at it. Relights it. "If I go fight," he murmurs, "it won't be because of that."

Frost waits; watches the moon sink. The belly is gone. All that's left is the raised arm, like Liberty holding up her torch, sinking into New York Harbor.

Now just the torch.

Now gone.

"It's just that . . ." Thomas's voice comes out of the darkness. "It seems to me that everything I've written or said about my love of England is pure foolishness if I'm not willing to die for her. England has never been mine, and she'll never be mine, unless I'm prepared to fight. If I don't, I'll lose the only thing that has ever meant anything to me—the ability to look at that betony, or that poplar, or listen to those rooks, with composure."

Frost broods for a long minute. He loves this man.

And so (after casting two or three more stones into the darkness, not without anger) he does what Orpheus did, for whom love proved too strong. He looks back. "I see what you mean," he says.

Another minute passes.

He goes on, "You said that England would never be yours. I guess you could say as truly, or maybe more true, that you would never be England's. Do you really mean you want to possess the poplar? That's what a landlord does, and he's got his gamekeeper to keep out riffraff like you and me. No, you want to be possessed by them. You fight for England like a son, and the door the betony stands sentinel to is home."

They descend the hill. It's four miles back to Ledington, and past ten o'clock when they see through trees ahead the lights of the Chandler farmhouse, where the Thomases are renting rooms. Chandler is a soldier, forty-four years old, who's already seen twenty years of service. He was called back two weeks ago to a camp in Hereford.

"Come on to our place," Frost urges. "You really intend to bicycle off in a day or two?"

"I've promised an article for the *English Review*, on rural attitudes toward the war."

"Satisfy Helen, then come on with me."

Frost waits on the path. He hears Helen's voice, a steady stream. Nothing from Thomas. A minute later he appears out of the dark, walking fast. "Let's go." They cross the field, descend to the plank across the stream, cut up through the cow pasture. "Chandler was back at the farm again yesterday, to check up on things," Thomas says. "He seems very cheerful about the prospect of going to France."

"This happy breed of men," Frost says.

"This little world," Thomas says.

The two men say the lines between them as they go:

> "This precious stone set in the silver sea,
> Which serves it in the office of a wall,
> Or as a moat defensive to a house
> Against the envy of less happier lands;
> This blessèd plot, this earth, this realm, this England."

77

NEW HAMPSHIRE STATE HOSPITAL, CONCORD, NEW HAMPSHIRE

JANUARY 11, 1950

Irma, divorced by her rat of a husband, forcibly separated from her dear little boy, imprisoned against her will, has in her cell (they call it a room) a bed, a desk, a chair, a dresser, a plastic vase with flowers. There's a view of the grounds that her visitors say every time—every time!—is lovely. (She *hates* that.) The only other thing she has in all the world is all the time in the world.

With all the time in the world, and nothing to do but watch the sun go up and down, and fear her doctors' designs on her, she thinks of England, when she was a little girl of ten or eleven. Her family lived in a little house in Gloucestershire, and she and her sisters had a bedroom upstairs. At night sometimes the girls were enthralled and mystified by a gleam of light that darted around the room. They told Papa, and he came to see. After a moment he ran downstairs and out the door. Behind the house he caught the village constable, who was patriotically keeping his eye peeled for spies by peeping in the girl's room, purely coincidentally of course, just when they were undressing for bed.

78

THE DERRY FARM, NEW HAMPSHIRE
JUNE 1908

Lesley is telling the children how big the world is, that the very long ride they took in the wagon the other day (Carol said it was "clear around the world") wasn't almost, or half, or a tenth the way, but just a tiny bit compared with the whole world.

"Oh I don't believe that," Irma says.

"Go and ask Mama if it's true then."

"No."

"Why not?"

"Because if I ask Mama I know she'll say yes, and then I'll have to believe it. But I don't want to think it's true, so I won't ask her."

79

Frost is led in jacket and shirt cuffs into the courtroom. Merfyn is seated at a table, looking frightened. They've hauled him up from the detention cell he slept in last night. Three lawyers look down on Frost from a dais. Atropos speaks: "In the case of Merfyn Thomas, a citizen of the United Kingdom, aged fifteen years old, the law is clear. Any alien under sixteen, upon entering the United States, must be met at the immigration office by at least one parent, or by a sponsor who can offer acceptable evidence of ability to provide financial support, so as to prevent the minor from becoming a public charge. If you, Mr. Frost, are offering to serve as guardian for this underage alien, how do you plan to earn a living?"

Frost struggles not to say, "I'm a tramp just off the steamer, can't you tell?" He struggles not to say, "I could lick all three of you." He says, "I'm a teacher and a poet."

America has no use for poets. "Do you have a position now as a teacher?"

"No, but I plan to get one. I can get one easily."

"Until you do, would you be able to support yourself, your family, and this boy on the earnings from your poetry?"

"I recently published two books in England, and one of these books has also been published in the United States—"

Foolish of him to answer; it was a joke question. "How much money have you received for these books so far?"

Ask the mermaid! Drop her a line. Hook her and cook her. The check's in the mail. I've got forty dollars in my pocket for a poem you wouldn't call a poem. And eight hundred a year from my dead grandfather, who disdained poets as much as you do. *Give me twenty years*, I said to him, to become a poet, and if he was alive today he'd be tickled to death to see me on trial—*Rob, they'll happily give you twenty years.*

"None so far, but . . ." Oh, he's made their day. Tedious work, this bullying of schoolboys, but he's got them breaking out in grins. "Look," he says, "I was told this had been resolved. I spent yesterday on the phone with a lawyer, Charles Burlingham, who vouched for me as a sponsor to the commissioner of immigration."

The three confer. Atropos speaks again. "We've received no word from the commissioner." Snip! He shifts his attention to Merfyn. "Do you have anything to say in your own behalf concerning why you should not be sent back to England?"

Merfyn casts a mute appeal at Frost. The boy seems close to tears. Boiling over, Frost shouts to Merfyn across the room, "Tell them you wouldn't *stay* in a country where they treat people like this!"

Gavel. Order in the court. They break for lunch to allow the dangerous character to cool off. During lunch the message from the commissioner is found, and after lunch, the dangerous character is allowed to be Merfyn's sponsor.

One month later, in New Hampshire, Frost dreams a dream:

He's back in the courtroom on Ellis Island. It's also a classroom in the Lawrence High School. Frost sits at a desk that's too small for him. The lawyer hands him a written examination. On it are two questions:

1. Who in Hell do you think you are?
2. How much do one and one make?

80

7:36 a.m., April 9, 1917; Easter Monday. What was it like, Edward?

(You were schoolboys, calling each other Frost and Thomas, up to the moment you left England. With the Atlantic between you, you grew up; you became Robert and Edward. Were you afraid before?)

Edward wrote to you about how the shells moaned as they came in; how they seemed to hover; how the air sagged when they went over. He said they burst with a black grisly flap.

Did he see the burst on April 9, 1917?

He'd been a poet for twenty-nine months, a soldier for twenty-one. He'd been in France ten weeks. He was at his observation post. His battery was in an orchard. (With you, he was always eating apples.) The Germans were lobbing Five-Nines—5.9-inch shells. They moan, he said, then savagely stop with a flap.

Was seventy days unusually short? Was he marked?

It was the beginning of the Battle of Arras, and he was at the Beaurains observation post. He was one of the first to die. The English were laying down a suppressing barrage, the infantry had yet to go up and over into Dead Man's Land.

No, you mean No Man's Land.

There's a poem you included in *Mountain Interval* only because Edward liked it. Later, he said it was an exact description of No Man's Land. You wrote it before the term existed—in 1902, at the Derry farm—not knowing you were prophesying:

> The battle rent a cobweb diamond-strung
> And cut a flower beside a ground bird's nest
> Before it stained a single human breast.
> The stricken flower bent double and so hung.

And still the bird revisited her young.
A butterfly its fall had dispossessed
A moment sought in air his flower of rest,
Then lightly stooped to it and fluttering clung.

On the bare upland pasture there had spread
O'ernight 'twixt mullein stalks a wheel of thread
And straining cables wet with silver dew.
A sudden passing bullet shook it dry.
The indwelling spider ran to greet the fly,
But finding nothing, sullenly withdrew.

You called it "The Little Things of War," but changed the title to "Range-Finding" when Edward started training for the artillery in the summer of 1916. Prophecy—Edward was looking through binoculars, finding the range for his battery, but the Germans found it first and the Five-Nine came in. Edward must have been some feet away because his body was found intact. It was the shockwave: his heart had stopped, his watch with it (7:36 a.m.). He was killed by air; killed by the Muse.

He was a poet.

August 1914 was your month with him. You'll never see another like it. You imagined him a poet, and three months later he wrote his first poem. In its opening lines he sent you a secret message.

"I could wring the old thing's neck that put it there!
A public-house! it may be public for birds,
Squirrels and suchlike, ghosts of charcoal-burners
And highwaymen." The wild girl laughed.

Months before, he'd written to you that he wanted to follow your ideas about speech sounds in literature; he wanted to "wring all the necks of my rhetoric—the geese." He was killing off the public prose-writer he once was and celebrating the murder in his first line as new-born poet.

And the poet was a prodigy. In his little study on top of a hill in

Hampshire, Edward poured out poems, sometimes two or three a week. He turned your walks with him into a poem.

> The sun used to shine while we two walked
> Slowly together, paused and started
> Again, and sometimes mused, sometimes talked
> As either pleased, and cheerfully parted
>
> Each night

The lines run past their ends like your mutual musing that never stopped, that spurred each other continually on. (*How much do one and one make?*) Edward was the only man who could ever match you in talk. Yes, the sun shone on those fields you walked, the asphodel fields of the upper air. But from the beginning, Hades was calling. It was your month with him, a month like no other, and it was also August 1914.

> We turned from men or poetry
>
> To rumours of the war remote
> Only till both stood disinclined
> For aught but the yellow flavorous coat
> Of an apple wasps had undermined;
>
> Or a sentry of dark betonies,
> The stateliest of small flowers on earth,
> At the forest verge

Every detail was true—except the moon, which Edward changed:

> The war
> Came back to mind with the moonrise
> Which soldiers in the east afar
> Beheld then.

Rising instead of falling, east instead of west, so that the soldiers along the Meuse and the two poets bemused could behold it at the same time. And full instead of new—for surely that unrivaled month of friendship took place beneath a waxing moon.

By the time Edward wrote the poem, he was a soldier, with one foot in the underworld, and the voice toward the end grows ghostly:

> Everything
> To faintness like those rumours fades—
> Like the brook's water glittering
>
> Under the moonlight—like those walks
> Now—like us two that took them, and
> The fallen apples, all the talks
> And silences—like memory's sand
>
> When the tide covers it late or soon,
> And other men through other flowers
> In those fields under the same moon
> Go talking and have easy hours.

Even after August 26 he wavered between America and France, between teacher and soldier. He wavered for eleven months while you called to him from across the sea. Both of you saw the too-easy metaphor in the fact that he lived in Hampshire and you hoped to draw him to New Hampshire.

> Today I was out from 12 till sunset bicycling to the pine country by Ascot & back [he wrote to you in May 1914]. But it all fleets & one cannot lock up at evening the cake one ate during the day. There must be a world where that is done. I hope you & I will meet in it. I hardly expect it of New Hampshire more than of old.

You proved, in the end, the dreamier one. You wondered, just before he shipped out to France, if the army might allow him to visit you for a week in New Hampshire, and he answered that the idea had made him smile: "It is one of the impossiblest things."

Impossiblest—unless blessed? Might it indeed be possible, in God-blessed America, to both eat your cake and keep it, and be one eater? You wrote for him a poem that you called "Two Roads":

> Two roads diverged in a yellow wood,
> And sorry I could not travel both
> And be one traveler, long I stood
> And looked down one as far as I could
> To where it bent in the undergrowth

So much went into that poem that means so much to you, so deeply and obscurely (about you and him, about choice, about fate and the dark glass), that you've never been sure what the poem actually says, still less what a reader sees. Edward was puzzled, so you called it a joke (you were hurt). Your public loves it as a homily, which it isn't.

> I shall be telling this with a sigh
> Somewhere ages and ages hence

Did you mean at the time what it seems to you now—that that damned troublesome sigh (oh, the mountain of letters demanding the meaning of that sigh!) has something to do with what is, at least for sublunary human beings, one of the impossiblest things: to communicate correctly, somehow purely (*I shall be telling this*), when all words are metaphor, and truth itself is metaphorical? In short, to speak truth without lying? (And be one speaker.) Where is the place in which that is possible? In that world, whether you call it the New Jerusalem or the New Hampshire, "you & I" will not collide, but merge.

> Two roads diverged in a wood, and I—
> I

Edward was puzzled, and you were hurt. But the poem did spark something in him.

> Yet knowing how way leads on to way,
> I doubted if I should ever come back

"I dreamt we were walking near Ledington," he wrote to you later, "but we lost one another in a strange place & I woke saying to myself 'somehow someday I shall be here again.'"

By then he was a soldier, both too reserved and too clear-eyed to promise to come back to you except in a dream. And you, through your poem, were prophesying that he would not. By then you had changed the title of the poem to "The Road Not Taken."

> long I stood
> And looked down one as far as I could
> To where it bent in the undergrowth

Goodbye, Edward. Goodbye.

The war made the poet, and the poet went to war. "I am in it & no mistake," he wrote you, but he wasn't talking about the war, not yet, he was talking about poetry. The war ended any chance of his earning his bread with prose, so he felt he might as well starve on poetry. And his poetry wove his love for England into such durable cloth that he cut it for a uniform.

> The Combe was ever dark, ancient and dark.
> Its mouth is stopped with bramble, thorn, and briar;
> And no one scrambles over the sliding chalk
> By beech and yew and perishing juniper
> Down the half precipices of its sides, with roots
> And rabbit holes for steps. The sun of Winter,

The moon of Summer, and all the singing birds
Except the missel-thrush that loves juniper,
Are quite shut out. But far more ancient and dark
The Combe looks since they killed the badger there,
Dug him out and gave him to the hounds,
That most ancient Briton of English beasts.

You knew. And despite his dream, Edward knew. Being a poet, he
also could prophesy. He wrote a song with the refrain:

I'm bound away for ever,
Away somewhere, away for ever

What was it like? The fall, the flash—
It was beautiful, how he chose it, and you loved the beauty while
hating the choice. He beat his New Hampshire plowshare into
a Hampshire sword. He went forth and spent himself strongly. And
strongly spent (as you've written somewhere) is synonymous with
"kept." Whereas you— You kept in a different way. You—

But why declare
The things forbidden that while the Customs slept
I have crossed to Safety with?

The things forbidden were your American children, your precious
American hide. Wherever you two sojourned together, he cut walking
sticks and you cut lances. For you, playing Indian was enough, while
he smoked his war pipe and brooded.

He is that fallen lance that lies as hurled

You walked down the chicken stairs; you crossed the ocean to safety.
What was it like? The Germans lobbed a Five-Nine, it rose and
fell.

> And, Hob, being then his name,
> He kept the hog that thought the butcher came
> To bring his breakfast. "You thought wrong" said Hob

These are the last words Edward wrote to you:

> You are among the unchanged things that I can not or dare
> not think of except in flashes. . . . Goodnight to you & Elinor
> & all. Remember I am in 244 Siege Battery, B.E.F., France
> & am & shall remain 2nd Lieut. Edward Thomas
> Yours ever

Remember me.

The shell rose and fell and blew him to New Hampshire come. Did he think of you, in the flash?

He's buried in Agny, France. They say it's grassy there. On his grave is planted Old Man. A bush of it grew by Edward's door in Hampshire, along the garden path, and his young daughter Myfanwy used to pick the leaves and shred them. Edward wrote about it in one of his first poems, three months after August 1914.

> As for myself,
> Where first I met the bitter scent is lost.
> I, too, often shrivel the grey shreds,
> Sniff them and think and sniff again and try
> Once more to think what it is I am remembering,
> Always in vain. I cannot like the scent,
> Yet I would rather give up others more sweet,
> With no meaning, than this bitter one.
>
> I have mislaid the key. I sniff the spray
> And think of nothing; I see and I hear nothing;
> Yet seem, too, to be listening, lying in wait
> For what I should, yet never can, remember:

No garden appears, no path, no hoar-green bush
Of Lad's-love, or Old Man, no child beside,
Neither father nor mother, nor any playmate;
Only an avenue, dark, nameless, without end.

81

When the crowd filling the backstage corridor spots the sprung white hair behind the Younger Poet, it cheers. The Younger Poet runs interference. Frost has just read to four thousand. It was standing room only—a relief, because the Younger Poet has heard that Frost in his old age rages, inconsolable, at empty seats.

A good reading. Another relief, because the Younger Poet heard Frost read in Stanford years ago and was appalled. Frost pretended to be the simple rustic his audience wanted him to be. He cracked jokes in the middle of his poems, made fun of professors who read hidden meanings into the honest work of an old farmer. He betrayed his own poetry.

But not tonight. And the Younger Poet (now a professor at this university) was afraid Frost would say something rude about him to the audience. That happy malice of his, which is always happy, too, in its expression—part of its appeal to him. But instead the old poet sang his praises; said he had returned to Ann Arbor after many years to "see a young poet I helped to bring up." Frost called him a son.

Pushing down the hall, through a thicket of hands held out for a shake, a touch, holding scraps of paper the poet might sign, hoping the tough old tree might carve its initials in their skin. Frost is close behind, shuffling and thanking, refusing to sign anything.

His son. Of course the Younger Poet knows about Carol. And Irma and Marjorie. Impossible to know what that would do to a man. Make him inconsolable; make him rage. In the past he's been wary of Frost, anxious for him, angry at him, admiring of him, afraid of him. Now, for the first time, he feels close to him. On the way to the press conference this morning, Frost said, "You're getting taller every time I look at you." The Younger Poet was moved. It was as though Frost were watching some belated replacement for his son grow on time-lapse film.

They squeeze past the last fans through the stage door to the street, and find hundreds more milling on the sidewalk around the limousine. Another cheer, a coalescing, a surge forward. The Younger Poet moves through sideways, hand out to slice through. When he reaches the car, he opens the rear door, but Frost hesitates. Turning to face the hundreds of faces, he raises both arms. Blessing, embrace, exorcism?

None of these. The old poet calls out over their heads, in a tremulous voice, "Remember me."

The crowd stirs and breathes, as though a wind moved over a field of flowers. "We will," the voices come, from nowhere, from all around. "We will."

82

A horse snorts in the darkness. The long face appears in the firelight, floating, chewing. Disappears. Snorts. (Frost opens an eye. Plastic window. Bright contrail scratches on blue. Was he snoring? Closes the eye.) Russian boys around a campfire. Beyond is pitch-blackness. A clap from the river, a whispering among the reeds. "The carpenter went into the forest," says the melancholy boy with the piping voice. He's speaking Russian, and Frost is unutterably pleased that he can understand it. He's sitting with them around the fire and he's also lying on a haystack nearby and can't see them, so he watches the stars and listens to their drowsy voices. "To gather acorns," says the young boy.

"Acorns," repeats another boy.

"He got lost in the woods."

"Lost!"

"By a pond he met a water sprite, a nixie. . . ."

A clap from the river. "What a splash!" a big boy says, peering into the blackness. "Must be a pike." (The reeds whisper.)

"Her voice was high and piping, like a frog's. A ghost of sleighbells. She called to him. . . ."

"Hyla . . . Hyla . . . Hyla . . . ," the boys sing, arms around each other's shoulders. They're dancing around the fire, a Russian dance, but Frost understands every word. The head of the horse floats in the air, chewing, and among the reeds Echo crouches and whispers. "She reached out to him, like this. . . . Come . . . come, my love. . . ."

"Hm?" Bright window. "What?"

"We're coming in for the landing," Frank says.

"What? Oh." He sits up. "What time is it?"

"Ten-thirty."

Rubs sense into his face, tightens his seat belt. Lets his head fall back against the seat. He feels half dead.

Too much love.

Why is he thinking that? Was he dreaming? He can't remember. Too much love. What doomed Eurydice. Orpheus turned back. Makes the gods jealous. 'Tis a fearful thing to love. The evil of good born.

The stomach of the plane rumbles for a long moment, burps. Landing gear. He's going to meet Khrushchev. Godfrey mighty, the invitation came. Come, my boy, come closer. Closer . . . (He's falling!) It was just a dream—saving the world! Galahad asked him. Dobrynin buttonholed him. Stewart trapped him. He never wanted this. He will fail. Worse, he will make things worse.

Fear and fatigue roll through him, synchronizing with his pulse, pounding in his ears. His stomach hurts like hell. Yesterday morning, Stewart flew down to Khrushchev's Black Sea villa without him. He yelled at Frank and Freddie, *Don't lecture to me! I'm the lecturer! Everyone shut up and listen to me!* He had a television interview scheduled and the boys were afraid he'd throw a tantrum on the air. They didn't know him enough to know he would never do that. The show must go on. The lights came up and over at the side poor Franklin was standing half turned away so he'd only half see the disaster. Frost smiled, thanked his hosts, made nice. And the more he made nice, the better he felt. Well—he'd tried, hadn't he? Pretty good for an eighty-eight-year-old man. Now he could go home. Let Galahad save the goddamn world. Dinner that night was at the Matlocks', and Frost found he had an appetite. He sat on the couch afterward and joked with Jack's children. Then the telephone rang and Matlock came into the room beaming. "The invitation's come through! You're meeting Khrushchev tomorrow. There's a commercial flight at eight in the morning."

He'd felt sick ever since. In his hotel room last night he said, "I don't know if I'm well enough."

"Robert," Freddie said, "I'm worried about what you'll think of yourself afterward if you come all this way and don't go."

You mean, failure? Frost thought. Chicken? Go ahead, say it. You can't despise me more than I despise myself. (Edward used to say that out loud, to Helen. Wonderful way to shut her up.) Poor Frank looked distraught. And maybe it was for him, for the brave young man who didn't know him so well as Freddie did, that Frost managed to play the false part. In the morning he said, "I feel worse, but I'll go. That's what I came for."

They caught the plane, and rose and fell, and now Frost is in the back of a limousine with a hearse's curtains across the windows, and maybe the driver will spare him by killing them all, he's going so fast around the curves, leaning on the horn. Frank sits next to him. Since the invitation was only for two, and Frost needs Frank to translate, Fred had to stay behind in Moscow. "We've crossed into Georgia," Frank says, peering through the curtain. He leans forward and volleys with the driver. "We'll be at the guesthouse in half an hour. How are you feeling?"

"Terrible." It's true. It's his fault, but he can't help it. His body has always obeyed him: 4-F any time he needs it.

They arrive. Frost's room is on the second floor. Up my knee! He climbs and climbs and collapses on the bed. "My stomach hurts more," he says.

"The premier's dacha is twenty minutes away," Frank says. "We're supposed to lunch here first. Do you want anything to eat?"

"No."

"Anything to drink?"

"No! Leave me!" By which maybe he means, *Don't leave me!* "Wait!"

"Yes?"

"Do you think they have perry? I'd like a glass of perry."

"I'll ask." He disappears.

Frost dozes, wakes.

"No perry," Frank reports. His head floats, chews.

"There never is, is there?" Frost says.

He decides he might die here, right on this bed. By turning his head, he can see a glass sliding door, a balcony, a lemon tree, the blue sea. A path down to the shore. Why not die here? Maybe that's the way to save the world. *Kennedy and Khrushchev stand shoulder to shoulder on the platform in the bright light and shade the paper of their joint statement, Kennedy with his top hat, Khrushchev with his crushed Panama. "This great man who died in the cause of peace . . . we honor his sacrifice by declaring all issues touching on the Berlin problem resolved. . . ."*

He wakes again. "Do you want to see a doctor?" Frank asks.

"Yes." The doctor will see. He will declare Frost unfit. He'll straighten from the bed and round with anger on the others, "It's too late now for me to do anything." K., Khrushchev, Kennedy, everyone will be sorry! Except Larry. He'll dance a jig.

Frost dozes. He wakes with his face turned to the glass door, the balcony, and he sees, through the iron railing, a mermaid walking up from the sea. Dressed in white, carrying to him in a black bag all of his books of poetry fished up, still dripping natal water. He hears her weedy rustling on the floor below, and then she's standing in the doorway, the bag creaking at the end of her arm. His doctor, sea-changed.

She's impossibly young, elfin pretty, with wide-set eyes, a low forehead. Murmuring a stream of her liquid language, she holds his hand and gazes in his eyes, unbuttons his shirt and unlocks the secrets of his heart. Oh, he loves her. He wants her to take him away with her. She speaks to Frank with a grave mien, and Frost's instinct is not to trust the translator (he has suspected at every step that they're lying to him, even Franklin, misunderstanding his metaphors, shielding him from the truth) when he says, "Good news! She doesn't think it's very serious. A case of indigestion and the strain of so much traveling." He must read between the lines. So much traveling—exactly. Too much. He's strayed too far from home. Lost!

"I can't go any farther," he tells Frank. "I just can't. You have to tell them that." Take this cup. A bed, a balcony, a lemon tree, the blue sea. His eyes plead with the mermaid, *Don't leave me*. Frank goes. The mermaid stays. Black eyes, ivory skin, small mouth and chin. Dark smudges under her eyes. "You look tired," he tells her, and she smiles, uncomprehending. She pats him on the forearm and says something in an affectionate voice. He reminds her of her great-great-grandfather, Poseidon.

Frank returns. "Surkov's on the phone to the premier. I told him you were done in."

Frost lies back. Well, he almost did it. He would have done it, if he hadn't gotten sick. Damn his frailty, his old age! When's the next plane to Moscow? "Can the doctor come with me to the plane?" he asks. But Frank isn't there. She's sitting in a chair in the corner, all his poetry at her feet. "You should sleep," he tells her, and she smiles.

Frank comes in again, excited. "Khrushchev is sending his own doctor; then he's coming himself. You'll have your meeting after all!"

"Oh, good," Frost says to the ceiling, and dozes. Or maybe he faints.

Khrushchev's seal head breaks the surface of the water. He stares at Frost, his head floating, and he grins, showing off the mountain gap between his front teeth. "Every snipe praises his own bog," he says. Yes, home! Frost thinks, or maybe says. My Vermont farm! My upland pasture! I want to go home. "I am afraid that would be difficult," Khrushchev says. I'm afraid, Frost thinks or says. "Your ship sails without you," Khrushchev says, and as his head sinks back into the water, he blows a jet.

Frost wakes. A man he's never seen before is standing over the bed.

"This is the premier's personal doctor," Frank says. "He'll examine you."

A tanned, glossy man. At home among the lemon trees and beaches, at home with power. Fingers on wrist, watch, arm cuff, rubber bulb, hiss, cold probe in mouth, cold coin on chest, thump, breathe, thump, breathe, open wide and say ah. "Aaaahh!" Frost says.

"You have a fever of 101.5 degrees," Frank says. "But the doctor's judgment is that mainly you're just worn out. I've told him that we absolutely must be on the flight back to Moscow tonight."

"Good boy," says Frost.

"Khrushchev will be here soon."

Frost lies back again and closes his eyes, but this time doesn't doze. Some of his nervousness has left him. He can do nothing; he need do nothing. Khrushchev will not be stopped. A man used to wielding power, he will come and roll over Frost. A wind through the reeds. *Every snipe praises its own bog.* Was Frost having some dream about that? It's something Khrushchev said on his visit to America in 1959, and Frost liked him for it. He liked the earthy turn of phrase, and he agreed with the sentiment. Of course Americans were proud, and thought they were right, Khrushchev meant. But Americans should know that Russians were proud, and thought they were right. *Vive la différence!* And when you needed to fight, you fought hard, but you didn't pretend the other fellow didn't have his own reasons for fighting. Where was the glory in fighting someone you despised?

It was the American trip that first got Frost interested in Khrushchev as a man. The coverage was all over the papers. The illiterate shepherd boy who'd fought his way to the top, who now held the fate of the world in his hands. He was both the czar and the boy with the acorn. (Two roads converged.) He taught himself to read. He had no formal education until he was twenty-six. He worked in a coal mine. He threw a hazel lance and hit the moon. He denounced Stalin. Every night he talked past midnight, exhausting his comrades. His rockets were twice as powerful as ours. When he landed at Andrews Air Force Base in the largest airplane in the world, the crowd gasped. He pulled from it, with a wave of his wand, his wife, whom the West had never seen, who'd existed only in rumor. Round like him, beaming like him, exactly his height, seal wife to a seal husband.

It reminded Frost of a poem he'd written forty years ago about Paul Bunyan—how Paul cut a length of dark pith or maybe dried snakeskin out of a log of white pine, tossed it in a millpond to drink, and ran off with the rehydrated girl who resulted.

> Paul was what's called a terrible possessor.
> Owning a wife with him meant owning her.
> She wasn't anybody else's business,
> Either to praise her, or so much as name her,
> And he'd thank people not to think of her.
> Murphy's idea was that a man like Paul
> Wouldn't be spoken to about a wife
> In any way the world knew how to speak.

And if an American's mermaid speaks Russian, it turned out a Russian's mermaid spoke English. Mrs. Khrushchev had that miraculous ability. Everywhere she went, she squinted in the light of day, beaming. The press loved her, and so, it seemed, did Khrushchev. Now that the newspapers knew Khrushchev had a family, they reported he was a family man. He'd raised two sons and three daughters, plus several nieces and nephews as members of his own family. Frost liked that.

He liked the way Khrushchev talked, so unlike any politician he'd ever heard. Other politicians derided the premier for his crudeness.

He said if you pulled down Adenauer's pants and looked at him from behind you'd see that Germany was divided, and if you looked at him from the front you'd see that a united Germany could not stand. But Frost wanted to say to American reporters and senators, Have you read Shakespeare lately? (Of course the answer would be no.) Khrushchev seemed naturally to think in terms of concrete metaphor. Maybe it was his shepherd background. Pan-Slavic pipes. Nothing to fix his abstract thoughts on but rocks and fleece and milk and sheep shit.

Russians say every good job should be started in the morning.

If we were weak countries, then our quarrel would not matter, because when the weak quarrel they just scratch each other's faces.

If our atoms and our rockets are used for destruction, the earth will be covered with ashes and graves.

We have not come here with a long hand to try to get into your pockets.

Two mountains can never meet, but two people can meet.

The United States wants the U.S.S.R. to sit like a schoolboy with its hands on its desk.

If I am struck on the right cheek, I will hit the ringleader so hard on his right cheek that his head won't stay on his shoulders.

Every evening for those two weeks in the late summer of 1959 Frost read the newspaper out loud to K. in his hot cabin on the Homer Noble farm, and talked about Khrushchev and the Russians and democracy and power, until K. started snoring, and finding himself alone he found himself addressing a strange, silent thought to this Russian bear, this boor, this shepherd in wolf's clothing who threatened to blow up the world if it didn't acknowledge his worth as a man: *You have the soul of a poet.*

A knock on the door. Frank enters.

"The premier is downstairs. They'll bring him up as soon as you're ready."

Frost sits up, swings his legs over the edge of the bed. He buttons his shirt, palms his hair. Does he need to pee? He'll survive, he's too shaky on his pins to bother. But his feet are bare. He looks around the room. The mermaid is gone. "Where are my shoes and socks?" Frank brings them. Frost pulls them on, leans forward to tie the shoes but feels dizzy, tries to lift his feet to the bedside table but it's too high. "I'm sorry, Franklin. Can you—?"

Frank ties his shoes. Lacing his boxing gloves. On the beach. His father's grip on his forearms. *You can take him.*

After the Paris summit, Eisenhower called Khrushchev a "scoundrel." That was the sound of a gentleman refusing to duel a shepherd. *Respect me*, Khrushchev says. *Fight me.* You and I, Frost thinks. Shepherd versus farmer. Age-old. Give me your best shot.

"I'm ready," he says. Frank goes out, and Frost is alone.

By the blue sea, under the lemon tree.

Tityre, tu patulae recubans sub tegmine fagi

Why, Tityrus! But you've forgotten me.
I'm Meliboeus the potato man

In America in 1959, in the newspaper, in Frost's Vermont cabin, Khrushchev said the thing that made Frost like him most of all: "Let us shake hands and turn to peaceful competition. We will see which system—Communist or capitalist—can create the better way of life. If history should show that capitalism proves more capable than the Communist system, I would be the first to raise my hand in favor of capitalism." A noble rivalry. Frost's aim, acorn in fist, is to get the emperor to keep his word. Or perhaps, as published poet to unproven one, to get him to take his own metaphors seriously.

In his first hour on Russian soil, at the Moscow airport, Frost spoke to the assembled reporters, and one of the things he said was "If the Russians beat my country in everything, then I'll become a Russian." They didn't get it, which was no surprise. It was a secret message to Khrushchev: *I am here; I understand you.* Unfortunately, the next day Frank told him none of his comments had been printed in the papers. Maybe now—

The door opens and Khrushchev walks in. He's in the room. He's wearing a light-tan suit, smiling. It's him.

There are other men—four or five. Chairs are brought out from somewhere, scraped along the floor. Frank sits on the opposite bed, while Khrushchev takes the chair immediately in front of Frost. The other translator, the Russian who flew down with them from Moscow—Frost can't remember his name—sits next to him on the bed.

Looking at Khrushchev, Frost can only see him in snatches. Tanned, healthy face, a horseshoe of white hair at the back glowing in the sea-light from the balcony, matching the gleam of his unkempt teeth. That famous wen on the side of his nose. He talked about it in America, his metaphor for how the West had to accept noninterference in Communist countries: "The wen is there, and there's nothing I can do about it."

The wen is here. Khrushchev speaks; Frank translates. "I hope you're feeling better. You've traveled a long way for a man your age. I'm impressed you've managed it at all." He waggles a thick finger and forms a frown. "But you must take care of yourself." They say he also holds men's lapels when he argues with them, intimate and coercive at once. But Frost has no lapels. "You must follow the doctor's orders if you want to live to be a hundred."

Is this Khrushchev's secret message back to him? Because Frost has joked of late that when he reaches a hundred the U.S. will be two hundred (it almost works; anyway, no one contradicts him), and isn't it something to be half as old as your country? "I'm very glad to have come," Frost says, and waits while the Russian translates it. "I was very pleased by the invitation. As for doctors and their orders, you can never trust them, anyway."

He and the premier continue like this for a while. Pleasantries: Galahad says hello; your fine country. Meanwhile, Frost takes in more of the man across from him. He's short, but he looks taller when he sits. Homer said that of Odysseus, who used words (delivered in council, seated) to amplify his stature. Khrushchev, too, has his vivid rhetoric—and he has his finger in your face, his grip on your lapel, his shoe in his hand, his calling card on the moon, his big missiles. And that happy, voracious smile. One of the cheap tricks the press played on him when he was in America was to publish a photo of him eating, his head down almost in his plate. Peasant! Some children on a bus yelled at him, "Hey, meatball!"

The last curtsey is made, acknowledged; there's a pause. Khrushchev tugs his summer jacket open, spreads his legs, leans forward. He puts his hands on his knees. Frost is too tired not to slump, so he finds himself looking up at the shorter man. Hail, Caesar! "The premier would like to know," Frank says, "if you have anything special on your mind that you wanted to speak with him about."

Frost swallows. Here goes. "Tell him I've wanted to talk with him about East and West, about coming to a better understanding of each other." He waits; it's awkward, this translating business. He looks Khrushchev in the eye and pretends he can understand him as he speaks. "I agree with you, you know—about rivalry, about a noble rivalry between your system and ours." Not "coexistence"—Khrushchev's word. To Frost, that sounds like stalemate, like death. "Republican friends of mine, I've got a lot of 'em, they talk it down, rivalry, but I don't see it that way. I say the Soviet system is here to stay, like it or not, we in the West, there's nothing we can do about it. Socialism is inevitable, you can see it in the way the Western democracies are straining upward toward their own brand of it, through welfare-statism, and so on, and how your own system is easing down toward socialism from the severity of Communism." Maybe now it's just rubber bullets in the back of the head, hey? "Everyone taking care of everyone else." Too much brotherly love. The evil of good born. "I don't say I like it, but it's there; it's happening. And I'll say right out, I admire you—and here's also where I disagree with some of my friends—I admire you for the audacity and the courage you show in your use of power. Don't be afraid to use power, I said to Kennedy." He's beginning to get the rhythm; every couple of sentences, he pauses and watches Khrushchev's face while the translator speaks. "You know, liberals, in my country, they cry down power. I like to say that a liberal is someone who can't take his own side in a quarrel, a man who'd rather fuss with the Gordian Knot than cut it. They say 'on the one hand,' and 'on the other.' They sit on their hands." Like a schoolboy with his hands on the desk. *Where are you going, old man?* "A real leader is ultimately—at the core, you know—arbitrary. 'I bid my will avouch it,' and it's so. *Fiat.* The first word spoken, see. Nothing else can happen without it." *Fiat lux. Fiat poeta.* "What I mean to say is, power is meant to be used. The question is how. A noble rivalry is conducted by noble leaders. I'm talking about morality—not sex morality, but what Aristotle called character, the character of politicians. We had that in the last election, you know. This Kennedy, he's young, but he's not weak, he's no Adlai Stevenson. He's vigorous, and he knows what strength is, and he knows what poetry is, too. Augustus was young. I wrote a poem about that, it's in my book that I want to give you, 'a golden age of poetry and power,' and I mean that."

What exactly is he talking about? Is it possible to talk of it exactly? Is to talk of it exactly to betray it? A new age. In Augustus's time, it was Jesus Christ, and Virgil was his prophet. That was a one-power world, the Pax Romana, so what Augustus had coming to him was the universal Prince of Peace. But this is a two-power world. What's coming is the Age of Leo. Not the saphead liberals' peaceable-kingdom guff, the lion lying down with the lamb, but lion to lion, lionhearted, magnanimous. The other fellow drops his sword, you pick it up, hand it to him, then lunge at him and aim for the heart. Is East Berlin the dropped sword? No, it's less important than that, it's a misunderstood word, an accidental insult. To be waved away. Frost doesn't know if he's putting this in words right. (He sometimes can't remember what he said two minutes ago.) But this, this—for the past year, this year that's maybe his last on earth, this is the lump in his throat, the prophetic fumes in his head, the thing around which words will form or not form, as luck will have it.

> Weave a circle round him thrice,
> And close your eyes with holy dread,
> For he on honey-dew hath fed,
> And drunk the milk of Paradise

"That's the poet's role in government," he forges on. "I mean character. The top thing a government bestows isn't welfare, it isn't security or equality, it's character. I've said before, a great nation makes great poetry, and great poetry makes a great nation. Aristotle talks about magnanimity. That great word—magnanimity! He calls it the crowning virtue, because you can only have it if you already have the other virtues. It's like a salt to virtue. A great nation is magnanimous. It doesn't descend to petty squabbling or dirty play. It doesn't black-guard the other fellow. Aristotle recognized that virtue was particular to each man. What counted was that a man develop the virtue appropriate to him, to his character. It's the same for nations. Call it metaphor. Each nation's metaphor is different, but the only important question is, is it carried through with conviction?" Khrushchev is listening intently, with a slight frown of concentration.

"At our level," Frost goes on—he means Khrushchev and himself, Power and Poet, Caesar and Unacknowledged Senator—"there must be candid understanding. Squabbling over Berlin is beneath us. You are a great leader, and Russia is a great country. As you've said, it's a two-power world, Russia and America. Two grand visions for mankind. The arena is set between us for a grand contest of maybe a hundred years." The magic number: a Frost's age for a noble Cold War. "But it all should be on a high level. We're laid out for rivalry in sports, science, art, democracy. That's the real test, which democracy's going to win? And then add the salt: let's be rivals in magnanimity. We should keep surpassing each other. That's the only way progress is made."

The Russian finishes translating, and Frost glances at Franklin. Well? Has he made any sense? Has he gone on too long? Frank gives him an uncertain smile. "Is he getting my words right?" Frost asks him.

"He's doing a good job. As good as I would."

Khrushchev puffs out a breath and sits back, makes a "Well!" gesture with his hands, glances at one of his men. They confer for a moment. Then Khrushchev looks at Frost and smiles—is it a comrade's grin, or a horse-trader's?—and his words start to trickle in through Frank. Emphatically agree about maintaining a high level . . . some Western leaders wouldn't agree, or don't act as if they do . . . pleased to hear America's greatest poet recognize greatness of Russia . . . of course Russians don't need that recognition, they know their worth . . . his wise words about contest of democracies . . . premier has said that himself . . . respects

President Kennedy . . . hopes the president will visit him soon and bring his beautiful wife . . . he knows socialism is inevitable . . . but interesting to hear Mr. Frost say it . . . Mr. Frost is a Marxist, maybe . . . isn't it beautiful here, perhaps Mr. Frost would like a dacha of his own, enjoy the sun, become Russia's greatest Marxist poet . . . ha-ha . . . however, Mr. Frost surely came here with something more specific on his mind?

"Yes," Frost says. "Exactly! You understand. I've wanted to speak with you about Berlin for a long time." Khrushchev once called Berlin "the balls of the West." That was the ruffian in him speaking: *I've got you by the balls.* But another part of him says, *Respect me; duel me.* It's that part that Frost must appeal to, the imperial side. Make him see his greatness, seize it, become it. Dream him into being, as a true emperor. "I have a modest proposal. I call it modest because it's simple, and I suppose everyone thinks it's impossible because it's simple, and maybe that's why only a great man could do it. The Gordian Knot, see. Alexander had the greatness to cut through all the reasons, all the rules. He showed they weren't rules, they were pieces of string. Lordly impatience, see. There are things too trivial to waste time on. Berlin is one of them. You and we, together, Russians and Americans, we trounced the Germans, we shook hands—what a grand moment! East meets West—on top of the rubble heap. And now we're squabbling over this scrap of spoil. This dented pot." This is where, in poetry, Power says, Speak one wish and, on my honor, it shall be granted!

"Honor then the gods, Achilleus, and take pity upon me."
"Your son is given back to you, aged sir, as you asked it."

"It's a two-power world, as you say. But there are times when promises entangle both sides in a position neither wants to be in. Both sides are honorable, but it takes one side to act. Just cut the Knot. Relent. Graciously give, and prove your strength by giving." Speak, my boy! You've won my heart! One wish! "My proposal is this: act unilaterally. Deliver East Berlin to West Berlin. Guarantee something like a Polish Corridor to the West. Put an end to the whole argument."

He'd been canny about his idea. He'd told everyone he had one, but wouldn't say what it was. His secret proposal. For Khrushchev's ears only. Then he'd told Frank and Freddie a couple of days ago. It was at the end of a long day, and he'd just read to seven hundred in Moscow. It had gone well, the audience had understood everything, and he'd found his memory was like ten years ago, he said his poems flawlessly, and they cheered him at the end. So he was riding high, he felt anything was possible between East and West. Back in his hotel room, he told his two companions about his proposal—and he saw the blank, stiff dismay in their faces. *This* was his great idea? *This* is what he'd brought them to Russia for?

But didn't they see? That's the nature of cutting the Knot. It seems impossible, it seems foolish—until you do it. (Frank and Freddie didn't topple the Stalin cult; they didn't stamp their name on the moon.) One impossible thing has already happened: Frost has made his way into the emperor's presence. This is the second.

Weave a circle round him thrice

Khrushchev is speaking. What's in his expression? Is he intrigued, nettled? His eyebrows have drawn together, a slight flush has come to his heavenly dome; a pink sunset among the clouds. "Mr. Frost, what you suggest is impossible. East Berlin is the capital of the German Democratic Republic! I have long proposed a solution to the problem—turning West Berlin into a free city garrisoned by UN troops, in conjunction with a German peace treaty. In the current situation, West Berlin is a malignant tumor growing in the heart of the GDR. No country should be asked to accept this. No West European country would accept this. The West howls at the wall the GDR has built to protect itself from Western bribes to lure workers from their homeland, but what are the West's own actions? What far more dangerous and aggressive wall have they built? NATO threatens Eastern Europe and the Soviet Union. Why have the Western allies allowed the recrudescence of Nazi power in West Germany? Why have they allowed Germany to once again become a threat to peace?"

"Germany wouldn't be a threat," Frost says, "if it were united and demilitarized, and given a commercial trade route."

Khrushchev doesn't merely wave this comment aside, he swats it like a shuttlecock. "Germany isn't a threat to us, anyway, and neither is NATO. Do you imagine we fear them? Those days of Russia's cowering hat in hand are over. Our rockets could blast all of Europe into little pieces in less than thirty minutes." He sweeps out both arms, palms down, and cities of millions are carried away. The ruffian is speaking. "If the West really wants to regularize the situation, it will sign a peace treaty with the German Democratic Republic. That's what happened in Austria, and look how stable it is there. Schnitzels and tourists! Even your President Kennedy told me he wanted to sign a peace treaty, but he said he couldn't because of conditions in his country. He meant your reactionary senators, and your generals eager to fight another war."

"But a war over this!" Frost exclaims. "I'm no pacifist. But if the United States and Russia are to come to blows, let it be over something big. Something basic. For two great powers to destroy each other over something neither has inherent interest in—it's abhorrent. It's—it's—" What he wants to say is that it's unpoetic, a stupendously bad metaphor. But he suspects Khrushchev would not hear that the right way. "It would be a terrible tragedy."

"I agree."

"And that's why I'm suggesting a way out. If you prefer, call it a bit of horse-trading."

"Trade what? The West has no claim to East Berlin. We liberated it with no help, not one bullet, from the West. There's nothing to trade."

They're on the wrong track. Argument! It will get them nowhere. Reasons will drift around their legs and hold them fast. Frost has to give Khrushchev the wings to rise above argument, above reasons. "You said President Kennedy couldn't act because of political considerations in America. That's true, and it's why I've come to Russia to speak to you. Ours is a senatorial democracy, like the Roman Republic, whereas Russia is an imperial democracy. You are the most powerful person on earth. You are more powerful than Kennedy, and you are a great man, a courageous and magnanimous man. You have done great things for your country. You've shepherded it out of the Stalin era, built the economy, led the way in space. The world admires you, and I admire you. The next hundred years belong to the two giants of the world, my country and yours, and you are the one who can ensure that this will happen. God wants us to contend."

As the words are translated, Khrushchev flushes pink again; this time, it seems, with pleasure. He raises one hand, palm cupped and fingertips together, and bounces it gently in the air above his eyes. It could be a mimed toast, or the hint of a salute, or maybe he's hefting this praise like a bag of gold. "The fundamental contention between us is economic," he answers. "At one time not so long ago, the West could spit on our production, but that is no longer true. The Warsaw Pact countries are forging ahead economically, and they will soon overtake the Common Market. The Soviet Union and the Warsaw Pact nations are young countries, vital and full of energy. The United States and Western Europe, on the other hand, are old men, trapped in a defunct economic system. This reminds me of an anecdote the great Russian writer Gorky put in his memoirs about Tolstoy. Tolstoy was talking about what it was like to be too old and weak to be able to fuck, but still having the desire. That is the Western economic system."

Frost chuckles. This is the ruffian speaking, but it's also the part of Khrushchev that he likes. The ruffian poet. One of Virgil's shepherds accuses another of taking it up the ass—and in the temple, too! "That might be true for the two of us," he says, "but the United States is too young to worry about that yet." It occurs to him too late that the premier is twenty years younger than he is, and calling him an impotent old man is hardly the way to urge him to don the mantle of greatness. He glances at the clock on the bedside table. They've been talking for an hour. He guesses he has only one chance left. "Pardon me if I return to my proposal. President Kennedy wants a solution, but he can't act, for reasons that you know. Berlin is like a dropped— No, that's not ... It's a ... it's a ... *problem* that he can't solve on his own. He needs your hand. Yours is the stronger hand here. You've said you'll surpass us, and this is a grand way to do it, to surpass us and outdo yourself. You are the Augustus. He's waiting for you to extend your hand, and I promise you, he will take it. Any simple solution you offer on Berlin—forget the details I gave, you know better; any simple solution. By acting generously, you will disarm the senators and generals you've complained of, who argue you bear us only ill will. You will strengthen Kennedy, who would be your friend. If the danger of a one-power world is tyranny, the danger of a two-power world is stalemate. Stalemate by its very nature cannot be escaped through jockeying or negotiation. Magnanimity is the salt. In a bilateral world, magnanimity is the grace of unilateral action. You are Augustus." Is he repeating himself? "You can be the liberator. You've liberated your country, now liberate the world. Usher in the golden age. You bid your will avouch it. *Fiat pax!* No one will doubt your greatness then." Frost has run out of steam. He knows it. He doesn't have the strength anymore.

He holds out his fist. Inside is nothing, and everything. "Something simple. Save the world."

His words, such as they are, are translated. Khrushchev nods and smiles and frowns and purses his thick lips and runs a broad hand up and over his heavenly dome, maybe sweeping clouds away, maybe stirring up a storm. He nods a final time at the last words muttered in his ear, then looks in Frost's eyes for a long moment. He sits straight, while Frost slumps (Frost can barely keep himself from collapsing backward on the bed, and Christ he needs to take a leak), so he looks down into Frost's eyes with a gaze that is—what?—sorrowful, understanding, weighing, rejecting, admiring, pitying, recognizing. A half-smile forms. An almost imperceptible shake of the head. He says, "You have the soul of a poet."

Frost can only nod. A few more sentences are traded, but later Frost won't remember any of them. He remembers only Khrushchev looking penetratingly at him one last time and asking, "Aren't you tired? I've overstayed my time."

"No," Frost says. "No, not at all. I'm glad we've had such a frank, high-minded talk."

"Give my greetings to President Kennedy and the American

people, and urge your president to consider these issues as you and I have discussed them."

"Yes. Yes I will."

"It is a great pleasure to have met such a famous poet." Khrushchev is standing, and Frost struggles to his feet. The room sways. They shake hands, which Frost rarely does, and Frost trembles on the end of the premier's arm like a leaf on a branch. Khrushchev lets go and walks toward the door and Frost is probably already falling backward before he gets there, but at least he doesn't actually hit the bed until after the premier is out of the room.

He gazes at the ceiling. Christ on the crapper, the bathroom is miles away. "Well," he says to Frank. "We did it, didn't we?"

Did what? Showed up at the battle; survived. Now he can face K. when he goes home. "He's a great man," Frost says. "He's a great man, all right."

"Don't you want to sign your book for him?" comes Frank's voice.

"I forgot!" Frost sits up. The copy of *In the Clearing* is on the bedside table. Pen in the drawer. He writes in a trembling hand:

> To Premier Khrushchev
>   from his rival in friendship
>   Robert Frost
>
> Gagra
> Sept 7 1962

Frank takes the book and Frost falls back. The world turns.

> I slumbered with your poems on my breast
> Spread open as I dropped them half-read through
> Like dove wings on a figure on a tomb
> To see, if in a dream they brought of you,
>
> I might not have the chance I missed in life
> Through some delay, and call you to your face

First soldier, and then poet, and then both,
Who died a soldier-poet of your race . . .

You went to meet the shell's embrace of fire
On Vimy Ridge; and when you fell that day
The war seemed over more for you than me

Finally he accepts that he must get up or he will wet his pants. "Franklin?" He turns his head, but his translator is not there. Instead, it's his mermaid, sitting in the corner chair. She comes to the bed and leans over him. "Hello," he says.

She helps him to the bathroom, and afterward takes his temperature. She holds up the thermometer between her cold, greenish fingers. His fever is gone.

"Will you come to the plane with me?" he asks.

She sits silently in the front seat next to the driver, glancing back at him now and then to see if he yet lives. The driver drives even faster than he did that morning. Frost doesn't care. He survived the meeting, and this is nothing. Maybe he should roll down the window and flog the car's flank: Faster! Gee up! As they race down the airport's access road, the jet to Moscow roars overhead, climbing.

Your ship sails without you.

83

The chairman's Chaika convertible is about to start back to his dacha when the young American translator runs out of the guesthouse holding a book. "He forgot! He's inscribed it."

"Ah," Khrushchev says. "Tell him thank you. Tell him I will read it so that I may understand his country better."

He glances at the cover as the driver next to him starts up the allée of pines and turns onto the road south to Pitsunda. The title is . . . The premier cogitates for a moment. *In the* . . . something. He's briefly embarrassed for the hundredth time that he knows hardly any English. Well fuck that! Frost can't say a single word of Russian. "Hel-lo!" he says in English, to the warm sea air buffeting in around the windshield, to the palm trees and shrubs whizzing past. He turns to look at his secretary, Lebedev, in the back seat. "Hel-lo!" He holds up the book, with the old poet's photograph on the cover. "How-are-you?"

"I'm fine," says Lebedev in English. The premier laughs and leans over the seat to punch Lebedev in the shoulder. He turns back around, glances at the photo again before putting the book aside. An old man. Sun-mottled, head like a square stone turned up by the plow, a peasant's hand of boiled beef. Khrushchev likes all that. And he liked the praise the old man heaped on him. But everything else puzzled him. The proposal couldn't be serious, of course. What are they testing? To see if he's lost his marbles? That's what he's afraid Kennedy might think, or what those rabid senators will tell him to think. The question is, does Kennedy have the balls to stand up to the pressure? He's younger than the premier's own son. At the Vienna conference he let the premier bully him. That was a good sign then. Bad sign now.

The Americans know about the buildup on Cuba, of course. But they don't know about the missiles. The senators forced Kennedy to say the day before yesterday that "the gravest issues would arise" if there turned out to be an offensive force on Cuba. Khrushchev immediately ordered a speedup in the delivery of the medium-range missiles. They'll be on the island within a week. Get the goat's ass all the way into the peasant's hut. The Americans will hate the smell, but they'll get used to it. Keep them from trying another invasion. Their dearest wish. Strangle the Bearded One. Khrushchev would be blamed for losing Cuba. Give his enemies just what they needed. The precipice at his back. Americans like Senator Keating and that madman LeMay would push him right off. They'd be fucking sorry when they saw what replaced him.

So he's thrown a hedgehog down Uncle Sam's pants. Ha! Make him dance a little jig. Give the Americans a taste of their own medicine. Those fucking Jupiter missiles in Turkey, aimed right up his ass. And Kennedy was one of those responsible, back when *he* was a rabid senator, forcing Eisenhower to counter the Russian ICBMs. (It's a game they play. The hotheads in Congress, the statesman in the White House. Stalin's not the bad one, no, it's his Jew advisers.) Yeah—those big Russian cocks, those ICBMs. Which mainly don't exist.

Khrushchev looks pensively out on the coast gliding past, on the sunlit blue water. Good day for a swim.

That's the joke of it. He bluffed about his intercontinental missiles so he could reduce the army and save the fucking economy, and now everybody believes it except himself and his own generals. He's got barely a handful, and they take hours to fuel up for a launch. The Americans have solid fuel. They're miles ahead and rich as shit. The old man talked about how the U.S. and Russia could avoid a stalemate. Fuck! Khrushchev would love a stalemate. If only! American generals can't really believe Russian nuclear forces are any match for theirs, they're not that stupid. It's another game, a lie to enrich the arms industrialists.

Give the bastards what they want. What they say he's got, whether he's got it or not. He may not have ICBMs worth a rat's ass, but he's got enough medium- and intermediate-range missiles to make the Americans drop a load. If he can get them operational on Cuba before they discover them. Then the Soviet Union can finally speak to America as an equal.

Why didn't the old man say anything about Cuba? He's in Kennedy's inner circle, must be getting instructions every day. That's why Khrushchev asked him down. Udall yesterday didn't have anything new to say on the subject, so the premier wondered if the court poet had a personal communiqué.

An old man. He looked half dead. Maybe he forgot! (Khrushchev laughs. His driver looks across at him. "Watch the fucking road," he says.) Maybe the old man was armed with a secret message, something only a family friend could be trusted to carry, something that would have solved everything. And he just plain forgot.

Khrushchev shrugs. He's disappointed. And worried. What's Kennedy going to do when he finds out about those missiles?

The car pulls up at his villa. "Vladimir," he says to Lebedev, "come with me." They go up to his study. Well he's in it now. As they say in America, he's holding his cards and his bet's been called. The only thing to do is raise. "Take this down." He's got thirty-six medium-range missiles and twenty-four intermediate on the way to Cuba. The first could threaten U.S. cities almost all the way to Washington, the second could reach New York and Boston. Pull your ass cheeks wider, Kennedy, see what this feels like. But what if the Americans really invade? He's not going to fire those missiles. The U.S. would launch against Russia. By the time his ICBMs were ready to fire there wouldn't be a wet spot left of anyone in Moscow or thirty other cities. He needs something he could actually use. "I've decided to send battle-field nuclear weapons to Cuba. That short-range rocket, with the two-kiloton warhead."

"The Luna?"

"Yeah. I'm sending a dozen Lunas. Cable Pliyev about it." Blast them to the fucking moon.

He's worried. He's fucking worried. He's got this voice in his ear telling him he's made a fucking gigantic mistake. "Pah! It's hot! I'm sweating like a pig! And I'm hungry!"

They go downstairs. He eats a horse, swims a mile, slaughters his doctor at badminton. Afterward, he sits out on the shingle beach in a deck chair, Lebedev next to him. The sun is going down over the water. Fuck, he needs to get his mind off Kennedy. "What's that manuscript you've been threatening to read to me? A day in a life. By that ex-convict, the one Tvardovsky wants to publish. Bring it here." Lebedev hurries up to the house.

Khrushchev settles himself more comfortably in the chair. Fuck.

Lebedev returns with the papers in his hands. "Read." Khrushchev suddenly remembers the book Frost gave him. What did he do with it? Must have left it in the car.

Lebedev reads.

"Reveille was sounded, as always, at 5 A.M.—a hammer pounding on a rail outside camp HQ. The ringing noise came faintly on and off through the windowpanes covered with ice more than an inch thick, and died away fast. It was cold and the warder didn't feel like going on banging."

The premier closes his eyes. He feels with pleasure the warmth of the setting sun on his face.

84

Cold!

He stands briefly by the window but can't see the thermometer through the ice. He hurries back to the stove. Last night it reached forty below. He's used to houses popping in cold nights, but this one cracks as loud as a rifle shot. He half expects to see part of a wall blasted open, the blue air streaming in with rigid fingers to grab him by the throat.

During the Derry years he'd only been up here in the hay-fever season. And it was a sunny day in April last year when he first walked up the hill south of town and saw this fifty-acre farm and its little house with the magnificent view of the Franconia Range across the valley of the Ham Branch. For him, farms are like friends—he loves them at first sight. He offered to buy, and maybe he should have wondered why the farmer was so agreeable. He wouldn't have credited how much of a difference it makes, the way the frigid air flows down the mountainsides and pools in the valley. August frosts killed the garden he and the children planted last year. (Elinor was laid up with the pregnancy that scared them all half to death; his new friend Louis Untermeyer helped them take care of that.)

After their exile in England, the children, Margery in particular, want another Derry. Margery was five when they moved off the old farm, and she's ten now—shy and quiet, their little bird. Derry is the lost paradise, and Franconia is supposed to make it up to her. Franconia forever. There's a barn and a cow and a pasture and a woodlot and a sugar orchard, and two swimming holes, and high- and low-bush blueberries to pick. And the view.

But too cold! He who likes to joke with his name finds it bitter to-night, huddled by the stove, to think that he must live his life trapped between frost lines: north of the one that kills ragweed and south of the one that kills fruit trees. Is there a space between? If there is, it's as narrow as the crack he sometimes breathes through in his lungs, the crack he feels like he's got his fingers wedged in, trying to keep it from closing, trying not to panic.

He knows they can't stay here forever, or even for long. He feels guilty about dragging Elinor and the children from place to place. He feels guilty that, even while they live here, he spends so much time away, giving the readings that are their main source of income. When he came back from the last tour, he was in disgrace. Margery, crying, asked where he'd been, when was he leaving again, why. Carol didn't speak to him for a day; Irma closed her door. Elinor wishes he were still writing his poems only for her. He feels guilty that he can't wave a wand and give Derry back to them. He feels guilty (while he's on the subject) that he got Elinor pregnant again. He feels guilty that, because Elinor was sick with her pregnancy, he wasn't able to take in Merfyn as Edward hoped, when Merfyn started complaining about the man he was working for down in Keene. He feels guilty that he didn't help more when Merfyn went back to England at Christmas, and he feels guilty about the reason Merfyn went back—Edward has become a soldier. He wanted to see his son in case, when he went to war, he liked it so much he stayed.

What do you do with guilt? With all the things you can't apologize for, because you can't do anything about them, or won't? You write a poem. He's been working on a longish one lately, and he thinks it's nearly finished. It's about a middle-aged couple, long married, wea-ried, wary, moving into a country house. They're uncertain they've made the right choice, they're a bit scared by the loneliness and the dark. They don't know if this house will ever be a home; all they know is, their lives are in the home stretch. And that's what he'll probably call it, "In the Home Stretch."

He put in the dirtiness of these little New England towns, which surprised him after three years in England, where the yeomanry know to keep themselves well scrubbed for their lord's sense of fitness.

> And now and then a smudged, infernal face
> Looked in a door behind her and addressed
> Her back. She always answered without turning.

> "Where will I put this walnut bureau, lady?"

He put in the frailty of this house, which might be the frailty of the future:

> "Bang goes something big away
> Off there upstairs. The very tread of men
> As great as those is shattering to the frame
> Of such a little house."

He put in the fear of the cold:

> "The stove! Before they go! Knock on the window;
> Ask them to help you get it on its feet.
> We stand here dreaming. Hurry! Call them back!"

> "They're not gone yet."

> "We've got to have the stove,
> Whatever else we want for. And a light."

He put in the sense of dread that lies just beneath the New England soil like the bone-white stones—those couples before them, in their own home stretches, who made the same mistake (if it is a mistake) that this couple makes:

> "I don't know what they think we see in what
> They leave us to: that pasture slope that seems

The back some farm presents us; and your woods
To northward from your window at the sink,
Waiting to steal a step on us whenever
We drop our eyes or turn to other things,
As in the game 'Ten-step' the children play."

What children? They're nowhere in the poem. Maybe that's a guilt that lies too deep for expression. Or maybe Frost, in his garrulous middle age, is just rewriting "In Neglect," his short ardent burst about himself and Elinor before the children came:

They leave us so to the way we took,
     As two in whom they were proved mistaken,
That we sit sometimes in the wayside nook,
With mischievous, vagrant, seraphic look,
     And *try* if we cannot feel forsaken.

Ah, youth! And here's what that feels like in the home stretch, when the young, loud movers bang out the door and head back to the lighted town:

"Did they make something lonesome go through you?
It would take more than them to sicken you—
Us of our bargain. But they left us so
As to our fate, like fools past reasoning with.
They almost shook *me*."

What's left, when the seraphim have stopped singing, and the cozy nook has become a narrow crack?

"I know this much:
I'm going to put you in your bed, if first
I have to make you build it. Come, the light."

That's the woman speaking. Her husband, like Odysseus, builds the marriage bed. No longer young, he and his Penelope mount the stairs. *They then gladly went together to bed, and their old ritual.* The cold is kept out, at least for tonight, by their bed-warmth, their squirming heat, which finds its reflection on the kitchen ceiling below them:

> When there was no more lantern in the kitchen,
> The fire got out through crannies in the stove
> And danced in yellow wrigglers on the ceiling,
> As much at home as if they'd always danced there.

Ah, guilt! And the exorcism thereof. Note that the woman seems not ever to get pregnant. And that, perhaps as a consequence of the foregoing, she seems to welcome sex.

85

He wrote to you from Hampshire in September 1914: "There are some apples about here. So come if you can." He wrote to you from London in August 1915: "Ledington & White leaved Oak seems purely paradisal, with Beauty of Bath apples Hesperidean lying with thunder dew on the warm ground." When he heard you were looking to buy the farm in Franconia, his first question was "Are there any apples there?"

But you had to disappoint him. You wrote back, "About all it raises is grass and trees. Some time we must have a real fruit farm again further down along."

You've always wondered if apples would have tipped the balance. (*Stay me with flagons, comfort me with—*) You wrote, "We have gone too far into the wilds for you or something."

He wrote, "Last week I had screwed myself up to the point of believing I should come out to America & lecture if anyone wanted me to. But I have altered my mind. I am going to enlist on Wednesday if the doctor will pass me."

When you wrote "In the Home Stretch," you put in a message for him. You gave your farm of pine sap and maple sap an impossible orchard:

> "Before we set ourselves to right the house,
> The first thing in the morning, out we go
> To go the round of apple, cherry, peach,
> Pine, alder, pasture, mowing, well, and brook.
> All of a farm it is."

I hope you & I will meet in it.

86

FRANCONIA, NEW HAMPSHIRE

MARCH 1919

"He gets along beautifully with the children," Elinor says of Walter Hendricks. Rob and Elinor have been wanting to visit Lesley in her first semester at Barnard, but didn't see how they could leave Marjorie, Irma, and Carol alone in Franconia. Then Walter came to stay for a while, and they saw that the children liked him. Or maybe what was just as important, they saw that he liked the children.

Rob is not unaware that many people can't stand his kids. People, for instance, who expect obedience and politeness from children. He's raised a brood of brooders, incipient artists, or maybe incipient failures. It amounts to pretty much the same thing. They take the world strangely and hard. Walter, with his shot nerves, his jumpy diffidence, feels rapport with them rather than repulsion.

Agoraphobes like their mother or paranoiacs like their father, or each a unique blend of creative and destructive lunacy. Lesley went to Wellesley College as a freshman savage and fought with everybody—teachers, classmates, roommates, team coaches. She came out of it happier and stronger than ever. Then she quit with a flourish and went to work for the war in an airplane factory, where each morning she drank like coffee the thought of annihilating the German people. Now she's at Barnard, and already quarreling over a poetry contest. Go, Lesley! Rob cheers from the stands. Smash that line! Frosts: 1; Enemies: 0.

> O saw ye bonnie Lesley
> > As she gaed o'er the border?
> She's gane, like Alexander,
> > To spread her conquests farther.

None of them can bear schooling, and he doubts he's helped them to bear it. Marjorie has just started at a school in Franconia but is already talking about leaving. She says it's "awfully sleepy." Irma boarded at Dana Hall last fall for one semester, and within a week concluded she hated every girl in her house. She wrote home daily and was frantic whenever Elinor didn't answer in kind. Carol, seventeen now, is gratefully done with the whole aborted business. He gives up too easily, but he's got his own smoldering to prod him out of his chair. He escapes out the back door and goes hunting, finds nothing, returns to sulk, then flares to his feet again. He takes a hatchet to cut pea sticks with such inarticulate anger he gashes his leg and requires stitches. Another of his many accidents. (What makes Frost's poem "Out, Out—" so terrifying to him is the thought that if anyone could lose his hand to a buzz saw, it's Carol.) The other day he fought a college freshman who'd taken a hockey stick from a younger boy. He knocked the college boy down and sent him off humiliated in front of the crowd. Go, Carol! Frosts: 2!

Rob loves his children for what they are, for the unseasonable way they run out of song and speed, for the trouble they experience doing things other children do without thought or feeling, for the stomach upsets and long grudges he bequeathed them, for the way Marjorie shrinks sweetly, Irma hides sourly, Carol escapes bitterly. And for Lesley, who fights for them all (when she's not fighting with them).

Perhaps Irma is the oddest, and Rob's love for her is full of fear and regret. She clings to her parents like a drowning person, threatening to drown them to save herself. She takes most things said to her the wrong way; she objects to questions nobody asked. When she quit Dana Hall, Elinor set her up by herself in the front downstairs bedroom, because she knew Irma valued above all a sense of peace and security, a solid door to close. She works at her drawing in there. She closes the door with such a dark look Rob imagines he hears locks and bolts rattling home. (Home is the place where—) But there's only silence.

Lucky, then, that Walter seems to understand them. Elinor put him in the upstairs front bedroom, which gets the most heat from the new furnace. After three winters, that furnace finally makes the house feel capable of surviving a winter. For example, a late-March snow squall is blowing outside this very moment, and Rob is not even shivering as he puts clothes in his suitcase. Now if they can only solve the problem of the spring on the hillside freezing. No water in the pipes again. Instead, they're collecting it in buckets in every room, because the furnace warms the house enough to melt the snow on the leaky roof. Carol's got to get up and shovel the snow off. Rob can only hope he doesn't shovel himself off, break his neck.

They'll be in New York for three days. Elinor will worry every minute about the children. Lesley will announce some new adventure she's dead set on, partly for the pleasure of seeing her mother pale. Elinor will want to hug her, and Lesley will hang back. Rob regrets, almost as much as Elinor, that the children are growing up, that someday they will marry sons of earth and move to other oases. It's natural, of course, that they do. But can't it be natural that he follow them? He'll build an ell onto each of their self-sufficient farmhouses with a room just for him. He'll ajudicate their quarrels, meddle in their affairs, warm himself at their fires.

He closes the suitcase and goes downstairs, looking for Elinor but finding Walter. "Where is she?"

"Carol's room, I think."

"Fretting over the boy's cold. If he coughs once, the trip to New York will be off. You'll be off the hook."

"Doesn't seem too serious."

"Doesn't matter what you think. Or me, either."

Walter was one of Frost's better students at Amherst. He wrote poetry that showed promise. Then Wilson declared war on Germany, and all the boys enlisted. Walter went into the Air Corps, won his commission early and taught three hundred men to fly. Not a few of his students crashed their planes and died in front of him.

Frost has been fascinated by man's flight since Kitty Hawk. Humans taking wing; matter soaring into spirit; playing with gravity (grave play). The metaphors seem too good for a poet to quite believe in the reality of flight, and that edge of unbelief keeps him hooked. Reality rich as dream. Or nightmare. That was Walter's contribution to Frost's understanding. He stayed with Frost on leave toward the end of the war, and his matter had indeed turned to spirit: he was a ghost. He didn't hear you, couldn't sleep. It turns out the reality of flying is mainly boredom, hours and hours of practicing the same few moves, then now and again a nosedive into a field and you get the engine in your lap, which burns your lower half off, or more mercifully kills you. Hendricks was in hospital once next to a fellow flyer, and he said a picture he'd never get rid of was the doctor holding the boy's teeth apart while he died, so the blood could gush through and he could draw his last breath free. Walter unheroically feared the end of his leave as only a hero deserved to.

Since the war he's come partly back from the dead, put on a little matter, regained some color. But Frost expects he'll never be the same. He's a soldier who suffered as badly as any, without ever going to war. Against the Germans, anyway. He warred against gravity, which for Frost is the greater heroism for being futile and perverse.

Ah, when to the heart of man
   Was it ever less than a treason
To go with the drift of things,
   To yield with a grace to reason,
And bow and accept the end
   Of a love or a season?

Go, Walter! Spirit: 1; Matter: 0.

"There you are. How's Carol doing?"

"Oh, the poor boy!" Elinor says. "I've told him not to go out while we're gone, but I'm sure he won't listen."

"No, he probably won't. The air might do him good. And there's the roof."

"Is the snow abating?"

"It's ended. Didn't amount to much. Roads should be all right. Walter can take us over to Littleton."

In the sleigh behind Beaut, Rob and Elinor sit cozily together under a robe while Walter handles the reins. Rob holds his girl's hand where Walter can't see. The sky has cleared, and everything is white; the Franconia Range, the muffled stream smoking through ice holes at the bottom of the hill. Rob looks over his shoulder, but the farm is already out of sight.

He planted twelve apple trees on a northerly slope above the house a week ago, when it was rainy and almost warm, but he doubts they'll make it. These Franconia springs that alternate fifty-degree days with weeklong freezes on into May and even June will coax the buds out and kill them. He's just begun a poem about that. A line came to him when he was planting the trees:

Keep cold, young orchard. Good-bye and keep cold

He said that over to himself a few times while he worked, and then another line came to him:

Dread fifty above more than fifty below

Now he's got an opening sentence:

> This saying good-bye on the edge of the dark
> And cold to an orchard so young in the bark
> Reminds me of all that can happen to harm
> An orchard away at the end of the farm
> All winter, cut off by a hill from the house.

It occurred to him only after he'd begun writing it that he was also writing about Lesley. Those adventures of hers out in the cold world. She's an attractive girl.

> To see her is to love her,
>   And love but her for ever;
> For nature made her what she is,
>   And never made anither!

He's kidding himself if he thinks she only likes to see her mother turn pale. She's tormenting him, too. Lesley: 1; Rob: 0!

When she was working at the airplane factory in Marblehead, she wouldn't look for a room with a family who'd watch out for her. No, she had to live by herself in a teahouse. Every time she said the word, Rob heard "cathouse" and "geisha girl." And there was a Mr. Wheeler, some dirty-minded fellow as old as Rob, with fine manners and a yacht as lure. Trolling the town, he snagged Lesley, invited her out for a day's sail. Alone, of course. Here's the stateroom; looks like a storm's coming on; better batten down the hatches; stay below, ride it out; ride and ride. And she went! Rob was as sleepless as Walter when he heard that. Nothing happened, but the thought of Lesley pulling some trick like that again with some other fellow—Rob wrote to her about it. He can only hope that admitting to his worry won't goad her into going farther.

His Bonnie Lesley, young in the bark, his forbidden fruit.

The engine is in his lap.

87

For years you wanted to kill him. He knocked; the wolf at the door. He invaded her room like a blast of cold air. He fell on her like a shell.

She was only fifteen.

He didn't rape her, thank God. But he made a pass. Put his hands on her. Pulled her to him. The girl he left behind. The soldier come home. Recompense for his suffering. Fall into her arms.

You blamed yourself. Why had you taken him in?

Because (you saw only later) he was a substitute for Edward; he was a poet-soldier who survived the war. (You told yourself his poetry was better than it was.) Wilson declared war on April 6 and Edward was killed on April 9. You learned of it a week later, and that week and the next you encouraged your students to enlist. You hated the pacifists, and you hated the socialists (whom you'd hardly thought about before then) because they were pacifists. Go, Amherst! Kill Germans!

> In the days of Captain John
> Sanborn Sem had nothing on
> Pinkerton! Pinkerton!

You flirted again with the idea of going yourself. (Now it *was* your war.) You thought you were serious, but really you only wanted to make Elinor worry; make her demand that you not go, make her admit that, if she didn't exactly love you, at least she slightly preferred living with you to without. But she knew you better than you knew yourself. She snorted and said you'd never dare. So you showed her, all right. You spent a day drilling on the Amherst common with other middle-aged patriots, the Awkward Squad, and then you broke the news to her: you were going down to the enlistment office the next day.

Silence. She knew.

So your students went for you. Walter went, and came back a shell of his former self, and you took him in. You left him to look after your children.

So for years you wanted to kill him. You forced him out, bad-mouthed him, insisted your friends ostracize him. And now you can blame yourself for that, too, because you suspect Irma imagined it all. (Look at all she's imagined since then.)

You've made some restitution. Agreed to be a trustee at the college Walter started, to give it some stature. But you still can hardly stand him. Is it because his poetry is sappy, his early promise betrayed? Or because he reminds you of your false accusation? Or maybe you're not entirely certain that it was false. Look at your sister, Jeanie. Like Irma, she thought every man was out to seduce her—rape her, if that's what it took. Yet some men are rapists. More are heartless seducers. Your boyhood friend Mills, who dated Jeanie when she was seventeen, possessed her and threw her aside. That broke her. And there was the story you heard only in whispers, in snatches. One of the San Francisco hotels the family stayed in, when your mother needed a break from the housekeeping she didn't do. Jeanie was three years old, and some older boy "toyed" with her.

That word. You didn't know why it burned your ears. A child's word turned sinister. There was a ruckus; the boy was whipped badly by his mother, and you can still hear his screams filling the hotel.

> When that I was and a little tiny boy,
>   With hey, ho, the wind and the rain,
> A foolish thing was but a toy,
>   For the rain it raineth every day.

Jeanie always said her touble was that nobody liked her the way she wanted to be liked. She was right. But she carried the metaphor too far. Her tragedy was that she became wrong in her very rightness.

And Irma? Your pretty one?

88

Pulpiteers will censure
Our instinctive venture
Into what they call
The material
When we took that fall
From the apple tree.

He calls it "Kitty Hawk," and he's been laboring over it for years. More than four hundred lines. It's about his flight to the Dismal Swamp in 1894, the Coast Guard savior he met on the beach near Kitty Hawk, the flight he didn't make into words about all that then, the flight he's making now, the flight of man into the air and beyond, rocket flights into space, the flight of the moon around the earth, the earth around the sun, the sun around the galactic disk. Headlong flights that are a courageous return to where you started.

"Nothing can go up
But it must come down."
Earth is still our fate.

It's the most important poem he's written in a decade, it's his whole philosophy. And no one seems to get it. His editor at Holt won't come out and say so, but he's hoping Frost won't put it in his next book. He's subtitled it "A Skylark," and of course his hawk has its precursor in Shelley's bird, which also stayed aloft on wingbeats of three:

Hail to thee, blithe Spirit!
  Bird thou never wert—
That from heaven, or near it,
  Pourest thy full heart
In profuse strains of unpremeditated art.

Sixty-four years ago, there was a boy named Robert Frost:

You might think too poor-
Spirited to care
Who I was or where
I was being blown
Faster than my tread—
Like the crumpled, better
Left-unwritten letter
I had read and thrown.

Like Dante's ladder of terza rima, the interlocking rhymes pull the
poem down and down, to where the silly and precious boy went to lose
himself, too callow to know what all must learn soon or late: wherever
he went, why, there he was. Or as that brightest of all angels says,

Which way I fly is Hell; myself am Hell

Another silly boy, who ran north instead of south, said it in his
own skylark, "A Song About Myself":

There was a naughty boy,
  And a naughty boy was he,
He ran away to Scotland
  The people for to see—
    There he found
    That the ground
    Was as hard,
    That a yard

Was as long,
That a song
Was as merry,
That a cherry
Was as red,
That lead
Was as weighty,
That fourscore
Was as eighty,
That a door
Was as wooden
As in England—
So he stood in his shoes
And he wonder'd,
He wonder'd,
He stood in his shoes
And he wonder'd.

This jeu d'esprit by a teenaged John Keats seems to eighty-four-year-old Robert Frost, living alone in the house his poetry built, to sound the heights of human wisdom and the depths of human fate. Doesn't anyone else see it?

Though our kiting ships
Prove but flying chips
From the science shop
And when motors stop
They may have to drop
Short of anywhere . . .
Don't discount our powers;
We have made a pass
At the infinite

His audience chuckles too readily, applauds itself. Professors turn their backs. His editor shakes his head.

89

Irma, Lesley, and Marjorie are taking a walk deep in the woods far away from the Lynch farm, where they've all come again for the summer because of Papa's hay fever. One of the Lynches' dogs is with them, running up ahead. Lesley peers left and right as she walks. She says, "This is a beary region." Irma feels nervous and looks, too. Rounding a turn in the path, Lesley calls out, "Here!" In front of them is a patch of lovely red bunchberries. The children pick and eat for a minute. The dog is off ahead among the trees; suddenly it runs back, barking. "It's a bear!" Irma cries. The next thing she knows, they're all running down the path. Lesley turns to look back. "I see him!" she yells. "He's in the old wood road!" Irma runs twice as fast. All of the children are screaming. Finally they reach the edge of the woods and run across the yard and into the house. "We saw a bear! It chased us!" They tell it over and over to Papa and Mama, while they catch their breaths.

Later, Irma asks Lesley, "If a bear got hold of us, how would he kill us?"

"He'd probably hug us to death," Lesley says.

This sounds so funny, Irma laughs.

90

Rob always suspected that leaving Franconia broke Margery's heart. (When he feels especially tender toward her, he sees her name as Lesley spelled it in her childhood journal, twenty-five years ago at Derry. She was a baby then, and she has never quite stopped being a baby for Rob and Elinor. He supposes it's not impossible she's been for them the replacement of that unnamable child who never grows up.)

Margery wanted a family that was hermetically sealed, that would never change. But in Franconia Rob was often away balancing poems on his nose, and his semesters teaching in Amherst dragged the family with him. Carol married in 1923, Irma in 1926, Lesley in 1928—and it's no coincidence that over the course of these years Margery fell increasingly into depression. She became an invalid; she became what Rob and Elinor wanted, in spades—their baby, lying on the couch, being fed by them (when she was willing to eat), fussed over, temperature taken.

She pulled through, thank God. Rob and Elinor took her to England and France, and maybe that helped her decide there was a world beyond the walls worth looking into. Now she's training to be a nurse in Baltimore, and her letters, in the main, are cheerful and breezy. She likes the regimentation of a large hospital.

> I have never enjoyed anything in my life as much as I enjoy
> a feeling of being a lost private in the ranks just doing my
> allotted task.

But what he suspected about Franconia comes through in the letter he's holding now, arrived this morning.

> Dear Mama and Papa.
>
> A wonderful rainy night. With the window wide open, and the old, fragrant air coming in, all the places I have ever been come back to me just as they were then, not as I have found them to be since. The years between are as if they had never been, and for a moment I am sitting on the steps of the old stoop back of Lynches, inhaling horse-radish tops, listening to the pump inside, losing suction with every gasping pump of the old handle, and watching the sun slip down behind the ranges. Something lost behind *those* ranges, isn't there? Now that we are on the other side. You see what a little thing like rain does to me. Perhaps it's a good thing we don't have it more often.

Why does this affect him so strongly? There was always something about those mountain ranges. From the Lynch farm, on the western slope of Garnet Mountain, you had a clear view of five, range beyond range, and you could get the same view if you climbed Sugar Hill, behind the Franconia farmhouse. You were looking west, and the sun was always going down, and each range was mistier, vaguer than the one in front of it. It looked as if the ranges, one by one, were going to sleep, turning to dream.

When the Fitzgerald boy, Raymond, whom the Frost family knew, cut his hand off while sawing wood in his farmyard and died of the shock, it was those dreamy mountain ranges that kept coming back to Frost. They were the lump in his throat that started "Out, Out—":

> The buzz-saw snarled and rattled in the yard
> And made dust and dropped stove-length sticks of wood,
> Sweet-scented stuff when the breeze drew across it.

And from there those that lifted eyes could count
Five mountain ranges one behind the other
Under the sunset far into Vermont.

Did Raymond look up? Did the ranges make him dream about what
lay beyond them? Marjorie says that what lies beyond them is loss.
Five ranges, five fingers. Sixteen-year-old boy.

Frost never reads "Out, Out—" in public. Marjorie is now
twenty-five, and thank God it looks as though she'll make it, loss
and all.

91

THE GULLY HOUSE, SOUTH SHAFTSBURY, VERMONT

1936

When Margery died, Rob and Elinor gathered her poems and had
them privately printed. They titled the collection *Franconia*, after the
poem they placed third.

Franconia

> Long, long ago a little child,
> Bare headed in the snow,
> Lay back against the wind—and smiled,
> Then let her footsteps blow.
>
> Lighter than leaves they blew about,
> Until she sank to rest
> Down where no wind could blow her out,
> Deep in a mountain nest.

And to this day she's smiling there
With eyes alert and wild,
For she has lived on mountain air
And stayed a little child.

92

You kept looking.

You dreamed of the gap in the mountains, the hidden valley. You walked through the Dismal Swamp to the healing sea.

You read the parchment roll that said, *Flee from the wrath to come.* You peered across the wide field, and Evangelist asked, "Do you see yonder shining light?" You answered, "I think I do," and he said, "Keep that light in your eye."

You crossed the Ham Branch of the Gale River and walked up the road, and as you rounded the curve the fragile kite-white farmhouse appeared, the healing view of the Franconia Range in the east. The porch was unroofed and you knew in the twinkling of an eye that that would be changed. There must be shelter from rain, from snow, from fire and brimstone, while you sat for many years, for the rest of your life, on that porch and watched the streams carry the mountains to the sea.

You drove with directions from the general store at South Shaftsbury's one crossing and descended into the dip and rose, and the sturdy cottage was there on the right, barn-red clapboard atop thick gray stone, an apple orchard behind, a view of the Green Mountains before. You put in a furnace and ran pipes from a spring and planted apple trees of unforbidden varieties, and set out, on your knees, a thousand pine seedlings. When Carol married Lillian, you built the sheltering roof over their heads that your grandfather had refused to do for you—as a wedding gift, you gave Carol the farm outright, so that the farmer could be possessed by the land he possessed.

You wandered east across the fields, keeping the Green Mountains in your eye, and you discovered paths and followed them, raised a barbed-wire strand and lowered another, and when you rounded the knoll, you saw the ancient farmhouse, unpainted, the nine sway-backed barns, the scattered sheds and corn cribs. With a hill on its right and the knoll on its left, and a long view north (if the barns were knocked down) toward Mount Equinox and the North Pole, it sat comfortably in its saddle, its gully. You saw this in a moment and you bought it, and you swung a sledgehammer and knocked down barns with abandon, built dormers on the house, planted pine seedlings in the old pasture, dug a pond. You walked the 150 acres with acorns in your pocket, and when you found a clearing in the woods you thumbed a hole, dropped the seed, trod it with your heel. You built a retaining wall on the north side of the house and leveled the ground so you could sit by the front door for the rest of your life and watch the oak trees grow and the North Pole draw nearer.

Wade Van Dore, a younger poet, a wanderer, a sometime hired man, a thorough Thoreauvian, had done (truth be told) most of the work for you on the Gully House, and he deserved a hidden valley, too (none more so), his own five acres and independence, his own creature wife the world didn't know how to speak of, and you told him, "Go find yourself a farm and I'll pay for it." And Wade wandered through Vermont and Massachusetts, looking for a hilltop, a cabin, a spring, and at long last, lost, far in the back of the Berkshires, he found a place that was nearly perfect—the cabin was almost on the hilltop, it almost had a view—and you bought it for him. Wade slapped down rails of chestnut beams from a fallen barn, and laid across them old fence posts, and he took a lever longer than his long leg and single-handedly, like Bunyan, he rolled his house up the incline. It took a week, and every night his bedroom had a different view. The mountains across the valley rose in his window until on the last night he was on the stone ledge at the brow of the hill, and the view into the valley called Canaan was good. He brought his wife and kept her there.

You kept looking. You wanted nine bean-rows and a bee-loud glade. You wanted woodspurge with a cup of three. You wanted pale orchises and a bright green snake. You wanted a moon to follow you, a mountain spring to drink from, a local character to listen to. You wanted a view in front, a writing chair in the middle, an escape hatch behind. You wanted a return of Saturn's reign, Virgil's Golden Age.

> *cedet et ipse mari vector, nec nautica pinus*
> *mutabit merces: omnis feret omnia tellus*

Or, to give it living tongue:

> all trading will stop, all merchants leave their ships
> and the sea: every farm will produce every thing.

All of a farm it is.
You wanted to build walls, but you wanted to let down your defenses while building them. You wanted a door to your inner room, but you wanted it closed. Long ago you'd had a vision of the land you promised yourself:

> So desert it would have to be, so walled
> By mountain ranges half in summer snow,
> No one would covet it or think it worth
> The pains of conquering to force change on.
> Scattered oases where men dwelt, but mostly
> Sand dunes held loosely in tamarisk
> Blown over and over themselves in idleness.
> Sand grains should sugar in the natal dew
> The babe born to the desert, the sand storm
> Retard mid-waste my cowering caravans—

But the man from Porlock knocked. The babe *was* born to the desert—

incipe, parve puer, risu cognoscere matrem

—begin, dear child, to recognize your mother with a smile—
    —and wave to her, because your mother is dying.
  In the high plains of Montana, baby Robin was born and fledgling
Margery died. Years before, you'd seen it all, all of it:

> Your mother named you. You and she just saw
> Each other in passing in the room upstairs,
> One coming this way into life, and one
> Going the other out of life—you know?

Meeting and passing. Wave to each other, mother and child! A wave
offering is all you can give. No milk, no suckling. A desert.

> And thou shalt sanctify the breast of the wave offering, and
> the shoulder of the heave offering, which is waved, and
> which is heaved up, of the ram of the consecration

And for you, Orpheus, more guilt:

> Oh, should a child be left unwarned
> That any song in which he mourned
> Would be as if he prophesied?

When Marjorie died despite all your prayers, you cursed words,
and you found comfort in words. Praying that Elinor might survive
the blow, yet not knowing how, you clung to a poem by Matthew
Arnold.

> Far, far from here,
> The Adriatic breaks in a warm bay
> Among the green Illyrian hills

(And what should I do in Illyria? My daughter, she is in Elysium.)

And there, they say, two bright and aged snakes,
Who once were Cadmus and Harmonia,
Bask in the glens or on the warm sea-shore,
In breathless quiet, after all their ills

The summer after Marjorie's death, you took Elinor as far away as you could, you took her south to Florida, and farther south, to the Keys, and out along the chain, you kept fleeing, you took her to the very end, to Key West. And there at land's end you rented a house twenty feet from the warm sea-shore and the placid waters stretching unbroken to the red-eyed sunset.

There those two live, far in the Illyrian brakes!
They had stay'd long enough to see,
In Thebes, the billow of calamity
Over their own dear children roll'd,
Curse upon curse, pang upon pang,
For years, they sitting helpless in their home,
A grey old man and woman; yet of old
The Gods had to their marriage come,
And at the banquet all the Muses sang.

Therefore they did not end their days
In sight of blood; but were rapt, far away,
To where the west-wind plays,
And murmurs of the Adriatic come
To those untrodden mountain-lawns; and there
Placed safely in changed forms, the pair
Wholly forget their first sad life, and home,
And all that Theban woe, and stray
For ever through the glens, placid and dumb.

What worked for you didn't work for her. (You had the poem to cling to, and your own words, that endless supply of bubbles, to buoy you; you were placid and she was dumb; Elinor drowned in silence.) Since the South didn't help her, you struck out for the North, as far as America would allow, you passed Franconia, you forded a river and climbed out of its valley and crossed a marsh and ascended a hill. The mist parted, and you spied the lost hamlet: the crossroads, the cellar holes, the four last tumbledown houses, the overgrown cemetery, the granite sill (threshold to sumac and steeplebush) of a schoolhouse long gone. You'd seen the name surrounded by white on a map: Concord Corner. A wayside nook for your Harmonia. Your eye twinkled and you saw it all changed. Elinor would shed her skin here, she would be reborn, she would stretch and find herself at home, you and she would grow old as the Greeks together. You bought the Greek Revival house with the view of Shadow Lake at the bottom of the hill, you planted sugar maples along the road, and you bought the house next door (you would save it for a friend; you and the Friend would together build the wall between).

But nothing helped. Nine months later Elinor died in a rented room in Florida. You and she, the very day she collapsed, had found a house to buy for the winter months. (Concordia every summer, Illyria every winter.) She who never could take all the steps up from her private underworld, she died from climbing stairs, and Lesley and Carol blamed you, because Elinor had insisted that the two of you take the upper floor in the rented house, while Lesley and her girls took the apartment below. Yes, it was Elinor who insisted—but it was all for you. She said the sound of children's feet above you would disturb your work. Lesley was enough your daughter to take furious delight in wielding words: your poetry had killed her! And Carol was enough his mother's son to condemn more handily by saying nothing. He packed his bags and returned to the farm, his castle, that you'd given him. Where, two years later, in the kitchen that looked out on the old apple orchard, he shot himself.

By then you'd sold the Gully House. The floors were sea-blue, a color Elinor had chosen (and good Wade had painted); they were the waters she could cross without seasickness to her island of firelight. You couldn't stand to be there without her. And the house in Concord Corner? Oh, that you kept. But you had to keep off.

Irma lived there for a time, and by then your presence disturbed her. Her marriage was collapsing and she was descending step by step into her permanent home, the twilit antechamber to the house of the mad. You were the Plotter, the All-Powerful. You were practically God to her, and she hated God as powerfully as she clung to Him.

Do you see yonder shining light?
I . . . think I do.
Keep that light in your eye.

Is it a buoy you're swimming to, in the icy sea? And is that also you, back on the shore, the boy terrified that the old man won't make it? The water numbs you, you welcome the numbness. You keep the light in your eye, and when you reach the buoy and hug it, when you climb the ladder, you discover the rungs are verses, the buoy is another poem, a long one, obscure as Tom Eliot's stuff—it's his *Waste Land*, twenty-five hundred years before he wrote it. The book of Job.

Is it possible you're not quite human anymore? You're an Artifex, a machine for generating form. Maybe on the way to the buoy you died, and you've wakened in your self-promised land, an afterlife where the mind is on fire and the heart is ice.

> *A fair oasis in the purest desert.*
> *A man sits leaning back against a palm.*
> *His wife lies by him looking at the sky.*

Another world war is raging, many people you don't know (how very many people you don't know!) are dying, and Louis Untermeyer wants you to write propaganda, but you have your own soul to save. You write instead the forty-third chapter of Job.

> *The throne's a plywood flat, prefabricated,*
> *That God pulls lightly upright on its hinges*
> *And stands beside, supporting it in place.*

Your God says to Job,

I've had you on my mind a thousand years
To thank you someday for the way you helped me
Establish once for all the principle
There's no connection man can reason out
Between his just deserts and what he gets.

You call it *A Masque of Reason*, but it isn't really a masque, it's a play whose subject is the mask of reason, and also your own mask, which you wear for a reason. (Go on, keep playing with words. Joke your way through the most serious poem you ever wrote.) And Elinor is There! She has crossed to the safety of Art. On the public stage she speaks her most private thoughts, as she never did in the unstoried, unenhanced world:

I stood by Job. I may have turned on You. . . .
All You can seem to do is lose Your temper
When reason-hungry mortals ask for reasons.

Oh, there are all sort of jokes. There's a Kodak camera, and puns galore, and the Devil shows up looking like the bastard offspring of an Irish faerie and Yeats's jeweled nightingale. Job's Wife sums up the philosophy in the last line, when she lifts the Kodak to take everyone's picture:

You'd as well smile as frown on the occasion.

All your houses have been plagued, all your sheltering porches have burned. (*All my pretty ones? Did you say all? O hell-kite! All?*), so let a smile be your umbrella, hey? For the rain it raineth every day. Elinor is dead, and you crossed the wide field and lifted the barbed wire and you went down the path in the woods and found K., and you've written some of her into Job's Wife as well. You've given these two women of your life, joined in the person of the Wife, the name Thyatira, which in God's Book is the city that sheltered witches. Amid the laughter, your God says of Thyatira,

She wants to know why there is still injustice.
I answer flatly: That's the way it is,
And bid my will avouch it like Macbeth.

And you suppose it might as well be funny that if God exists, or even if He's just a literary character (and more and more you suspect it's the same thing), he reminds you most of the mad, haunted thane, of whom the witch said,

By the pricking of my thumbs,
Something wicked this way comes.

Do you see yonder shining light?
I think I do.
You walk up the dirt road from the state route out of Ripton, and Bread Loaf Mountain is on your right hand, and a pasture opens on your left (upland pasture! beautiful phrase!), and ahead you see a farmhouse, and in a moment, in the twinkling of an eye, you see it all changed, you prophesy like a male witch: an ell will be added, to make more space (maybe a wall) between K. and Ted, her husband-in-name, and you will live in the log cabin on the slope above, and you will keep chickens and a collie dog, you will plant a thousand pine trees, and every day you will take the path from the back of the cabin that goes out over the mountain.

93

After one of Robert Frost's inimitable lectures, the Younger Poet is thrilled to find himself in the great man's company for an evening of talk around a restaurant table. He strains to memorize every word. Frost says, "In the old days, I formed a habit of putting all unanswered mail into a large box until I should have the time to answer them. But when the box was filled, it was always a temptation to start a new box. Letters all the time—and sometimes from the most patient of letter-writers. And autograph-hunters. Continually people send me my books through the mail without enclosing return postage. They think I can well afford to do this. Why do they do it?"

Ah, fame! the Younger Poet thinks. And the burdens thereof. He resolves not to write any more letters to Frost.

Frost talks and talks, and it's all wonderful. While the others at the table tire, he seems only to gain energy. At one-thirty in the morning, they summon a taxi to take him back to his apartment. They crowd into the cab with him. He talks all the way, and when they arrive at his place, he shakes everyone's hand. As the taxi pulls away, the Younger Poet looks out the back window. Robert Frost is in his front hall, and through the glass door the Younger Poet can see him looking in his mailbox to see if there are any letters.

94

And now Jeanie's in jail. A druggist in Portland, Maine, called the police after she became hysterical in his shop. When the officers arrived, she thought they were criminals come to kidnap her for the white-slave trade. They had to subdue her by force. A doctor says she needs to be committed. Frost holds his head in his hands. Can he afford to pay for an asylum? Is she really insane? She's got her friend, her live-in companion (whatever you call her), Louie Merriam—equally eccentric and man-hating. They've managed to eke out an existence in their twilit world. Can't that go on?

He must go to Portland. He feels sick.

The last time he saw her he was in bed with influenza. It was Armistice Day. Jeanie had been teaching in a town north of Amherst, but the townspeople were persecuting her because she'd been flaunting her pro-German opinions. On Armistice Day she was in tears for the abdicated emperor, Kaiser Wilhelm. She stood up against the whole town. (They were the coarse and brutal world; she was spirit.) When she refused to salute the flag, they chased her out. She fled to Amherst in a taxi, burst into her brother's bedroom and harangued him while he lay there. She needed money for the driver, and would he find her another job, and why didn't he show more sympathy, he'd always been cold to her, and cruel!

The only man she loves is Kaiser Wilhelm. Isn't it funny—autocratic, belligerent, a man named William. Jeanie's lost him again.

95

The Old Bennington Church rises like sailcloth, clean-limbed clapboard blazing white in the sunlight. A perfect Vermont church. Too perfect for Frost. It reminds him of that museum village they've started in Sturbridge. Is that really a parishioner talking to a minister over by the door, or are they both actors waiting for the five o'clock bell? "He'll meet us by the gravesite," he says to Lillian and his grandson, Prescott. He means the minister, who is in fact something of an actor, a wily Scots-Italian who tricked Frost into contributing to his brag show four years ago, when the church was rededicated as a "colonial shrine," whatever that meant. They'd finished the historical restoration, which as usual meant stripping the building of its own history. Frost agreed to read a poem, thinking the affair would be all about poetry, but instead it was all about the minister and his rich donor friends.

But Elinor remarked on the church's beauty and she loved the view east toward the Green Mountains. When Frost grumbled, she said, wasn't he pleased his name was included on the pulpit plaque celebrating ten living Vermonters?

"Who are the other nine?" he said.

"Rob Frost," she scolded.

Frost walks through the graveyard, holding Elinor's ashes. Behind him, Prescott carries Carol's. The headstones are marble, half shrouded in the black mold that marble is liable to, pitted and blurred by rain. Turn to the right, then left, then farther down the slope to the edge of town, by the sugar maple. Two plots.

It's as though he was waiting. When Frost decided he couldn't bear to scatter Elinor's ashes at Derry, he and Carol at last bought these plots for the Frost family. (Gather them in, the wards of the wandering bard: Elliott from Derry, Marjorie from Montana, Jeanie from Maine.) There was some holdup on the deed. Frost didn't receive it until last October. He called Carol from Ripton to tell him they had a place for his mother. A week later, Carol killed himself.

So now he can lie with her. *You killed her, with your selfishness!* Well, no, let's be fair, it was Lesley who said that. But Carol thought it. That's why he hightailed it back to his farm. Frost sent a letter after him:

> There was nothing Elinor wanted more than to have you take satisfaction out of that home and farm. I wish you would remember it every day of your life.

Maybe Carol did. Maybe he felt it as another of his failures. Another wrong way Frost took with him.

It's been almost a year since. Frost was unsure what to do. Elinor didn't believe in churches. For three and a half years her urn had sat on a cupboard shelf in the Stone Cottage on Carol's farm. Why shouldn't it stay with Rob now, wander with him, to Ripton, Cambridge, Florida? But Carol wants his mother. And Lillian doesn't intend to wander.

Frost and Prescott set the urns on the grass. Frost nods to two workmen who are standing a few feet away, smoking, waiting to set the stones in place. All that's needed is the minister.

Something of an actor. Like most ministers. Elinor had no patience for them. Maybe that parishioner he's talking to is a donor. The organ fund, the Bible fund, the trick-the-poet fund. Prescott is staring across the Bennington valley toward the mountains, hands under his arms. He's sixteen years old. Was his father a cloud that's lifted? Or a shade tree cut down? Lillian is looking at Prescott. She told Frost that in all the years of their marriage not a day passed when Carol didn't talk of suicide. Nobody's speaking. "Where is he?" Frost says.

The sugar maple next to the plot is tinged at the top with red. Silvered bark, too young yet to split and curl. About Prescott's age.

Someday it will tower over the gravestones, drop leaves on them—flesh-colored hands, turning as they fall. "Where in hell is he?" (The workmen grin.) Frost looks at the two stones he ordered. No angels, no Biblical text. Just a poet's crown of laurel leaves framing the space for the names. He chose Barre granite. Five hundred years from now the laurel leaves, and the names of all the dead Frosts, will still be crisp.

We are gathered here— Yes, everyone except the goddamned minister. "We don't need any help to do what we came here for." Frost picks up Elinor's urn and puts it in the niche dug in the ground. "Prescott, that's your father's place. Put him there." Prescott's a good boy; he does what he's told. Lillian knows Frost too well to be shocked. "Cover 'em up, boys," Frost says to the workmen. They slide the two slabs off the pallets and lever them into place with rag-wrapped crowbars. Frost tips them. "Now don't give any of that to the pastor." Then to Lillian and Prescott: "Let's go."

Elinor would scold him: *Rob*. But they'd share a laugh later.

Frost hurries away from her ghost. Ah, the view. The view!

96

1963

Lillian told him, and to the Biographer it seems wonderfully typical of that ghoulish, crazy family. With relish he passes on the details to a surviving friend of Frost's: the old bastard in a snit couldn't wait for the minister, so he lifted the stone himself while his grandson slid his father's ashes into the niche. Then he had his grandson do the same for Elinor's ashes. What is this, *Wuthering Heights*?

97

It seems impossible that the sun should still be up. It was rising eighteen hours ago, when he took off from Moscow. Yet there it is, high in the west, bright in his eyes. "Could you answer a few short questions, Mr. Frost?"

Who's that? Stewart's holding his arm to keep him from keeling over. "Sure, sure. Go ahead."

"This way." They've commandeered a room in the terminal. Packed with reporters. Stewart whispers, "You don't have to—"

"No, I'm all right!" A seat is waiting; a microphone. Flashbulbs pop.

"Do you have anything for the president?" Who's asking? He can't see anything but spots in his eyes.

He says, "A secret message."

"Could you say what's in it?"

He shields his eyes. Where? He wags his finger. A swarm of young men smiling, hungry. Bear cubs. Cub reporters. "Oh no." More flashes. Someone comes up almost over the table and blinds him. He's alarmed, exhausted. But this is great fun. Great events, great time to be alive. K. will have to admit she's proud of him. "That's up to the president. I couldn't do that."

"When do you plan to go to the White House?"

"I don't plan. I wait for the president."

Other questions; Frost tries to stay focused. He has to be careful. At a press conference in Moscow right after he flew up from Gagra, he called Khrushchev a "ruffian." He meant it as a compliment, but some people misunderstood. They also misunderstood his saying

"Mending Wall" at one of his talks in Russia. Some idiots thought he was making a comment on the Berlin Wall. The press is always looking for juice, for sly digs. Blackguarding is their middle name. He's got to be careful. They want to bring what Khrushchev and he talked about down to a petty level, to proposals and rejections, to name-calling.

Khrushchev wouldn't cut the Knot for him. He had his own circumstances; so be it. But Frost and the premier understood each other. It was all on a high level. It's hard to put into words. But it was something K. would be proud of—Frost and the most powerful man in the world, agreeing on what's best in human nature, human action. Honest, not prettied up; a ruffian, yes. Not like the country-club liberals who talk and talk. Khrushchev knows that. He told that joke about liberals, the one Gorky told to Tolstoy, or maybe it was Tolstoy who told it to Gorky—interesting to find the old powerhouse so bookish—about how liberals are like the bald-headed row at a leg show, enjoying thinking about doing something they don't have the ability to do. It's exactly Frost's opinion; it shows how much he and the premier think alike. "Khrushchev said he feared for us because of our lot of liberals," Frost says. "He said we were too liberal to fight. I suppose he thought we'd stand there for the next hundred years saying, 'On the one hand—but on the other hand.'"

He takes a few more questions. The flashbulbs go off like fireworks and he can hardly sit up straight, but they're all grinning, and it's been a great success. The old man survived his trip to Russia and came home in glory.

98

The *Washington Post* lies on Kennedy's desk. On the front page:

FROST SAYS KHRUSHCHEV SEES U.S. AS "TOO LIBERAL" TO DEFEND ITSELF

Kennedy sits in the rocking chair that's supposed to help with his fucking back. The effects of his second hot shower of the day are wearing off, and the hungry red pain is climbing up the ladder, rung by rung. He's furious. "Why did he have to say that?"

Udall struggles to answer. "I think—"

"Khrushchev never said it—?"

"No. The translator assured me. I—I think he was paraphrasing, in his own way, a comment the premier did make. A general comment about the decline of the West."

"Well *fuck*! He should keep his paraphrases to himself. Give an egomaniac a microphone. As it is, half of Congress wants me to invade Cuba tomorrow. They'll use this! It makes me look soft. It makes everything worse."

99

Yea, though I walk through the valley of the shadow of death, I will fear no evil: for thou art with me

Really? Who? Rob is alone in the hospital room. Elinor is resting at the hotel, after watching all night by Margery's bedside. Margery is here, but not here.

For we are but of yesterday, and know nothing, because our days upon earth are a shadow

Nothing to do but wait. The doctors now admit there's little hope. (They mean no hope.)

If thy children have sinned against him, and he have cast them away for their transgression; if thou wouldest seek unto God betimes, and make thy supplication to the Almighty; if thou wert pure and upright; surely now he would awake for thee

Oh yes, Friend, Comforter? Does God sleep? Rob calls that blasphemy. It's what Elijah said of Baal, when he mocked the false worshippers.

There's no mystery, Elinor says. God doesn't exist.

But does fiction, then, not live? Oh, don't say so. Rob has devoted his life to the contrary religion.

Margery murmurs. She does that. She's been doing that for six weeks. Rob leans over the bed. She's as thin now as when she was sunk in nervous exhaustion, six years ago. Face flushed. Her hair very black, very heavy; from the pregnancy, from the sweat. Her temperature reached 110 degrees this morning. The doctors say it's the highest fever ever recorded at the clinic. Go, Margery! And yet she lives. For six weeks they've tortured her. At first they were optimistic—they had a new serum for her type of infection—and she proved them wrong. Now they're pessimistic, and every morning she proves them wrong again. They have no idea how much suffering she can stand. (Her mother's daughter.)

Go, Margery. Go.

Rob leans close. "Margery," he says. Her eyes flutter open and she murmurs. He puts out his hand and touches her lightly. "You," he says. Then he touches his own chest. "Me." He touches her again. "You." And himself. "Me."

For days he talked to her about her healthy, beautiful baby, Robin; about her husband, who was holding up, but looking forward, oh, waiting so patiently and lovingly, for her return home (poor Willard, paralyzed by shock and panic, is not holding up); about Carol's and Lillian's health, and their boy, Prescott; about spring in Montana and spring in Vermont (two states named for mountains, range beyond range). But she understood nothing. She slept, or tossed, or was on a journey, or made nursing motions with her mouth, or her hand grasped air or her fingers fluttered, or her arm lifted slowly, and then slowly, dreamily fell. Doctors came and went, infusions flushed in and dripped out, her temperature fluctuated, her face turned red, turned white, turned red.

He simplified what he said. It's sunny today. Today is Tuesday. You have a baby girl. You're at the Mayo Clinic. They're doing everything they can. I'm here with you. I'm doing nothing useful.

But none of it got through. Finally he reduced it to "You" and "Me," and occasionally she seemed to respond to that with a ghostly smile, or her eyes would focus on his for a moment, or the hand instead of grasping and releasing empty air would make a move toward his, so that when he put his thumb in her grip it seemed as though she'd met him halfway; or he just imagined all of it, he made a pleasing fiction that he was determined to believe, a cave with painted walls to hide in. Margery. Margery. He finds himself, in the long silences, saying her name over and over.

> What was it about her name? Its strangeness lay
> In having too much meaning. Other names,
> As Lesley, Carol, Irma, Marjorie,
> Signified nothing.

It was the only name Lesley, as a child, couldn't spell right.

> sundy we took are wack all of us margery and i and carol
> and irma papa and mama we all went out in the big grov
> margery liket it very much

That must have been fall of 1905. Margery was born March 29 that year.

> mama made some new close for a new baby becas we thot
> we would have a new baby

Robin was born March 16. Margery was not quite twenty-nine years old. A healthy baby girl, the cowboy doctor said. Is that what's lost beyond the mountain ranges? The Wild West, Willard's country, birth by the campfire, sand blowing, night surrounding, the weird sounds of pike or maybe pixie coming out of the darkness. The doctor rides up and dismounts, slaps his chaps; his black bag creaks in his dirty hand.

The West saved her, and now it's going to kill her. Colorado air cured her of her tuberculosis, it woke her up; she came alive enough to fall in love three times—first a doctor at the sanatorium bruised her heart; then a fellow talked all sorts and kinds of love to her, until she discovered he was only trying to get in with the famous Robert Frost. (His shadow—all his children have wilted in it; his strength, their weakness. *Keep me as the apple of the eye, hide me under the shadow of thy wings*.) "I never dreamed that any man could be so low, and at the same time so attractive," Margery wrote home. Her ironic voice in that. She had her mother's grimness, but she salted it. "Don't worry!" she commanded from Baltimore, when she was studying to be a nurse. She'd mentioned eyestrain, and Elinor and Rob nearly jumped on the next train. "If I really came down sick abed and almost dead I would have you duly notified."

> and margery la very still and lookt up in the tall pins but at
> last she gut fusy and mama had to hold her

She also had Colorado to thank for Willard. Lucky number three. He was an archaeology student at the university. "He is a dear, kind, and considerate man," she wrote home, and she was right. Willard's a good fellow, a far better choice than Lesley's playboy, or Irma's prig. He brought her home to Billings and married her, and for nine months she made her home on the dusty plain, gained weight, harbored her secret, and was happier than she'd ever been.

Willard the widower. Unnested Robin lying at the foot of the maple tree.

> and margery la very still and lookt up in the tall pins

Does he keep saying her name because he doesn't quite believe that this dying woman with the rank hair is the baby born at Derry, who fussed for the bottle and then lay still, who cried when she saw a steamroller, who drank the water in the tin washtub at Christmas instead of bobbing for an apple, who ran across the road after the other children, calling, "Wait for me!"? Everyone knows you can't be in two places at the same time, but Rob has always found it hard to believe that he could be in two places at two different times. As a boy he used to lie awake at night and recall where he'd been during the day. He could picture it all in detail, yet couldn't quite believe any of it; and the more vividly he pictured it, the less he believed.

Maybe you could say that he doesn't quite believe in Time.

Or maybe you could say that Time is the only thing he believes in.

He is Here. Today is today. Out the window is sunlight and a blue sky, and inside, the smell of medicine and metal and urine. He looks at his daughter and knows that she will die, and he knows that he will survive it. Whereas he can't say the same of Elinor. What does that mean?

He's always thought that Elinor was the one who stayed underground after Elliott died, but maybe all along it was he, locked away in a place where the death of another child would hurt, but not enough. Hasn't he already written about this?

> I long for weight and strength
> To feel the earth as rough
> To all my length

Did he replace the love of his children, whom death could touch, with the love of words?

> As Lesley, Carol, Irma, Marjorie,
> Signified nothing

He's always told himself that it was the birth of his children, year by year, that brought him back step by step into the upper air. But maybe, all along, it wasn't them at all, but the poems he wrote at the kitchen table while they slept, each line a rung, each verse a ladder pointing through this material realm, this tempting World Apple Tree of ours, toward heaven. It's as though his heart, long ago, crept too near a blast and went a little deaf. He sits on one side of a wall of scar tissue, and can only toss words to his daughter on the other side.

You (hot).

Me (cold).

He leans close again. "Margery." More than a hundred young people in Billings volunteered for the blood transfusions that have kept her alive, that have kept her suffering for so long. "Margery." She opens her black eyes. Her pupils like yawning well-shafts.

"You," he says, for the last time. "Me."

She smiles faintly. Her nursing mouth puckers and pinches, forms words, almost inaudible. "All the same."

He brings his ear close to her mouth. "You and me the same?"

She frowns, gives a head shake that seems, though small, to signal a vast struggle. He pulls his own head back. Her eyes focus on his. Her mouth works again, and she murmurs, "Always the same."

100

SUGAR HILL, NEW HAMPSHIRE

SEPTEMBER 1934

Frost is dreaming.

He's flying a plane.

He's trying from the air to find a farm to buy.

His fifth farm.

Nothing seems right.

Farms don't seem right.

Plane doesn't seem right.

He's lost his landing gear.

Hm. Must keep moving.

No farms for him, just air! Pollen-free air!

But he's running out of gas.

All gone!

Nose tips down.

Farm, anyone?

What do pilots call it, when you descend with the power off, fluttering the ailerons?

(Hendricks told him. A pretty phrase.)

He flutters the ailerons. The plane rocks. The ground comes up fast.

"Falling leaf," they call it.

Farm? Field?

He banks the plane, he falls, he skims the tops of trees.

An opening. A field with white stones. A graveyard.

He hauls up on the shaft. He cries in fright.

The plane comes in fast. He goes back and forth, row after row, knocking down every gravestone in the place.

101

A clear windy evening. In the orange maple woods down the slope and toward the sunset from his Sunset Avenue house, it seems all the leaves are falling at once. The annual genocide. He steps on the dessicated bodies, kicks through the pyres.

> Thy leaves have ripened to the fall;
> Tomorrow's wind, if it be wild,
> Should waste them all

Why not tonight? Get it over with. Bring on November! Ready December! The millionth first snow will paste down the million dead leaves, and he'll lift his knee for the sixtieth time to step on the snow. Which by March will be—where?

Waste. He thinks of his little orchard at Derry, how when the apples finally came they poured down on him in an avalanche.

> For I have had too much
> Of apple-picking: I am overtired
> Of the great harvest I myself desired

Overtired. Awful tired.

He looks with impatience and disgust at the sea around him of dead and dying leaves, and a new word occurs to him: "autumn-tired." He remembers a dream he had a few weeks ago, about a plane. "Falling leaf." He thinks of Margery, and his heart flutters like a leaf on a branch, wind-shaken, threatening to let go.

He stands still, closes his eyes. The wind is louder. Falling leaves touch his face. Fingertips on his eyes, urging him to cry; tickling his lips to make them tremble. Siren song.

> Come away, O human child

They're speaking to the dried leaf in his chest, leaf to leaf. Gently urging it under.

> Child—are you lief to leave?

He opens his eyes; kicks his way homeward. The sun is setting, and he's got a poem to write.

102

KEY WEST, FLORIDA

MARCH 1935

Frost has come to a land where there has never been a frost. He's deep among strangers: the summer people, the bathing-suit crowd, the beachcombers. He clambers over dead coral along the empty shore at midnight (the summer people are drinking in the hotel), and he wonders if that's Canopus, that bright star above the haze on the southern horizon. Second-brightest star, after Sirius—the two rivals of heaven.

But in the island's small and derelict library, he can find no book of star maps.

He and Elinor arrived here by train, crossing a shallow sea on bridges so narrow you couldn't see them from the window. It was like walking on water. It was the only way Frost could spirit her to an island without putting her on a boat; she swore she'd never sail again after her seasickness going to England and France in '28. But she got seasick anyway, by association of smell.

Angling inland, he walks on a million dollars' worth of government sidewalks past empty speculators' lots. Bust town. Half the population gone in the last ten years. He stoops to feel the spiny grass. Strange southern species.

> As for the grass, it grew as scant as hair
>   In leprosy; thin dry blades pricked the mud
>   Which underneath looked kneaded up with blood

He walks on, wondering why "Childe Roland" comes to him. Perhaps his punning mind is at fault. Childe, child. His child is dead. And God, or conscience, or some useless, brainless voice, says to the grieving parent: *Child, child.*

Elinor lies in the rented house, twenty feet from the glassy sea. He says they came south for her angina (medical Latin for a broken heart). She says they came for his grippe (medieval French for a choking rage). She says the moist tropical air is bad for her. She has taken on Marjorie's invalidism. Her memorial; the only piece of Marjorie she could preserve. And who can blame her. Oh, she does get out of bed. She does it early while he's still asleep, so she can be back under the sheet before he's up. The goal is to keep from keeping him company. She tells him from her bed that the clouds at dawn were something to behold. Not for lazy late risers like him!

He leaves her and plays tennis. He smashes the ball straight at his opponent's chest, sees with glee the chicken-dance as the man trips back and tries too late to interpose an awkward wing. The courts belong to the Casa Marina Hotel, and in their eyes he's riffraff, trudging along the line of coconut palms from his thirty-eight-dollar-a-month converted garage perched just above the sea wrack to play on their property. What *is* he? they wonder. An unelectrified rustic with a submarginal mind? Didn't they see him hugging his family Bible at the Scopes trial? He had Holt send some of his books to the hotel on consignment. Not that a winter poet would sell more than two or three. But he wanted this crowd to know, he might be a rustic, but after a hell of a lot of slow thought he could put two words together, and he was willing to have his books read even by rich people.

Speaking of rich people, Wallace Stevens is here. Staying at the Casa Marina. He can sip his afternoon cocktail and look down from his balcony on Frost doing his damnedest to kill his opponent on the tennis court. Frost met him for the first time the other day. A glossy presence; could be a college president. He hides his poetry from his country-club pals like a mistress kept in a boudoir near the cathouse. "The trouble with you, Frost," he said, "is that you write too much."

"Oh come now, Stevens," Frost said, "I've written just as little as you have."

That's a true fragment from the Age of Eliot, the emperor who's clothed himself in less verse than anybody.

> Because I could not write
> Because I could not
> Because I

The sound of the rabbit going back in the hat.

At dinner in the hotel, Stevens got drunk and made passes at the waitress. Frost excused himself early and went out walking. *Who are you?* Canopus asked, twinkling.

When Rob and Elinor first arrived, the rental agent took them to see the Administrator. The who? they asked. Julius Stone, a grinning, bustling man with white shorts and exceptionally furry legs. Elinor called him the Dictator. Rob called him the Rehabilitor in Chief. It turned out the Federal Emergency Relief Administration had come to the island's . . . well, relief. Key West had already died thrice—first when the piracy was stamped out, then when the nimble fleet of "salvagers" were ordered to desist, finally when the cigar business moved to Tampa—and Franklin D. had decided to stretch his benevolent wing over the outcropping of dead coral and give it one more life to lose. Thus the exquisite concrete sidewalks. And the interest in rehabilitating the citizenry. Cars are now supposed to have mufflers; drivers are encouraged to have licenses; dogs are introduced to leashes, children to the rod; someone has even floated the idea of sewers. And prospective renters are questioned to see if they're good enough for the heavenly scheme.

So Rob sat before the man with the furry legs, who asked, *Who are you?* It seems every time he gets near the border of America they put him on trial. Should they let him in? Kick him out? They were looking at his clothes. They were wondering about his pocketbook. I'm a Vermonter, he might have said. I'm from Massachusetts. I'm a Californian. Which would be modesty and which would be boast? He refused to boast. I came through Ellis Island, so I must be an immigrant. I'm a Devonshire Frost. No, I'm a Lincolnshire Frost. My coat-of-arms is a squirrel up a pine tree. Bark at me all you want. The house-renting clerk, a lady, said, "Mr. Frost, you remind me of a real gentleman we had in here yesterday, a Mr. Tibbets from Maine." I'm from Maine, too. Maybe you've heard of my ancestor, Charles Frost of Eliot, Maine. He was at least as much a gentleman as Mr. Tibbets, I'll have you know he was a major in the militia, *arma virumque cano*. He invited the local Indians to a barbecue and massacred them all. Well, not quite all. A couple of survivors killed him one Sunday on his way home from church. They later dug up his body and hanged it just to make sure. (Back then, everyone was gentle.) "Yes," he said, "my name is often mistaken for Tibbets on the telephone."

Oh la! A comedian! What do you do for a living? they asked.

You tell me. I'm old enough to be retired, but from what? Farming? Teaching? Would you believe I get paid for talking at random? Maybe I should charge you for this delightful interrogation. How about my first month's rent?

A man in the back of the office piped up, "Hey, you aren't the Frost who writes poetry for the University of Michigan?"

Just for them, yes. The shepherd in his campus.

> Hail, Michigan, heaven's brightest star!
> (And by the way, where's my company car?)

"There are five Frosts writing poetry," he said. "Two men and three women. I'm not one of the women."

They let him go with a fine—his winter's rent in advance. Me for the North! Call me Sirius. Let Stevens be Canopus, he likes this Southern haze.

So the dog walks the streets every night, tail between his legs. He hears a Spanish or Creole shout in the next block and heads in the opposite direction. He pokes his nose here and there, he sniffs at the stinks. He circles thrice, trampling the grass, before settling down with a groan. Or say (star that he is) he orbits. He gravitates back to the beach below the rented bungalow. He looks southwest across a sheet of shining black water. Stars above, stars reflected in the glass below, and between them, far off, five lighthouses strung along the outlying reefs. Behind him in the house is the silent woman, who didn't want to come here. "I am sure we don't want to lie around on beaches, anyway." Of course not, Marjorie is dead and their suffering must be complete.

> Alive? he might be dead for aught I know,
>   With that red gaunt and colloped neck a-strain,
>   And shut eyes underneath the rusty mane;
>   Seldom went such grotesqueness with such woe;
>   I never saw a brute I hated so;
>   He must be wicked to deserve such pain.

No, she doesn't want to lie on the beach. Yet she complains that the servants from the hotel gather on her and Rob's private pocketful of sand to tan in the afternoon. "But you know they can't tan on the hotel beach," he wants to say to her. "That's reserved for Stevens."

Meanwhile, Frost takes comfort in numbers. The island is three miles long, one wide, one hundred fifty south of Miami, three hundred south of Cairo, a hundred out to sea, and one foot above sea level. Winter rainfall is six inches. The temperature ranges from seventy to eighty. The waves break twenty feet from his door. He sleeps under one sheet. He's just turned sixty-one. The world thinks he's sixty. Woodspurge has a cup of three. He has three children left.

At one in the morning, while Elinor sleeps, he writes a letter to the strong one, to Lesley.

> You make the crowd around you, even some of the better ones, look as if they had wrinkles in their souls. They may be better than they seem to us. Their ways however are not our ways. You should not be broken to fit their mould.

He wants to tell her about the waves breaking twenty feet from his door. But he has never paced it off, and Lesley deserves accuracy. She alone among his children stamps both her feet in this world. He leaves the letter on the table, goes out into the warm night and counts steps down to the water. Stevens shines glossily in the south.

Well hang him for a liar. It's seventy-five feet. He returns to the house and sits back in his chair. While he's arranging his homemade writing board he notices a grass burr clinging to his pant leg, trying to mate with it. Tenacious seed.

> I think I never saw
> Such starved ignoble nature; nothing throve:
> For flowers—as well expect a cedar grove!
> But cockle, spurge, according to their law
> Might propagate their kind, with none to awe,
> You'd think; a burr had been a treasure-trove.

The sort of treasure a child can appreciate. Lesley's daughters, Elinor and Lee, are five and three. Frost eases the burr off the woolen fabric.

The water is exactly seventy five feet from our door by measurement made just now while the letter waited. Enclosed for Lee and Elinor is a grass burr I got making it.

The burr grips his thumb in an urgent kiss of microscopic lips. He pries it off, drops it in the envelope. A tenacious seed for his own tenacious seed.

103

BENNINGTON, VERMONT
AUGUST 1963

The world claimed him, but she's got him now. Lesley telephoned the secretary of the graveyard association only the day before, lying about special circumstances, emergency, whatever it took, and so got an appointment, and now she's here. Full summer, and the urn is warm in her hands. Nobody but herself, a friend as witness, a man from the association, and two gravediggers. She urged discretion on the secretary, but who knows—perhaps even now the Bennington paper is scrambling to get its arts man up the hill; perhaps reporters are forming convoys on the highways out of New York City and Boston. She'd better hurry.

The bulletins from his hospital room, the press conferences: it was as though the president were dying. A reporter broke into the room after it was all over and stole some of his personal items. Relics. "I think of you as Robert Coeur de Lion," she wrote him after she saw him in December. That was when he'd had his first embolism, when they thought he was going to die right then. She spent three days by his side. But he rallied, and she had to return to New York. She had a career, after all. Kathleen Morrison happily went back to operating the drawbridge. Kay's career was vampirism.

Robert Coeur de Lion. Lesley meant it. Her father was the dashing king, heroic in tragedy—also, like the other lionheart, never at home, yearned after from afar. And of course held captive by the enemy. Father spoke of the Pendragons in Russia, the two guides who no doubt were spies. Kay and her daughter, Anne, were the Pendragons of Father's last years. Lesley didn't blame Anne so much. Anne had known Father when she was a young girl, and Father was always splendid with children. His jokes, his toy javelins, his skipping stones. But Kay was a gold-digger and a lion-hunter. No better than a prostitute.

"You're something of a Lesley de Lion yourself," Father wrote in a letter he managed to sneak across the moat.

> I have deferred not a little in my thoughts to the strength I find in you and Prescott and Lee and very, very affection-ately to K Morrison and Anne Morrison Gentry, who are with me taking this dictation in the hospital.

Very, very affectionately: that was for Kay's ears—if she didn't just add the words herself. *Who are with me taking this dictation:* that was for Lesley. In other words, *I can't speak freely, my captors are present.* But a captivity he wanted. There's no fool like an old fool, hey?

But Lesley's got him now. God, the telegrams that poured in all that month—the world claiming him, playing to his vanity. Even the Russians had been Frost-bitten. Some Communist lackey poet ca-bled, "I am happy that you live on earth." What did he know of Fa-ther? He was playing to his tsar, some byzantine maneuver to stay out of Siberia. But she's got him now, and she's fooled everybody. The whore's not here, or Father's court jester Untermeyer, or his creepy biographer. Famous ashes. Would some reporter or fan try to steal them? Eat them?

Are they coming? *Tell 'em I like orchids,* Father said when someone asked him what he wanted in the hospital. And the orchids came in a deluge. They covered the chairs and crowded the bed. Father lay among them like a dying nature-god.

Lesley places the urn in the niche. Oh, Papa. She holds on to her friend and cries for a while. Then smiles at a thought. *Stay where you are until our backs are turned!* She turns away. Oh, the lovely view. The Green Mountains are gray in the summer haze. The Long Trail begins there. One of Lesley's first published pieces was about the hike she and her siblings made in the twenties, the first backpackers to traverse the entire trail. Father always said he wanted to die on the trail, not in a hospital. When he died, even the Pendragons weren't there. Kay could keep everyone else out, but—oops!—she had her own husband's bed to sleep in. So Father died alone.

Lesley can hear the gravediggers behind her, wrestling the granite slab into place. Because of the short notice, Father's name hasn't been added to the stone. In a way, that pleases her. Is he there, is he not? Let them guess. "Let's go," she says to her friend, turning abruptly up the path.

When she was a child, she was fascinated by the Brontës. Living in seclusion, strangers to the world, looked on as strange, all of them writing plays, poems, novels, family newspapers. Living half mad in their imaginations. And as a child she imagined (of course) that she would be Charlotte, Anne, and Emily all rolled into one. But the Frosts turned out to be a version of the Brontës in which the father, Patrick, was the world-conquering writer, while Charlotte, Anne, Emily, and Branwell were condemned to live in his footsteps, his footnotes. Half mad, whole mad.

She's at the gate. Beyond the iron spikes, she can see it, her long, dusty trail. She will spend the rest of her life answering questions from reporters and doctoral students.

Here they come.

104

The Biographer sniffs: couldn't Lesley at least have bestirred herself to arrange for a marker for her father?

105

NAPLES, ITALY

30 B.C.E.

It is right that Orpheus should turn, that Eurydice be lost forever. To turn, to be tempted, is human, and only the inhuman, the unfeeling, can have any sort of victory over Death. Publius Vergilius Maro, shy bachelor, slow of speech, shambling unsociable bear, licks into shape his precious cubs, these two lines he strives to perfect for this exact moment, when Orpheus looks back:

cum subita incautum dementia cepit amantem,
ignoscenda quidem, scirent si ignoscere manes

a sudden madness seizes the mind of the lover—
a thing forgivable, if Death knew anything of forgiveness

106

Alone in his townhouse on Brewster Street, Frost wakes. He looks at his Baby Ben. It's 3:00 a.m. For a few moments he stares at the ceiling. He can still hear it. He heaves himself up. His hams ache. He puts on a bathrobe and walks to the window. Not a soul out. Cambridge, Massachusetts, without a question. Yet he can still hear it, through the surf-hiss of blood in his ears—like geese who, in midair, suffered a change, lost their bearings, fell as changelings into the sea, then gathered for precarious refuge on a rocky point three thousand miles away. The crying of seals.

107

Frost kept going on farewell tours, then doing it again the next year, around and around like a planet. It seemed he'd live forever. Then he died.

He gave a farewell reading to four thousand at Ann Arbor in 1962, then died in 1963, and in 1964 someone in the theater program at the University of Michigan woke up crying out in fright, "Is the show really over?" Frost's audience was larger than ever, and if he didn't exist anymore, he'd have to be reinvented. So the theater department commissioned a piece, and the Younger Poet wrote it.

An Evening's Frost has four characters: Narrator, The Woman, Young Frost, Elder Frost. All words spoken on stage by Frost (or "Frost")—poems, letters, snatches of his conversation—were really written or spoken by Frost. But the Younger Poet would admit (if anyone thought to ask him) that his "Frost" is not quite Frost. His "Frost" is *his* Frost. *Frost is for everyone, for poets too.* The Younger Poet's Frost, for example, doesn't break off in the middle of a poem to cackle, "Now *that's* a good line." He doesn't snipe self-diminishingly at T. S. Eliot and his elite fighting corps of university professors. He just reads his poems. His quiet poems, his light poems, his magnificent poems. And he reads the terrible poems that Frost never read in public: "Home Burial" and "Out, Out—":

> They listened at his heart.
> Little—less—nothing!—and that ended it.
> No more to build on there. And they, since they
> Were not the one dead, turned to their affairs.

An Evening's Frost premiered in Ann Arbor in February 1965, and was a great success. It came to New York City in October and the run has just been extended for the second time. The theater management reports that twenty thousand students and teachers from five hundred schools across nine states have seen the play. It would seem that—as the Younger Poet always liked to believe—*his* Frost is not incompatible with the public's Frost. Though he made the taste of Frost more bitter, the whale still swallowed him.

He stands in the back of the packed house, listening. "Frost," wrapped in art's cured hide, is tougher than Frost. When "Frost" reads "Home Burial," it calls up for the Younger Poet the flayed Frost who couldn't read it, and he finds himself moved to tears.

The reviews have been good. But one thing the Younger Poet has noticed. Though the actor playing Young Frost has a substantial part, the reviews tend only to mention Elder Frost. Perhaps the whale can digest a battered Frost, hair turned white by more than age. But a fledgling Frost, an unfinished Frost? That, it vomits up.

108

Going north into the land of magic, where no ragweed grows, summer after summer, it saves Frost's life. He climbs up from the ocean depths, the Derry mucus, to take a breath of air in the White Mountains. In Bethlehem, in the long wooden hotels for the hay-fever refugees, it's all Anglo and Hebrew, but here on the south road toward Franconia, on Garnet Mountain, the families are Irish, and Frost loves them, loves the sound of their talk, loves the mountain and his children and his wife, loves the air deep in his lungs. His mother's Scottish was romance and dream; his father's English, chaos and tragedy; this mountain aerie, among the Celts, is his mother's country. Six weeks each summer, while Guay takes care of the Derry farm (he manages it better than Frost, so the longer Frost stays away the more his farm prospers), the children play in the fields and hunt for berries, and there are baseball games with the locals and walks down into Franconia for ice cream and evening gatherings of Lynch cousins and neighbors on the farmhouse porch (the Frosts stay every year with the Lynches), and since this is Celtic country, everyone tells stories and sings—they sing in parts, all of them. Frost is fascinated by the way Celts speak in a natural iambic, more than the English, who fall so often into anapests. Is it some echo of the old language most of them no longer speak?

Mrs. Lynch is telling Frost late one night, under the hanging lamp, moths tapping the porch screen, of how hard it is to get Mr. Lynch out of his newspaper. (A favorite story; there are many chapters.) There was the day the cow got out. "I say to him, 'The cow is in the corn.' 'Whose corn's she in?' says he, still reading in his paper. 'Our own, you may be sure,' I say, and he: 'Go drive her into someone else's then!'" With her rum voice, she laughs. A fine-looking dark-eyed woman, fifty years old, mother of four. And John Lynch, sixty, husband of thirty years, gazes long at her, deadpan behind his silver beard.

For Frost: bliss.

Bliss.

109

SOUTH SHAFTSBURY, VERMONT

JUNE 1938

Out through the fields and the woods
And over the walls I have wended

—all his poems have been about her, *to* her—

And lo, it is ended

Her ashes are in the cupboard.

But when she got there
The cupboard was bare
And so the poor dog had none

The cupboard is in his bedroom in Carol's house. Carol set up the room for him. Because he can't sleep in the Gully House. Elinor's presence, or absence, or both, is too strong.

He wends through fields and woods. He wakes in the room with the cupboard that holds her ashes, downs a raw egg and walks out—out, out—avoiding Carol, who might be in the orchard or the barn, he crosses the road (why?), he gets to the other side, he keeps the Green Mountains in his eye and heads up through unkempt cow pasture, skirts sloughs, tramps along ditches, ducks through barbed wire, reaches the Gully farm. He wanders through the woods, walks along the perimeter to see if anyone's been stealing his trees, hopes for a fight, circles back to the knoll to see if Mount Equinox is still standing, passes the front of the house, circles to the back, circles to the front again, walks through the house, across her floors, past her hearth, out the back, climbs Buck's Cobble to check on the Taconic Range, detours to see his paper birches, angles northwest and down to the lower edge of his property, he's got 150 acres, did he check the forty-seventh, the 105th?, the oak tree in the clearing, the wineglass elm, the pipe from the spring? and on down the public road to the crossroads where the country store is, then south along the Bennington road, down into the dip where the creek flows through the culvert, and up, and the Stone Cottage, Carol's house, appears on the right, and there's ninety acres here to wander and wend in (avoiding Carol, who's cutting pea sticks or building apple crates or has his torso under the automobile). Derry was thirty acres, Franconia fifty, and here he and Carol have 240; he's a lord, ain't he, a squire, a success, a self-made man, if his mother could see him now.

Last week—two weeks ago?—he went to Derry and saw it spoiled, no place for Elinor's ashes, so he put them in the cupboard, an urn on a shelf, otherwise empty, and he doesn't know what to do.

There was an old woman who lived in a shoe

He goes out and walks around in circles all day and comes back, and the ashes are still there.

Ring around the rosie. All fall down.

I watched her face to see which way
She took the awful news

271

When he reads Emily Dickinson, he sometimes wonders if something in her voice might have been Elinor's if Elinor had kept writing poetry after high school. Dickinson was an agoraphobe. Dressed in ghostly white. Elinor White. She sat next to him in school, a new girl. Extremely pretty, with eyes dark as wellwater. (His family was all sky-eyed lunacy.) She'd been kept at home for two years with slow fever. He remembers her eyes on him when he spoke in class, and she seemed to like him, and he started to speak in class for her. He liked her because she was even shier than he was. Then one day in class between one show-off word and the next, he realized he loved her absolutely and forever.

Paul was what's called a terrible possessor

But possessed by what he possesses. White and Frost.

You see the snow-white through the white of frost?

It was poetry, and therefore it was Fate. He weaved a circle round her thrice, slipped the circle on her finger, possessed her in the high grass by the Merrimack, out of whose water maybe she'd just emerged. She was his white lily.

He played with her name in his poems—

> There amid lolling juniper reclined,
> Myself unseen, I see in white defined
> Far off the homes of men

never obviously (she never would have allowed that)

> Our faltering few steps on
> To white rest, and a place of rest

and "white" of course was sometimes the only correct word (he's always been a black-and-white poet, not a color poet)

He thought that I was after him for a feather—
The white one in his tail

but he's never once used the word without thinking, somewhere in the back of his mind, of her, his tabula rasa, on whom he wrote, for whom he spoke (would she let him).

Elliott died, and the gap it opened between them never closed.

I watched her face to see which way
She took the awful news,
Whether she died before she heard—

He felt as though he were calling to her, never quite reaching her, or ever quite clearly seeing her.

One drop fell from a fern, and lo, a ripple
Shook whatever it was lay there at bottom,
Blurred it, blotted it out. What was that whiteness?
Truth? A pebble of quartz?

He wondered if all he really had of her was what he made of her.

like some snow-white
Minerva's snow-white marble eyes
Without the gift of sight

Maybe Frost and White are poetry's words for the artist and his raw material.

Paul sawed his wife
Out of a white-pine log

Was she therefore quite human? Or just the projection of his longing?

<pre>
                       He made out in there
        A slender length of pith, or was it pith?
        It might have been the skin a snake had cast
        And left stood up on end inside the tree
</pre>

Might have been, but was it? Paul lays whatever it is at the edge of the pond to drink, and it melts and rises up a girl. That snake, now—is it the same snake that rises unexpectedly in his poem about his old neighbor Guay, who carved the ax "elve" for him?

<pre>
        But now he brushed the shavings from his knee
        And stood the axe there on its horse's hoof,
        Erect, but not without its waves, as when
        The snake stood up for evil in the Garden—
</pre>

Maybe "erect" is a clue—

<pre>
                       He chafed its long white body
        From end to end with his rough hand shut round it.
        He tried it at the eye-hole in the axe-head
</pre>

Along with the death of Elliott, that was always between them, her dislike of the act, his shame before her of what he needed, his resentment of her that she made him feel ashamed.

<pre>
        It comes down to a doubt about the wisdom
        Of having children—after having had them,
        So there is nothing we can do about it
        But warn the children they perhaps should have none
</pre>

Or might that be to poison their minds, poison their wombs?

He wakes. Looks around. Where is he?

He's standing on a slope. Some other farmer's field of feed corn below on his left, a stand of maples above on his right. The sun is westering. There's a solitary lightning-scarred red oak against the north sky. He's northwest of Carol's house. Near the edge of the property. Should he head for the North Pole? The Amazon? He knows a little bog on the other side of the ridge. He'll go see what's growing there. He clambers up through last year's leaves.

Flowers were the only lovemaking he could press on her that made her grateful. He first learned about orchids when she was pregnant with Elliott. With their testicular roots, their spectacularly vaginal flowers—flagrant, fragrant, everted, inviting—they became his lifelong code to her for an Adam-and-Eve mutuality he otherwise couldn't have.

> I only knelt and putting the boughs aside
> Looked

And he thinks even Elinor took pleasure in them as such—a pleasure she otherwise couldn't have.

> There we bowed us in the burning,
>   As the sun's right worship is,
> To pick where none could miss them
>   A thousand orchises

Is the rose pogonia, say, cut from a log of the king's phallic white pine? Its Greek name means "snake-tongued," for the tickling, yellow, insect-licking landing pad it sticks out below the clitoral bud in its drawn-back hood. Thus the stalk, teasingly fingered halfway up its shaft by a single leaf, must be the snake that stands up—for evil, maybe, if you're evil-minded, or for children, also known as the good of evil born.

> Sometimes I wander out of beaten ways
> Half looking for the orchid Calypso

The calypso, being very rare, is the Holy Grail of orchid-lovers. (He's crested the ridge and is half sliding down through twigs and leaves toward the bog.) If he ever finds one—maybe here, maybe today!—he hopes a heart attack fells him the moment he plucks it, so that he pitches forward soundlessly into the bog, he and Calypso slowly sinking together, where no one will find them, where with the passage of years he will undergo a marsh-change, become deep-tanned and bodily immortal, a mastodon with his nymph. (He's in the bog. He balances on a tussock, wets his shoe stepping to the next.)

That poem he had such trouble with, years ago—the one he felt he had to write despite Elinor's disliking it, the poem about him and her and sex—for a long time he couldn't find the right form for it. And for once he couldn't take his attempts to Elinor for her comments. Then Emily ghostlike spoke to him in Elinor's voice.

> In Winter, in my room,
> I came upon a worm,
> Pink, lank, and warm.

Something stirred deep in him.

> But as he was a worm
> And worms presume,
> Not quite with him at home—
> Secured him by a string
> To something neighboring,
> And went along.

Three drumbeats are the sound of the Fall:

> Adam lay ybounden,
> Bounden in a bond;
> Four thousand winter
> Thoughte he not too long.
> And all was for an apple

Emily's worm swells, it stands up:

> A snake, with mottles rare,
> Surveyed my chamber floor,
> In feature as the worm before,
> But ringed with power

He saw what he might do. Three fatal beats. He didn't want to use a snake. His marriage with Elinor had always been couched in the language of flowers, and he would hold to that, but he would subvert it, just as, long ago, he'd subverted his White Lily by the Merrimack. He would make the flower phallic.

He pictured a man and a woman in a field of concealing goldenrod and cushioning brake. Her hair has come undone. Some encounter has just gone wrong. The man has sprouted; the woman has recoiled. This is not the posy she wanted.

> And he lashed his open palm
> With the tender-headed flower

After years of frustration, the poem came easily. It was like having a conversation with Emily/Elinor. Or rather, nothing so ladylike—a confrontation; they were the fearful spinster in the house, he the dog with a bone outside howling. She:

> That time I flew,
> Both eyes his way,
> Lest he pursue—

He:

> She dared not stir a foot,
> Lest movement should provoke
> The demon of pursuit

She:

> Then, to a rhythm slim
> Secreted in his form

He:

> A hand hung like a paw,
> An arm worked like a saw

She flees horrified:

> Nor ever ceased to run

He flees ashamed:

> A coward save at night,
> Turned from the place and ran

He wakes. He's standing wet-ankled in the bog. How long has he been there? Sunk an inch or two. Up my knee. He pulls himself up by a branch, gains drier ground. Skirts the bog. The sun is behind the ridge. He can't see well in the gloomy light under the alders. No orchises. He trudges north, up the slope. There's a grove of red pines up that way that Carol and he planted, oh, a thousand years ago. They make their own gloom now; maybe he can find a pink lady's slipper.

Elinor! Remember the little summer cottage we rented for our honeymoon in Allenstown? When we learned about the orchids?

> Age saw two quiet children
> Go loving by at twilight

Weren't we happy for a day?

> Be happy, happy, happy

But Emily gets the final word:

> I watched her face to see which way
> She took the awful news,
> Whether she died before she heard—
> Or in protracted bruise
> Remained a few slow years with us,
> Each heavier than the last—
> A further afternoon to fail,
> As Flower at fall of Frost.

He enters the pine woods. Quiet and dark; getting darker as the sun sinks. Right away, he sees it. White and glowing between the trunks. Is it—? He kneels. A showy orchis. The dangling white lips of the magenta blooms lean away from his breath, dance back, lean away. He shouldn't pick it. He picks it. Finds his way back in the dusk to the empty Stone Cottage. Lillian must be out with Prescott on an errand. Carol's probably milking the cow. He pulls down a thin, clear vase from a high shelf in the kitchen, fills it with water, puts in the flower. Then stands there.

The kitchen grows dark.

Stands there.

This poor dog doesn't know what to do.

Her voice comes to him. It's her voice from one of his poems, but it *is* her voice (isn't it?), it's the closest he's ever come to capturing her, that aggrieved tone of hers, and thus he's always loved this poem, slight though it is. It's about the time he and she, when they were a young couple, came across a colt way out in a mountain pasture when the first winter snow was falling.

> "I think the little fellow's afraid of the snow . . .
> Where is his mother? He can't be out alone . . .
> Whoever it is that leaves him out so late,
> When other creatures have gone to stall and bin,
> Ought to be told to come and take him in."

He takes the orchis up to his bedroom, opens the cupboard, and places it on the shelf next to her ashes.

Stands back.

Stands there.

110

Having spotted a car coming up the dirt road, he hurries out of the kitchen, ducks behind the barn, and from there makes it unseen to the woods. He peers out from behind a bush. The car stops in the yard and a woman gets out. He recognizes her—Ted Morrison's wife, Kathleen. Frost got to know them at Harvard two years ago, when he gave the Norton Lectures. Ted's director of the Bread Loaf Writers' Conference. Steady, quiet sort. His wife more lively. She has a slight Scottish burr Frost finds attractive. Those round, rich "o"s. What's she doing here? He sees her knock; glance around the yard. She writes a note and wedges it in the door. Drives off.

He comes down to read the note. Ted's inviting him to the August conference at Bread Loaf. Can do as much or as little as he wants. (Coddle the wreck.) And Kathleen's inviting him to stay with her and her children for a few days at a friend's summer home in West Dover. Without her husband? The wild Bread Loaf crowd. Benny DeVoto's harem. Louis tiptoeing in and out of rooms at night with his shoes in his hands. Is she one of them? Bit of a hussy?

He tosses the note.

111

". . . It is, therefore, both a delight and an honor to present the poet, my old and dear friend, Robert Frost."

Full again, to the rafters, they're on their feet again, and he's on his, walking to the podium, he one and they about six hundred, which of course is perfect, Poetry must be watching—

> Into the valley of Death
> Rode the six hundred

—he's going to die soon, and maybe they'll all die soon, too.

"Sometimes, lately," he muses into the microphone, "when I'm trying to go to sleep I see, on the backside of my eyelids, faces, and they seem to come from another world—very vivid, so vivid I can't go to sleep. To get rid of them, I have to get up and light the light, and look at the light. It's this audience that I'm having, and it's strange how they change as I look at them." One foot in the afterlife, maybe he's glimpsing the audience he'll have there, made up of all the audiences he's ever had, Vermonters, Californians, Georgians, New Yorkers, Russians, replacing each other one seat at a time in a random pattern through the hall, a twinkling of costume changes, a quilt of shifting colors. They'll never speak, but they'll all be looking at him, the changing eyes never changing their gaze, and his lecture will never end.

Interesting that he said *from another world*, the title of Louis's autobiography, with Louis here on stage, dear Louis, who just finished introducing him, who organized in his unmatchable, indefatigable way this National Poetry Festival (whatever that is!), three days of poets escaping their desks to get some free room and board. The first ever National Poetry Festival and probably the last.

They tell him it's his prostate, this urinary urgency and creeping gonadal pain that's got so bad, and he's prophesying right now that if they get him into the hospital he's never coming out. Marjorie always said she'd rather die in a ditch than in a hospital, and he always wanted to die on a Vermont trail. Why not a heart attack? That's how you end a lover's quarrel. But maybe it will all be solved by a missile attack. He and his audience packed off to another world together. He saw on the map in the newspaper this morning how Washington, D.C., was tucked for bedtime just inside the circle that lay everted, inviting, to the missiles ready to go in Cuba. If he were in Cambridge or Vermont, he'd be safe for another week or two, until they got the longer-range missiles set up. Louis, you saved me from the hospital. Hold my hand, Louis. Hurry. Something's falling.

Dear Louis. If Edward Thomas was Frost's poet-brother of tragedy, Louis Untermeyer is his repetition as farce. And he means that in the kindest way. Nobody can make Frost laugh and forget himself as well as Louis can. And he's not a good enough poet to complicate their friendship with rivalry. Instead, as editor, anthologist, popularizer, prize-committee member, he's been Frost's champion for fifty years, doing more than any other person to make Frost a public figure. "Louis here on the platform makes me reminisce," he says into the microphone. "You know, I'm sort of a figment of his imagination! That's very literally true." Could all of this be Louis's dream? Behind that rippling bald forehead, above those benign brown eyes. Louis dreamed Frost into existence, and he dreamed up the American appetite for poetry, he dreamed up this particular audience, this Poetry Festival that no one had conceived of before, and he's charmed the best poets in America to step within the magic circle stretching from Washington to the Panama Canal, with Cuba the secret sitting in the middle, and the Muse from another world is descending at six thousand miles an hour.

Ten minutes, they say it would take. It takes eight minutes for sun-light to reach the earth. Maybe the sun exploded seven and a half minutes ago. Maybe two minutes before that, the Muse lifted off from a sugarcane field.

Who's with him? (Who's against him?) He's reminiscing into the microphone: ". . . and then in England there were Edward Thomas and Lascelles Abercrombie and a publisher"—he has no name for the nameless one—"strangers to me. I owe lots to them, and I might go on. Mark Van Doren, with us here, he's been one of my faithful—some of them extraordinarily faithful. And some wavering." He's in the Garden of Gethsemane; his disciples are sleeping. But Mark is awake. Hold my hand, Mark. Can you hear it descending? It's the Holy Ghost.

He reminisces some more. More old friends that are with him, in the audience—Gordon Chalmers, John Crowe Ransom. At least they seem at the moment to be the best of friends. "And here we are to-night. These things thrown together these ways. Isn't it interesting?" So many people have died on him, and it has seemed sometimes like a betrayal. And here are the ones left, Mark and John and Louis, and this audience of vivid, shifting faces in the rows of seats before him, this stagelight on him, this microphone, and they can all go together, something is coming that will finally, finally kill him. "Well," he says, "that's a sort of introduction. You know, you feel strange about this day in our history." October 23, 1962. Think of it long enough, it be-comes a phrase with its own color, like April 19 or July 4. Think of it longer and it starts to seem uncanny, like the image that plagued him when he was a boy, that kept him from sleeping after a day when he'd gone fishing. He'd be watching the bob in the still water, minute after minute, nothing happening, when suddenly the bob would sink and ripples would start out from it. And that image would remain so vivid in his mind, it would trouble him all night.

He's known since yesterday evening, when Kennedy on television announced the blockade of Cuba, which poem he'd start with to-night. "This poem is called 'October.'" He wrote it at the Derry kitchen table, his children asleep upstairs.

Gentle Jesus, meek and mild,
Look upon a little child

But he's not saying that, he's saying:

"O hushed October morning mild,
Thy leaves have ripened to the fall;
To-morrow's wind, if it be wild,
Should waste them all. . . ."

He doesn't say,

Pity my simplicity,
Suffer me to come to Thee.

Instead, he finishes the poem. He starts into another one, "November." He's the Pied Piper, leading his pied audience underground step by step. This one is also about leaves and waste.

He's been thinking a lot about waste lately. And extravagance, which is the same thing. The sheer extravagance of this universe, the mind-boggling emptiness, the lordly waste of the sun's million nuclear bombs going off every second, to warm all that emptiness; and incidentally to shine on us. *Shine, perishing*— And those millions of leaves born every year to die; and all the world's people, and all that carefully stored-up, husbanded megatonnage reserved just for them. For every sinner, his own spoonful of Castro oil. The world is dead, long live the world.

In his grandfather's house in Lawrence, there was a room with drawers and boxes, and in the drawers were neatly folded newspapers, rescued wrapping paper, old paper bags, pieces of used string wound up in a ball, and the labels on the drawers, one and all, should have read in his grandfather's neat hand, "My soul."

If it's lordly to waste, maybe it's beggarly to save. All that New England thrift. Where did it get them, those pinched, vigilant husbands?

What makes New England rich is its decay, its compost. Waste turned under. The waste of laziness! Which his grandfather deplored. But Rob's laziness rotted and sprouted his poems. The practical crowd want to ignore the waste of leisure and of pleasure, and the pacifist crowd want to ignore the greater waste of human hate, which maybe can be as lordly and creative as love. "November" is about those people, who can only boast of their balls of string, their progressive schemes for other people's improvement,

> "By denying and ignoring
> The waste of nations warring,"

he says, finishing the poem.

"And then I'd like to add tonight," he can't resist, "'And the waste of breath deploring.'"

The audience stirs. Ah, he's making them uneasy. It's been nothing but easy deploring all day. Nuclear weapons should be banned! A fine idea. But first blast Cuba to kingdom come. Or nuclear weapons should be banned (oh, what a fine idea!) and let's ban aggression while we're at it. Let's ban sin. Everyone's scared, the young people in particular. This universe that blows up star systems owes them a life. Well, he's scared, too. But that's his and Pascal's advantage over the universe, ain't it? He can feel terror, the universe feels nothing. Glaciers advance and retreat, killing forests and species of man; the callused soul disappears into his cave ten thousand years ago. The president said last night that when the longer-range missiles are ready Cuba will be able to hit Hudson Bay.

> It's to say, "You and I"
> To such a ghost,
> "You and I
> Off here
> With the dead race of the Great Auk!"

But he's not saying that poem. He's begun to talk about his trip to Russia, and what happens to poems in translation. ". . . there is a

word—the word's 'play.' That you can't carry over . . ." That's all poetry is: wordplay. Or you could call it extravagance. Or call it waste.
People ask, what's poetry good *for*? "I've been seeing poets in Russia.
I've been seeing myself translated into Russian. Of course, I couldn't
tell whether it was any good, and they couldn't tell whether mine was
any good. It was all nowhere, just absolute loss. What is it Mark
Twain says—like an encounter of battleaxes at a hundred yards in a
fog. Something like that. You're just waving your weapons at each
other."

So he's back to weapons. Don't let them forget. Nature within her
inmost self divides. What's that he hears swimming toward them,
breasting the currents of the air? It's the universal translator!

Kennedy said last night that if a missile was fired from Cuba the
United States would respond with a full retaliatory strike on Russia. So
instead of a hundred years of saying, "On the one hand, but on the
other," we'll have a thousand years to measure the Geiger ticks winking at us from the drifting dust of Russians. What does the man in the
street think of that? What does Frost think of that? "They were nice
people," he says to his audience. "And I wish I knew their poems, could
get their poems." Maybe we'll all die because our theories are commu-
nicable but our play is not. "And my guess is that the best one of them
all is the liveliest one of them all." He's referring to Yevtushenko, but
he's not thinking of his poems. He wants to keep unsettling his audience. It might be their last night out. Wake them up with a good ghost
story before God's last *Put out the light* is spoken. "He was a lively,
youngish man, and I got quite an impression of him, quite bohemian,
and quite stirred up to heroic feelings about Cuba and all that, and
ready for some more revolution. His revolution was more than forty
years old, you know, and they need some new ones for refreshment."
Thomas Jefferson spoke in favor of a revolution every twenty years.
July 4, October 23. Cuba was theirs before they were Cuba's.

"Now I'll go on with some of these older poems and some new
ones. Supposing I turn to a political one of my own, see where it gets
more political. This is made on a poem by Robinson Jeffers, who's not
here in this world anymore." But Frost sees Jeffers's face winking on

and off in the audience. "It is a stirring poem. It's a despairing poem, and he speaks of us; he says, 'Shine, perishing republic.'"

The crowd stirs again; there's a soft, collective gasp. What's going on? The national bard of uplift is sniffing Yorick's skull. The farmer is using his hoe to dig a grave.

Frost repeats it: "'Shine, perishing republic.'" Then he rubs it in. "'Perishing'—I felt like being funny about that. Everything that shines perishes, shines by perishing: candles and firecrackers, everything." July 4, the fireworks rise; October 23, they fall.

He says his poem about the decline of all civilizations, "Our Doom to Bloom," and wonders if his restless, unhappy audience, six hundred younger poets riding into the valley of death, remembers Jeffers's lines:

> You making haste haste on decay: not blameworthy;
>   life is good, be it stubbornly long or suddenly
> A mortal splendor: meteors are not needed less than
>   mountains: shine, perishing republic.

Life is good. "Great times to be alive, aren't they?" he wrote to the president before he went to Russia. "How grand for you to think of me this way." Before he lost Kennedy as a friend. "And how like you to take the chance of sending anyone like me over there."

Never a word from him. Not one. *I wait for the president*, Frost said to the crowd of reporters at Idlewild, and it came true in prophecy's twisted way. It was Franklin the White House wanted to talk to, not him. There was a luncheon scheduled for all the poets today at the White House. Since poetry's good for nothing, and therefore is women's business, it was going to be hosted by Mrs. Kennedy. Frost hoped somehow to get word to the president. But the luncheon was canceled. They say Mrs. Kennedy is hiding somewhere in a cave. "Would we as a United States rather wilt than fade?" he asks his audience. But he's not asking. "No, we'd rather fade—go through it all."

Now they're really unhappy. Next he gives them "Provide, Provide," but he spares them a little, he tells them about the charwomen's strike at Harvard, he makes all the old jokes. He lays it on thick. But they don't laugh much. Jackie's hiding in a cave, and her husband is who knows where, maybe in a concrete bunker below the White House or aloft in Air Force One. And Frost wonders, a little bit, if it's partly his fault. He doesn't know how it happened, the newspapers took his words and somehow made it sound like he was saying Kennedy was soft and Khrushchev would roll right over him. Stewart told him that Kennedy was steamed, that it put him in a tough position. The national bard had called him a coward. And there was the president on television last night ordering a blockade starting tomorrow morning at ten— American ships stopping Russian ones, maybe firing on them. A Russian sub responds, a missile lifts off from Cuba, and Kennedy orders the nuclear destruction of Russia. No coward he. The poets Frost met, the bohemians in the cafés, the Pendragons, those children in the school with the red nooses around their necks—all gone.

HOW ROBERT FROST
CAUSED HOLOCAUST

"That leads me to another thought," he's saying into the microphone. "I've joked about liberals a great deal, and there's been something going around. I wonder how many of you've heard it: that I was told in Russia that Americans were too liberal to fight, or something like that. Nothing like that did I hear. What I heard was, rather, a pleasantry from the greatest ruler in the world, you know, the almighty"—*Fiat nox!*—"and in his genial way he just said, 'As Tolsoy said to Gorky'—or vice versa, I've forgotten which; it was a very literary conversation—'As Tolstoy said to Gorky, "There's such a thing as a nation getting so soft it couldn't . . . "'" Frost pauses. He can't say the nation can't screw. Has its prostate out and its balls, too. ". . . wouldn't fight." The bright sunlight in his eyes, the beach sand giving way under his feet. Fight! the men are shouting. Fight! You and I, Kevin. "See, that's all. He was just saying there was such a thing, and he might be suggesting that we better look out. See, that's all, it was a pleasantry. It wasn't a defiant thing, nothing was defiant. I'd like that straightened out, whatever happens." We're all ascending in an incandescent cloud, but let's get this one thing straight, anyway.

And Khrushchev—while he and Frost spoke, while they were agreeing about the need to be magnanimous, to be noble—Khrushchev the almighty was secretly sending missiles to Cuba. What should Frost think about that? He doesn't know. Maybe it would take him years to figure it out, and he hasn't got years.

> I'm going out to clean the pasture spring;
> I'll only stop to rake the leaves away
> (And wait to watch the water clear, I may):
> I sha'n't be gone long.—You come too.

"There were no lies, see," he says to himself, and maybe also into the microphone. "It's very interesting. I couldn't go to him and say I was lied to, but I could say that there was a sort of loss of faith." Is that what he means? "That we understood each other, that I was led to understand what probably I was partly mistaken about." Partly his own fault. Half-deaf, dying old man. "I wasn't very deeply, just a little. I could make that charge, that 'You've broken faith with me,' a little." Whatever you ask, my boy! It's yours! "I'd like to say that to him, like to see him here tonight." To accuse; to apologize; to try again. To say, Great times to be alive, aren't they? "I admire him, admire the power and all that; but I feel a little hurt that way." Isn't that the premier in the audience, in the back row, in the white suit? He stares at Frost, but doesn't speak.

They all stare up at him. *You come too.* He wanders on, they follow. He says a poem by Matthew Arnold, he talks about Emerson, he reads a couple of poems from *In the Clearing.* He glances at the watch he keeps on the podium. Miles to go. "Shall I go on in one or two more of the new ones, little ones?"

> Gentle Jesus, meek and mild,
> All my pretty ones? Did you say all?

The audience isn't with him. They're all poets, they're all younger. Six hundred healthy prostates. He says to the microphone,

"In winter in the woods alone..."

You and I, Hardy. Let's knock down this goddamn tree and go off together. He says,

"The mower in the dew had loved them thus,
By leaving them to flourish, not for us,

Nor yet to draw one thought of ours to him.
But from sheer morning gladness at the brim."

Minute by minute passes and the Muse doesn't descend. The audience gazes up at him. He says, "Now take this one—" He says, "And here, just for tonight—" And the faces in the audience are vivid, and they shift, and this lecture will go on forever—

In Massachusetts, in Virginia

—it looks like they're going to survive this evening. Maybe tomorrow's wind will be wild, when the first Russian ship reaches the quarantine line, or maybe the day after, when some Cuban bravo, a young revolutionary panting for a feather in his hair, steals the launch key from a tired Russian, lights off his firecracker with a happy war whoop. Or maybe not. Maybe the world will go on, and Frost's bladder will burst and they'll take him to the hospital and he'll die alone.

This is the way the world ends
Not with a bang but a whimper.

You and I, Tom. Yes, even you. I'll go off with you if there's nobody else.

112

His motto is: Keep Moving. Cambridge in autumn, weekends up to Hanover, Florida in January, Vermont for the summer. Townhouse, apartment, prefab cottage, log cabin. In between are the tours—halls great and small, professors' houses, inns, student unions, fraternities, Pullman cars. The arrows of outrageous fortune fall behind him, or if they lodge in his back he no longer notices. To get through a bog without sinking you keep moving with a fluid stride. Edward Thomas showed him that. On his coat-of-arms the squirrel leaps from pine to pine as the pack of hounds streams baying below. Inscribed on the crest are the initials of his motto: *K.M.* They also stand for K. Morrison, his fluid wife.

He thought, after that day in the woods, that she would divorce Ted and marry him. He thought her marriage couldn't be anything but a sham if she returned his advances. He wanted to make an honest woman of her. But she refused. She's given a dozen reasons, mostly to do with propriety, but he's never understood.

As he's hinted for thirty years about his real age, he hints now about his real relationship with her. Wordplay. Louis smiles urbanely; he knows all about puns, all about adultery. Benny DeVoto was outraged when it started; he called Frost a bad man. But that was jealousy. Benny had his own crush on K. Ted is blind, as he wants to be. K. and Ted are husband and wife in name only. He let her down on that score. (K. told Frost all about it.) Frost refers to her in public, with relish, as his Devoted Secretary, and every time he says it he thinks of vanquished DeVoto. In private, he calls her Egeria, his water nymph and wise councillor. He calls her Augusta, empress of this poor Virgil, and presiding spirit of that miraculous August day, when she saved him from drowning. His half-wife, his mermaid.

> My father was the keeper of the Eddystone Light
> And he slept with a mermaid one fine night.
> And from that union there came three,
> A porpoise and a porgy and the other was me.

At the age of sixty-five, he finally became a true ecloguist—he learned to play the panpipe, also called the recorder. It was so that he could play that song. One day he'd like to write a poem as good. The verses have everything—wildness and everything.

> One night as I was a-trimming the glim
> A-singing a verse of the evening hymn,
> A voice to the starboard shouted "Ahoy"
> And there was my mother sitting on a buoy.

That was six months after the August day in the woods. He'd dragged K. down to Florida with him, to Hervey Allen's place, but Ted had tagged along, and the situation was impossible, Frost was half crazy and K. was furious. He was exiled to a spare room in the guest cottage. Caged bear. There he had nothing to do for days but finger his recorder.

> "Oh what has become of my children three?"
> My mother then she asked of me.
> "One we exhibited as a talking fish
> And one was served in a chafing dish."

He couldn't figure her out. She prated about decency and reputation, but she and Ted kept separate beds, and it was she (wasn't it?) who'd spoken to him, in the first months of their screwing, in praise of the ruthlessness of poetic and political power that doesn't stick at scruples, but has its way to the great end.

Then the phosphorus flashed in her seaweed hair.
I looked again and my mother wasn't there.
But a voice came echoing out of the night,
"To Hell with the keeper of the Eddystone Light."

It's a rivalry between Ted and him, a rivalry of years, and he's determined to win it. Meanwhile, it drives him crazy that no one knows, that he can't aknowledge her openly as his savior, as the inspiration for his best poems since Elinor died, and it angers him to be dishonest, and to think that she feels at home with dishonesty, so he hints about their relationship, while she (fresh—or stale—from his bed) assures his friends that it's all in his imagination. She implies, in fact, that he's no longer a man in that way.

He plays his recorder. He's made up pornographic verses to "The Eddystone Light" about the anatomical difficulties involved in screwing mermaids. Sometimes when he and she are alone with friends he sings them to infuriate her. It works beautifully. She dives out of the room. But he can't live without her. He's never been good about writing letters, even to Edward Thomas, but when he's on tour he writes to K. every day. He begins them, "Dear Egeria," "Dear Augusta." He pours all his eloquence into expressing how much he loves her, needs her. After she reads the letters, she burns them.

113

ELIZABETHTOWN, NEW YORK

AUGUST 1941

"They're going to sleep in a double bed over there," Frost tells Larry with deep anguish. He shifts from foot to foot, near bellowing or breaking something.

"I guess there isn't anything you can do about that," Larry answers.

"Well there is. I won't stay."

K., Ted, Frost, and Larry (his new official biographer, a bright boy, devoted to him) have come to visit Louis and Esther Untermeyer on their Adirondack farm. When Frost went into the room he thought was his and Larry's, he saw K.'s and Ted's suitcase lying on the double bed. "How can a person devote his life to stimulating his imagination and then be expected to handle an image like that double bed?" he demands of Larry. "It's all Esther's fault. Why didn't she put them in our room, with the two single beds? You and I could have bunked in their room. I have to leave tonight."

"All right." But Larry is impatient. "I'll drive you home."

"That won't do. As soon as we're gone, they'll go to that double bed!"

They then gladly went together to bed, and their old ritual. "Well, what to do?"

"Tell Esther to change the rooms."

"I can't do that."

Rage at Larry.

"I'll talk to K.," Larry says.

When he returns, he says, "Come for a drive with me, and we'll talk it over." They drive into the dark countryside. After a minute, Larry says, "She and Ted are going back to Bread Loaf tonight."

"Then I have to speak with her."

"She doesn't want to talk with you right now. Let them go."

"You can't kidnap me, Larry! I *will* go back!"

In the room with the double bed, K. rounds on him from her packing. "You're acting like a child," she hisses furiously.

"How can I let you—"

"I've told you a thousand times, you have to let me handle these things. You only make everything worse with these tantrums. I was planning all along to go back to Vermont tonight, as soon as I saw the bed. And now you've made it so much harder. And you've made an utter fool of yourself and you've upset everyone for no reason at all."

Is she right? Is she? He leaves the room. "Larry? Larry?"

"Here I am."

"Take me for a ride. Into the mountains."

114

MEET THE PRESS, NBC STUDIOS, NEW YORK CITY

DECEMBER 25, 1955

INEZ ROBB: Mr. Frost, one of the most famous lines of modern poetry was written by an expatriate American, T. S. Eliot, who said, "This is the way the world ends, not with a bang but a whimper." Could you tell us if you agree with him or if you disagree?

ROBERT FROST: It's not ended with a bang and there are only a few whimperers around, and it isn't ending. That's an extravagance of his, it's a very pretty piece of expression, isn't it, but an extravagance. He just meant that everything is in a bad way.

INEZ ROBB: You think then that the world is more apt to end with a bang in this atomic age or are you hopeful for it?

ROBERT FROST: I've got my money on its not ending.

115

He burned his poetry.

Which train? Frost hurries, shoulders past people. Which platform? Where is the timetable? K. is trotting beside, trying to herd him. His collie. Her nurse's voice, trying to calm him. "It's the Berkshire Limited."

"I know that," Frost rasps. "But where—?" A conductor—how young he looks!—a confab. Platform Six. A whistle. A soul in torment. He burned all his poetry and all his letters. He burned his life in the bedroom stove.

Frost steps up into a car. Too crowded. He backs into K. She nudges him forward. "They're all like this." Where are all these people going? The Berkshires in October? Not hay fever, or summer cottages, or skiing. Must be the foliage crowd. Maple leaves falling, like hands seeking a touch. Beauty is death, death beauty—that is all ye know on earth—

But the strong go on. Like Prescott, who found his father's body and didn't run screaming from the house, as Frost would have done at that age. Imagine not quite sixteen, and waking to the shot, seeing the mess moments afterward. The kitchen floor. Blood. Oh, how much? And the rifle still in his hand? "There's nowhere to sit—"

"There. Right there."

He burned his poetry and his letters. All those letters—Frost tried so hard—

I feel more and more the power behind your poems.

Your apple-crating poem has a great deal more of the feeling of real work and country business than anything of mine could ever pretend or hope to have.

Maybe he overdid it. Carol could hear the anxiety to humor him, buck him up. *Stop hovering! Leave me alone!* Sometimes Frost in his letters was trying to make up for comments he'd let slip when he was with Carol, spurts of irritation. He's always been kinder in letters, where the conversation can proceed exactly as he wants it. In a person's presence, something gets him—fear he'll be touched, maybe; hugged, smothered. Fight, fight! The boy's poetry just was never much good. Frost found the ore in other young men—sometimes small veins, but true. Carol somehow didn't have the ear.

> In a lawn I modeled over once he drilled,
> Till I had wicked wishes for that gopher.
> Just as fast as I could get the holes refilled
> He cleaned them out to prove he was no loafer.

Oh! It hurt! Frost tried to talk Carol into writing up the family hike on the Long Trail in prose rather than in verse.

> You know the weakness of verse: one line of it will be strong and good and the next will be almost anything for the sake of the rhyme. That's why some people can't stand the stuff.

Maybe Carol heard: *That's why I can't stand your stuff.*

Maybe it was what Frost was saying.

Why isn't the goddamn train moving? Frost searches for his timetable. "May I?" A young man is leaning across the aisle, holding out his own. Two, even. Does he collect them? Maybe he stole Frost's in the first place. To offer it back, gain some advantage.

Frost is curt. "Thank you." He hands one to K., tries to read the one he keeps. But he looks back at the young man. Who, where, below what podium, in which classroom seat, behind\ what proffered copy of which first edition. "I've seen you before."

The young man smiles. He names a gathering in Boston half a year ago.

A poet. (Frost can't remember if he's any good; has he read anything?) Frost names him, and like a lamp switched brighter, he expands. Frost buries himself in the newspaper. Raids on London.

Carol hated his name. It's a girl's name! he charged. Accused, rather. *In those letters that were supposed to build him up, you always wrote "Carol," never "Carroll," as he wanted. Why not? A simple thing.* Because he was wrong! For five hundred years it had been a man's name. For Christ's sake, the word *means* "man"! Who cares that a few ignorant people have confused it with "Caroline"? It's a beautiful name. (Maybe if Carol had a better ear.) And anyway, what other man's name also means song, means poetry?

> From deep secluded recesses,
> From the fragrant cedars and the ghostly pines so still,
> Came the carol of the bird.

Whitman's hermit thrush, which sings of death, but with the shaping beauty that brings death alive.

> Come lovely and soothing death,
> Undulate round the world, serenely arriving, arriving,
> In the day, in the night, to all, to each,
> Sooner or later delicate death.

But is it a lie? Nothing beautiful or delicate about a rifle bullet in the head, a fifteen-year-old boy kneeling in his father's blood. Or this photograph in today's newspaper, a London bus destroyed by a German bomb. Those scorched tatters, lining the blown-out windows—are they children's clothes?

Christ, that Carol could do that to his son. Prescott stayed up most of the night trying to talk him out of it, finally slept in exhaustion. What kind of father says to his son, *Give me a reason*, when the reason is sitting in front of him?

Of course, he wasn't right in the head. The family curse.

And isn't it a lie, too, for Whitman to present so unambiguously the thrush singing to *him*, with a message he could understand? Isn't that the flummery of so much poetry, the world-hugging obverse of inward-turned paranoia? *The birds are talking to me! I hear America singing!* When Frost hears a bird deep in the woods, just he and the one bird alone in the night, he, too, could too easily imagine the bird saying, *You and me, Rob; come in for a confab.* The strong man holds back from the darkness, the strong poet holds back from riding the metaphor into a lather.

Frost feels a stir in the blood. There might be a poem there.

The young man is back, on his feet in the aisle, hanging by Frost's shoulder. He wants an audience. Why not? *Bask, you old fraud.* Take his mind off. Blood, brains—

> I fled Him, down the nights and down the days;
> I fled Him, down the arches of the years

Now Carol can haunt him for real.

Frost closes the newspaper and turns to his disciple and blurts out the first thing that comes into his head: "Paul Engle." A young poet who's gotten a lot of attention lately for his Whitmanesque effusions. He called his epic *American Song*, no less. Another who thinks birds and bridges have a special message for him. "What do you think of him?" Frost asks, the bile in him rising. But he must be careful. Mustn't shock the dew out of those young eyes. He goes on to Hervey Allen, Robinson Jeffers, the *Atlantic*. The young poet coughs up Sir Philip Sidney, Frost vomits back Keats.

Then they are in Springfield, where K. leaves him to catch a train back to Boston. The old goat is far enough down the chute, he can't turn around. Frost follows her out to the platform to say goodbye. He can't kiss her here; would never try. She'd make him suffer. He watches her walk away, trim and speedy, not looking back, and feels so desolate he turns up and down the platform, pilgrimming, until the last "all aboard" sounds.

Of course people are whispering as he makes his way to his seat. *Was that his mistress? Too young for him. He looks like hell. Maybe his son just put a bullet through his head.* The family curse. But when you're famous, people really do talk behind your back, signal to each other.

> Whenever Richard Cory went down town,
> We people on the pavement looked at him

Frost sits next to the young poet. Otherwise the damned kid, too deferential to take K.'s seat and too mothlike to keep from the lamp, will stand in the aisle all the way to Williamstown. But God, he can't face talk right now— "My son, Carol, died last night. He killed himself." That ought to shut him up.

"My God! I'm sorry—"

"Please don't talk to me any more."

"Of course."

The curse. And heartbreaking that it comes on so gradually, that you watch the true, by becoming more itself, go false. Carol from birth was wary, serious, earnest. When do you call those Yankee virtues paranoia, depression, obsession? Carol lately thought the drivers in the cars passing the Stone Cottage were spying on him. He dragged Lillian down to the basement in the middle of the night to help him search for the wires to the hidden listening devices. *Stop hovering! Leave me alone!*

The thought of Carol in an institution, peering for thirty years around the edge of a barred window. Looking for codes in Lillian's letters. Whispers in the hallway. *Son of* — "Carol was sensitive," Frost says to someone, anyone, in this case the young poet. "He wrote poetry. But without much success. That is, no success." That is, failure. "What about your poetry?" The young poet says something. Frost doesn't catch it, or give a shit, either. He starts lecturing. Poetic framework, texture . . . Frost glares at the young poet beside him. Promising? Talented? Sunny? Sane? Who in hell is he? Frost racks his memory. He's spoken with the lad; somewhere gold-green; maple flowers; a May evening after a reading. He's from New Hampshire. He's farmed; kept poultry. Didn't go to college.

On that May evening, Frost asked him, "What kind of chickens do you have?"

"New Hampshire Reds."

"Do you raise apples to sell?"

"Mostly for applesauce."

Frost liked him. "Are you married?"

"No." Frost considered playing Cupid. Marry him off to some tender girl who inhales poetry, send them straight to the bedchamber, get them started on a new crop of poets. Putting in the seed.

Now he asks, "So has a college caught you yet?"

"No."

"Ever been to Bread Loaf? The MacDowell Colony?"

"No."

Frost's heart flushes. Rage flees. He gazes at the youth: shy as Pan, writing his poems under red McIntoshes, shin-deep in red chickens. He says, "You are like me."

Carol tried so hard, he sacrificed so much. But the earth opened and swallowed him.

> I don't understand the system of blank verse. Is there some way of grouping the words? I'm sending along thoughts I had and would like to know what type of verse they would best be adapted to.

How to condescend to that, yet not wound? Frost often failed to find the middle way. One April in the sweet-pea field behind the Stone Cottage, he came upon Carol lying full-length in the turned earth, sifting the soil through his fingers to remove the quack-grass roots. A rate that would take him a fortnight to clear the plot. Frost was indignant: "Don't you know you can't make a success of farming that way?"

And Carol shot him his brow-shadowed look, armoring himself

too late with anger: "But isn't this the way you write your poetry?" Frost stood dumb.

> Slave to a springtime passion for the earth.
> How Love burns through the Putting in the Seed

Was the metaphor valid? He didn't know. (And here, on the train, he still doesn't know.) Frost could have said to his son, "But I only played at farming. You farm in earnest." He could have said, "You are the parent; I am the child." He could have knelt in the dirt and begged his son's forgiveness. But he only walked away, dumb.

Or (to flee to a different example), whereas the father made play and poetry of splitting wood, often running short in the Derry years because the fun ran out before the work did, Carol went at it in a sullen rage of literalness, piling up the cords that kept his parents comfortable. Before going to California (when Lillian was tubercular), Carol in two afternoons felled, cut, and stacked an ash tree at the bottom of the slope leading up to the Gully House, leaving only the chore of transport to Frost. And even then, Frost played. He never touched the wheelbarrow; he tucked a stove-length under each arm whenever he happened to be walking up from the Stone Cottage. It looked so unfarmerish—maybe like going after quack-grass roots with your fingers—he preferred doing it at night when the neighbors wouldn't see him.

Frost was called out to the Stone Cottage a week ago by an alarmed Lillian (who was in the hospital for a hysterectomy), and he spent three days talking Carol out of a desperate act. He called on nature, on duty, even on poetry. *You're going your own way, and you'll get there if you stick to both the farm work and poetry. Your style will be different from other writers'.* He knelt in the dirt and waved the white flag: *I need you! There are those two cabins in Florida to build. You and me together. You're much more capable than I am.* He enlisted the boy's dead mother: *There was nothing Elinor wanted more than to have you take satisfaction in your family and your farm.* Oh, his eloquence! A pity there wasn't a packed hall to listen to him. Carol didn't stand a chance. In the end, Frost asked him to promise he would never do more than talk about suicide. Carol promised. Frost packed his bags for Boston. But Carol's last words to him were "You always win an argument, don't you?"

The train is pulling into the Williamstown station. Frost stands to get his bag down from the rack. A glance at the younger poet suggests he might try to offer some final condolence, something embarrassing and irrelevant, and Frost will have to be polite. So he forestalls him. Opening the newspaper to the picture of the bombed-out bus, he presses it on the boy. "They were probably all killed. There are more sadnesses than mine. It was fine talking with you."

He hurries up the aisle. He remembers the worst wreck he ever saw. In Cuba, last year. The bus drivers there were fired if they were a minute late, so they drove like mad. Frost came on an accident moments after it had happened, a head-on collision between a bus and a family car. Kids were all over the road. A little girl was under the bus.

Can't make poetry out of that. Or shouldn't.

Or something. Frost can't formulate how he feels about it. (He waits in the crush by the door.) He did write "Out, Out—":

> They listened at his heart.
> Little—less—nothing!—and that ended it.
> No more to build on there. And they, since they
> Were not the one dead, turned to their affairs.

Perhaps, to be more honest, it is the poet who turns away. Poetry is the making of form. How—why—give form, which never comes untinged with pleasure, to the little girl under the bus? Shakespeare knew these desert places, beyond words. The unexpressible country from whose bourne no poet returns. At the moment Lear dies, he says, "O, o, o, o."

"Don't, don't, don't, don't," she cried.

Frost stands in the doorway. A conductor reaches up to help him with his bag. *Old man.* He declines, steps down to the platform. He looks around for Prescott. What will he say?

Carol was a good, safe driver. He was good with all tools, and he understood cars. Frost didn't own a car until he was forty-five, and Carol taught him how to drive it, when to shift gear going uphill, what speed to maintain on a long trip to keep the engine from overheating. Frost wrote with pride to Carol (this wasn't bucking him up: he *was* proud) when the car Carol had tinkered with, listened to, crawled under, fine-tuned, made the 150-mile trip from South Shaftsbury to Franconia averaging thirty-five miles an hour. He was proud of Carol, and proud of himself for the driving.

And Carol was good with horses. He wasn't afraid of them, as Frost has always been. And he was never afraid of hard work. Damn it, he was a real farmer, the real thing. So what if he wasn't a poet? He was a real farmer. He thought he wasn't, because his farm was failing. But didn't he know that New England has been defeating real farmers for three hundred years? Didn't Frost make this clear to him? Maybe if Frost had said— (He will do this for years to come.)

Cars and horses. If Carol could have lived only among them. No people with their obscure expectations, their unexplained glances, no fathers, just horses to talk to when their ears lie back and their eyes roll, and cars to crawl under and listen to. In Vermont, years ago, in mud time, there was a bad patch at the dip in the road just north of the Stone Cottage. Drivers were always getting stuck there. One April night, past midnight, there came a hammering at the front door. City folk. Three cars were up to their axles, and could the farmer help. Frost was awake, but laid up with a cold, so he stayed in while Carol (who, a real farmer, had been asleep at that hour) stamped out to harness up the horses. So Frost didn't witness the scene, but he can see it—

Between his two half-Morgans, Carol arrives at the slough and stares with disapproval at the cars he would never have got stuck in the mud in the first place. He gives that angry shrug of his; responds to the drivers' comments with a rude grunt; turns his back on them, as nothing, to attend to the interesting problem of where to tie the ropes.

These city folk don't know him. They don't know he's struggled to write poetry, or that he knows more about the flowers of Gloucestershire than they'll ever know. To them, his taciturnity and sullenness are right and proper: it's past midnight, and he's the Yankee farmer roused from his bed. Two dollars for each of the smaller automobiles, he demands, three for the big one. The canny Yankee presses his advantage.

In short, Carol *fits*. And oh, Frost wants to leave his son there, under the cold stars, first gentling the horses, then urging them, hauling those cars out of the Vermont mud while the city folk stand by with nothing to do but sit on their hands.

The platform: Prescott, his grandson, is standing in front of him. Frost drops his bag, fights down his aversion to physical contact, hugs the boy. Neither of them speaks.

116

CAMBRIDGE, MASSACHUSETTS

1941

You always win an argument, don't you?

And children! He was splendid with them. After Marjorie's death, when her baby, Robin, was with the family in Vermont, or in winters down south, it was Carol who devoted all his time to her. One of the things he kept returning to, those three days Frost argued with him, was that Lillian couldn't bear any more children. Well, he had Prescott. But maybe he wanted a daughter. He had so loved his mother. Or maybe he just wanted a baby, a blessed innocent, as unjudging as his farm animals.

Frost tried so many ways, and every one wrong. On a perfect May day, he restlessly walks the streets of Cambridge. Turgenev's golden clouds, those Blessèd Isles, are at the top of the sky, where they will always be, golden apples of the sun on the topmost branch, always out of reach. Perfect happiness. If you ever got there, you'd find they were only mist and rain.

Maybe if Frost had said . . .

117

Getting away from it all in a rented car with K., who drives like a demon lover. They're headed for an island named Captiva, just the two of them, a rented house for a week. Shells, rare birds, no telephones. A cold front is moving in, and soon the rain is slashing down in sheets, but K. hardly slows. The wipers throw their hands up in horror, the low trees hold their heads and sway. Leaves batter the windshield like a plague of frogs. Frost is happy. He starts to sing:

> Love, oh love, oh careless love
> You see what love has done to me

A big roast beef sits in the back seat, guarded by—well, all right, they're not alone—Helen Muir is back there. K. asked her along. So it won't be quite like last year, when Frost and K. had the island to themselves. K.'s secret machinations, they always mean something, but Frost doesn't want to think about it. He'll have the garage apartment, and she'll come each day at lunchtime, leaving Helen behind.

> What, oh what, will Mama say
> When she learns I've gone astray

The young folk were singing that song up at Bread Loaf. Things you couldn't sing in Frost's time without getting a beating. Careless young. The rain drums. Let it come, let it drum, I'm a-going to get Captiva-ted! The car rocks on its springs. Frost puts back his hoary head and sings it loud,

> Once I wore my apron low
> I couldn't scarcely keep you from my door
>
> Now my apron strings don't pin
> You pass my door and you don't come in
>
> Love, oh love, oh careless love
> You see what love has done to me!

118

HOMER NOBLE FARM, RIPTON, VERMONT

SEPTEMBER 1945

After supper, Frost walks to the barn to feed Steeple and Chad. The warm weather deserted last week and after a couple of bright cool days the clouds have settled in for a long rain. The light is failing. The first wind-harvest of maple leaves lies matted and sodden in the path.

He gives hay to the horses, then stands by the open barn door, looking out. It's raining harder. Maybe he's waiting for it to slack off before going back to the house. Or maybe he's imagining the rain is gray watercolor, washing back and forth over the picture. Or maybe he's waiting for that puddle to overflow and go trickling down the rut it's made in other rains. Or maybe he's waiting for

Margery to appear at his elbow and say softly, "What's the matter, Papa?"

He and K. have been alone together for a week, while Ted was back in Cambridge preparing for the new semester. But tomorrow she's going to him. And he'll go to his Brewster Street house, and every night he'll think of them in their house three blocks away. Clearing the dishes from the table, then Ted sitting with his pipe and book, K. knitting. Their old ritual.

He steps forward until the rain is falling just past his cheeks. He can feel the mist flung off by the drops. Why is he alone? Does he deserve it? Did he kill them all? Talk them past endurance? Have his way, until they left him to his way? Now the rain's really coming down. It roars.

The last lone aster is gone

His skin crawls. Some creature is standing next to him. Some monster, some instrument of divine vengeance.

But when I came, alas, to wive,
With hey, ho, the wind and the rain

One must not look. Frost hums, pretends indifference.

"Wind and rain
Wind and rain
Wind and rain
Wind and rain
Wind and rain
Wind and rain."

"Stop that!" the creature cries.

One must not look. He looks. It's K., just swum up from the depths, dripping. "I came looking for you," she says, with no love in her voice. "What's the matter?" (—*now?*)

He chooses to be reasonable. He looks through her and says,

> "Wind and rain
>   And wind and rain
> And wind and rain
>   And wind and rain."

This frightens her. He likes that. Evil spirit, I conjure you! Come out of this creature! But he takes pity on her lost soul. He speaks in mermaid. "I'm all worked up inside, and when it rains like this there are times when I just want to go out into it and run and run and run."

"Go ahead," she says, with no trace of love or affection or patience in her voice.

All right, he will. And she'll be— He runs. Down the road, splashing through the puddles. The rain soaks him; he can't see. Keeps running. Life, life, eternal life!

> A great while ago the world begun

It's in a large puddle that he trips and falls. He lands full-length, and his wind gusts out of his mouth, rises free of him and disappears.

> But that's all one, our play is done

In two inches of water, he groans. Rough earth; cold water. Might as well live here. No one will find him. He can drink the water. But some creature, some hellhound, comes flying down the road. It stands over him and barks. Three inches from his ear, it delights in the torture.

> Bark!
> Bark!
> Bark!
> Bark!
> Bark!

And now he can hear her coming after. Drown him in two inches. Terrified, with all his strength, he shouts, "Goddamn you, get the hell out of here!" The rain roars.

He hears her running back up the road. He lays his cheek in the water.

Ah! Bliss.

119

CAMBRIDGE, MASSACHUSETTS
DECEMBER 31, 1946

Coming up on midnight. No one to get ahead of him in shouting Happy New Year. Lesley is in Madrid, working for the U.S. Information Agency (informing said agency that everything they do is wrong). Irma straggled in unannounced at Christmas with her six-year-old son, hoping to live with him, but Frost chased her out. K. is at a party somewhere with Ted-Ted-Ted. She told Frost if he wanted to celebrate he should invite his own friends in.

The clock strikes twelve. He doesn't say it. Instead, he writes to Louis Untermeyer, a long letter that takes him a couple of hours. He deals in a lively manner with a number of poets and puts in lots of puns. Oh, he's content to be alone! At the end he writes briefly about how miserable Irma is. Then he goes into the living room and kicks the chairs around. Crumbles some cheese and crackers on a plate. Pours whiskey into a glass, spills most of it on the dining-room table, drops the glass on the carpet, covers it with a napkin, stamps on it. Throws the napkin away. Gets out a pincer and the cigars he keeps for guests; holds one after another in the gas flame of the stove until the place reeks. Gathers up the ashes and distributes them in ashtrays. Flings some of it around. Confetti!

Goes to bed. Tomorrow K. will have to help him clean up from the party.

120

"Stop here," he tells K. at the end of Irma's street. "I'll walk the rest. Wait here." He doesn't want K. to see, if anything unseemly happens. Something out in the street. He heads up the sidewalk. Her house is around the bend.

Her house—*he* bought it. And he bought the house in Hanover for her. And the farm in North Bennington before that. And he paid John's way through two colleges, the first for landscape design, the second for architecture. John, who's divorced her, and taken up with another woman. And not in that order.

Can he blame John? She ran away from him when they were newlyweds; ran howling back to Rob and Elinor from his Kansas farm with her baby, calling her mother-in-law a fiend. John later blamed it on sex. No surprise there. Still, Frost never liked John. He seemed to care more about Frost's approval than he did about Irma's. His father was sickly with TB; he was raised by women. His mother controlled him. Frost was the father figure. And maybe the sugar daddy. All his children had to deal with that.

Irma lost her love for John when she saw how his mother controlled him; fled with the baby, like Belle fleeing William. Runs in the blood. And she went back to him, like Belle. At his graduation from Yale, in architecture, John led the class. Irma sat in the bleachers and cried through the whole ceremony. She said, "Look at that goddamned schoolboy. I can't stand it." Now she insists that in addition to the woman he left her for, he's keeping a long string of whores on the side. The older son, Jackie, is out of the horror: a soldier with the occupation army in Germany. But Harold is only six, and he's with Irma. She asked for police protection last week, to keep intruders away from the house. She asked the family friend Merrill Moore for a revolver, for self-defense. Of course Moore refused. Speaking professionally, he says she'll have to be committed, sooner or later. Says Harold may not be safe.

She can't stay in a boarding house if there are any men in it. She was renting a place in White Plains last fall, but was acting so wild she was told to leave. Then she stayed with friends until they couldn't stand her anymore and kicked her out. She was spending all day in the bathroom washing every stitch of clothing she and Harold had worn the day before. She showed up at Brewster Street on Christmas Eve. "I don't see why I can't share your house with you," she said. Frost said, "Well you can't." She said, "But why can't I?" And Frost bellowed at her: "Because you can't!"

She would drown him. She would drown him.

He put her and Harold up in an inn in Groton for a month, while he found this house in Acton and bought it for her. Moore is trying to keep an eye on her. And Frost is near enough to stop in now and then. When he can stand to. The house has a flower garden she can work in. In the past she has sometimes enjoyed that. (She told him the neighbors were stealing her trees.)

An asylum for her? He'd have to be the one to commit her. John refuses to have anything to do with it. Frost remembers the first time he visited his sister in the Maine asylum. Jeanie hated him for signing the committal papers. She sat in her room with her eyes shut, her face wrung tight into a grimace. She answered him in monosyllables, and the muscles in her face twitched as though the words were being forced out of her.

Irma accused him a few weeks ago of having plans to kill her. She said he wanted her "out of the way" because he knew she was a better artist than he was. That her sculpted heads were better than any of his poems. Those heads—she's done them for years. Twisted expressions, horrible mouths. As though they were melting. She had one in plaster she lugged around. The head was huge, something for a statue at the top of a victory column. Sensual, leering lips, a crushed forehead. K. thought it looked like Mussolini.

He's worked his way around the bend to the point where he can see her house. It's a snug little bungalow. Has a nice view. He can see the flower garden, but Irma's not in it. She must be in the house with Harold. One of the upstairs windows is open.

He creeps closer. If she's looking out any of the windows on this side, she can see him. Cover him with the revolver. There's something in that open window. He creeps closer until he can make it out—a line of her heads, leering at the neighbors, at him. Gargoyles.

Half church of God, half castle 'gainst the Scot.

Or jack-o'-lanterns. If he could slam the door. If he could lock her out. His melting child.

What kind of parent—?

One who will survive.

He turns around. This Scot creeps away, to fight another day.

121

RIPTON, VERMONT

AUGUST 3, 1947

She's run away from the Acton house and been wandering the streets of Cambridge. Trying to foil the best-laid plans of white-slave kidnappers. Exactly like Jeanie; the chickens home to roost. He'll have to commit her. He sent the telegram to John today. John will refuse to help. Wash his hands. Frost will have to be her kidnapper. He'll be the gopher, just to prove he's no loafer!

He drinks another daiquiri. He never drinks. He grew up on two things—Korah swallowed by the earth, and William Frost swallowed by the bottle. Papa went in, a crazed genie came out. He drinks another. It's after dinner at his doctor's house, with K. and Ted. His doctor says a little liquor's good for you. Relieves tension. Little nips through the day. Nip, nip! I'll have another! "I've got a song to sing, O!" he announces to everyone. He's spread out on the sofa.

"My father was the keeper of the Eddystone Light. . . ."

That lovely look of alarm on K.'s face! How far will he go? Ho ho ho! And a bottle of rum! Ted could handle it. Have to. But Frost keeps it mild. What with his hosts. Still, K.'s panic—how might he get it back?

It's time to go. Near midnight. Goodbye, good doctor! Ted drives. Frost lies down in the back seat. Bumps and rumbles; tops of trees going by. Comfy. "I'm going to buy a whole case of liquor," he tells K., who's sitting up front next to the eunuch. Keeps her from getting kidnapped. "Dr. Porter knows what he's talking about!" Cure what ails him. Hair of the dog. His father drank a full tumbler of lime juice every morning, then went right back to the sauce. Fed it to his dogs. He said it made them young. Glazed looks from man and beast.

At the farm Frost gets out and heads up the path to his cabin. He looks back and sees a light on in the barn. No light in the main house. K. and Ted in the barn together. Feeding hay to the horses. K. and Ted in the hay. Hey! He turns around. He'll protect her! He marches down, shouting with each step, "Hey! Hay! Hey! Hay!" The eunuch stands in the barn doorway, blocking his way. "Where's K.?"

"She's gone to bed."

You lie! Frost looks past him into the barn. She's hiding somewhere. Tramp.

Frost looks at Ted for a moment. Then he wheels around and weaves back toward his cabin. Coward! He veers off into the upper pasture. A really good poem occurs to him and he marches up and down, shouting it.

> "Goddamn!
> Goddamn-damn!
> Goddamn-damn-damn!
> Goddamn-damn-damn-damn!"

When he enters the darkened porch he bumps into his writing desk. So he finds a hammer and claws it to pieces. Then he goes into the kitchen and throws all his dishes out on to the porch, to lie with his desk. Shatter clatter! Lighten his load. Hit the road. He's bound away! He cannot stay! His father's eyes—in his last months, he never lost the glazed look of a drunken dog. When Robbie was young, Papa often couldn't go to sleep alone. He'd make Robbie lie on the couch with him. Hug him hard. Robbie would lie very still, waiting for the beast to fall asleep. Hot whiskey breath in his face.

Robbie hits the road. He shouts some very good poems to the stars. Comes back to the cabin at dawn. Drinks some lemon juice. Goes to bed. Wakes at noon. K. comes up with his lunch at one. He looks at her ugly face. Irma is still crazy. At least he is sober. He says to K., "I don't think I'll buy that case of liquor after all."

122

POMONA, CALIFORNIA

1931

Frost can hardly believe he's here, the Golden State of his childhood, the golden weather minus the fog, weather even Elinor can't complain about, and the *dorado* names that tickle his ears like the sands of time: San Bernardino, San Fernando. Beyond the open car window yellow hills rise and fall against a blue sky, greenhouses flash, and in the north the San Gabriel Mountains are Olympian black teeth chipped by debris slides that (Frost, fascinated, read yesterday in the local paper) sweep bungalows down the slopes like boats on a tide, carry away orchards and nurseries, close the lifeline, Route 66. Carol and Lillian and six-year-old Prescott arrived two days ago on 66, having driven clear across the country (mind-boggling) in his Model A, while Frost and Elinor raced them on a train out of Colorado and Utah. California! The future!

Carol is driving, and the dry wind bathes Frost's face, and he remembers, savors, the dust in his mouth. A few more grams for his peck of gold. A sign says Pomona, three miles ahead. "Goddess of orchards!" he says. "A good omen!" Carol doesn't answer, but nods, gripping the wheel, glum. Damn him. Orange trees across a valley dance in parallax, fruit like sunset eyes staring up from under dark green brows.

Frost and his son are house-hunting. Hallelujah! Lillian has tuberculosis, and they're moving to California to save her life. Back in Vermont, Carol's apple trees, after years of work, are just coming into production. But all flesh is grass, and all gold is dust. Lillian, the capable one, the cheerful one, may die—la!—and so may Marjorie, who's got her own case (childhood girlfriends, it's as though they decided to share the adventure) and wastes away at a sanatorium in Colorado. And Lesley, with a newborn babe at her breast, wants a divorce from her husband, Dwight, who cheats like mad on her, and might in fact be mad, or maybe he's just pretending, with his glib talk of compulsions and compensations, to excuse his behavior. And Irma, with her husband off at college, is as nerve-racked as Dwight, only she's not pretending. To top it off, Frost fears he's tapped out as a poet. But the sun is bright. God doesn't seem to care, so why should he? And he's house-hunting!

A road is joining from the right. Dust comes in a swirl. Carol tromps on the brake. "What?"

"That fellow cut me off."

Frost leans out the window. "Watch where you're going!"

"Watch yourself, son of a bitch!"

La! The sweet swell of rage! "Chase him, Carol!" The fellow chugs off, spitting gravel. "Catch the bastard!"

But Carol is reluctant. He downshifts, waggling the stick. "It's not worth—"

"Get some gumption!"

Carol scowls. But he speeds up. "You're so—" He shakes his head.

"Proud? I was born here! That fellow's probably a damn Easterner in the movie business." Frost pounds the outside of his door with the flat of his hand. "Faster! Gee up!"

"Don't dent my door." Carol is smiling. Maybe he wants to see what the car can do. So off they go. Frost switches to pounding the dashboard, yelling, and Carol drops his reserve, or anyway he takes it off and folds it on the seat beside him. He urges the shuddering car past fifty miles an hour (as fast as mad Dwight, who's had three accidents), and father and son chase the frightened bastard all the way to Pomona.

123

PRIVATE CUSTODIAL CARE, CUTTINGSVILLE, VERMONT
JANUARY 1959

Irma is lying in her bed, unable to sleep. She's never liked poetry. But for some reason, whenever, such as now, she stares and stares into the dark and sleep won't come, rhyming words come instead. She tries to hold them off, but they won't be held off, they come in, and she can't get rid of them.

124

A doctor stood in the doorway. Frost ran for the hills. But first he yelled, "This is when I walk out of your lives—all of you!" He fled up the stairs and lay facedown on his bed. The doctor followed and spoke to him, but he played dead. After a while the doctor and K. went away and let him be king on his own.

His royal highness rose and went downstairs and swallowed a raw egg. He wondered if it was time to stop playing, time to lie on his real deathbed.

This perfect moment of unbafflement

When K. returned, he could see the impatience and contempt in her eyes, and he was contrite. "Help me pack my bags for the hospital," he said. He was quiet as she drove him there. The stores were getting ready for Christmas. When she left him in his room, he said to her, "I will do this on the highest plane—don't fear."

But he fears he hasn't kept his word. He's yelled. He's thrashed. He's seen K.'s eyes roll, and her daughter, Anne, quail from him. Then he's good. When friends visit, he's kind. They're saying farewell. That angers him, but he hides it, because they might be right. Then he's sure they're wrong. Then he knows they're right. When he's a spoiled baby, his friends take heart: "That's the Robert we know!" It's when he's gentle, when he opens his heart to them, that they look worried. Ain't that funny.

He's been here how many weeks? A lifetime. Early December K.

brought him here. Then left him for days and days. She had a funeral to go to in Vermont, and when she came back she had a bad cold and the doctors wouldn't let her see him. She said. Anne stayed with him most of that time. And he's got the nurses K. hired: one from 7:00 a.m. to 3:00 p.m.; another from 3:00 to 11:00; then whoever K. can scrounge up for the night shift. It was hard to find people over Christmas, and she let him know it. But he can't bear to be alone in the room, night or day. That's when he yells, and eyes roll. But why not yell? They're all paid. Boughten friendship. He's bought a dozen homes. This is his last.

Metal, linoleum, fluorescent light. Window view down to the hospital entrance, where new patients are carted in every day. He's in Margery's hospital bed. At night he wakes and sees himself sleeping in the chair in the corner, keeping his bedside vigil, such as it is. "Hey, you!" he barks. "Wake up!" And the person who comes to his bedside is a stranger. "Who are you?"

They won't tell him, but he's not an idiot—they found cancer in the prostate. Maybe in the bladder, too. But it won't be the cancer that kills him, it'll be the blood clots. He's had two pulmonary embolisms. He's seen what the world looks like through an oxygen tent. (Watery.) He knows what a catheter feels like. The doctors tied off the veins in his legs to keep more clots from reaching his lungs. But it won't work. Elinor's heart killed her. What could kill Frost but his lungs?

Most of the weeks here he planned to go home. He's still two months shy of his ninetieth year. K. arranged for a couple to live in at Brewster Street and take care of him. He held court in his room. Doctors came round in the evening, and he offered them delicacies he had K. stock in the hall refrigerator. Entertained them. Robert Frost went on and on and on. Sometimes he sat in a chair. Sometime he drank a little champagne propped up in bed. He's a king. This room's a suite, the best in the hospital. The last occupant was the king of Saudi Arabia. He's got a fireplace, his own bathroom. Flowers everywhere. Telegrams in piles. Long live the king! In Florida once long ago, in the time of myth, K. stormed out, hissing over her shoulder, "You can stay in your cabin and be a king," and he'd shouted after her,

"But I don't want to be a king—alone!" He's only wanted to crown her, all these years. Elinor returned his engagement ring. K. throws her crown at him.

And there he sat alone and dreamed his dream

She left with Ted today—a getaway. Somewhere in western Massachusetts. She said she was exhausted. Or was it yesterday? He looks at his Baby Ben on the table next to his bed. One a.m. Yesterday. It's Monday now. A new day. New patients coming to the hospital, under his window. She'll be gone two or three days. Maybe he'll die while she's gone. (The dead go out the back way.) Make her sorry. Or will she be sorry? Are they sharing a bed on their getaway? Can he finally admit to himself, on his deathbed, that he doesn't know? That he can't be sure of anything K. tells him? She sat in this room a week ago, two weeks ago, and he shooed out the nurse and told her for the thousandth time that he hoped his biography would do her the honor of telling the true story of their relationship. She gestured angrily. "For the thousandth time—!"

"The story should be told."

"And what story is that?"

"Why . . ." And he told her.

"I've been your secretary, and I helped you out of your despair when you were lost—"

"In the woods—"

"—*when you were lost*, and so did Ted, and I've always been a good wife to him, and a good secretary to you, and it hasn't been easy."

"But the world should know. . . ." And he told her.

"That didn't happen," she said.

"That's what you insist the biography should say—"

"It didn't happen, and I've asked you over and over and over again to stop insinuating that it has, it just robs you of your dignity, and it dirties my name, and I won't have it."

And there he sat alone and dreamed his dream

He knows it happened. He knows. She can't take that from him. She's burned all his letters. But he's got the poems in his briefcase. (He can see it on the chair by the window.) All the secret poems he's written about her, for her, to celebrate her, punish her. She calls them dirty. Well it's their dirty little secret, isn't it? Obscene—which means "off-stage." Behind the painted backdrop sewn from the stuff of silken tents, off the beaten forest-path, he lies with K., and her drawers are off, and never again will birds' song be the same.

Do you hear it, Robert? Edward crooks a finger. The nightingale—there. Do you hear it?

I . . . think I do.

He's seen her eyes go straight to the briefcase when she comes into the room. She locates it before she looks to see whether he's alive or dead. If his soul is in there, might it be appropriate that it won't survive five minutes longer than he does? She'll swoop down on it and carry it off, make a burnt offering. Their little secret. The one thing Lesley and K. can agree on. Pretend it never happened. They'll have their way, bury him together. The world will think he was a mad old man, with no idea what his madness was. *Cum subita incautum dementia cepit amantem.* The letters and secret poems will be gone. There will be only a few photographs, and none of them private. But look. See. Dear posterity, read between the lines—in the Bread Loaf photos, year after year, the rows of faculty standing and sitting, Ted is always at the side with his inseparable pipe, K. is always in the center, at Frost's feet. The king is on his throne, his concubine at his feet. He gives her a crown, but when he walks away it comes rolling after him like a hoop.

How hard it is to keep from being king

Lesley wrote a letter. She called him Robert Coeur de Lion. After all the fights between them since her mother died, this moved him deeply. He knows how much she dislikes K., and it pains him to think, to know, that they'll quarrel over his death. There's been bad feeling about how he's distributed his property. He dictated a letter to Lesley.

"I trust my word can bind you all together as long as my name as a poet lasts." *Fiat pax!* Couldn't his poetry charm them, at least *them*, to step into the magic circle? He feared not, and his fear brought tears to his eyes, and the tears brought shame. "I am too emotional for my state," he said, apologizing to those present, and Anne took it down in shorthand for the letter and K. typed it up.

It's been on his mind more and more during his stay here. That word. Not "peace," the other word. The word the sapheads wallow in. Love your neighbor as you love yourself, Rabbi Reichert said to him, oh, a thousand years ago. And hate your neighbor as you hate yourself, Frost answered.

Only half the equation. *Omnia vincit Amor:* the conquering madness of the Love-god, the evil born of that good. Jeanie loved her brother's friend Mills, and when that love broke her, she loved Kaiser Wilhelm. Wilhelm loved Belgium, and Edward Thomas loved England.

> Anyway all he talked about was love.
> They soon saw he would do someone a mischief
> If he wa'n't kept strict watch of, and it ended
> In father's building him a sort of cage

But it's what he's been thinking about. He's going to die very soon. He's in constant pain, and the past three days he's slipped in and out of consciousness. The doctors are arguing with each other. He's been vomiting.

Yesterday who should show up but Ezra's daughter. An Italian countess! This was where all Ezra's troubadouring was headed, fifty years ago. Can't get much farther away from Idaho than that. Poor Ezra. People think Frost dislikes him, but really, how could he not feel for the man's fight with madness. If Frost's words have been bubbles that buoyed him, Ezra's were doubloons and argent chains that helped drag him under. His daughter said she'd come to thank Frost for his help in getting Ezra out of the loony bin. "He'll be glad to know you consented to see me."

"I've never got over those days we had together," Frost said.

"My father didn't say much when he was released from Saint Elizabeth's, but I suppose you and he understand each other." She meant Ezra didn't thank Frost for getting him out.

"Politics makes too much difference to both of us," Frost told her. "Love is all. Romantic love as in stories and poems. I tremble with it. I'd like to see Ezra again." He meant it. Oh, to be back in Ezra's bohemian room on an alley in London in 1913, Ezra in an Oriental dressing gown reading the first bound copy of *A Boy's Will* while Frost stares unseeing at a magazine, waiting for the verdict. "You don't mind our liking this?" Ezra intones. (If Frost's desire was to be king, Ezra's goal was the papacy.) "Oh no," Frost says. "Go right ahead."

Frost looks at his Baby Ben. Two a.m. Time to write poetry. But he can only dictate, and Anne's not here. He tried yesterday but couldn't get anywhere with the poem he's working on. It's about a king who wants prophets brought in so they can interpret a dream he's had. But the twist is, he can't describe the dream to them. He needs a prophet to tell him what his dream was, and *then* interpret it. (Where's Anne?) The prophets say they can't do that, so he has them all executed. He's left sitting alone with his dream. Then a bum comes in. Riffraff. The king says to him (it's the last part of the poem so far), he says to him . . . What's the line? "Tell me . . ." Where the hell's Anne?

The night nurse comes to his bedside. "Did you say something?"

"Where's Anne?"

"She's home asleep. You should try to sleep, too." She starts fussing with his sheets.

"Don't tell me what to do. Get away from me." He's always telling K. to tell the nurses he doesn't like them holding his hand, he doesn't like them sitting on the edge of his bed, he doesn't like them tucking him in. He doesn't like them jollying him, he doesn't like them combing his hair. He doesn't like them bathing him. Putting him in the zinc washtub. Playing games with him. His father hugging him tight as he falls asleep, drunkard's breath bathing him. He doesn't like them beating him hard when he's awake. Taking his pants down. Don't touch me.

The unembarrassed flesh of the bathing-suit crowd. Oily handshakes. Robert Frost goes on and on and on. Words as deeds. The king sat alone and dreamed his dream.

Frost wakes.

The room is dark. The nurse dozing. Light comes from the corridor. The door is open, framing a silhouetted figure. Dressed in white. The angel of death. He steps in. It's Dr. Thorn. He comes through on his rounds at nine or ten each morning, interns in a cloud behind him. But Baby Ben says seven. And Thorn's alone. "Traveling light today, aren't you?" Frost says to him. The better to tuck Frost under one arm, leap.

"I just wanted to check on you," Thorn says.

He had a feeling. A premonition. Woke early. Something's wrong. Drove straight in. When doctors take up prophesying, it's time for poets to die. Frost looks again, and the doorway is empty.

The only certain freedom's in departure

He dozes; wakes at noon. Anne is sitting in the chair. "Where's K.?"

"She's away for a couple of days, remember? She left yesterday."

"Anything from the president?"

She shakes her head gently. "Not yet."

Piles of telegrams. But not a word from Kennedy. Go home, old man. Even Russians visited him. When was that? They drank champagne. Katayev was there, whom he'd met in Russia. And one of the Pendragons; Frida, who fought with his driver on the way to school. It was lovely to see her. Come to bounce him out of bed, show him a palace, marry him to a Russian poetess. He said to them, "I had a heart-to-heart talk with Khrushchev." Who played his cards magnanimously after all. Pulled back the ships, dismantled the missiles. Saved the world. Frost said, "We were charmed with each other. I'm very fond of him. He's a lovable man."

Love. He trembles with it.

This perfect moment of unbafflement,
When no man's name and no noun's adjective

But summons out of nowhere like a jinni.
We know not what we owe this moment to.
It may be wine, but much more likely love.

He saw Frank Reeve. Was it the same day? No, it was earlier. New Year's Day. 1963. They had a lovely party. Drank champagne. (Or was that with the Russians?) Frank brought a note from his children and a calendar with a picture they'd drawn. (Was a date circled? *Here dies Robert Frost.*) January 28, 1963. Frost said to Frank, "You have the world before you." *All the world, the saved world, the charming, earnest world.* He confided that the poem he was working on, something about a king and his dream, was no good. "I'm close to giving up," he said. There was only one last thing he wanted. "I want to go back to Russia to see Khrushchev. He and I understood each other."

"Tell me my dream then," said the king

He saw Frank, and Al Edwards one day, and Stewart Udall, and Louis, and Fred Adams, Stanley Burnshaw, Ed Lathem. They all say get well, but they're really saying goodbye, and Frost is gentle and open and they know it's a sure sign. He'll miss them all; he trembles with it. Only Larry hasn't come. The others come to praise him, but Larry will bury him. He doesn't want to come, and Frost doesn't want to see him. And K. detests Larry, and Larry loathes K. His word will never bind them together, that quarrel over his dead body will be Homeric, and he thought he wanted it, but now he only wants everyone to get along. He's had a deathbed conversion, he's a member now of the saphead communion.

Take this wafer. He vomits. They're feeding him some gruel, a spoon or two every half-hour. The doctors say he's not getting enough of something. Some balance. He pushes the spoon away, he grimaces, turns his mouth out of reach. "We'll have to do it intravenously if you don't cooperate," the doctor says. Or maybe it's the nurse. He swallows a spoonful, vomits it back up. What goes down must come up. Fall and rise. "There's something wrong," he says. "I shouldn't be like this." They try again; he vomits again. They leave him alone. He cooperated, so he doesn't get the needle. He was a good boy.

He thinks of the earth going round. 1963. Eighty-nine trips around the sun since he was born, and always back to the same place. What's he or the earth accomplished? He said a thousand years ago that he seemed to manage a volume of poetry every seven years, and it's worked out about right, if you count Derry as the beginning. 1900–1963: nine collections. Every seven years is a climacteric, and the ninth is the grand climacteric. The grand climax.

Last scene of all,
That ends this strange, eventful history,
Is second childishness and mere oblivion,
Sans teeth, sans eyes, sans taste, sans everything

And the earth? Survived another one. Go, Earth!

He's been troubled by an image for some time now. He sees the earth getting tired of the eternal round, Mother Bard visiting the same celestial colleges year after year. He sees her breaking free of the sun's gravity, a ball loosed from a chain, sailing majestically straight out of the solar system, blowing a goodbye kiss to Venus, fighting past Mars, trading a jovial joke with Jupiter. Heading maybe for a confab with Sirius, or a closer look at the Crab Nebula.

We'll cast off hawser for the universe

Why does this appeal to him? Because it's rise without fall? Eating your cake and locking it up at night, too? He's never believed it possible. But death is close now. Death's in the doorway. And he wants to know: where's the back door? The escape hatch to the peaceable kingdom. This lion wants to lie down with a lamb. Man can go either way with the knowledge he got from biting the atom. The peaceful use—atomic energy, rockets to the stars. Or the other kind—rockets that rise and fall. Earth's the right place for death. Earth's the right place for love.

So have I heard and do in part believe it.

"Jack Sweeney and his wife are here," Anne says. "Do you feel up to seeing them?"

Yes. I tremble with it. Did he say that? He must let the nurse touch him. She helps him sit up in bed. He closes his eyes and opens them. Jack is there. "How's Harvard treating you?" Frost says. Jack's curator of a poetry collection there.

They talk about this and that. Jack's lovely. And his wife. Frost looks at them. They should be holding hands, somewhere where he can't see. Stay married, he wants to tell them.

Be happy, happy, happy

Or maybe he should say,

O, o, o, o

He says, "I feel as though I were in my last hours."

They leave. Then Anne goes for the night. Baby Ben says 6:00 p.m. The nurse gives him gruel and he vomits, but she gives him some more and he keeps it down. He dozes. Wakes at nine, feeling better. The night nurse asks him if he's strong enough to sit in his chair while she changes the bed. He is. While he's sitting there, the phone rings. The nurse says, "It's Anne. She wants to know how it's going."

"Fine!" Frost calls across the room to the receiver. "How's it going with her?"

K. is still gone. She'll be sorry. The nurse helps him back into the clean bed. Clean just to get dirty, then clean again. Round and round. A January bed. A 1963 bed. What's it for?

Ten p.m. When the Russians were here drinking champagne, Katayev said something from the Book of Saphead Prayer. It was for the reporters. "If all humanity had men like Frost there would be no wars."

Frost wasn't a member of the communion yet, and when the reporters crowded into the room afterward, seeking a comment, he said, "Men are men. I'm not always so hopeful. War has its rules. We must not cut down the apple trees, and we must not poison the wells."

He trembles with it. He looks up into the apple tree, he looks down into the well. White blossoms above, a glimmer of white below, white chickens milling about his feet. He looks at them, and beyond them, across the yard, and he sees that it's mud time. Precious mud time! You don't see it much anymore, with all the country roads paved. The old pleasures of mud time. Helping each other out of the mud.

> But the Prince drew away his hand in time
> To avoid what he wasn't sure he wanted.
> So the crown fell and the crown jewels scattered

Why is he thinking of that? He wants to think of mud. Wallow in it. Mud's the right place for love. It's a wonderful world—

He opens his eyes. Eleven p.m. To hell with it.

Why is he thinking that? He said something once. There was an audience. He stood at the podium and said "Two Tramps in Mud Time," and then he said, "Play for mortal stakes. Life's a gamble, and you bet nothing less than your life. There's no sweeter expression than 'You bet your sweet life.'" Sweet, muddy world. He said, "The most inalienable right of man is to go to hell in his own way."

> So the crown fell and the crown jewels scattered

He said, "It's a wonderful world—to hell with it," and his audience was uncomfortable.

Do you see yonder shining light? he said. And his audience breathed, it stirred: *We . . . think we do.*

Keep that light in your eye, he said.

He opens his eye. Baby Ben says midnight.

Something is happening. Something's rising in him. He gags. The nurse looms, and he tries to speak. He gags again. Something comes out of his mouth. The thing is blooming in him, filling him. It takes his fingers and waggles them at the nurse. She hurries out of the room. *This is when I walk out—* He looks at the ceiling, at the window, at the walls, at the foot of the bed, at the calendar Frank's children drew for him. *There may be little or much beyond the grave.* Soon he'll know. Or he won't. He opens his eyes. There's a young man leaning over him. A stranger. The resident on the floor. Frost tries to speak. He wants to say to him, *The butter's by your elbow, Father Hart.* He wants to say, *Shall I go on? Or have I said enough?*

But that's not his job anymore, is it? The cow's in the corn, and they're calling him, *Schneider!*, and he flows off the porch like water, he runs up the Berry Road, barking joyfully.

125

1967

Why are you laughing, children?
The Younger Poet writes:

> Sexual intercourse began
> In nineteen sixty-three
> (Which was rather late for me)—
> Between the end of the *Chatterley* ban
> And the Beatles' first LP.
>
> Up till then there'd only been
> A sort of bargaining,
> A wrangle for a ring,
> A shame that started at sixteen
> And spread to everything.

126

Standing at the hotel-room door, Margaret Bartlett Anderson is startled to see that Robert Frost is not the big man she remembers from
her childhood in Boulder, when her parents would drop everything to
go to Denver and meet him off the train. He's shrunk without having
aged. But perhaps that's because when, at eight years old, she first saw
him, he already seemed as old as the hills.

He invites her in. He looks tired. She's heard he's finishing up a
tour of some twenty colleges. The presidential election is tomorrow. She read somewhere that he'd predicted Kennedy would win.
What a disaster that would be! Her parents would spin in their
graves.

They talk for an hour. Margaret has been left the letters between
Frost and her parents that her mother so desperately wanted to publish. Frost blocked her, even when she was dying of cancer. It seemed
cruel of him. But Margaret doesn't forget, while talking with him,
that he's the man who brought her parents together. In a way, she exists only because of him.

His schedule is busy; she rises to go. He apologizes for being so
tired. "For fifty years," he tells her, "I've given lectures, and every
summer I go away from people, hide out in Vermont. Then in the
fall I start the lectures, the talks, and it all comes over me again, the
old fears, the anxieties. Why do I do it? I don't have to anymore. I
want out, you see, I want out! But then I go on . . . and it's all right."
When he walks her to the door he pauses at the threshold. Something about the way he looks at her makes her feel her youth. He

seems to want to send her off with something to think about, something to remember him by. She probably will never see him again.

"Remember," he says, holding the door open for her to pass through, "remember, nothing is momentous. We always think it is, but—nothing is momentous."

127

COBBETTS POND, WINDHAM, NEW HAMPSHIRE

1891

The hired man on John Dinsmore's farm goes down the long line turning the hay with a fork in the morning sunshine. Beautiful weather. The pond glimmers.

He takes a step, turns over a forkful. Steps, turns. Right, left. Make, hay. Warm, work.

Morning gladness.

He looks up. *Morning gladness.*

Glass. The still pond. He looks down into the sky.

Steps, turns. *Morning gladness.* He repeats it as he goes down the line. Morning, step. Gladness, turn. At the end of the line he pauses. Stretches. Warm muscles. Make money.

Sheer morning gladness.

He starts up the next row. The farmers say, "Leave the hay to make." Make in the sun. Bake in the sun. Mow it and make it and put it in the mow. *Sheer morning gladness.* He swings it more, down the row. Warmer and warmer. *Sheer morning gladness.*

He stops again at the end of the line. Wipes sweat. His eyesight glitters. The pond gleams. Gladness, glass. The pondwater brims.

Sheer morning gladness at the brim.

Warmth floods him. He writes the words down when he gets back to the bunkhouse, and he's happy for three days.

128

The Younger Poet lays him down, and as he sleeps he dreams a dream:

Midway on his career's journey, he finds himself in a lovely dark wood. Far ahead he makes out, masked by gloom, a shambling creature, linking tracks through the snow. A peripatetic bear, shaggy head wagging, lower lip hanging. Or is it a leopard? Or a wolf? The Younger Poet pursues. The beast zags, seeming to want to keep off, but it is slow, awkward. At last it stops and the Younger Poet catches up. Without turning it speaks over its snow-crusted shoulder. "You find me punished here, because I was too selfish of my career, too jealous of Eliot, who mongered Dante, who didn't know Virgil any better than I did, though the Harvard gang could never see it."

"You were Herrick to his Donne," the Younger Poet says with feeling.

The beast turns. Frost's cold blue eyes gaze full on him. "A volume of Herrick's poetry was the first I ever remember laying eyes on. I was seven."

"Like you, Master, in rural solitude, made joyfully sad by the quotidian, Herrick flaunted neither his learning nor his suffering."

"I must be imagining you. You are the Perfect Reader."

"I am the Younger Poet."

"Ah." He smiles, not noticeably happy. He looks upward, past the snowy boughs. All the stars are falling, as flakes. "The earthly approximation. But as I was overfond of saying, I wasn't a Platonist, so why was I so haunted by that Ideal? The Perfect Friend. I kept to my wife, and later my mistress, but I kept trying to find—"

"I have found *you*."

"Tracked me down, yes." Frost shudders, or perhaps shivers. "I dreamed of this encounter long ago, you and I in this whiteness." Gesturing broadly with an arm, he nearly falls; his feet are gripped by the deep snow. "You find me here because I fled to woods too often. I ran from Methuen's poisoned well and Derry's poverty, I buried myself under thatch in England but deserted England's war to burrow in Franconia, I fled the August frosts of Franconia, breaking Marjorie's heart, to tend my garden in South Shaftsbury, I retreated from the grippe of Vermont winters to hide in the glare of Florida. In Ripton, it was an annual ritual that I ran from a friendly game of baseball, if I lost, to lose myself in the trees and make the sorry winners worry. Unlike Virgil, who carried his lamp behind to light the way for those who followed, I was a light only to myself. Through poetry, I made my words into deeds, because in prosaic deeds I was poor. I embraced my laziness and my freedom. My punishment here is to have, of all the dead, the most regular hours."

"You are—?"

"I am the Watchman of the Night, I am the Coward on Duty, I am the Resident on the Floor. Not my will, but thine."

"Could I ask you—"

"I was the Monologuist, but here I am dogged by dialogue, my feet tangled in unanswerable questions like leashes, my spaniel protégés polishing my heels."

"You still seem a monologuist."

Frost's eyes turn a colder shade. "This is Hell. If you want change, go to Purgatory. Tom and Ezra are there, vomiting up their undigested Latin. They'll be ready for Heaven in about a thousand years."

"Whereas you will always be here, only more sure of all you thought was true."

"*I* don't mind eating my words. And by the way, you can go to hell." Frost turns away.

The Younger Poet is contrite. He says to the back, "But you were a great poet."

Frost turns again. He seems more contrite than the Younger Poet. He seems stricken. (This is a competition he will always win.) "Forgive me." He makes a movement as though to grip the Younger Poet's arm, but stops short. His hand describes a little wave instead. "We are good enough friends to forgive each other, aren't we?" He leans close. Into his pale eyes comes that old insatiable hunger. "I *was* great, wasn't I?"

It takes a moment for the Younger Poet to recognize this as a question. "Yes."

"You hesitated!"

"I—"

Frost looks away. He speaks into the darkness between the trees. "Poetry is love, and earth is the right place for it. Not here." He wrenches one foot out of the snow. "You shouldn't stay."

He takes a weary step, and another. But he turns back a last time. He seems to brighten at an idea. The orchidous lower lip that can look so sadly lost draws itself into a cup to nestle the famous impish smile. "In poetry, there is a law of seriousness, also known as gravity. Aquinas said that gravity was love. The apple loves the earth it falls to—or Newton's head, if it's in the way. Einstein showed that gravity was a bending of space itself, like grain in wood." He holds up a thumb. Is the whorl on it an example of the grain he means? "See. We naturally fall toward each other. See. *Felix culpa!* We fall into the arms of everything, along the grain of space-time. We roll down the slope with rocks, stones, trees, apples, and the moon. Even missiles. Even they fit in somehow." He shivers.

He turns for good. Starts away through the snow. The Younger Poet calls after, puckishly, "Should I come, too?"

But the old man (they say) is deaf as a post. The shaggy head, the white spots of powder on the coat—the bear, the leopard, the wolf— doesn't answer. The beast goes doggedly into the pillared dark, lifting knees to mount the ice crust for a moment before punching through, so that every step jolts, the shoulders heave. It stumbles once, but catches itself and keeps on.

∽

AUTHOR'S NOTE

Although this work is properly called a novel, I've approached it in the spirit of a biographer who wanted to stretch his usual form to accommodate more speculation than nonfiction generally allows. None of the known facts of Robert Frost's life have been changed; all of the letters quoted or paraphrased are real; Frost's public utterances are drawn from transcripts; most of the private conversations are either close paraphrases of reported interchanges or elaborations of a participant's description of a conversation. (Exceptions are noted below.) My contribution, for the most part, has been confined to selecting a few events from a very long and full life to trace what I consider important contours of Frost's extraordinarily lush and difficult mental landscape; adding concrete detail, drawn as much as possible from facts gleaned from a wide variety of sources; and, of course, presuming to guess what Frost might have been thinking during those incidents. In particular, my interest has been to suggest how a great writer's language flows out of his life and back into it, how certain mysteriously fecund words and their associated ideas are turned under in the writer's mind, whence they sprout daughter ideas, seedlings that are turned under again, until the mind "can contain itself no more, / But sweating-full, drips wine and oil a little." Because this subject is perforce highly speculative, straightforward literary biographies tend to undertreat it.

I should point out that what might seem to be the least plausible aspect of my text—i.e., Frost's ability to remember flawlessly hundreds of lines of his own and other poets' verse, so that *le vers juste* seems always to be dancing on the tip of his tongue—was attested by many witnesses during his lifetime. Everything by another poet or writer that I put into Frost's mind was mentioned, quoted, or identified as important to him by the real Robert Frost; the few exceptions are poems or prose works that seem to have inspired a poem of his own.

"The Younger Poet" is not a composite character, since I've changed no facts and thus have not suppressed inconsistencies; rather, it's a common label for various poets, some well known and some not, who could be considered at least in part to have been influenced by Frost's poetry and personality. Presented in the plural, they might have been a chorus called Legacy. I've rendered them in the singular to stand for that perfect Other that most of us hope for, that artists pursue with such ardency, and that Robert Frost hunted with his own peculiar tragic force.

In the chapter notes that follow, I mention only my more unusual sources. Most of the straightforward biographical facts, such as the deaths of children, family histories, well-attested incidents, purchases of farms, and so on, are drawn from Lawrance

Thompson's three-volume biography, *Robert Frost* (I: *The Early Years*; II: *The Years of Triumph*; III: *The Later Years*, Thompson and R. H. Winnick). Other excellent sources of biographical information that in general I don't specify are Jay Parini's *Robert Frost: A Life*; William Pritchard's *Frost: A Literary Life Reconsidered*; and John Evangelist Walsh's *Into My Own: The English Years of Robert Frost*. Much of the detail regarding Frost's time in Russia is drawn from F. D. Reeve's *Robert Frost in Russia*. Unless otherwise mentioned, all letters quoted can be found in the biographies, or in one of the following sources: *Selected Letters of Robert Frost*, edited by Lawrance Thompson; *Family Letters of Robert and Elinor Frost*, edited by Arnold Grade; *The Letters of Robert Frost to Louis Untermeyer*, edited by Untermeyer; *Elected Friends: Robert Frost and Edward Thomas to One Another*, edited by Matthew Spencer. Lesley Frost's delightful juvenile writings appear in *New Hampshire's Child*.

Where I've followed a source in unusually close detail, I say so. I also name the various faces of the Younger Poet, and acknowledge my debts for particular insights. If I don't specify a conversation or an incident as an invention, then it is based on fact.

Plagiarism police, take note: if I name a book or article as a source, it means I've felt free to use any reported dialogue therein, and in some cases I've taken the written thoughts of the writer and converted them into spoken expression—or, in the cases of the chapters that are not told from Frost's point of view, the thoughts of my narrator occasionally incorporate phrases that the real person in question wrote in his or her account of the incident being described. Frost's own thoughts throughout the novel are extensively larded with phrases from his letters, and with lines and fragments of lines from his own and other people's poems. (Poetry lovers: happy hunting.) I've tried in the notes that follow to raise the white flag at all those places where my larceny has been grand rather than petty. If I've failed to mention anything, the omission has been unintentional (in other words, don't shoot!); just as whatever factual mistakes I have surely made can be laid at the door of my ignorance and sloth, rather than evil intent.

Finally, a word about Frost's copyrighted poems. Readers may have noticed occasional awkward spots in my text, where I quote only a brief snippet from a poem and then paraphrase the rest. Works first published after 1922 will not enter the public domain until 2018 at the earliest (and perhaps not even then, given the interest of powerful corporations in extending copyright), and anyone wishing to print more than a small fraction of any of Frost's later poems must secure permission from the Estate of Robert Frost. That permission was not forthcoming for this work. I was never granted the reasons for the refusal, but I suspect they were a combination of discomfort over a complex portrayal of a man who has already been unfairly mauled by his official biographer, and nonspecific unhappiness with the genre of biographical fiction. The irony is that I could legally invent a scene in which Frost commits murder (since in American law you can't libel the dead), and I could just as legally fill this novel with my own atrocious doggerel that I insisted, hand over heart, was Frost's, but I'm not allowed to freely quote his actual, still-copyrighted poetry, much of which is widely available (despite copyright) online.

The ever-lengthening arm of copyright protection is proving to be a burden and often a bane to more and more scholars and creative artists. At least in this case I can comfort myself with the thought that my difficulties have been metaphorically apt. Frost really did write to Lionel Trilling, "No sweeter music can come to my ears than the clash of arms over my dead body when I am down." The fight over Frost—plaster saint, monster, or human being?—has always been, and continues to be, Homeric. My ears are still ringing from the ax-blow to my helmet, but I'd like to think that somewhere Frost—or maybe I just mean Poetry—is enjoying the music.

CHAPTER NOTES

1. F. D. Reeve, *Robert Frost in Russia.* Frederick B. Adams Jr., *To Russia with Frost.*
3. The Younger Poet is Daniel Smythe. I've closely followed his account in *Robert Frost Speaks.*
6. Louis Mertins, *Robert Frost: Life and Talks-Walking.*
9. This is the only chapter for which I've invented a precise date; Parini places this meeting in "early May." RF's conversation with Dobrynin is elaborated from a brief comment RF made to Fred Adams. Anatoly Dobrynin, *In Confidence.*
10. The original final line of "The Lockless Door" is in a letter from RF to Untermeyer.
13. "I was brought up on" the Korah story: letter, RF to Untermeyer. RF did clean the well at Amesbury after spilling milk in it; that he may in retrospect have feared contamination of the well in Methuen is my own speculation.
18. The Younger Poet is Robert Francis; poem and diary entry are in his *Frost: A Time to Talk.*
20. Landor died at age eighty-nine, but RF thought he died at ninety; RF's curious linking of Landor's age with the North Pole occurs in a letter to George Whicher, *Selected Letters.* Once RF enters the Little Theater, everything he says out loud is drawn verbatim from a transcript published in Reginald Cook, *Robert Frost: A Living Voice.* The couplet on the Swedish ore that I can't quote is "From Iron: Tools and Weapons."
21. The Younger Poet is Galway Kinnell.
22. Thompson aired this bizarre theory to Stanley Burnshaw, who reported it in his *Robert Frost Himself.*
24. Slightly elaborated from an anecdote told by RF in Mertins.
25. Elaborated from an account in Sidney Cox, *A Swinger of Birches.*
27. Verbatim from a transcript made by Thompson from a sound recording of the television broadcast of the inauguration; included in his "Notes on Robert Frost," Dartmouth College Library, Rauner Special Collections.
28. Stewart Udall, "Robert Frost's Last Adventure," *New York Times Magazine,* June 11, 1972.
29. Mertins. The exchange between RF and Belle is invented.
30. Reminiscence of Alan Cheuse, recorded in *Whose Woods These Are: A History of the Bread Loaf Writers' Conference, 1926–1992.*
31. Thompson reports this as really having happened; Parini makes the plausible suggestion that Lesley dreamed it.
32. Reeve. William Taubman, *Khrushchev: The Man and His Era.*
33. Letter, RF to Gertrude McQuesten, August 30, 1914, quoted in Walsh.
34. Margaret Bartlett Anderson, *Robert Frost and John Bartlett: The Record of a Friendship.*

35. Lesley Frost, *New Hampshire's Child*. N. Arthur Bleau, "Robert Frost's Favorite Poem," *Frost: Centennial Essays III*, ed. Jac Tharpe.
36. The Younger Poet is John Ciardi; the biographer is Thompson; the critic is Richard Poirier, *Robert Frost: The Work of Knowing*; the encyclopedist is David Mesher, in *The Robert Frost Encyclopedia*, ed. Nancy Lewis Tuten and John Zubizarreta.
37. Transcript in Cook.
38. It's Poirier's good idea that "The Woodspurge" helped inspire RF's "The Vantage Point." The poem about the diver that I can't quote is "Despair." It's uncollected, but it can be found in The Library of America edition of Frost's poems.
40. The use of "fill" instead of "keep" in the antepenultimate line is per RF's first published version of this poem.
41. Lesley Frost, *New Hampshire's Child*.
43. The Younger Poet is Robert Lowell.
46. Lesley Frost, *New Hampshire's Child*.
47. Lesley Frost, *New Hampshire's Child*.
48. The visit to the school is closely based on Reeve's account. RF on Hardy, "He has planted himself on the wrongs that can't be righted": *The Notebooks of Robert Frost*, ed. Robert Faggen.
50. Frost's interest in white pines as the king's trees is reported by Robert Francis. This conversation is invented.
51. RF told Mertins that all his life he imagined he heard seals in the night.
54. RF's Schneider stories, in their copyrighted entirety, are in *Stories for Lesley*, ed. Roger D. Sell.
55. The Younger Poet is Padraic Colum. This is based closely on his account, quoted in Thompson.
56. The poem I can't quote much of is "A Cliff Dwelling," a charming lesser-known lyric.
58. Sell, *Stories for Lesley*.
61. Elinor's use of the phrase "robs life of its grace and charm" is in Thompson's "Notes on Robert Frost."
64. Telephone interview with Edward Lathem, July 24, 2007.
66. Letter, RF to Susan Hayes Ward, Febuary 10, 1912. Walsh points out that the concluding line of "The Road Not Taken" echoes "She Dwelt Among the Untrodden Ways."
68. Reeve and Adams. Frost did read some Russian poetry in translation before traveling to the Soviet Union, but I haven't found any references to specific poems. He would certainly have read something by Akhmatova, and he would at least have been told of Yevtushenko's "Babii Yar."
70. RF's intriguing view of Mrs. Nutt as a quasi-mermaid is reported by Robert Francis.
72. Lesley Lee Francis, *The Frost Family's Adventure in Poetry*.
74. A good deal of the material involving Edward Thomas is drawn from Helen Thomas's *Under Storm's Wing* and Eleanor Farjeon's *Edward Thomas: The Last Four Years*.
75. Thompson, "Notes on Robert Frost." Helen Thomas.
76. The conversation on May Hill is elaborated from hints in Thomas's poem, "The

Sun Used to Shine," as well as his article, "This England," reproduced in *Elected Friends*.

77. Letter, Irma Frost Cone to Alma Elliott, Dartmouth College Library.

78. Close paraphrase of Lesley's account in *New Hampshire's Child*.

79. RF's dream is described by him in a letter to Nathan Haskell Dole, *Selected Letters*.

81. The Younger Poet is Donald Hall (no relation). Much of this is partly verbatim, partly close paraphrase of Hall's beautiful account in *Their Ancient Glittering Eyes*.

82. RF's conversation with Khrushchev is elaborated from Reeve's account, which is part paraphrase and part a general description of the topics covered. No transcript exists. Some of the descriptive action is a close paraphrase of Reeve, and some of the incidental dialogue is verbatim.

83. It's wonderfully true that Khrushchev, on the day he met RF, also listened to Solzhenitsyn's *One Day in the Life of Ivan Denisovich* and ordered battlefield nuclear weapons sent to Cuba. Taubman, *Khrushchev*. Richard Reeves, *President Kennedy: Profile of Power*. Khrushchev, *Khrushchev Remembers: The Last Testament*.

84. Elinor's abortion: Thompson, "Notes on Robert Frost."

86. Much of the material on Hendricks, some of it close paraphrase, is drawn from *Family Letters*. The brief exchanges between RF and Hendricks, and between RF and Elinor, are invented.

87. There's no positive evidence that RF continued to suspect Hendricks after Irma's mental illness became clear. But his dislike of Hendricks remained, and Thompson's "Notes on Robert Frost" reveal that Jeanie did suffer real abuse that may have sparked her paranoia.

88. The Holt editor who didn't like "Kitty Hawk" was Stanley Burnshaw; *Robert Frost Himself*.

89. Irma Frost, "An Adventure in the White Mountains," printed in the children's family newsletter, *The Bouquet*, June 1914, University of Virginia Library.

90. Marjorie's letters are in the Dartmouth College Library.

92. The material on Wade Van Dore is drawn from his *Life of the Hired Man*.

93. The Younger Poet is Smythe again; this is closely based on his account.

96. Letter, Lawrance Thompson to G. R. Elliott, Amherst College Library, Robert Frost Collection.

98. This conversation is elaborated from brief hints in Udall, and in Robert Dallek's *An Unfinished Life: John F. Kennedy, 1917–1963*.

99. The spoken exchange between RF and Marjorie on her deathbed is reported in RF's letter to Untermeyer, May 15, 1934.

100. RF describes this dream in a letter to Untermeyer, September 15, 1934.

101. The poem RF goes off to write, which I can't quote, is "A Leaf Treader."

102. "Hail, Michigan": my invention.

103. Some of the material here is drawn from Jeffrey Meyers, *Robert Frost*. The perceived kinship with the Brontës is reported in Lesley Lee Francis.

104. Letter, Lawrance Thompson to G. R. Elliott, September 10, 1963, Amherst College Library.

107. The Younger Poet is Donald Hall.

111. All of RF's spoken words are drawn verbatim from a transcript in *National Poetry Festival*, U.S. Government Printing Office.

112. Material on Theodore and Kathleen Morrison is drawn from Thompson, "Notes on Robert Frost," and Donald Sheehy, "(Re)Figuring Love: Robert Frost in Crisis, 1938–42," *New England Quarterly*, June 1990.
113. Through "I *will* go back," the spoken words are a slightly shortened transcription of Thompson's account in "Notes on Robert Frost." The exchange between RF and K. Morrison is inferred from accounts of other exchanges.
115. The conversation is closely based on Smythe's account. Carol's poem, quoted partially, is "The Gopher, Man and Maker." "I don't understand": letter, Carol Frost to RF, Dartmouth College Library. Quack grass anecdote: Van Dore. Cars stuck in the mud: letter, Elinor Frost to Ethel Manthy-Zorn, Amherst College Library.
116. Cf. Frost's moving couplet "An Answer," which I can't quote.
117. Helen Muir, *Frost in Florida*.
118. This is closely based on Thompson's account in "Notes on Robert Frost."
120. Thompson, "Notes on Robert Frost." RF refers to John Cone's "confessed adultery" in a letter to his lawyer, April 29, 1948, Dartmouth College Library.
121. This is closely based on Thompson's account in "Notes on Robert Frost." Thompson doesn't seem to have noticed that RF sent a telegram to John Cone conceding the necessity of Irma's committal on the day he uncharacteristically got drunk.
122. Elaborated from a brief reference in a letter from RF to Carol Frost, November 19, 1931.
123. Letter, Irma Frost to Alma Elliott, Darmouth College Library.
124. Much of this material is drawn from Kathleen Morrison, *Robert Frost: A Pictorial Chronicle* and Thompson's "Notes on Robert Frost." Nearly everything RF says is drawn verbatim from various accounts; the only exception is his argument with K. Morrison over telling the truth about their relationship, which is inferred from accounts of similar exchanges in "Notes on Robert Frost." I can't quote much of RF's fascinating last (incomplete) poem, and unfortunately it can only be found, as far as I know, in the third volume of Thompson's biography.
125. The Younger Poet is Philip Larkin.
126. Frost's words are taken verbatim from Anderson.
128. The Younger Poet here is part my invention, part Galway Kinnell. In Kinnell's fine poem "For Robert Frost," the narrator encounters Frost as a creature slogging through snow in a dark wood and speaking of love.